Restoring Love

Jennifer Slattery

CENTER POINT LARGE PRINT
THORNDIKE, MAINE

This Center Point Large Print edition
is published in the year 2018 by arrangement with
New Hope Publishers.

The text of this Large Print edition is unabridged.
In other aspects, this book may vary
from the original edition.
Printed in the United States of America
on permanent paper.
Set in 16-point Times New Roman type.

ISBN: 978-1-68324-716-6

Library of Congress Cataloging-in-Publication Data

Names: Slattery, Jennifer, 1974- author.
Title: Restoring love : a contemporary novel / Jennifer Slattery.
Description: Center Point Large Print edition. | Thorndike, Maine :
    Center Point Large Print, 2017.
Identifiers: LCCN 2017057924 | ISBN 9781683247166
    (hardcover : alk. paper)
Subjects: LCSH: Large type books. | GSAFD: Christian fiction. |
    Love stories.
Classification: LCC PS3619.L3755 R47 2017b | DDC 813/.6—dc23
LC record available at https://lccn.loc.gov/2017057924

Restoring Love

Center Point
Large Print

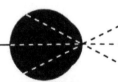

**This Large Print Book carries the
Seal of Approval of N.A.V.H.**

Dedicated to the man who saw the writer in me long before I did and who sweeps me off my feet daily. Love you!

Acknowledgments

So many people helped me with this novel, from talented critique partners who pointed out every repetitive phrase to industry professionals who shared their realty, house-flipping, or mold-eliminating knowledge with me. Shannon Vannatter, I cannot thank you enough for all the ways you've helped and encouraged me over the years. I really appreciate your prayers and all the fun, writerly, and random emails we've exchanged. Thanks also to critique partners extraordinaire, Marji Lane Clubine and Carole Towriss, for poring over this novel word by word and helping me to make it the strongest story possible.

Amy Pfortmiller, you knew your name would land in one of my novels eventually, right? Thanks so much for all your support and encouragement, for reading through each of my stories (pre-edits!), and for having the courage to offer honest feedback. Thanks also for continually pointing me to Jesus. I cherish you, girl, and this story in particular is stronger thanks to you!

To my sweet, incredibly patient husband— you're a gift to me! Thanks for always standing beside me, nudging me forward, and encouraging me to keep on keeping on. So glad I get to do life with you!

To all the staff at New Hope, especially Sarah Doss and Natalie Hanemann, thanks for all the help, encouragement, and guidance you've provided over the years. I've learned so much, not just in regard to writing but also in watching how your actions and interactions proclaim Christ.

Doyle Ollis, my favorite realtor in all of the Midwest—thanks for answering my plethora of questions, whether shot your way via email, text, or a random midday phone call. I also want to thank my sister in Christ, Beth Walman, for sharing her house-flipping knowledge with me. The insight was great; the time spent over dinner was even better! Donna Gay, you have been such a blessing to me! Thanks for sharing your knowledge of the inner workings of the nursing home industry with me.

I also want to thank Steve from A1 Mold Testing and Remediation Service for the information you provided on dealing with mold issues in regard to remodels and house sales. Finally, Abby Johnson, I know you're incredibly busy fulfilling the life-saving ministry God has assigned to you, and yet you patiently and graciously took time to answer questions from a random stranger working on a book. Thank you for that, and may God expand and bless your ministry as you seek to serve Him.

Chapter 1

"I don't know why you stay with that loser anyway. He can't keep a job, eats up all your money, and you better believe he's out running around on you right now."

Bianca's molars gritted together. "Hardly." Slamming her kitchen drawer shut, she whirled to face her co-worker, who had once again barged, unannounced, into Bianca's home. "Not everyone's a cheater."

Dawn shrugged. "Whatever. I still say it's time you left the jerk. Find a real man. One with a big bank roll." She laughed then blew a puff of air toward her bangs. "Can't you turn on some air already?" She fanned her face, her cheap rings flashing. "For real, girl, it's hotter than a sauna in here!"

"You wanna pay for it?"

"My point exactly."

As Dawn continued to gripe about everything from the heat and humidity to the taxes on cigarettes, Bianca checked her phone. Where was Reid, and why hadn't he responded to her messages? She wanted to catch some time with him before she headed to work. More than that, she needed to know he wasn't out getting into trouble.

A bedroom door creaked, and Cassie Joe, her 14-year-old daughter, emerged from her room. Wearing one of those romper ensembles, the fabric see-through, the hem much too short. Heavy-handed eyeliner made her hazel eyes look like a raccoon's.

"Hey, girlfriend." Dawn eyed C. J. with a raised eyebrow. "Nice shoes."

Bianca frowned. "For a stripper maybe." She thought of the princess her daughter used to be, decked in tiaras and glittery dress-up shoes. That princess was still there, only hidden by trashy clothes and cheap makeup. If only Bianca could help her see that. Could help all her kids realize they were better than this.

"Lighten up, B." Dawn leaned back in her chair and folded her hands across her protruding belly. "I say the girl looks good." She stretched out the last word. "Ready for a night out with the ladies, right, girlfriend? Speaking of—"

Bianca glared, effectively shutting Dawn up, then turned back to her daughter, arms crossed. "Where'd you get that trashy outfit?"

C. J. scowled. "It's not trashy."

"Well?"

"McKenzie. We traded."

"Uh-huh." Bianca grabbed her glass of water and brought it to her mouth, watching her daughter over the rim. The last time she caught C. J. with something new, it'd been stained with

10

ink left from a broken security tag. "You might as well change because you're not leaving the house like that. Matter of fact"—she glanced toward the stove—"I'm about to cook dinner, so settle in."

"Whatever." C. J. huffed and stomped back to her room.

After another glance toward the empty drive, Bianca sighed. What if Dawn was right? Not about her husband cheating—he'd never do that. He loved her too much. But about her needing to leave him.

She faced the living room. Her two boys sat side-by-side watching television. Her six-year-old edged as close as he could to his older brother without getting punched. Her ten-year-old, slumped against the couch, focused on the screen.

They looked so small, so . . . fragile, swallowed up by the cushions. Their profiles revealed tiny, soft features and wide, ever-watching eyes. Except most folks didn't get to see that side of them.

If only she could whisk her kids away from this place, away from her husband's hoodlum friends . . . to where? Poverty followed her like maggots to rotting meat. But not her kids. No. Things would be different for them. She'd make sure of that.

"You know what tonight is, right?" Dawn

grabbed her leopard print purse off the floor and plopped it on the table in front of her.

Bianca opened the fridge and pulled out half a block of cheese and a container of bologna. "Yeah. The night I pull a 12-hour shift."

"Wrong." Apparently not finding what she wanted, Dawn plunged both arms into her bag, elbow-deep. "Ladies' night. And you know what that means."

"You're gonna get drunk and . . ." She glanced toward her boys. They might not seem to be listening, but their ears were crazy sharp.

"It means we need some girl time, on someone else's dime." Laughing, she slapped the table, her bracelets clanking.

Bianca rolled her eyes and moved to the cupboard to search for bread. She found two slices, four heels, and a partially smashed hamburger bun. And one can of tomato soup with a dented side. Her paycheck couldn't come soon enough.

She checked the clock on the stove. *Reid, where are you?* The gnarled lump in her gut told her she didn't want to know.

Heels scuffed on the linoleum, followed by a rush of much-too-sweet perfume as Dawn approached. "Bologna? Nasty. Don't tell me you actually eat that garbage."

"At half the cost of ham? You better believe it." She planted a hand on her hip. "And unless you've got funds to throw into the family pot . . ."

Dawn leaned back against the counter. Twirling a lock of frizzy hair around her thick finger, she gazed toward the window. "I guess you can't expect to eat steak when you're sleeping with a felon, huh?"

She faced her, muscles tense. "You wanna talk trash, you best take it somewhere else."

Dawn raised her hands, palms out. "I'm just saying." She pulled a pack of cigarettes from her back pocket. "Old habits die hard."

"Uh-uh. You need to take that outside."

She dropped the pack on the counter. "Like Reid doesn't smoke more than a freight train."

"Not in here, he don't." Bianca glanced at her sons, grateful they were mesmerized by the television. Why'd she let hateful, foul-mouthed Dawn hang around? "And for your information, he's on the straight and narrow."

"Uh-huh." She slinked to the window and rested her forearms on the sill, her large rear end sticking out. "Then why's he hanging with the dope crew?"

"He's not. Hasn't hung with them for a while. Over three months, in fact."

Dawn faced Bianca. "Oh, really?" She planted a hand on her hip, her silver nails contrasting with her black jeans. "Then who's the dude with the red Camaro?"

Bianca's mouth went slack as images of Mean-

13

man Marvin and his crew flashed through her mind. No. Reid had promised.

And how many other times had he broken his word? When things got tight and the cupboards bare?

Rubbing her neck, she approached the window. There in her driveway sat Marvin's fast car, the rest of his gang packed inside. And Reid? He stood beside the rear passenger door, as if he'd just stepped out. With a parting nod, he turned, heading up the stairs. When he saw Bianca, his face blanched.

"I'm outta here." Dawn slung her purse over her shoulder, reaching for the door as Reid walked in. "Look who finally came home. Prince Charming himself."

"Shut up, Dawn," Bianca said.

"Girl, when you gonna wake up and smell the garbage?" Glaring at Reid, she pinched her nose. "Because it sure stinks up in here." Laughing, she shook her head and maneuvered around him.

Reid scowled, and Bianca held her breath, waiting for a fight. But instead, he turned to her with a tight and clearly forced grin.

"Hey, beautiful." He reached for her, mouth puckered, but she pushed him away. His eyes widened, but then his lazy smile reappeared. Further verifying his guilt. "Dude, am I hungry." He moved to the fridge, opened it, stared at the empty shelves, then closed the door. "What's for dinner?"

"Where you been?"

"What do you mean? It's not even seven o'clock." After a quick glance at the items Bianca had set on the counter, he rummaged through the cupboards. "Nothing. Time for us to do some shopping, huh?"

Bianca frowned. "I asked you a question."

"Baby, what's with you?" He moved closer, placed his strong, warm hands around her shoulders. "Don't I always take care of you? Huh?" He leaned in for a kiss but she looked away. He placed a callused finger under her chin and gently turned her face back. "Haven't I always?" Speaking softly, he brushed his lips along the edge of her jawline. "Let's not fight. You're just stressed about getting the kids off to school Wednesday."

"Because we're broke, Reid. We don't have money for school supplies. Barely have enough to feed their bellies. And I'm tired." A tear slid down her cheek. "So tired."

He wiped her tear with his finger. "I know. I'm trying to make things better. Can't you see that?"

She stepped away and turned her back to him. "Not like this." She busied herself with meal preparations. "You promised."

"We just need to get our feet under us. That's all."

Her bottom lip trembled as more tears fell silently. She shook her head. "Not like this."

His footsteps receded and Bianca focused on making the kids' dinner. A moment later, his voice, soft and husky, drifted from the living room. Her heart shredded as she watched him ruffle Robby's hair before snagging Sebastian, his birth son, in a bear hug. "Hey, bud. Robster." He held her gaze, his blue eyes soft, apologetic. "I gotta step out, and since your momma's got to work, your sister will be manning the fort tonight." He studied Bianca who turned back to the simmering soup and stack of bologna sandwiches. "Be good?"

After a few more clichéd phrases, he left.

Chapter 2

Angela fought a wave of nausea, and it wasn't from motion sickness. *I can't do this. I can't. I'm too old. Much too practiced in the art of failure.* Sitting in the passenger seat while her daughter drove, she felt as if the doors of the vehicle were closing in on her. With every mile, her desire to turn back intensified. But she couldn't. Wouldn't. If only to prove she could actually follow through with something.

Even if that follow-through landed her under the freeway overpass.

She swallowed hard, casting frequent glances at her sweet daughter. Ainsley gripped the steering wheel with both hands, looking straight ahead. Was she glad to see Angela go? Would she miss her, visit on occasion? Or would their relationship fade into distant phone calls and the occasional holiday gathering? It'd only been a few years since they'd begun to heal their relationship, a relationship Angela had nearly destroyed by her selfish, irresponsible behavior. Despite the distance, Angela was determined to hold tight to what God had restored. What Christ had helped them build.

Breathing deeply, Angela shoved her anxious thoughts aside and focused instead on the stretch of road in front of them. They were two and a half hours from Kansas City. Less than ten minutes from her new home, her new life. A life she longed to embrace, if only the thoughts from her past would relent.

After decades of poor choices and shameful behavior wracking up debt and bouncing from job to job and relationship to relationship, what made Angela think she could do any different? Common sense said she was well past the career-launching age, which was why she'd received zero hits on all the résumés she'd sent out. But at least she'd found something, even if it wasn't in her preferred school district. Or her job of choice.

Low pay or not, it was a stepping-stone to teaching. Hopefully.

She closed her eyes and leaned her temple against her window.

"You OK?" Ainsley eased off the freeway. "It's not too late to change your mind."

"I'm fine."

A giant gentleman's club sign caught her eye. Classy. And according to her daughter's GPS, less than seven minutes from her new house. *Oh, Lord Jesus, please tell me I'm doing the right thing here.*

Fighting against a debilitating case of the jitters, she offered her best attempt at a smile. "I've got a plan." Wednesday she'd start as an assistant teacher—a paraeducator, they called it—subbing for a woman on medical leave. Her position would last four, five months tops, but hopefully, it'd get her foot in the door. "If all goes well, I'll have a teaching job by next fall. If not sooner."

"Are you sure this is the right thing? I mean . . . I'm proud of you and everything. Incredibly proud. But you're hiring on as a sub, Mom. Long-term or not . . . Can't you sub as a teacher rather than an assistant? You'd make more money, and that's something you could do in Kansas City."

Angela studied her. How could she make her daughter understand how much she needed to do this? To prove she could actually stand on her own. "I felt like this was a great opportunity." The only one she'd found. "Plus, the Martins needed a house sitter."

"I guess I just don't understand why you're in such a hurry."

"I figured it's about time I start acting like the parent, quit mooching off my daughter and her kindhearted husband." Moreover, she needed to start paying them back.

"It wasn't like that and you know it."

Angela gave a half shrug. "I appreciate you and Chris taking me in and everything, but it's time . . ." Past time. Long past.

"Well, I guess if it doesn't work out, you can always come back, right?" Ainsley grinned and nudged Angela with her elbow.

Angela offered a slight smile. Failure wasn't an option. Not anymore.

An awkward silence followed as they wove past nineteenth-century houses with stone chimneys and porch swings.

Less than five minutes later, Ainsley turned onto 35th Street and pulled into a gravel driveway. "Here we are."

Angela surveyed her new residence. A brick and stucco, single-story home with peeling, maroon trim. Patches of dirt dotted the lawn, and a splattering of unkempt plants overtook the flowerbed. It needed work—a lot of it—but she had time.

Exiting the vehicle, she inhaled as a gust of late August heat swept over them. One hundred degrees and climbing.

Chris, her son-in-law, pulled to the curb behind them, parked, and stepped out. He hooked a thumb in his belt loop and shaded his eyes with his free hand. "A bit neglected but seems sturdy enough."

Angela bit her bottom lip, eyeing her daughter's swelling stomach before meeting her eyes. She grabbed her hands. "I'm going to miss our morning walks. And coffee. And . . ." She touched Ainsley's belly. Angela's first grandchild.

"Oh, stop." Ainsley gave a tight laugh that failed to hide the concern radiating from her eyes. "It's not like you're leaving the country.

Or that we won't visit. Especially when the baby comes. Date night!" She gave Angela a sideways hug. "Now, what do you say we check out the inside and leave the heavy lifting to that strong, handsome man of mine?" She looped an arm through Angela's and led her up the cracked walkway and stairs to a quaint, covered porch.

Chris began unloading Angela's meager belongings while she and Ainsley toured the place. The owners, a military family stationed in Japan, left it furnished. A hodgepodge of what looked to be garage sale finds contrasted with the yellow-striped wallpaper. It wasn't plush by any standards, but it was free and welcoming. Peaceful.

Chris strolled in, set down a box of dishes, and dusted off his hands. "Guess that's it." He approached his teary wife and wrapped a protective arm around her shoulder. "Don't worry so much, Ains. God's got this." He offered Angela a soft smile, one she'd grown quite accustomed to over the past four years. "Besides, we've got unlimited texting."

Ainsley nodded. Blinking rapidly, she swiped her thumbs beneath her eyes.

"Which reminds me." He pulled out his car keys. "As promised, here's your shiny new ride." He jingled the keys, then handed them over. "It's not much, but it's oiled, tuned, and should get you to work and back."

Angela's face burned. She hated feeling like a mooch. Except she really didn't want to navigate Omaha on foot. Especially come winter with its blizzards and white outs. Swallowing her pride, she accepted the gift. "I appreciate it. Really."

"And to hold you over until your first paycheck comes in . . ." He pulled a series of bills from his wallet and held them out.

She raised her hands, palms out. "Oh, no. I couldn't."

"Mom, don't be silly." Ainsley rolled her eyes. "I saw your bank account, remember?"

Angela's mouth went slack. A surge of heat shot up her neck and settled into her face. "Sweetie, I know you mean well, both of you, but I'm a grown woman." And after nearly 50 years of living like an irresponsible child, she'd finally begun to act like one. "I can take care of myself." Scratch that. God could take care of her. Without Him, she'd be back in Kansas City wracking up debt with her impulse shopping and running from one sleazy man to another. "Besides, if things get tight, there's always mac'n'cheese and peanut butter."

"So save it for a rainy day." Chris pressed the money into Angela's hands, closing her fingers around it. "Or a new alternator." He chuckled and glanced through the opened doorway to the rusted, 1984 Volkswagen Rabbit parked in the drive. "Please, for us. It'll make us feel better. Help Ainsley sleep at night."

Angela studied her son-in-law's deep-set eyes. He wasn't one to back down once he set his mind to something. "Fine. I'll keep it under the mattress, and I'll return every dollar." She refused to add one more debt to her ginormous list. Rather, she planned to start paying things off, paying people back. Including her mother, if she could find her.

Hooking her arm through Ainsley's, she led the way out the door to the covered porch to say their good-byes. "Don't be strangers."

"Never." Ainsley gave her a squeeze, then Chris did the same. The three walked to the couple's remaining car and said their final good-byes.

Angela started to head back to her house when loud rock music turned her attention to the house across the street. A low-riding Cutlass pulled up along the curb then idled. The driver, who looked about 17, had long, jet-black hair streaked with blue. Studded bracelets circled his pale wrist.

Catching Angela's eye, his gaze narrowed. A moment later, a younger-looking girl stepped out of the vehicle, and the guy sped away.

Clutching a duffel bag to her chest, the slender brunette stared down the road until the car disappeared. When her gaze met Angela's, she squared her shoulders, her slumped stance taking on a stiff defensiveness. Though her face was hard, her eyes held a haunting desperation. One Angela understood.

The door to the house lurched open and a petite, young woman with short, tousled hair poked her head out. "Cassie Joe, get inside. Now. And wash that garbage off your face."

The door slammed shut and the teen flinched. With a visible sigh, she turned and trudged up the walk into a single-story, boxlike home.

Painful memories from Angela's past resurfaced. She stared up at the evening sky. "Why have you brought me here, Lord?"

Chapter 3

Mitch pulled to the curb on 35th Street alongside a tan two-story bungalow. It was kitty-corner from their rental property, and his business partner wanted to buy the place on auction. Said they could flip it for a pretty profit. The property was a mess with a moss-covered roof, what looked like dry-rotted trim, and a thick layer of grime on the windows. A lilac bush, at least four feet high and six feet wide, pressed against the left side of the house, its dead, shriveled flowers sagging toward the ground. Even so, the location was good, the neighborhood in flux, which could mean rising house values.

He made a visual sweep of the area, his gaze catching on a car parked at the Martins' house. The military family was serving overseas and not due back for at least another year. Strange to see someone at their house now. Maybe someone they'd hired to deal with the yard or something, but Mitch would shoot the owners an email to check.

He shifted to survey the yellow, single-story across the street, one of his and Dennis's rental properties. If the Douglases didn't pay rent soon, he'd be forced to evict, something his partner had been pushing for.

He caught a glimpse of young Sebastian's bike, leaning against the side of the house, and frowned. Poor kid. Rent or not, Mitch couldn't throw that family out. But if they didn't step up soon, he might not have a choice.

With a heavy sigh, he grabbed his comparables, pen, and notepad, and cut his engine. He opened the truck door, and a gust of sweltering air assaulted him. His phone rang. Probably his business partner saying he was running late. Mitch checked the caller ID. His ex-wife Sheila. Just who he didn't want to talk to right now. Or ever.

He exited his truck. "Hey. What do you need?"

"I'm calling about your son."

Their youngest. "What's Eliot done this time?"

"Nothing." She threw the word out with enough bite to silence a jackhammer. "Maybe if you quit expecting the worst of him, he'd actually make something of himself."

"I'm not. What I'm expecting, what I'm praying daily for, is that he'll get the help he needs—something he'll never do if you keep bailing him out."

Mitch's partner, Dennis, pulled up in a green pickup, parked, and stepped out. He wore his signature purple knit shirt and tan slacks, a swatch of curly gray hair encircling the peach-fuzzed baldness on top of his head. He waved.

Mitch raised a finger and pointed to the phone, mouthing, "Sheila."

He nodded. "Good luck." Clipboard in hand, camera dangling by a cord around his neck, he shot a mischievous grin. He'd been a good friend, tried and true since he and Mitch had roomed together in college. Their house-flipping-rental business had been Dennis's idea, and he'd done a chunk of the footwork to get things started. He'd pulled the weight when Mitch had fallen into a six-month depression after his son died and came over with Chinese takeout after Sheila left. Every time an emotional blow hit, Dennis was there.

But lately, for the past few years actually, things between them had tensed.

As Sheila's high-pitched voice ran her breathless, Mitch leaned against his truck, ankles crossed. He watched Dennis survey the property, then the neighborhood. A handful of the houses, although older, were well maintained—had great curb appeal.

A few of the others could use major overhauling, and their renter's yard and fence needed work.

"Mitch Kenney." His ex's snippety voice jolted him back to his phone conversation. "Have you heard anything I said?"

"Uh-huh. Eliot's hungry, says he's off the pipe, and you want me to hire him on."

"Yes."

"In other words, you want me to reward him for bailing on rehab."

"No. I want you to act like a dad and help your son."

And so went their arguments. In truth, he had no idea how to deal with the kid, but he knew for sure enabling him wasn't the answer. "You know it's not entirely up to me."

"So talk to Dennis. Surely he won't turn away his business partner's son."

"Right. Because drugs, hangovers, and nail guns are a great combination."

"Just talk to him. Please?" Her whiny voice grated on Mitch's ears. "Tell him Eliot's clean and sober now."

"So he says." And for how long? A day? A week? Most likely until his next paycheck—yet another reason why Mitch shouldn't hire him back on. But he couldn't prevent Sheila from slipping the boy cash and food. Maybe putting him to work would be the best thing for him.

"We should be starting another remodel soon," Mitch said. "I'll talk to Dennis. If I can convince him to give Eliot another chance," which was highly unlikely, "I'll let Eliot know." Mitch hit call end and slipped the phone back into his pocket. Hopefully he wasn't making a huge mistake.

Turning, he caught sight of a woman sitting on the Martins' steps. Shiny, silver hair reached just below her chin, and a hint of smile accentuated high cheekbones.

Who was she, and how did she know the Martins?

Flicking a wave, he locked his truck. He crossed the overgrown lawn and rounded the property to find Dennis in the back, inspecting the foundation.

"Looks solid." His partner straightened, eyeing a peeling windowsill. "But it's got a bit of dry rot."

"When's the auction?"

"Tomorrow morning. Which means it's all on me, huh, being a Sunday and all?"

Mitch shoved his hands in his front pockets and gave a slight nod. They'd discussed this a hundred times. "If you don't mind."

Dennis studied him, cracking his knuckles one finger at a time. "How much you think?"

"Not sure." He handed over the comps he'd printed. "I think we can low-ball them. If we don't get it, we'll walk away. No harm done."

Dennis chewed on his pencil. "I don't know. I think this one's worth some risk."

"How high you thinking? Because the way I see it, we could blow through a load of cash and end up with a lot of vacant properties collecting cobwebs."

"The very reason we need to get rid of our freeloaders."

Mitch tensed. He knew this was coming. "I'll talk to the Douglases."

"I'm done talking. This isn't a charity." His frown deepened, his eyes boring into Mitch. They stood like that for some time, Mitch at a loss as to what to say. He understood the logistics, the rules of good business, but those kids . . . he just couldn't do it. Not yet. Not until he'd given Bianca every chance to get her feet under her.

He released a gust of air. "Fine. I'll take care of it." Somehow. Without tossing that family on the street.

"Good." Dennis smiled and tucked his clipboard under his arm. He turned back to the property. "As for this place . . . if we can get it for the right price . . ." He paused. "We'd have to turn it fast."

"True."

"Two weeks. Three tops."

He nodded.

"Let's do it." He checked his watch. "I better go." His smile turned lopsided as the skin around his eyes crinkled. "Got me a date tonight."

Mitch raised his eyebrows. "Really? Let me guess, the girl from Dan's Hardware?"

He chuckled.

"It's about time."

"All right then. Guess I'll call you tomorrow. Let you know how we fare at the auction." He started to leave.

"Wait."

Dennis turned back around, an eyebrow raised.

"Never mind." Now wasn't a good time to talk to him about his son.

Chapter 4

Early Sunday morning, Angela shuffled into her new living room, the anxiety she'd gone to bed with replaced with a rising sense of hope.

Lord, You've been so good to me. Much better than I deserve. I'm not going to waste one ounce of Your grace. If only she'd grabbed hold of His grace sooner, or acted like an adult, period, she wouldn't have made such a mess of her life. Over two decades, living like an irresponsible, impetuous teenager, taking advantage of others and never considering or caring about the consequences for her actions. She'd spent the past three years trying to live differently, with integrity and an eye on her future.

Today started a new chapter, and this time, she was going to do it right. Beginning with making a debt repayment plan. But first things first—*coffee.*

Pot and grounds already unpacked and waiting, she started them percolating. She checked the time on her phone. Seven a.m., which meant that between all her tossing and turning, she'd slept maybe six hours. Enough to get her through, though maybe she'd take a nap.

She snatched a cup of coffee while it continued

to brew and meandered to the living room. Her sketchpad and charcoal pencil lay on the end table. Drawing helped her unwind. Process. Today she hoped to capture a knotted tree she'd spotted in the adjacent yard. Ivy climbed its trunk, its thick branches stretching out like gnarled arms. Its vibrant green leaves shimmered beneath the sun's rays.

Sunlight radiated through the dusty blinds, casting lines across the maroon carpet. Outside, birdsong mingled with the distant sound of traffic.

Male voices drew her attention to the neighboring house. In the overgrown and browning yard, half a dozen men of varying shapes and sizes milled about, taking notes as they went. A younger couple, a blonde, cheerleader-type and a tall, dark-haired man with broad shoulders, conversed in the shade of an overgrown tree. From the way the woman's arms flapped about, the conversation appeared ssheated.

She'd seen a *For Sale by Auction* sign in the yard. Maybe the auction was today? Now that would be interesting. What led to something like that anyway? Did that mean the property had been foreclosed?

She'd scout out the area later and maybe see why the other men had been canvassing the vacant house the day before. She smiled, thinking of the taller man of the two. Though trim, it was clear he was well-built, and he walked like someone with authority. His short hair specked with gray and what resembled a three-day beard reminded her of those men in outdoorsman catalogs.

Angela Meadows, what are you doing? You're done with men, remember?

Understatement of the millennium.

Right now, she needed to figure out where she stood—income, debts, everything—as daunting as that was.

She eyed the sparse boxes lining the far wall. Thanks to Chris, most of them were labeled, the one containing items from her "junk drawer" top and center. Her Bible lay in the box beneath it, along with her journal and three years' worth of carefully recorded sermon notes jotted on the back of church bulletins.

After a quick sip of coffee, she set her mug down to search the box for a notepad. Not finding it, she settled on a scrap of moving paper, which she spread out on the coffee table. She then proceeded to list out all her debts.

Her school loan topped the list. Four maxed-out credit cards, two of which her daughter had cosigned for, followed.

Dropping her head into her hands, she sighed. "Oh, Ainsley-bear, I'm so sorry." *How could I have been so thoughtless, so irresponsible and selfish?* But never again. From here on out, not only would Angela stand on her own, she'd be a blessing. A giver, not a taker.

She grabbed her Bible from her tote, the binding stiff with newness. Opening the cover, she lifted an old Polaroid taken 43 years ago of her and her mother. Angela wore a yellow blouse and bell-bottom pants, her long, blonde hair parted down the center. Her mother looked radiant in a flower dress and lace-edged apron. Beneath it lay an old letter, folded and unfolded so many times, tiny rips had formed in the creases and the inked words had faded.

Written almost ten years ago, and never sent. Because truly, what could Angela say? *I'm sorry* felt insufficient. Moreover, they hadn't spoken in over four decades, their last conversation ending with her mother's ultimatum. *"Shape up or don't come back."*

"I'm trying, Momma. It took me a while, but I'm trying."

Was she too late? And what would her mom say when she found out what Angela did all those years ago? She'd have to tell her. There'd be no way to hide it.

Her mom would hate her. If she didn't already.

She tucked the note and photo back in the Bible and opened to her favorite book—the Psalms. David's prayers and songs always soothed her, reminded her of God's power and grace.

"Help me, Lord. I want to do the right thing. For once."

She set her Bible down and stood, brushing the dust from her pajama bottoms.

"Where should I start?" Cobwebs hung from the corners and a long, thin web draped from the ceiling fan to the curtain. And clearly, the place hadn't seen a vacuum for some time. Years, maybe.

Nor had she brought one. Now that was smart. Surely the Martins had one? Most likely buried in the cluttered garage. No matter. Angela would pick one up at a garage sale. In the meantime, she really needed to tackle the mess of weeds out front. After dashing to her bedroom for a quick change of clothes, she pulled her hair back and shoved up her sleeves.

She stepped outside and humid air enveloped her, filling her lungs with a mixture of lilac and sunbaked earth. With a deep, refreshing breath, she turned to what she suspected was once a beautiful flower garden. Tall tufts of grass nearly swallowed two overgrown rose bushes. A gnarled vine wound around and through a blossoming rose bush, dandelions clustered along its base.

She knelt in the warm dirt and reached for a patch of clover when her cell rang. She sat on her heels and pulled her phone from her pocket, smiling as she read the return number.

"Ainsley, good morning." She swiped a lock

of hair from her forehead, dirt tumbling onto her nose. "You miss me already?"

"Of course." Music played in the background. "But don't worry. I hope to fix that soon. Chris and I are already planning when we can come your way again. We plan to hold off on booking any more concerts for a while once the baby is born."

"I wish I could watch the little guy for you when you go on tour. I feel bad that I can't."

"Honestly, I don't think I'll be ready to leave the little-bit for a while yet, at least, not for more than a few hours. Although Dad's new wife offered."

"How's your father doing?" The one good man Angela had in her life, and she'd blown it. Big time. But he'd stayed by Ainsley. Had been a good dad. Still was.

Ainsley paused. "Good. But enough about me. How are you liking your new home? You settling in all right? Did you sleep well?"

Minus the frequent jolts of adrenaline that came every time she thought of what lay ahead, and her dangerously low bank account? "I slept like a rock. Thank you."

"Meet your neighbors yet?"

"You mean the handsome man who was surveying the property next door?"

"Mom!"

Angela laughed. "I'm just playing with you,

sweetie. Don't worry. I have no intention of getting romantically involved with anyone."

"Good. Because with your history . . ." Ainsley's exhale reverberated across the line. "I'm sorry. That was uncalled for."

"No, you're right." How many of Angela's past poor choices were because of a man? Too many.

An extended silence followed.

Angela pressed a hand against her lower back and stretched. "I suppose I should let you go. I've got a long list of chores ahead."

"Not so many to keep you from church, I hope. Because I did a quick Google search this morning. Seems there are three within walking distance of your house.

"Um . . ."

"I'll text you the names and addresses."

Angela frowned and rubbed her brow. She wasn't opposed to going, it was just . . . most Christians didn't like her much. Well, except for those at Ainsley's church. They were lovely. But here . . . ? Besides, her clothes were all in boxes.

"I haven't unpacked yet." Sandwiching her phone between her ear and her shoulder, she returned to her weeding.

"You've got time."

"Everything will be wrinkled."

"So wear what you had on yesterday."

"Those are sweaty and covered in grime."

"Mom, we talked about this. How can you

expect to grow in Christ if you never spend time with His followers?"

Telling her she didn't belong wouldn't help. Ainsley would only counter that with one of her "saved by grace" slogans.

Angela sighed. "I'll go next week. Once I get more settled. Have a chance to breathe."

"Promise? I'm not trying to pester you or anything, it's just . . . you've gone through a lot of changes in the past few years, and you've got a lot of challenges ahead."

"Don't worry. I won't come crawling back with suitcases in hand."

"That's not what I'm worried about, and you know it."

The fact that her daughter worried about her at all only added to Angela's guilt. Yet another reason she needed to make this new transition work. And she refused to add yet another failed life-plan to her already jumbled history. "I'll be fine. Better than fine."

"Just don't isolate, OK? And if you feel yourself getting depressed . . ."

"Sweetie, please, let that go. I'm a different person now." Thanks to God and a phenomenal counselor from her old church. "I promise."

More silence. Then, "Of course, you're right. Enjoy your day."

"You too, Ainsley-bear." Hanging up, she sat in her yard a moment longer, the sun warm on her back, birds fluttering overhead. The Bible said she was a new creation. She turned toward the sky and smiled. *Thank You for that, Lord. Help me to believe the truth in those words.*

Standing, she brushed the dirt off her hands and went inside to get cleaned up. She wasn't quite up for church. That'd take a bit of a pep talk. She knew with every fiber of her being that Christ loved her. She just wasn't so sure His children here in Omaha would feel the same. Though she'd never know until she tried . . .

She ambled toward the back bedroom and pulled out her cell phone. Chuckled. Five new text messages, each one from Ainsley. She'd provided addresses and links to numerous churches in the area.

Maybe Angela would walk toward one, check it out. If she didn't like it, she could always leave.

A twinge pricked her heart as she thought of Jesus, arms outstretched, nailed to the Cross. If He could undergo such brutality for her, surely she could endure a bit of public scorn.

"Forgive me for being so selfish, Lord. It doesn't matter what anyone thinks of me. It doesn't even matter if church folks don't want me there. You do, so I'll go. To be with You."

Ten minutes later, hair damp and tousled, she stood in front of the closet mirror. Squished into a pair of skinny jeans that had tightened after her 15 pound weight gain, she fought, unsuccessfully, to close the zipper. And no amount of wiggling, cajoling, and sucking in her growing gut helped. Peeling them off, she fell back on the bed with a huff. Five outfits later, she settled on a skort—black and blue with bold, geometric shapes outlined in orange and a matching, sleeveless top.

I may be a new creation, but I've still got a long way to go. First step—forgo the ice cream therapy.

She exited her room, continued to the door, and stepped out onto the stoop, breathing in the cleansing air. Across the street, a young boy, about five or six, sat on the curb, chin in his hands. No shoes or shirt, and his hair was disheveled. Hunched over, he appeared to be watching the road.

She thought of the hollow-eyed teen she'd seen the previous evening, the one the woman had called Cassie Joe. Something about the teen drew her.

She wrapped an arm around her torso, remembering a story Ainsley often told of how God first called her into the homeless ministry.

Angela would be wise to mind her own business. She had enough to manage getting her own life put together.

Chapter 5

Sunday morning, Mitch manned the church's welcome center, waiting for first service to conclude. As a greeter, he'd spend a chunk of the day positioned right here, with a few hours' break mid-afternoon. Normally, he didn't mind. Enjoyed it, actually. But today, lack of sleep coupled with an empty belly fought against him.

"Hey, there." Bones, a longtime friend, clomped toward him, his heavy work boots smacking the tile. "Meant to call you last week." He gave Mitch a fist bump, his rolled up sleeves exposing a giant eyeball tattoo bisecting his forearm.

"Oh, yeah?"

Bones nodded. "Got a call from Jason down at the Streets." He stepped back, feet planted shoulder distance apart. "Told me about a girl that just got the boot, been living out of her car." Weighing in at 260 and change, his rough appearance—overgrown beard, trunk-like neck, and leather vest—hid one of the softest hearts Mitch had ever known.

"And you're wondering if I know of anywhere she can crash."

"I know things have been . . . tense between you and Dennis, but figured it didn't hurt none to ask." Bones leaned against the wall behind him.

"How are things going with you two, anyway?"

"Same. Worse, actually. Seems we're always fighting about something."

"Money."

"Basically." He relayed their last conversation.

"That's tough, man."

"Honestly, I haven't got a clue what the right thing to do is. I mean, I know we can't save everyone, but . . . he wants us to start the eviction process on the Douglases."

Bones gave a slow nod. "The broad with all the kids and the felon husband."

Mitch chuckled. "When you say it like that . . ."

"Didn't mean nothing by it. Hey, I was a thug once too, remember? Praise God someone had the courage to stick by me, otherwise I wouldn't be here today." He gave a low whistle. "Who would've thought—Bones Simmons, turned churchman."

"Hiccupping Bones now." Mitch suppressed a laugh and clamped his friend on his shoulder. It hadn't taken long for the man to earn his new nickname, the way he blubbered and sniffled through nearly every sermon. But if you crossed someone he loved? Mitch had only seen that once, and that was plenty.

"Nothing wrong with a few tears. Jesus wept." He gave a rattling cough. "So, you gonna do it?"

Mitch raised an eyebrow.

"Evict those folks?"

"I probably should." He stretched the fingers on his hand backward, cracking the knuckles. "They're always late with the rent, and now they're slipping behind. The last two months, they only paid just over half what they owed. But whenever I pray about it, I feel like I need to wait."

"No harm in that."

"Actually, there is. I'm trying Dennis's patience." Things would be so much easier if his business partner shared his faith. Something he'd been praying about for almost five years now, ever since Mitch accepted Christ himself. "If I'm not careful, I could tank our business."

"That's tough."

He nodded. "But back to your question. I can do some asking around. Talk to the elders. Maybe they know of a shelter."

"Everyone in the Omaha metro is booked." He coughed again, releasing the scent of stale cigarettes. "You know what that girl needs, what a whole slew of folks around here need? A lot more than a bed and a meal, I'll tell you that much."

"What? A job?"

"Nope. I mean, yeah, but more than that, they need a mentor. Someone to walk beside them, show them how to live different. 'Spect that's what the Douglas family needs too."

"A great thought but finding people with

the time to do that . . ." He glanced left as the doors to the sanctuary opened and folks started streaming out. "Time's up." He fist bumped Bones's shoulder. "I'll call you."

With a parting nod, Mitch moved to the church's entrance, ready to greet newcomers. As usual, Frances Archer was one of the first to arrive.

"Mitch, so good to see you." Offering a flirty smile, she sandwiched his hand with both of hers. "Beautiful day, isn't it?" With her carrot-orange hair, pink dress, and matching heels and purse, she reminded him of an old Strawberry Short Cake commercial.

Funny he'd remember that now, or ever, considering he'd raised three boys. "Great fishing weather."

"Or picnic."

Sensing an invitation coming, he offered a slight smile, then turned to help an elderly gentleman with the adjacent door. By then a sizable crowd had begun to trickle in, making further conversation impossible.

Thankfully.

He felt his phone vibrate and checked the number. Dennis, calling with good news?

Mitch moved away from the incoming throng to answer. "Hey. What do you got?"

"The Tonka Twins are here." His nickname for a house-flipping couple who were quickly becoming Mitch and Dennis's biggest competitors. "Word has it, they came with some serious cash."

"And you wanna raise our top dollar."

"If we want a shot at the place, yeah."

Mitch frowned. "How much?"

"I say we'll get it at another $20K."

"You think it's worth that much?"

"If the neighborhood shifts."

Meaning if people like the Douglases left, houses got flipped, and families moved in. "That place needs a lot of work."

"We could make it pop with $20K."

No, closer to $50K, but Mitch wasn't going to argue. Not with all the other battles wedging between them. "Were you able to do a walk-through?"

"Briefly. Cosmetically the property's a mess. Needs major updating. Fresh paint throughout, new appliances, new flooring in the kitchen. Might be a few leaks in the roof. But the place appears sturdy."

That was the problem with auctions. Nothing was ever how it appeared, and you never learned what a money pit a place was until you started gutting the place. But every once in a while you found a gem.

Muffled voices sounded in the background.

"The trustee's here," Dennis said. "I gotta go. Yay or nay?"

Things were pretty tight, but if Dennis's instincts were correct, this little jewel could earn a pretty penny. Maybe even enough to get him off Mitch's back regarding the Douglases. "Your call. I trust you."

Mitch slipped his phone back in his pocket and turned back toward the church entrance. An unexpected sight caught his eye—a petite older woman dressed in teenage attire. Was that the lady he'd seen at the Martins' place? With silver, chin-length hair and blue-gray eyes, her loud skirt landed at least an inch above her knees with an equally bold, sleeveless blouse. Her wedge shoes had to be at least four inches high. Clutching a ginormous sequined purse to her chest, she watched, wide-eyed, as other ladies streamed in.

Poor thing looked as out of place as a three-legged sawhorse . . . and downright terrified. Like she might be sick, even. That wouldn't bode well for her sparkly shoes.

Leaving his post, he ambled over, donning his most gracious smile. "Hi. Welcome to Abiding Fellowship. I'm Mitch." He extended his hand.

She stared at it, then him, before shaking his hand. As she tilted her head, a crease formed between her smoky blue eyes. "Angela. Angela Meadows." Her cheeks flushed pink, heart-shaped lips covered in a shimmering gloss. She was a pretty little thing with a sweet smile, though she did dress weird. Kinda loud for someone her age.

"I saw you yesterday, out at the Martins' old place."

She nodded. "Just moved in yesterday. Are we neighbors?"

"Not exactly." He studied her with a lowered brow. "You a friend of theirs?"

"Who? The Martins?" She gave a nervous laugh. "Not really. My daughter knows them. She's a musician." A sparkle lit her eyes at her last statement, and her chin lifted. "She met Mrs. Martin at a women's conference last summer, and well . . . I'm sort of watching their house."

"Yeah? For how long?"

"I . . . uh . . . they won't be back for at least a year."

The Martins were way too trusting, especially considering they were serving halfway across the world. And, from the sounds of it, barely knew Angela.

Though the woman seemed normal enough, aside from her attire, this situation warranted extra attention. For the Martins' sake.

Chapter 6

The full cloak of darkness surrounded Bianca's house when she pulled into her driveway on Tuesday night. A sliver of a moon emerged behind a tall brick building poking up from behind a row of homes. A distant horn merged with the loud, steady buzz of crickets.

Cutting the engine, she stretched her neck, massaging cramped muscles. Her feet burned. What she wouldn't give for some time off, but someone needed to pay the bills. And considering Reid still hadn't returned . . .

Tears fought to surface. *Why, Reid? Why you got to toss your family in the gutter like this?*

How many times had she told him he'd have to choose, live like a criminal or be the man she needed? That the kids needed. True, only one was his, but he'd been good to all three of them. Like a real dad.

Minus his extracurriculars.

Waving a hand in front of her face to dry her eyes, she pulled an old church flyer someone had stuck on her car windshield the week before. "Back to school items giveaway, August 12th, 5:00 to 8:00 p.m." She'd missed it.

Didn't matter. They'd make do. Always did.

Good thing her kids would be getting free breakfasts and lunches come tomorrow.

She slung her purse over her shoulder and stepped out into the humid night. Mosquitoes buzzed around her head, one landing on her nose. She swatted it away and hurried up her porch steps, aching for bed.

Her youngest, Sebastian, met her on the stoop. As usual, his face was dusted in dirt, his pants hung cockeyed, his blond hair slicked to his forehead by sweat.

"What you get?" Glancing back at the car, his blue eyes danced.

She pulled him into a sideways hug, resting her chin on his head. "Not this time, little man. We'll get what you need soon's I get paid." She could feel his entire body slump beside her. "Maybe we'll go shopping together. That way you can pick out what you want." Forcing a smile, she tickled his ribs.

He squirmed away, a dimple denting his cheek.

"Boy, you need a bath something awful." She angled her head, nose scrunched. "Might need to hose you down." She ruffled his hair and lumbered inside.

Robby sat in his usual spot on the couch, focused on the television. At least it wasn't MTV. Best thing about not being able to afford cable.

"Hey, big man," she called out to him. "You have a good last day of summer?"

He groaned.

She laughed and shuffled into the kitchen, cluttered by dirty dishes, empty macaroni-and-cheese boxes, and a dry milk carton lying on its side.

Milk! She'd forgotten to buy any. Not that she had the money to spare, not when so many bills were waiting to be paid. She and Reid had fallen behind, in part, due to having to buy a new car when their old one had died. Plus, she'd sent a chunk of change to help her brother make bail when he got busted on assault charges. She lost that money when he skipped out on his court date. It felt like they'd never climb out. It didn't help that she barely made over minimum wage as a nurse's assistant and was never given full-time hours, on account then her employer would have to pay for benefits. She had 20 bucks and change to get her to payday and needed to save that for gas. No matter. Water was cheap, and they had plenty of that.

She moved aside plates crusted with partially eaten dinners and dropped her purse on the table. "Where's your sister?"

Sebastian shrugged and plopped into the chair beside her. Her little shadow. She loved that about him.

Giving him a love-squeeze, she looked over his sweaty head to her oldest. "Hey, Robby, where's your sister?"

"Don't know. She left with Gabe."

Bianca rubbed her face. "I thought I told y'all to stay home tonight." Not to mention the fact that C. J. was supposed to be looking after her brothers. Added to the fact that Bianca absolutely hated that lowlife boyfriend of hers. That girl was heading straight down the road Bianca had trekked, one that ended in nothing but a bunch of dead ends.

She grabbed her phone and shot her daughter a text: *Get home. Now.*

That girl needed grounding. Bianca snorted. Lotta good that would do without an adult around to enforce it. With her working evenings and Reid gone . . . She shook the thought aside. No sense dwelling on things she couldn't change. She'd do the best she could, that's all she could do.

She'd just settled onto the couch, an arm around each son, when a car crunched on the driveway. Sitting up, she glanced toward the window, the reflecting television images marring her view. She checked her phone. No response from C. J. None from Reid.

Her pulse quickened as she watched the door, waiting. Air expelled from her chest, her heart skipping when her husband walked in lugging two bulging grocery bags. With his buzz cut, chiseled jaw, and icy blue eyes, he stole her breath even now.

Still, he had some explaining to do. "Where you been?"

He set his bags on the table and closed the distance between them. Pulling her from the couch, he pressed a kiss against her temple. "Taking care of business, baby." He grinned and began unloading his items, slapping a thick slab of meat on the counter. "Too bad y'all already ate, because these steaks look good." He winked at her. "What do you say I grill these babies up tomorrow as a sort of back-to-school celebration?"

She crossed her arms. "Where you get the money for all that?"

His grin widened, a dimple protruding that matched his son's. "I told you I'd take care of you." He raised a finger. "Hold on a minute."

He went back outside, returning with a single red rose. "Something sweet for my sweet." He closed the distance between them and wrapped an arm around her waist, nuzzling her neck. "Why do I love you so much?"

Her body—and her heart—melted to him, but she refused to be lulled by his charm. Not until she had answers.

She pushed him away and searched his eyes. "Tell me, Reid. Because I know you don't got no job." He'd lost that three weeks ago, claiming unfair and prejudicial treatment.

His smile vanished. "I got what we needed, baby." His voice deepened, and he looked from her to the kids.

She straightened. He was right. No sense fighting in front of the children. Forcing a smile, she turned to her youngest. "All right, little man, let's see about degriming that sweaty body of yours." She ushered him toward the bathroom, following to make sure he actually got into the shower.

C. J. came home 20 minutes later dressed in painted-on jeans and a crop top. Based on her scowl, the girl was looking for a fight.

Bianca slammed her hands on her hips. "I thought I told you to throw that shirt away?"

Reid stood beside Bianca and placed an arm around her shoulder. Always supportive. Mad at him or not, she appreciated that about him.

Holding an energy drink guaranteed to keep her up all night, C. J. took a swig. "I bought it with my own money."

"I don't care if you found it in the gutter," which was where it belonged, "no girl of mine is going out dressed like a tramp." C. J. harrumphed and started to walk away but Bianca grabbed her arm. "You're too good for this, C. J."

Her face softened and for a moment, Bianca thought C. J. wanted a hug but then she rolled her eyes and jerked her arm away.

Bianca slumped against Reid, any resolve, any energy she'd come home with, sapped. All she'd ever wanted was a close, loving family. To be a good mom. To give her children what she'd never had. But wanting and doing were different things.

Once the kids were all tucked in bed, she and Reid migrated to the couch. She let him hold her, breathing in his musky scent. But only for a moment because she had to know. If he were up to his old tricks . . . she couldn't allow that. Not in her home.

Facing him, she sat cross-legged, spine pressed into the corner of the couch. "You in trouble again? Because I know you've been hanging with the crew."

"Baby, why you got to worry so much? I got me a little something on the side, to pay the bills until something better comes around."

"Is it legit?"

"You know I won't let anything mess up what we got here." He bopped her on the nose and pulled her to him again.

She started to press him further but his phone rang. He wiggled it from his back pocket and stared at the screen.

His face tightened. "Hello?" He cursed then stood. "I knew this would happen. I told you not to bring him." He paced and cursed again. "This is messed up. Messed up." Still swearing, he marched into the bedroom.

Bianca followed, heart hammering as he crammed clothes into a duffel bag. "What's going on?"

"I got to go."

"What do you mean you got to go?" She fisted her hands, using every ounce of self-control not to scream at him.

He continued rummaging through drawers, pulling things out and shoving them into his bag.

As he approached Bianca, his expression softened. "Baby, you know I'll watch out for you. Always." He leaned forward to give her a kiss, but she turned away.

"Yeah? And why should I trust a word you say? You told me you wouldn't do this anymore, either."

Eyes pleading, he pulled out his wallet and produced a wad of bills, which he handed over. When she wouldn't take them, he placed them on the dresser. "I love you. You know that, right?"

"Apparently not enough."

Chapter 7

Bianca jolted awake to banging and the shouts of deep voices.

"Omaha P. D. Search warrant!"

Adrenaline ignited her nerves. "Reid!" She reached for her husband then froze, a scream building in her throat. He wasn't there. Tears blurred her vision as the reality of the situation fell upon her with full force, rendering her immobile.

"What's going on?" Her voice came out in a shriek.

"Police search warrant! Open the door." The banging continued, followed by a sickening crack.

A barrage of heavy footfalls followed, voices ricocheting off the thin walls.

"Mom!" Sebastian's voice called to her from the hallway. "Mom, what's happening?"

My babies! She sprang to her feet, lunging for her bedroom door when it whipped open. A pack of armed men advanced, guns pointed at her. One of them held a German Shepherd by a leash.

Reid, what have you done?

"Hands where we can see them, ma'am."

Behind them, more men, wearing ballistic

helmets and armor plates, guns raised, headed toward the kids' bedrooms.

"No!" Bianca sprang toward them but was hurled to the floor, her chin grinding in the carpet.

"Momma!" Sebastian began to cry.

"Mom? What's going on?" C. J.'s shrill voice rang out above the clamor, shredding Bianca's heart.

She grimaced as the officer holding her down wrenched his knee in her back. "Let me see your hands!"

Her children continued to cry, louder now.

She closed her eyes and gritted her teeth in an unsuccessful attempt to restrain her tears. "It's OK, baby. Just do what they say." Following her own orders, she forced her trembling muscles slack. Arms yanked behind her back, carpet fibers scraping her skin and clogging her nostril. "Everything's going to be all right."

That was a lie. Reid had really done it this time, and nothing would ever be the same again.

She winced as cold metal snapped around her wrists, pinching her skin.

"Ma'am,"—a deep but gentle voice cautioned— "we'll help you up, but you need to stay calm. Can you do that?"

She nodded then struggled to get her feet under her as strong hands pulled her up.

The yelling stopped but the children's cries,

though softer now, continued. Officers began rummaging through drawers, lifting the mattress, tossing items from the closet. There had to be a dozen of them, maybe more. Their stares—some filled with pity, others disgust—tore into her. All of them saying the same thing: *You're garbage. What kind of mother marries a thug?*

The kind who hoped for better, just like Reid promised.

Where was he? Had the police already gotten to him? If so, did he go down without a fight?

Oh, Reid. I don't want to lose you. I hate you! Man, do I hate you.

Down the hall, Sebastian continued to wail, calling out for her. C. J. urged him to calm down, tried to reassure him. But that only made him cry all the harder. Robby said nothing. Probably was too terrified.

My babies!

"Please." Bianca made eye contact with one of the officers, her legs weak and wobbly. "Let me go to my children. Please."

The men in the room grew quiet and looked from one to the other. Finally, a tall guy with red scruff covering a pointed jaw nodded. "Go ahead and uncuff her. Take her and the kids outside while we search." He jerked his head toward a squat man to his left. "Y'all watch 'em."

Chills crept up her arms, and tears she'd been fighting flooded her face.

She and the kids spent the next three hours on the porch, guarded by armed officers while the others tore apart every inch of the house.

It had rained the night before, the porch floorboards damp and slick beneath them, drops of moisture falling from their gutters. As the sun rose, pushing back the inky dawn, drivers passed, slowing, staring. Nosy neighbors began to emerge, soon to be talking. Bianca raised her chin.

You don't know nothing about me. About us.

She never cared what others said anyway.

Except her kids did. The thought stabbed her heart with such force, it squeezed the air from her. She looked at C. J. who stood, arms crossed, scowling. Acting angry, but Bianca knew better. She couldn't be more broken.

Oh, baby girl, I'm so sorry. So very sorry.

Sebastian clung to her side, face buried into her nightgown, tears dampening the fabric. Robby stood, shoulders hunched, at the other end of the porch.

Bianca pulled her youngest closer and rubbed his back.

"Great husband you picked there, Mom." C. J. glared at her.

Her insides crumbled at the hatred pouring from her daughter's eyes. "We'll get through this."

"Whatever. Like you care. Just leave me alone."

Their relationship had been shaky before, but had Bianca lost C. J. for good now?

No. Never. She lifted her shoulders and looked at each of her kids.

This wouldn't break them. She wouldn't let it.

Chapter 8

Wednesday morning, Angela awoke well before her alarm, prework jitters overpowering her exhaustion. If only her brain had an off-switch. She must've obsessed over every what-if scenario a hundred times, all of them resulting in eventual unemployment. And crawling back to Ainsley and Chris, begging them to take her in.

Clearly melodrama was her specialty.

She glanced at the clock on her bedside table: 4:45. Ainsley would probably just be waking up. Oh, how Angela missed their morning coffee and prayertime. Missed her sweet daughter, period.

Breathing deep, she tossed the covers aside and slid out of bed. She headed straight to the kitchen for a much-needed caffeine fix. A brisk walk afterward would help expend her nervous energy. Since she didn't have to be at the school until 8:30, she had plenty of time.

Moments later, steaming mug in hand, she meandered to the living room to search for her Bible. But distant voices—it sounded like a group of men—drew her attention to the window.

Parting the blinds, she expected to find a work crew gathered at the house next door. Instead, a row of police cars lined the street and uniformed men flowed in and out of her neighbor's home.

The young family—a woman with short hair, Cassie Joe, and two young boys—huddled on their porch. The lady held the youngest, a waif of a kid with ash-blond hair, close to her side, his face pressed against her.

The teen sat in the corner with her legs pulled to her chest, head buried in her knees.

Angela's maternal heart ached. Poor girl. She looked so . . . sad. Defeated. All of them did. What was going on? A burglary? Or worse? A shiver ran through her.

Perhaps this wasn't the best location. At least she hadn't signed a lease, not that she could afford to move anywhere else.

What about those children? They had to be terrified, and she couldn't imagine the kind of lifestyle that brought cops—half a dozen, in fact—to one's door. Actually, she could imagine. That was the problem.

Morning walk nixed, even after her Bible reading, she still had a great deal of time on her hands. She might as well make the most of it. And the cobwebs draped all over the house gave her the heebie-jeebies.

She filled a large bowl with hot, soapy water. Sloshing suds on herself and the floor, she carted it to the living room where, it appeared, an army of spiders had taken up residence.

Elbow deep in bubbles, she spent the next hour scrubbing and humming until the living room nearly shone. Only a hint of the stale, mildew aroma remained, most likely wafting from the carpets. She'd tackle that soon enough, before she finished unpacking. She tilted her head and noted the yellow-and-green striped wallpaper, envisioning a coat of deep orange paint in its stead. Or maybe a celery green. But she'd need to clear that with the Martins first.

Another hour later, Angela stepped outside, dressed in her favorite outfit—a swoop-necked, leopard-print blouse edged in green and matching skirt, both slightly snug but not terribly so. She glanced at her red three-inch heels. Too high for an assistant teacher? Should she change to tennis shoes, considering she'd have recess duty? No. It was always better to overdress rather than underdress. Especially on the first day.

New job, new life, starting now.

Her cell chimed a text, and she glanced at the screen with a smile. Sweet Ainsley.

Praying for you today. Have a great one.

Angela responded with a heart emoticon. *Love you.*

Outside, a pale blue sky and a rising sun replaced the dark, heavy clouds that had unleashed torrents of rain the night before. Almost 8:00, and it felt like the temperature was already in the mid-eighties.

She got into her car and eased out of the drive, casting frequent glances at the family huddled on the porch across the street. The middle child, a boy with dark hair and large, brown eyes, looked up and held her gaze. Poor thing! It was almost as if he were crying out to her, to anyone, to come and help him. But what could she do?

She arrived at Rockhurst Elementary 22 minutes later, grateful she'd left her house early. But still late, thanks to a random, unintentional detour . . . also known as getting lost. Most likely she was the only woman in all the Omaha metro without a smartphone.

Located in a rougher portion of town, the flat-roofed, brick building centered a circular drive. A fair number of cars, some newer, most old and rusted, dotted the rain-slicked lot. An empty police car was parked along the east curb. Floral beds decorated with small bushes and clumps of wilting red daylilies flanked the entrance.

She parked, wiped sweaty hands on her thighs, and checked her appearance in the mirror one more time. Despite the humidity, her carefully styled and heavily sprayed curls remained limp free. She said a quick prayer for peace and confidence and stepped out, crossed the lot, and continued through the double glass doors.

Once inside, she headed straight for the administrative office and approached the nearest desk.

A round woman with deep wrinkles fanning from her slate-toned eyes flashed a wide smile.

"Good morning. May I help you?" With short, corkscrew, silver-streaked hair, she appeared to be in her mid- to late-sixties. The nameplate on her desk read Mrs. Lynn MaCarthy, Receptionist.

"Yes, hello." Maybe Angela should clock in first? Or stop in at the principal's office? "I'm here to . . . I'm covering Melodie Hanson's position—teaching assistant, I mean, para. Is Mrs. Allen in?"

Lynn stood and extended her hand, her grin widening. "Welcome to Rockhurst." Her gaze swept the length of Angela, her smile faltering before returning full force. "I bet you're shadowing Reuben today." She wrinkled her face. "He can be a bit of a stink pot, least until he gets to know you. But he's harmless. Have you checked in yet?" She gave her blouse a tug, releasing the fabric from between two belly folds.

"I . . . um . . . no." Angela rubbed the palm of her hand with her thumb. "I'll do that now."

Lynn glanced around then gave an almost indiscernible shrug. "Follow me."

She led Angela down a short hall to the teacher's lounge, chatting the entire time. "Being a para can be tough. Some teachers are helpful and appreciative. Others are . . ." She raised her eyebrows and shook her head. "Well, you know how it is. There are roses and thistles in every job." She laughed. "But don't worry. The nice

ones, like me"—she winked—"stick together."
She glanced about. "Would you like some
coffee?"

The rich aroma of freshly brewed grounds
filled the air, merging with the scent of bleach
and burnt microwave popcorn.

"I'm fine, thank you." Any more caffeine
would give Angela the shakes.

They continued through a doorway to a small
enclosure boasting a narrow table and metal
folding chair. The electronic time clock stood
next to a large corkboard covered with memos.

"Reuben should be here soon." Lynn checked
her clock. "Actually, he might already be out at
the crosswalks."

Angela blushed. "I meant to get here earlier
but—"

"No problem." Lynn flicked a hand. "Let's get
you checked in, then you can follow me to Mrs.
Allen's office." The principal. "You'll report
directly to her."

Angela nodded. She'd met the woman twice
over the summer, prior to accepting the position.
Though stern and focused, she seemed nice
enough. Fair.

Ten minutes later, printed schedule in hand,
Angela stood on the corner of Briarhedge and
Landcaster wearing a yellow vest that escalated
her body temperature by at least ten degrees. She
followed as Reuben, the man she was shadowing

for the day, guided a group of kids and parents across the walk.

Peering down the street, she hoped to catch a glimpse of the neighbor kids. Did they even go to Rockhurst? Probably. It was the closest elementary school. But would they make it to school today? Once again, she wondered if something terrible had happened, terrible enough that they'd be ripped from their home. Worse, what if they needed to be removed?

She was about to turn back around when two boys emerged from a distant alleyway. Holding her breath, she strained to make out their faces. One taller than the other, they trudged forward with slumped shoulders. They bore a resemblance to the boys she'd seen huddled on her neighbor's porch that morning. But as they grew closer, the resemblance faded.

She frowned. It wasn't them. Not that she could've done anything if it had been, other than pray.

Yes, prayer. Prayer was good!

"Hi!" A chubby little girl with long, blonde hair stood in front of her, grinning. She looked to be five or six and, based on the green gunk dripping from her button nose, in the throes of a bad respiratory virus.

Angela smiled, wishing she had her purse with its supply of tissue. "I'm Ms. Meadows, your new crosswalk attendant."

"Where's Mrs. Hanson?"

"I'm not sure. On medical leave of some sort." Which meant, she'd be back, and then Angela would be out of a job. Unless she could find another position, hopefully a permanent one.

The girl gave a half shrug then sneezed, the goop from her nose increasing until it hovered dangerously close to the child's upper lip. She raised an arm.

"No, sweetie, let me—"

Before Angela could stop her, the child wiped her nose on her bright pink sleeve, leaving a trail of slime on her cheek. The sleeve of the same arm that zeroed in on Angela, almost as if in slow motion.

She gasped, stumbling backward, as the child enveloped her in a tight, gooey hug, her sticky face pressed into Angela's gut.

"Uh . . ." She blinked and looked at Reuben then back to her affectionate new friend. And still the child remained, her snot-covered arm digging into the folds of Angela's back. Glancing down, Angela patted the girl's back, then patted her back again. "Thank you, sweetie. It's good to meet you too."

She shot another glance to Reuben, who was watching her with a hint of a smile as he ushered the other students onto the curb.

"Uh . . . you should probably get to school

now." She pried the child's hands off her, careful not to touch the goo.

The little girl beamed. "You're soft and squishy, just like my grandpa."

Ouch. That was a description she hadn't heard before. "You mean grandma?"

"Nope." The child sniffed and wiped her nose again. "My grandpa."

"What's your name?" Sidestepping toward the curb, Angela nudged her new friend forward. She flinched as something cold and wet splattered her leg and foot, trickling between her toes. Squeals and giggles followed.

"Stop!" Reuben's voice commanded silence. "Get out of the water." He glared at a short boy with glasses and pointed to the curb.

Hand to her neck, Angela whirled around to see the water splashing culprit, standing in a puddle, grinning. The boy, maybe six or seven years old, was drenched in mud to mid-calf, the children near him splattered as well.

Holding her breath, Angela glanced down. Splotches of mud clung to her nylons and covered her shoes. On her first day, no less.

With a quick, apologetic wave to an angry businessman sitting in the car in front of her, and a long line of cars behind him, she spun around. As she scurried across the street, her left heel landed in a blotch of oil and mud, sending peripheral spray up her other leg and upsetting her balance. Slipping, she shrieked, wobbling and flailing about.

Moments before face-planting, she reached out for Reuben, her fingers closing in on thin fabric.

A ripping noise ensued, followed by a chain of gasps and giggles.

She cringed and glanced up to survey the damage. She'd torn her co-worker's sleeve—and from the looks of it, an expensive one at that.

Righting herself, she smoothed her blouse. "I'm so sorry."

He stared at her, lips pressed together so firmly, the skin around them had turned white. His eyes looked ready to bug out of their sockets.

He remained silent, despite her ceaseless apologies, until the last of the children trailed into the building. "Forget it." He turned and stalked away.

Angela surveyed her color-coordinated outfit, decorated by kid-snot and mud-splatter.

This was going to be a long, mortifying day.

Chapter 9

Wednesday morning, Mitch left to meet his business partner at their latest remodel, the nineteenth-century bungalow next to the Martins' and kitty-corner to the Douglases'. Mitch had wanted to size up the place Monday, but there'd been a delay at the title company. They didn't get the keys to the property until late Tuesday evening.

He arrived at the 35th Street house early to find police officers clogging the road. Uniformed men swarmed the Douglas property as the family gathered on the porch. All of them but Reid, who was either conveniently missing or had already been hauled away. Though he hated to admit it, Mitch hoped for the latter. Maybe then Bianca would get her act together.

His thoughts shifted to the pretty new neighbor. How was she holding up? She had to be pretty unsettled, waking to cops storming the neighborhood. Especially considering she lived by herself.

Did that mean she was single? Not that it was any of his business.

A knock on his window startled him, and he turned to see Dennis standing beside his truck, scowling. There was no way he'd let up on the eviction now. But Mitch couldn't throw Bianca and the kids out. Where would they go?

He cut his engine and stepped out. "Hey."

"Great tenants we got over there, Mitch." He motioned to their rental. "Aren't you glad you took up for them?"

Mitch's neck muscles tightened. "When's the roofer supposed to be here?"

Dennis stared at him, his mouth twitching as if containing an explosion worth of words. But the roofer pulled up before he got the chance. Thankfully.

With an appropriate albeit tense smile in place, Mitch greeted the roofer. "Thanks for coming out on such short notice, Grant."

"Not a problem." Shielding his eyes from the rising sun, the man turned toward the remodel. In his mid-sixties, his deeply wrinkled face and chapped lips showed the results of a lifetime of sun exposure. "What's your time line on this?"

Dennis scratched at his chin. "I'd like to get this place listed by the month's end."

Grant nodded, widening his stance. "I should be able to knock this out by Saturday. Monday at the latest, so long as I don't find anything major."

That was the dominating question. What condition was this house really in?

"I'll take a look." With a grin that showed tobacco-stained teeth, Grant returned to his truck and pulled a ladder from the bed.

Mitch faced the road, making eye contact with Bianca's middle child. The kid always touted an attitude, acting like he didn't have time for anyone. Yet, he often lingered whenever Mitch stopped by their place, like maybe he wanted to ask something. Or just be noticed.

When the family first moved in, Mitch had determined to mentor those boys. But their dad made his feelings clear—he wanted Mitch and his "Bible thumping" to stay away from his kids. Soon they'd be gone for good, unless he could figure out a way to change Dennis's mind. After this morning, that was about as likely as a late-August cold front.

He faced his partner. "When does Jeremy get here?" Jeremy was their lead contractor and the most talented and efficient remodeler in the Omaha metro.

Dennis checked his watch. "Any minute now." He straightened, cracking his neck. "How about we go inside? See what we've got to work with."

"Sounds good."

Leaving Grant to inspect the shingles, Mitch and Dennis strode up the walk and ascended the cracked cement steps to the front door. The porch, blackened by mold and dirt, sagged left, suggesting ground erosion. Either that or poor construction. Based on a one-inch fracture separating the walkway from the bottom step, probably the latter.

"We'll need to get a mud jacker out here." Mitch jerked his head toward the fissure. That'd add another $500 at least. "Maybe bury the gutters."

"I'm aware."

The lock stuck, but after some muscle, the door opened with a squeal. "Rusted hinges." Mitch inspected the frame, the rough wood poking through peeling paint. "Might want to replace the door altogether. To increase curb appeal."

"All it needs is a fresh coat of paint." Making a slow, visual sweep of the interior, Dennis jotted notes on his clipboard.

The carpet, most likely the original, was pea green, stained with large splotches of brown. Well-worn, some areas were visibly indented. The light fixtures, rusted and covered in a layer of grime, looked straight from the sixties.

A pile of junk—a stuffed garbage bag, an old vacuum, a rolling chair, and a mound of clothes—lay in the corner. Other random items littered the floor. None of this surprised Mitch. Based on the trash he'd found in the backyard, he came expecting a mess. Hopefully, it was all surface level.

After a cursory inspection of the first floor and the small bedrooms and bathroom that made up the second floor, they headed for the basement. It was unfinished with a cement floor, exposed pipe, and wiring lining the ceiling.

Dennis sniffed, walking the perimeter. "You smell that?"

"It's a bit sour. Does the place have a sump pump?" Canvassing the room's perimeter, Mitch didn't find anything concerning until he reached the northeast corner. Above him, a patch of wood near one of the pipes had darkened, suggesting a leak. A splotch of dried rust on the floor provided additional proof.

"Think I found the source of the stench." He motioned Dennis over. "Least, I hope this is all it is." And that mold hadn't invaded.

"Sure'd be nice if Jeremy'd show up." Dennis grabbed his phone and studied the screen. "I need to know how many guys he wants working on this project." He paused. "What kind of repairs do we have out with our rentals?"

The conversation was steering dangerously close to the Douglas place. "Nothing major. We should be able to pour our focus into this place. And . . ."

Now wasn't the time to bring his son into the mix. But he'd promised Sheila. Besides, if Eliot truly was clean . . . "I've been meaning to talk to you about something."

Dennis dropped his hand, expression wary. "Yeah?"

"Sheila called."

Dennis swore and shook his head. "Not again. Besides, I thought he was still in rehab."

"He's out." Mitch swallowed. "Says he can kick his addictions on his own."

"Uh-huh."

Dennis didn't need to remind him of all the times Eliot had said that in the past, and all the times he or Sheila had found the kid passed out in his own vomit.

"What about what that drug counselor said? About enabling?"

Mitch swiped a hand over his face. "I know. It's just . . ." Who really knew the best way to handle a drug-addicted kid? Sure, tough love worked for some. It killed others. "He's clean, Dennis."

"So he says."

"I gotta trust him. Give him a chance to change. You know that." His voice grew husky. "He's my son."

Dennis blew air through tight lips, his eyes softening. "All right. Bring him on. But this is the last time." His gaze intensified. "If he blows it, that's it."

Mitch nodded, a lump lodging in the back of his throat.

At what point did a parent walk away?

The words spoken by the therapist replayed in his mind. *I know you love your son, Mr. Kenney. But sometimes love says and does the hard thing.*

Chapter 10

Dressed in work scrubs, Bianca watched her daughter gather her things. "I hope you have a good day."

C. J. gave a half shrug.

"Can I have a hug?"

C. J. pulled her bottom lip in over her teeth, like she always did when trying not to cry. Then she gave an almost indiscernible nod and buried her face into Bianca's chest, her thin frame shaking.

"It's gonna be OK." She rubbed her daughter's back, holding her tight. "I know your dad and I messed up."

C. J. stiffened, pulled away. "He's not my dad."

"I messed up." She grabbed her daughter's hands. "But I'm going to make this right." She lifted C. J.'s chin until their eyes met. "I promise."

C. J. studied her, tears welling behind her lashes. "I got to go." She hoisted her backpack on her shoulder and stepped toward the door.

"Love you, Ceej. Don't ever forget that."

With one last glance over her shoulder, eyes red-rimmed, her daughter left.

Bianca took in a shuddering breath. They'd get through this. Whatever she had to do, they'd make it.

She checked her watch and urged her boys out

of the house, following close behind. "Come on, now. You're gonna be late."

Robby frowned. "How come you got to walk us anyway?"

"Because I said so." In truth, she didn't have an answer except she needed more time with them. Maybe because it felt like her whole world was falling apart, and her children were all she had left. Besides, today would be tough, with all the kids who saw the raid. She couldn't shelter her boys from the cruel taunting they'd soon receive, but she could walk with them.

"Why can't you drive us?"

"I already told you, I need to save my gas." She'd be lucky to make it to payday as it was. She didn't even have the money Reid had left her—it'd been seized, along with a mess of other things, in the raid. Not that she would've spent the cash, knowing where it came from.

Sebastian dropped his backpack onto the ground with a huff. "I don't want to go. Can't you write us a note?"

"Uh-uh." And stay on Mrs. Wright's radar? That was the last thing Bianca needed. That woman was bugging her enough already. "Who would watch you?" One of these days someone would call Child Protective Services. "Besides, you need to go to school. How you ever gonna make something of yourself if you don't, 'specially since you missed yesterday?" They'd been so broken, so scared, she hadn't the heart to send them off. But now they needed to step up. Move on.

Both boys groaned but complied, trudging forward with slumped shoulders.

Nearing the school, they slowed. Face downcast, Robby began swinging the stick he was holding faster, clearly agitated, casting frequent glances from the sidewalk to the school.

A few dawdling kids walked behind and ahead of them, and a girl with a butterfly backpack skipped down the sidewalk across from them. When they reached the corner of Brianhedge and Landcaster, Robby stopped completely and began rubbing at his forearm.

"Boy, what's holding you up?" She surveyed his tight expression and pale skin.

He shrugged, watching a pack of students gathered around the bike rack. "Nothing."

She wrapped an arm around each of her boys and pulled them close. "You got nothing to be ashamed of, you hear me?"

Robby shrugged again and she turned him to face her. She squatted to eye level. "You got *nothing* to be ashamed of. Ain't nobody can beat you down unless you let them. Got that?"

His chin dimpled as tears pooled in his eyes.

She grabbed his hands. "You're a great kid, Robby. You're smart, fun, honest." Her voice intensified. "Don't let no one tell you different."

She gave his shirt a tug and straightened, looked at each of her boys in turn. "You walk in there holding your head high. You hear me?"

With a deep breath, Robby nodded. "Come on, Sebastian." He nudged his brother toward the school.

If she were a praying woman . . .

But she stopped believing in fairy tales long ago.

Giving their shoulders gentle squeezes, she squared hers and continued forward, following the same advice she'd given to them. At the crosswalk she stopped and studied the woman across from her. Was that . . . ? She angled her head. Yeah, it was her, all right. That nosy lady from across the street, the one who always watched her house—she stood on the opposite corner. Her yellow reflector vest hung loose over a paisley blouse. Her capris matched, like exact pattern and color. The woman's heels reminded Bianca of an old eighties rock video.

"Hello." Holding a stop sign, the woman greeted Bianca with a cheesy grin. "I'm Angela Meadows, your new neighbor."

"Uh-huh." Bianca kept walking.

Footsteps scuffed on the asphalt behind her. "If you ever need anything . . . eggs, a cup of sugar . . ."

Because women like Bianca couldn't afford those things? "We don't need nothing from nobody."

She shook her head and gave her boys a sideways hug. Anything else would embarrass them more than they already were. Then, spine straight, she turned around and walked home.

Reaching her drive, she checked her watch. Almost 9:00 a.m. She was cutting it close. Hopefully she'd hit every green light on her way to Hillcrest Manor, the nursing home she worked at. Her stomach growled, reminding her that she hadn't eaten breakfast. She resisted the temptation to dash back inside for a few slices of bologna. Fran, the head cook at Hillcrest, would slip Bianca some hash browns or something.

In her car, she cranked the engine, then held her breath as it sputtered to life. The arrow on the gas gauge wobbled near E—less than she'd expected. Great. A scrounge through her purse provided enough for two gallons—50 miles. But she'd need to hurry.

She peeled out of her driveway, down the street, and eased into the first gas station she passed. Outside the convenience store a worker with long, straight hair pulled into a loose ponytail smoked a cigarette. Upon seeing Bianca, she rolled her eyes and took a drag. She flicked her butt onto the concrete and ground it with the toe of her heavy, black boot. Following Bianca inside, the worker made no hurry to round the counter.

"Prepay?"

Bianca nodded and dropped her cash—coins

and all—onto the counter. "Number nine."

The woman—her name tag read Shari—punched numbers into the cash register. She cursed. "Stupid thing's stuck." She jammed her hand down again and again.

Bianca checked her watch. "Can we use that register?" She indicated the vacant cash machine on the other side of the counter.

"It's not open."

"Can't you open it?"

"Hold up." She pulled out a cell phone and dialed.

Bianca sighed, heat climbing her neck. She really didn't have time for this.

"Hey, it's me." The lady leaned sideways, resting an elbow against the counter. "The register's stuck again. . . . He's not here. I don't know. . . . I tried that." She let out a loud, exasperated exhale."I've already rung a lady up. Whatever." She jabbed a finger against her screen, glanced at Bianca with a quick, "Wait," then approached the other register. Obviously in no hurry to proceed.

Ten minutes later, Bianca was back on the road. Three obscenely long red lights later, she arrived at work with two minutes to spare.

Hillcrest Manor was a large, southern-styled facility spanning five acres. It sat in an older, established neighborhood, the kind with massive trees with knotted branches, covered porches, and couples sitting on swings or rocking chairs.

One man in particular, short, bald, and back bent from age, always seemed to be outside, trimming his bushes or riding his lawnmower. Whenever Bianca drove by, he'd grin and wave, as if genuinely happy to see her.

Or just happy in general. What would it be like to be truly happy? To have nothing to do but sit and sip iced tea, while watching the sunrise? No way Bianca would ever have that kind of life. She'd be busting her behind until her feeble legs gave out. But not her kids. They were gonna do better. Graduate high school, maybe even go to college, like Bianca always wished she'd done.

She pulled to the back of the massive brick building edged in peach trim and parked near the far east corner of the lot. She looked around, surprised at the large number of cars. Strange. Maybe they wouldn't be shorthanded for once. That'd make her shift lighter, but it could eat into her paycheck, take away the need for her to work overtime.

How would she make it without Reid's help? Her heart sank as an image of his handsome face came to mind. Mercy, she loved that man! She sure knew how to pick 'em.

She cut the engine and stepped out into the hot, humid air tinged with the scent of fresh cut grass. Once inside, she headed straight for the break room, where she grabbed a blueberry muffin from a plate on the table. *Thanks, Mrs. Wiles. Appreciate you.* Bianca would supplement her impromptu breakfast with some strong coffee.

Slow, shuffling footfalls approached from behind.

"Girl, where you been?" Dawn, also a nurse's assistant, entered wearing her usual frown and cherry red lipstick. Her cheerful scrubs—today a periwinkle blue with rainbow and smiley face print—posed such a stark contrast to the woman's typically surly mood, they struck Bianca as comical.

"I'm working swing this week." She brought her steaming mug to her mouth, inhaling the rich aroma.

Dawn shook her head, eyebrows raised.

"Why?"

Dawn shot a glance behind her then moved in close. "A couple of suits-and-ties showed up this morning."

"What do you mean? Like corporate?"

"Uh-uh. Worse."

Bianca rolled her eyes and checked the clock. "Spill it already." She didn't have time for games, but she didn't want to stumble into a mess unprepared, either. And around here, there were plenty of messes to fall into—people stealing from residents, upset family members making accusations. Knowing Bianca's luck, she was about to be the perfect scapegoat, thanks to Reid and all his extracurriculars.

"According to Don, they're with the FBI or something."

Adrenaline shot through Bianca, and she nearly dropped her coffee. She wanted to find out more—why they were here, what they were looking for—but was afraid to ask for fear of implicating herself. Living with a felon had a way of making one paranoid. Besides, it wouldn't take much to stir the rumor pot.

"You heard about the stink Ol' Man Abbot's daughter raised, right? Saying her papa wasn't getting all his meds."

"Angry families throw fits all the time. This'll blow over. None of this involves us, anyway. It's not like we have a key to the med carts or anything."

"Yeah, but according to night shift, Don's been pretty careless, leaving his cart unlocked more than once. Coming in late all the time, acting scatterbrained. Like a user, if you ask me. Course, to hear him tell it, someone tried to jack with his lock."

So the guy was looking to point fingers. Great. It wasn't hard to imagine who he'd target.

If word got out about the raid, which was sure to happen, it wouldn't be long before everyone in the place started watching her. Waiting for her to foul something up so they could pin this drama— whatever it was—on her.

Chapter 11

Friday morning, Mitch arrived at the 35th Street job site to find Angela sitting on her porch sipping coffee. He watched her for a moment, a strange sensation filling his gut. The kind he got at estate auctions, just before making his bid. Which was crazy.

She wasn't even his type, not that he really knew what that was, anymore. He hadn't dated in almost six years. And his last relationship had ended badly. Like horrifically so, with his ex-girlfriend stalking him, showing up at the office, remodel locations, his church.

He glanced at the time on his dash—7:30—then toward the remodel. Dennis and Jeremy stood on the stoop, discussing something. Guys were already on the roof, tossing old shingles down. The landscapers would be out in 20 minutes to give them a bid on their drainage issues.

Mitch grabbed his briefcase and stepped out of his truck, once again eyeing Angela. It'd be neighborly to say hi, see if she'd gotten settled in, needed help with anything.

Breathing deep, he squared his shoulders and strolled over. She glanced up as he approached. Her delicate eyebrows rose before her features smoothed into a smile that lit up her eyes.

"Morning," he said.

"Hi. Beautiful day."

"It is." He shoved his hands in his pockets, rocked on his heels. Scratched his jaw, shoved his hands in his pockets again. "You need help with anything? Getting unpacked. Whatever."

"I'm good, but thanks."

He surveyed the house behind her—siding, trim, the large, overgrown oak hanging over her roof. "Rain'll come pretty hard soon enough, when the weather shifts. I'll check on your gutters, if you want. Make sure they're cleaned out."

"I . . . uh . . ." Her brow furrowed for a flash before smoothing back into a relaxed smile. "I'd love an estimate, thanks."

His neck warmed. She thought he came over to make a sales pitch? "No, I mean," he raised his hands, palms out, shaking his head. "I wouldn't charge you. Just trying to be neighborly."

"Oh." She studied him long enough to make him uncomfortable. To make him feel like a creep. Then, smile back in place, visibly stiff this time, she raised her mug. "I appreciate your kindness, but I can manage."

"Right." He paused. "Well, then. I guess I'll catch you later."

She nodded, and he started to walk away.

"Mitch?"

He turned back around.

"What happened the other day?" Her gaze

flicked to the Douglas place, hands wrapped around her mug. "With the police and everything?"

"Not sure." The hint of vulnerability, of insecurity, in her eyes stirred something within—his protective side. The side Dennis always taunted him for, calling Mitch a sucker for strays and underdogs. Not that Angela was either of those, but she was a single lady living across the street from a thug. A thug who hung out with drug addicts and dealers.

Not the best neighborhood for a little lady like Angela Meadows. All the more reason for Mitch to keep his eye on her.

He leaned against her porch railing. "If I were to guess, I'd say Reid, the man that lives there, stepped into something. Seems that guy can't stay out of trouble for long." Why Bianca didn't leave the man was beyond him. Except they were married.

"Is he dangerous?"

"Nah." Least Mitch hoped not, but if the guy was slinging, who knew? Drugs changed people. Made them do crazy things. "Tell you what . . ." He wiggled his wallet from his back pocket and pulled out a business card. "Here's my number. You need anything, get spooked, whatever, call me."

Her cheeks colored as she accepted his card. "Thanks. I appreciate it."

Another awkward silence. "Well . . ." An engine hummed behind him, and he turned to see the mud jacker's truck pull up. The driver parked along the curb of the adjacent property and stepped out.

Mitch faced Angela again. "I'll see you Sunday?"

She hesitated, features tight, then nodded. "Yeah, sure."

With a brief wave, he sauntered off, a bit confused by his pretty new friend, even more confused by his reaction to her. Seemed the best thing he could do was steer clear of her.

But she was a single lady living across the street from a felon. She'd need some watching over.

When he reached the remodel, he found the mud jackers inspecting the foundation, one of them crawling beneath the sagging porch. Dennis stood a few feet away, holding his clipboard.

He met Mitch with a tight-lipped scowl. "Your boy's a no-show."

"I'll give him a call."

"Hey, fellas?" Jeremy stood in the property's doorway with a strained expression. "Looks like we've got mold."

Dennis cursed.

Mitch suppressed a moan. "Where?"

"The half bath."

A room that had been too jammed packed with

garbage and pet supplies, including decade old dog food, to get more than a cursory glance. An image of the darkened wood on the basement ceiling came to mind, spiking his pulse.

"How bad?" Dennis stomped across the lawn. Mitch followed.

"Not sure." Jeremy led them to the tiny, wallpapered room. With garbage still piled on the floor, there was only enough room inside for Jeremy. Mitch and Dennis leaned in from the doorway.

The stench of stale urine wafted from the stained linoleum and merged with the smell of lemon cleaner—an overturned cleaning bottle lay on a mound of towels.

"See that?" Jeremy pointed to a blackened splotch located on the far corner of the ceiling.

Dennis swore again. "With a leak like that and how long this place has been vacant, spores could be everywhere. In the walls, the heating ducts."

If there was anything that could make a house flipper's blood run cold, it was mold. Once airborne, spores spread like termites on rotting wood. Cleaning it up could cost a chunk. In some cases, it was cheaper just to tear the place down.

Dennis leaned forward and opened the cupboard beneath the sink. He released another slew of curse words.

Mitch peered over his shoulder and blew air

through tight lips. *What a mess.* "Did you walk through the place at all, bud?"

Dennis scowled. "There's no way to check for everything. You know that."

"And you didn't think the bathrooms should warrant extra attention? Seriously, man."

The veins in Dennis's temple bulged, telling Mitch to let up. Besides, griping about the situation wouldn't help any. And now they had an audience as the crew, drawn by Dennis's loud, foul mouth, gathered, wide-eyed, in the hallway.

Seeing them, Dennis glared. "Get back to work!"

"Actually," Mitch glanced back toward the bathroom. "They should probably hold tight. Until we know what we're dealing with." The last thing he needed was to have his guys tearing up mold-infested walls and inhaling toxic fumes.

"The bottom of the shelving's pretty wet, and black." He glanced at the stained and peeling linoleum beneath his feet. "We'll need to check the floors." This little jewel just kept getting better. "Jeremy, you know how to deal with mold?"

"Yeah. This room's got to be sealed off. The guys will need gloves, face masks, the whole deal. But honestly, it might be best for resale if you had the professionals come out. We'll have to disclose the water damage."

Mitch nodded. "That way we can show we

took care of the problem, had it professionally remediated."

Apparently, Dennis had run out of cuss words because he just stared at Mitch, his eyes bugging from his head. Now wasn't the time to remind the man he'd been the one pushing for this house. Regardless, it didn't matter. They'd shucked the cash and signed the contract. Now they needed to make the best of it. Hopefully without driving their business into the ground.

Chapter 12

Monday morning, Angela sat in the back of Mrs. Wright's fifth grade math class. As the teacher's assistant, she needed to focus on the lesson so she could reteach it, if need be. But her mind kept drifting to Mitch. He was nothing like the type of men she was used to, guys who threw tired, cheesy lines at her. Lines she normally fell for, not because she actually believed them but because . . . honestly, she had no idea why she'd done half the things she had.

Ainsley said she'd been trying to fill a God-sized hole in her heart. As cliché as that might be, she was probably right.

So why, now that her hole had been filled with Jesus, was she attracted to Mitch? She gave a mental shrug. Ainsley had always said right living and thinking would take time. That Angela would have to fight against old temptations. Especially when they landed on her porch. Course, that didn't mean she and Mitch couldn't be friends or that Angela couldn't keep his card, for emergency purposes. Which she quite likely could need, considering the police action she'd witnessed across the street.

"Mrs. Wright? Violet's doing it again."

Angela glanced across the room, first to the

blond kid who sat three rows from the pencil sharpener, then to a girl with short, black hair and thick glasses. She sat straight, stiff, forearms resting on either side of her textbook, eyes on the teacher.

Mrs. Wright huffed and crossed the room. Reaching the girl, she leaned forward, palms flat on the desk. "Violet, you must stop this behavior. You're disrupting the class."

"Sorry." The girl's gaze darted about the classroom before dropping to her desk.

The teacher watched her a moment longer, then returned to the front of the classroom. The moment she faced the smart board, the girl began mumbling to herself again, moving her hands as if engaged in conversation. Almost as if arguing with herself.

Angela watched with raised brows then noted the children around her. One rolled her eyes. Others snickered. A girl with braids and more freckles than not, whispered something to another child sitting beside her and the two erupted in laughter.

Mrs. Wright clapped her hands. "Violet!"

The child stopped, her arms falling to her desk once again, until she was no longer the center of attention. Then her animated dialogue continued. Eventually, the teacher sighed, shook her head, and ignored the girl altogether.

What made a child talk to herself like that?

Angela had never seen anything like it. She observed the girl, enthralled, until a series of high-pitched sneezes drew her attention to the other side of the room where her young neighbor, Robby, sat. She'd been so absorbed in her thoughts, she'd almost forgotten about him entirely, and her desire to reach out to him.

Wearing a gray T-shirt and faded jeans, a backpack tucked by his feet, he was hunched over, staring at his desk. When he'd entered, the other children had created quite a ruckus, some taunting him outright, others smirking as they whispered to one another. Even now, a handful of children shot frequent glances his way.

Clearly word had gotten out about the mess that had occurred at his place. Poor boy. Kids could be so cruel. If only there was some way Angela could brighten the sweet child's day.

"Pay attention, class!" Mrs. Wright clapped, and Angela startled.

Jerking her focus back to the front of the class, Angela straightened and folded her hands on her desktop. The teacher eyed her students a moment longer before resuming the lesson.

Angela stole a sideways glance at Robby and found him watching her. She wiggled her eyebrows and made a funny face, eliciting a slight smile.

Five minutes later, the lesson ended, and everyone dispersed into groups, pulling, pushing, and sliding their desks into circles.

Angela stood. Hands twined in front of her, she approached Mrs. Wright. "Where would you like me?"

The teacher regarded her with a deep frown, her eyes sweeping the length of her. Angela followed the woman's gaze from her flowing silver blouse, wide red belt, to her ruffled paisley skirt, which suddenly felt three inches too short. Giving the hem a tug that simultaneously caused her swoop-necked blouse to slip off one shoulder, she met the teacher's gaze.

Mrs. Wright fingered her necklace. "You can help the D group." She motioned toward the far back corner where Angela's young neighbor and a handful of other students had gathered.

Angela inwardly winced at the way the teacher spoke the group's name, as if the very words tasted foul on her tongue. With a terse nod, she turned and marched across the room, smiling at students as she went.

Reaching the D group, she found them engaged in all sorts of ruckus. Two were taking turns punching each other in the shoulder, the boy on the left falling forcefully against Violet, who sat beside him. The girl shoved the boy backward, telling him again and again to stop it.

Meanwhile, her young neighbor hunched over

his textbook, pencil in hand, frowning. With stiff, almost jerky movements, he wrote his name on the top right hand corner of his paper—Robby Oden.

Angela looked at Mrs. Wright, who appeared oblivious to the chaos on the other side of the classroom. Most likely, she'd given up on these kids, which meant they'd probably given up on themselves. Angela wondered again about Violet's odd behavior. Was the child lonely? Or was she struggling with a disorder?

The D group. Angela suppressed a sigh. Seriously? The teacher might as well have used the F word—*failures*. With what she hoped was an encouraging smile, Angela pulled an empty chair over. Though she'd grown to recognize these children, had even come to know some by name, she'd never officially met them. Had yet to make a connection.

"Good morning. How about we start by getting to know one another." She made eye contact with each in turn. Some responded with looks of curiosity, others with apathetic frowns. Robby looked up for half a second before staring at his paper again.

She touched the shoulder of the girl with glasses. "You're Violet, right?" She'd heard the teacher address the child on a few occasions.

"Call her schizo-four-eyes!" The short, stocky boy to her right made an ugly face. He had a noticeable overbite and a large gap between his front two teeth. "She's crazy." He crossed his eyes and made a circular motion with his finger at his temple.

"Shut up!" Violet gave him a shove then grinned at Angela. "I'm Violet, but I'm only in this group because of I lose my homework a lot and get freaked out when I take tests."

"Liar!" A lanky kid with black hair and a round, cheeky face slammed both fists on the desktop. "You're here because you're stupid, just like the rest of us."

"You're not stupid." Angela laid a hand on the shoulders of the students to her right and left.

"Yeah?" The round-faced kid pulled a miniature candy bar from his pocket. "How would you know?"

Angela studied the boy for a minute, searching her brain for a response that would matter. Finally, she repeated something one of her old professors used to say. "Most likely, you just learn differently."

The kids looked at her with wrinkled brows. Robby raised his head, held her gaze.

She smiled. "My job is to figure out how, and to teach you in a way you can understand."

Hope glimmered in Violet's eyes, and suddenly Angela's role as a paraeducator, or teacher's assistant, as she preferred to call it, carried more weight.

Holding Robby's intense gaze, she wondered for the umpteenth time since coming to Omaha what the Lord was up to. Whatever it was, she wasn't sure she was prepared.

Chapter 13

The Hillcrest Manor dining room was quieter than usual, the tension so thick it sent goose bumps up Bianca's arm. It didn't help that many of the staff walked around like a bunch of stressed out martyrs. When the big wigs came in, everyone seemed on trial. Those stiff-necks were worse than a state inspection. At least with the state, you knew what was required, and they usually gave you a second chance to get things right. So long as you didn't do nothing major, didn't hurt nobody.

Betty, the resident Bianca had been feeding, sneezed, refocusing Bianca's attention. A glob of mucus dripped from the woman's nose, and bits of mashed peas splattered her chin.

"Bless you, Miss Betty." Bianca grabbed a napkin and began wiping the woman's face, an act she squirmed against.

A waif of a thing with angular shoulders jutting from her blue blouse, Betty'd recently gotten into the habit of refusing to swallow. And no amount of cajoling seemed to help. If anything, it only increased the woman's stubbornness. Not that Bianca blamed her. Poor thing was on a pureed diet.

"One more bite?" She brought the spoon to

Betty's lips, raising an eyebrow when the woman actually opened her mouth. "Good. Eat up, now."

Betty's face puckered, and her entire body shivered. Sticking out her tongue, she blew a raspberry, spewing green gook all over the table.

Bianca jerked backward, raising her hands, palms out. "Girl!"

Betty kept spitting, her bright pink tongue vibrating faster than a hummingbird's wings, her blue eyes twinkling.

Bianca couldn't help but laugh. "Miss Betty, you're something else." She wiped spittle from the woman's cheek and hand, noting the smile tugging on Betty's thin, wrinkled mouth. "All right. All right. You had enough. Got it." Shaking her head, she sighed and surveyed the woman's barely eaten plate of food. "Let's get you cleaned up and back to your room before you start hurling those mashed peas at one of your Bingo buddies."

Betty mumbled, slapping her hand on the table. After two strokes, the woman's speech had become garbled, unrecognizable. Bianca engaged her anyway, to help her feel valued, noticed.

"I know. You want me to hurry so's you don't miss *Jeopardy*. How much you think the winner will get this time?" She kept talking as she wheeled the woman down the hall, smiling and nodding at other residents along the way.

She turned the corner and slowed. Ahead, Don

Matthews, the morning charge nurse, poured pills into tiny paper cups. He looked down both sides of the hallway. Noticing Bianca, he scowled then disappeared into a resident's room.

Nearing the opened doorway, she peered inside. Rumors said he was the reason for all the corporate drama. Some said he stole pills, others that he was careless and left his cart unlocked. Still others said one of the new hires was being investigated for allegations of patient abuse.

In truth, there wasn't a staffer who could avoid being the center of facility gossip. At least no one had singled Bianca out yet.

When they reached Betty's room, the woman's granddaughter Shanna greeted them.

"Nana, how are you?" The willowy blond stepped forward and, hands cupped around Betty's shoulders, kissed the woman's cheeks. Standing, she smiled at Bianca, her eyes soft. "Thanks for bringing her down."

"Course."

"She really likes you. I can tell. I can see it in her eyes, in how relaxed she is, whenever you're around."

Bianca shrugged, her heart warming. "I like her too." She gave her old friend's shoulder a nudge. "She keeps me on my toes. Isn't that right, Miss Betty?"

The woman didn't answer, but her lips twitched toward a smile.

Shanna tucked a loose lock of hair behind her ear. "I've got her from here. Thanks."

Bianca nodded and moved aside, allowing the girl access to Betty's wheelchair handles. "You two have fun." As she stepped into the hall, her phone chimed.

She checked her screen. *Reid!* Her heart soared and sank at the same time. Tears stung her eyes as she read his message: *Stay strong. Keep your chin up. Love you.*

After all the messages she'd left him, all her desperate pleas for answers, now he chose to respond? And still, she had no answers. Not that she expected any. Not really. She'd been around thugs long enough—had been raised by one. The less she or anyone else knew the better. One slip of the tongue could land Reid in jail.

She dashed into an empty room to type a response. *Where are you? When you coming home?*

Did she even want him to come home? To risk having the police barge into her house again, to watch her kids crying on the porch, terrified? The next time she could lose them.

Sinking onto the empty bed, she dropped her phone in her lap, and covered her face in her hands. She straightened at the sound of approaching footsteps, then Dawn's familiar voice singing off key and off tempo.

Bianca stood, stepping out just as Dawn was about to enter.

"Woman, where you been?"

Bianca wiped sweaty hands on her scrubs top. "Hey. What do you need?"

"Help getting Henry in bed." She twined her fingers together, then stretched them backward, cracking her knuckles. "That man's like a stack of bricks. Come on." She motioned with her hand then led the way to Henry's room, three doors down.

Inside, the television was on, the volume high. Dawn grabbed the remote and lowered the sound, initiating grumbles from their patient.

"My man, I'm getting a headache." She glanced about, lifted a lace doily and a wad of tissues. "Where's your hearing aids?"

A plastic plant with purple flowers collected dust on his windowsill next to a Nebraska Cornhuskers water bottle. On his bedside table sat a box of half eaten chocolates, a crossword puzzle, and a folded newspaper. No hearing aids.

Bianca moved to his right and waited until Dawn secured her gait belt around Henry's waist. Then, suppressing a grunt, she helped hoist the man onto his bed.

Grabbing the man's remote, Dawn shook her head. "Whoo-whee, are things messed up in here!" She looked behind her then stepped closer.

"You know the big wigs sent the Anders sisters home, right?"

"What do you mean?"

"They left, that's what I mean."

Bianca huffed. "Duh. Why?"

"Ain't been to the break room yet." She grinned. "Give me till the end of the shift. I'll get the low down for you."

"No. You'll get the most interesting rumor."

"Whatever. All's I know is Don's acting strange, like he's sweating something."

"Don's always acting strange."

"Girl, ain't that the truth!" She laughed and sauntered off.

Watching Dawn leave, Bianca hugged her torso, fighting off the growing uneasiness churning in her gut. The truth would come out soon enough. In the meantime, she had people to attend to, and now wasn't the time to fret.

With a deep breath, she hurried down the hall to the room of one of her favorite patients.

Virginia sat in her wheelchair, chatting with a plump woman with kind eyes and shoulder-length brown hair. The woman held an opened book in her lap.

"I thought for sure it was in Luke." She flipped through the thin pages.

Bianca knocked on the door. "Excuse me."

Both ladies looked up, offering equally wide smiles, though Virginia's touched Bianca the most because with Virginia, she knew the smile was real. That she really cared. Why, Bianca hadn't a clue, except maybe that she didn't know what Bianca was really like, the type of husband she had.

"Come in, dear!" Virginia opened her arms wide, and her guest stood.

Bianca accepted the sweet woman's embrace, breathing in the scent of roses and talcum powder.

She stepped back and turned to the brunette with an extended hand. "Hello. I'm Bianca."

"Joan." The woman took Bianca's hand in both of hers. "Virginia's niece."

"Bianca here is one of the best Hillcrest has." Virginia squeezed Bianca's arm. "Isn't that right, dear?"

Her cheeks warmed. "I don't know about that."

"I do." Virginia winked and then shared a few of the things Bianca had done, all minor. Soon she was talking about her childhood days on the farm, the old country store two blocks away, and how she'd spend her weekly allowance on a candy bar.

Listening to her lifted Bianca's mood. Just standing in the woman's room, with the midafternoon sun filtering through her thin curtains and the smell of antiseptic tingeing the air, brought Bianca much needed peace. So much so, she lingered longer than necessary.

"Oh, my!" Joan looked at her watch and stood. "I hadn't realized it was so late. I better go. I'm watching the grandkids today." She patted Virginia's hand. "That means I better hurry, if I don't want to get stuck in the back of the school pick-up line." She gave her aunt a hug and kiss, Bianca a parting wave, and left.

"Guess I should go too." Yet Bianca remained standing, gazing without focusing on the woman's afghan.

"Bianca?"

She glanced over.

Virginia's eyes were soft, compassionate. "How are things going? How are your kids?"

She longed to share her heart with this kind woman, a woman who always spoke words of wisdom, of hope, even when she'd been knocked back by a nasty case of pneumonia.

But this woman—this honest, sweet woman— liked, even admired, Bianca. She couldn't shatter that by sharing the garbage of her life.

She forced a smile. "We're good. The kids are growing like weeds."

"I'm praying for you."

"For what?"

"That you would know how much God loves you." She paused, her gaze intensifying. "I made something for you." She reached into a bag hanging from her wheelchair and produced a delicately embroidered dishtowel, then handed it to Bianca.

Normally, staffers weren't allowed to take gifts from patients, but the director never seemed to mind when it came to Virginia. Maybe because her gifts were handmade.

Running her fingers along the lace, Bianca read the quote stitched in purple floss. "Come to me, all you who are weary and burdened, and I will give you rest. —Matthew 11:28"

Rest. What she wouldn't give to spend a day doing nothing. To close her eyes, prop her feet up, and take a long nap.

"This is beautiful." Her chest felt tight. "Thank you." Sweet Virginia. She meant well, with her platitudes and verse cards. But Bianca wasn't even on God's radar. Unless it was to squash her flat.

"Well, I guess I best get back to work."

She spent the rest of her shift wrapped up in her thoughts, replaying her last conversation with Reid in her head, reading his text message again and again. By the time she finished with her last patient, her tense muscles felt like stale taffy. She was so preoccupied with her Reid drama that she almost left without her paycheck. If not for seeing one of her co-workers holding his check, she would have.

Slinging her purse over her shoulder, she slammed her locker shut, then strolled down the hall to the front desk. As Dawn said, Summer

Anders, the person in charge of payroll, wasn't there. In her place stood a tall man with boxy shoulders, thick brows that curled upward, and a deep frown wrinkled between them. He eyed Bianca, as if sizing her up.

Resisting the urge to cringe, she stood tall and maintained eye contact. "I came to get my paycheck."

He stared at her a moment longer, then glanced behind her before turning back to his desk. He picked up a stack of envelopes from beside the computer screen, he faced her again. "Name?"

"Bianca Douglas."

Frowning, he flipped through the envelopes before handing one over.

"Thanks."

He nodded and crossed his arms, looking past her again.

She turned, walked slowly at first, then quickened her step to a near jog to the break room where she anxiously tore open her envelope. She pulled out the green check and studied the numbers, her stomach dropping.

How could that be? It was almost $200 less than normal. She whirled around, ready to march back to the office when it hit her. She'd called in three days in a row when Sebastian got the flu. Now she wouldn't have enough to pay her bills, and she was already two weeks behind on rent.

So much for sweet Virginia's prayers.

Chapter 14

Angela paced her kitchen, eyeing the pot of spaghetti on her stove. She wasn't the kind of woman who walked up to strangers, especially those who wanted to be left alone. Her neighbor had made that quite clear the day she and Angela met at the crosswalk. *"We don't need nothing from nobody."*

In other words, stay out of my business. But Angela couldn't do that. Her heart wouldn't let her.

She knew the children received free breakfasts and lunches. What'd they do about dinner? She thought of the police raid and shivered. Those poor kids.

Returning to her stove, she gave the sauce a stiff stir. "Lord, what should I do? I can't just go barging over to the woman's house. What if I offend her?" *I'd look like an idiot.*

She paused. And now she came to the ugly truth. No matter how hard she tried to justify her hesitation, when it came down to it, she was worried about appearing foolish. She was allowing her pride to hinder her obedience.

"Fine!" With a huff, she dropped her spoon on the stove and rummaged around for Tupperware, which, of course, wasn't unpacked yet. Twenty minutes later, sauce forming a cooked-on film around her pan, she spooned a serving of pasta for herself and covered it in tinfoil. Pouring the remainder in a large plastic container, she sucked in a deep breath and prepared for a healthy dose of humiliation.

Mitch kicked at the stump of an old, past-dead lilac bush standing in what he hoped to turn into an attractive flowerbed. From what he could see, the plant's roots stretched down deep. To make matters worse, someone had planted the thing right up next to the house, apparently not realizing it'd grow. When it got too large, their solution? Whack off the top.

"We can always make a chair out of it." The landscaper they'd hired to tackle the yard grinned. He was a short, squat man with beady eyes nearly swallowed by sagging lids.

Dennis cracked his neck and surveyed the dirt-packed yard. "Seems to me we might be better tearing everything up and starting fresh."

"You want the lawn resodded too, right?" Rocking on his heels, the man hooked his thumbs in his belt loops. "And the gutters buried? Drain pipes running down the side of the property to fix your erosion problem?"

It was no secret Mitch and Dennis had completely different budgets in mind. Matter of fact, completely different ideas on how they should run this business. If not for their long history, starting way back when they shared a dorm in college, Mitch would cut his losses and run. Losses that were growing bigger every day.

He glanced toward the Mold Remediation and Restorations van parked along the curb and shook his head. They'd finally showed up, after half a dozen phone calls.

"Shoddy work will cost us more." Dennis narrowed his gaze as if inviting a challenge. Mitch was through fighting for the day. He started to say as much when his phone rang, saving him from what probably would've been a public and humiliating argument.

He glanced at his screen. Kaden, their Realtor. "Hey, how'd the showing go this afternoon?" Hopefully Kaden had good news on the Ida Street property, a renovation they finished two weeks ago.

"I just heard back. The couple liked the location, said the house was nice, but they're really wanting a basement."

"At $75K?"

"I know. But according to their agent, they're young and googly-eyed in love, looking for their dream house."

Dennis nudged his shoulder and motioned toward the street where Bianca pulled into her driveway. His stomach dropped. Inhaling, he nodded. A perfect end to a frustrating day.

"Well, keep trying." Ending the call, he faced the Douglas property. Bianca climbed out of her car, shoulders slumped, and trudged up her stairs. Poor lady looked about as beaten up as Mitch felt.

As if his temporary frustrations compared in the slightest to hers—out of money, kids to feed, police banging on her door.

He slipped his phone into his back pocket and trudged across the yard. As he neared the edge of the property, a flash of color passed through his peripheral vision.

Turning, he watched with growing amusement as Angela Meadows crossed the street, dressed in dangerously high heels. That woman was something else. Pretty, petite, seemed kind, generous. But man, the way she dressed . . .

He shook his head and suppressed a smile. It appeared her mid-thigh, rainbow-colored skirt made it impossible for her to take steps any longer than a foot and a half. She wore a ruffled, maroon apron tied around the back and matching oven mitts, her hair pulled up in a clip. Well, most of it. The stiff, late August wind did a number on the back, swirling the loose locks every which way.

She hobbled up the Douglases' stairs, tripping over a large crack in the concrete. By the time she reached the door, Mitch was exhausted just watching her. And more than a little intrigued.

He chuckled. What was that silly little lady up to now? Playing reverse welcoming committee?

The door opened, and Bianca appeared. Angela thrust her food out. This appeared to initiate a conversation of sorts. Doing his best to keep from laughing out loud, he strained his ears but couldn't catch anything.

Three cars whizzed by in close succession, the last with music blaring from its open windows. When the street finally cleared, he found Angela heading his way.

His face heated. Ducking his head, he started to turn around when she called out to him. "Mitch, hello!"

He glanced up with a slight smile, hoping the heat in his cheeks wasn't an indication of their color. "Ms. Meadows." Why did he suddenly feel the need to hide from her? He was acting like a child.

Hands in his pockets, he sauntered over. "Lovely afternoon, isn't it?"

With a mitted hand, she brushed her hair from her face, strands catching on her lashes. "A little hot, but yes." She grinned and slipped off her oven mitts. "I saw you at church last Sunday, thought of saying hi, but you seemed pretty busy." She gave a one-shoulder shrug then turned to survey his renovation. "So, how're things going in the remodel business?"

"We're making progress." Sort of. In a lunge-forward, slide-back kind of way, but she didn't need to hear about his house-flipping drama. "How about you? Where'd you say you work, again?"

"I'm not sure I did." Her smile accentuated her high cheekbones. Her eyes were a smoky blue, rimmed in gray, dotted with icy flecks. In the absence of the heavy, glittery eye shadow, they were quite pretty. As was she. "I'm a paraeducator, until I can land a teaching position."

"Yeah? Which school?"

"Rockhurst."

"Really? You got any of Bianca's kids in your class?"

"Classes."

"Huh?"

"Classes. I float around quite a bit from one grade to the next."

He nodded. "So you've probably seen the Douglas boys, then. Well, I 'spect they might have a different name. Different dads." He clamped his mouth shut, wishing he'd learn to think before speaking. There was no sense airing Bianca's dirty laundry. The woman carried enough shame—and judgment—as it was. Not that she hadn't earned a good chunk of it, but even so. Maybe now that Reid was gone—at least Mitch assumed he was—he hadn't seen the man since before the raid—Bianca would get her life back together.

Angela chewed her bottom lip and looked across the street. When she faced Mitch again, her expression softened, turned maternal. "It's probably none of my business, but . . . I saw the police the other morning, and those poor kids gathered on the porch . . ."

He sighed and massaged his forehead, grains of dirt scraping beneath his fingers. How much should he tell her? That depended on why she wanted to know, and yet, her sad frown answered that. And the fact she'd just brought the family a tub of something. "It's an unfortunate situation. A case of a tired, lonely single mom falling for the wrong type of guy."

"But is he . . . ?" She hugged her midsection. "I guess I thought he was out of the picture."

"Could be. Don't know." Though he might find out soon enough, when he hit Bianca up for her rent money.

Angela rubbed her tricep, as if cold. "Well, I shouldn't keep you." She flashed a toothy smile that returned the light to her eyes. "I've got a plate of spaghetti getting cold on my counter."

"I could—" He stopped moments before asking her to dinner, as if he had the time or gumption to mess with romance. "I can understand why you'd want to get back."

She nodded, lingered a moment longer. "Well . . . I'll see you Sunday." She excused herself with a wave and started to walk away.

"Angela?"

She turned, rays from the low-lying sun lighting her delicate face. "Yes?"

"I . . . uh . . ." What? Wanted to take her to coffee? He hated the stuff. Wanted her to join him for dinner? That'd seem too much like a date, and he certainly wasn't ready for that. Nor the church gossip that'd initiate. Why was he even entertaining the thought? "You been to the zoo?"

Brow wrinkled, she angled her head. Hesitated. "Ever?"

Heat crawled up his neck, inching dangerously close to his face. "No, I mean . . . the Omaha Zoo. I know you like to—"

"Oh!" Her eyes widened as a grin emerged. "You thought maybe I could invite the Douglas boys. That's a wonderful idea, except . . ." She frowned and shook her head. "I don't think they'd go. I can barely get them to talk to me as it is. But I love how you think." She brought twined hands beneath her chin. "You know, we should tag-team those kids."

"Excuse me?" How had the conversation taken such an odd detour?

"You know, partner up in our efforts."

"I'm sorry, but you lost me."

"To reach out to Bianca and her children. Seems neither of us are making much headway." Her smile turned sheepish. "I get the sense you'd like to do more."

"I . . . uh . . ." That was true enough. And apparently, he'd flubbed his zoo invite. Who asked a grown woman to the zoo anyway? "Sure. What'd you have in mind?"

"I don't know. Should we pray on it?" That adorable grin returned, her eyes sparkling. "Hopefully the spaghetti helped pave the way."

"Next time bring cookies."

She laughed. "Great idea. With some to spare. You like chocolate chip?"

"I do." Was she flirting with him or just being neighborly? Another reason he didn't like the dating scene—too many gray areas and hidden messages.

"I'll have to make you some, then."

"I'll look forward to that."

An awkward silence followed.

"Well then." No sense standing there, grinning like an idiot. He shifted, rotating toward his property. "Guess I'll see you around."

She nodded. "Have a great day, Mitch. And good luck on your house."

Mind still spinning—and face still flaming—he watched her leave, totter down the walk and up her stairs, apron ties flapping behind her. That was one intriguing lady. Based on her clothing, he'd initially pegged her as flighty and shallow. Maybe even promiscuous. But after today's conversation, his opinion of her had taken a 180.

"What're you waiting on?"

119

He turned at his partner's gruff voice.

Frowning, the man approached, arms staunch. "You gonna talk to that woman, or do I need to do it for you?"

"What? What woman?" Heat rushed to Mitch's cheeks as his thoughts snapped to Angela.

"Our freeloader, Bianca Douglas. Because we both know how that conversation will go." He made a hitchhiking sign and tossed his thumb over his shoulder.

"I told you I'd take care of it."

"And how long have you been saying that?"

Mitch couldn't stall much longer. If Bianca didn't have the rent money, there wasn't much he could do to stave off the eviction process. Maybe he shouldn't even care. This was a business, after all. But the idea of throwing that family out made him physically ill.

Maybe I'm not cut out to be a landlord.

Chapter 15

Bianca stepped away from the window, allowing the curtain to fall back in place. That woman was insane, bringing over a pot of spaghetti in that getup. Someone needed to tell her the eighties were done and gone. And old ladies had no business wearing skirts that tight or bright. Or short.

She looked at the slip of paper her new neighbor had given her. *Here's my number. Call if you need anything or just want to get together for coffee.*

Right. Bianca would do that right quick.

Shaking her head, she ambled through the living room, pausing to watch Robby. She frowned. He sat hunched forward, elbows on his knees, hands fisted under his chin. His scowl was so deep, it nearly swallowed his entire face.

Her sweet boy was so angry. Same with C. J., not that Bianca was hugely surprised, the girl being a teenager and all. Even so, Bianca needed to find a way to connect with her. They needed some one-on-one time. All her kids did.

Unfortunately, time was something Bianca lacked. Still, she'd figure out something.

She walked into the kitchen to put away the chicken she'd been dicing. The groceries she'd asked C. J. to put away remained on the counter next to the container of spaghetti. Loud music blared from the girl's bedroom. Bianca started to holler, then stopped. There'd been enough fighting in their home lately.

She contemplated barging in to her daughter's room and shaking her thing, as she belted out the lyrics. Wouldn't that shock the stink right out of her? Except the girl would probably video it, post it online. Now that would be something.

Chuckling, she grabbed the chicken by the leg. She'd barely shoved it into an old potato-salad tub—her makeshift Tupperware—when her doorbell chimed.

Crazy woman, what'd she want now?

With a huff, Bianca washed her hands, plucked a frayed hand towel from the counter, and marched to the front door. Then stopped. Might not be her neighbor. Her stomach flopped, and a burst of adrenaline shot through her. Could be one of Reid's no-good friends, trying to track him down. Or maybe the police had come back, looking to rifle through her things again. Or CPS, asking questions about the raid.

"Who's there?" Sebastian sprang to his feet.

"Shh!" Bianca whirled around, finger pressed to her lips.

He startled, eyes wide, mouth ajar. Then, revealing a fear that can only come from waking to a house full of armed men, he backed into his chair.

Her already queasy stomach cramped to see her kids—all of them—living in fear. All the time. And it wouldn't go away until Reid got locked up.

The doorbell chimed again, making her jump.

Holding her breath, heart thrashing, she tilted sideways to catch a peek through the side window. She exhaled, her shoulders going slack. It was only her landlord. But then she remembered how much money she owed him, and she tensed once again.

Maybe if she ignored him, he'd go away. Think she wasn't home. Except he might've seen Miss-Diva-Chef drop off a big ol' container of food. That and Bianca's car sat in the driveway.

The doorbell chimed a third time, and with a heavy sigh, she answered.

"Good afternoon." Mitch Kenney stood on her porch wearing a sweat-stained shirt, faded jeans, and heavy boots.

She nodded, one hand on the door, her shoulder resting against the frame. "Mr. Kenney."

He shifted. Scratched his whiskered jaw. "Listen, I know things have been rough . . ."

She stiffened. "We're making do."

"Rent's late. Den—I came to collect."

Now what? She said she'd have the money when she got paid, and payday had come and gone. Besides, that preppy-dressing partner of his hated her. Was waiting for a reason to kick her and the kids out. He'd said as much himself. Called her a leech. "Hold on."

She closed the door an inch from latching and trudged to her bedroom. Her purse sat on her dresser next to a stack of bills. Like the electric, water, cell phone. Visa. She had no business using a credit card, but she signed up for it back when Reid was working. A real job.

She plopped onto the edge of her bed and covered her face with her hands. What was she going to do? How could she choose between rent and groceries? And she couldn't cut off her cell service. That was how work reached her when they needed someone to cover an extra shift. And her kids' school.

And Reid.

She squeezed her eyes shut to keep the tears from falling, but a few escaped. They trailed her cheeks and dropped off her chin.

It wasn't supposed to be this way.

She sat like that for some time, long enough her landlord might've given up on her. 'Cept she knew he wouldn't. Not unless he planned to return with an eviction notice, but he couldn't do that, not this quickly. Sure she'd been late on rent, a lot. But she'd always paid eventually. Would now too. Except she knew Mr. Kenney and his business partner were itching for a reason to toss her out. Regardless of how nice Mr. Kenney tried to act.

Drying her cheeks with both palms, she stood and crossed to her purse. She pulled her checkbook out and studied the numbers in the ledger. She didn't have enough. But if she wrote the check anyway . . .

It'd only make things worse. She had no choice but to offer Mr. Kenney her best and hope for mercy.

As if mercy ever came her way.

She snorted and pulled out a pen, scrawled out a number—half of her rent but all she could spare. Then, tearing it off carefully, she folded it and returned to the front door. She ruffled Sebastian's hair en route, wishing she could snatch the boy up. Hold him close, soaking up every last ounce of comfort the sweet child gave her. But she couldn't do that. She had to be strong.

Mr. Kenney still stood on the stoop, shifting from one foot to the other. Upon seeing Bianca, he visibly relaxed, and his expression softened. It almost looked like his eyes got misty. Probably from the wind.

She held out her folded check, unable to meet his gaze. "It's all I got."

Mr. Kenney studied her for several seconds before taking the slip of paper. Then, unfolding it, he looked from the check to her then back to the check again. He stood there for a long time, long enough that Bianca's feet began to burn. Long enough that it became awkward. Long enough that she began to wonder if he'd really boot her out this time.

But then he slipped the check in his pocket, looked her in the eye, and left.

She watched him cross the street, nausea mounting.

She needed to catch a break. Soon. Real soon.

Chapter 16

Noisy children jostled past Angela as she made her way to the cafeteria for lunchroom duty.

"Walk!" A deep, male voice boomed from behind her.

She jumped and quickened her step while the children slowed theirs, falling back in line in what resembled a hop-jog-shuffle. It was quite comical. And a bit embarrassing, considering she'd probably been negligent in allowing them to run. Though technically they weren't her responsibility until they actually made it into the cafeteria. In fact, she still had a minute and 30 seconds of break remaining.

A memory from when she was a child resurfaced. She'd been in the third grade, and their family had recently moved. As the friendless newbie, she'd hated going to school and pretended she was sick numerous times. But her mom never budged. She'd give her a quick hug, turn her toward the school entrance, and nudge her forward. But then one day, when the lunch bell rang, Angela trudged out of her classroom, dreading eating lunch by herself yet again, only to find her mom waiting for her in the hallway with a special packed lunch. They'd eaten it together on the front lawn of the school, and though the days following had still been hard and lonely, at least for a while, somehow that time with her mom had helped.

She missed her mom. Would she ever find her—and find a way to reconnect? To make up for all she'd done, all the lies and sneaking around?

A few feet ahead of her a kindergartner with auburn, French-braided hair hugged the wall, eyes wide. She held an insulated lunch bag decorated in rainbows and ponies in one hand and what appeared to be a stuffed bunny in the other.

Angela veered her direction. "Hey, there. What's your bunny rabbit's name?"

The girl's head snapped up, her previously tense features smoothing into a smile. "Radishy."

Angela laughed. A fitting name for the patched and tattered toy. She patted the animal's head. "Hello, Radishy, I'm Ms. Meadows." She looked at the girl again. "What's your name?"

"Sarah."

"Well, good to meet you, Sarah. You enjoying school?"

The child frowned and shook her head.

Angela suppressed a laugh. "It'll get easier. Promise." She watched as the girl continued down the hall, soon engaged with two other children.

Nearing the teacher's lounge, Angela slowed.

Reuben, Mrs. Wright, and a tall, heavyset man Angela had seen on numerous occasions in passing gathered outside the doorway. They all looked her way. Eyebrows raised high enough to be painful, Reuben made a slow, visual sweep of Angela's attire, then shook his head as if she disgusted him.

What had she done to land on his hate-radar?

Telling herself again and again she didn't care, she tugged on the bottom of her blouse and hurried down the hall. Her heels clinked against the shiny black linoleum as she entered the cafeteria. The aroma of fried chicken and something sweet she didn't recognize filled the room. She glanced at one of the children's trays on the table beside her. Nope. Still didn't recognize it.

As usual, she took up her position near the far-east corner for easy view of the tables. She offered kind words to passing students, many she now knew by name. Some she'd come to know a bit deeper—what foods they enjoyed, what classes they hated. Learned to recognize their hints of fears or insecurities. It touched her how easy it was to form a relationship with these sweet children. How easy it was to brighten their day.

But then there were others, like Robby, who remained aloof, guarded, no matter how hard she tried to connect. In class today, she could hardly get a word out of him. It hadn't helped that he hadn't done his homework and that Mrs. Wright chastised him for this—publicly. It was almost as if the woman had given up on the child. And she wasn't the only one. From what Angela could tell, Robby had a reputation for being a slacker.

But she knew that wasn't the case. The boy was just sad. Discouraged. Couldn't the faculty see that?

She scanned the cafeteria to catch a glimpse of him and his little brother. Robby sat at the far end of the fourth grade table, watching a group of rough-looking sixth graders across from him with what appeared to be admiration. Or fascination. She couldn't see what the older boys were doing, but she'd heard enough about them to know it probably wasn't anything good.

She frowned. A moment ago, she was condemning teachers for making assumptions, and here she was doing the same thing. Even so, she needed to see what was keeping those boys so enthralled.

She smoothed her hair behind her ears and approached them.

"Hot momma!" someone behind her called out.

She startled and whirled around to find a group of boys snickering.

Someone else whistled, this time from the sixth grade table. She whirled again, only to encounter more snickering. Breathing deeply, she squared her shoulders, ready to reprimand only to catch a glimpse of a smug-faced Reuben standing a few feet away.

Once again she wondered why that man hated her so. Sneers and sarcasm from children she could understand. Ignore. They were, after all, elementary-aged boys. But a colleague?

She looked him in the eye, initiating an extended, nonverbal standoff. One that only embarrassed her further, when she realized how incredibly childish she was being. A phrase her grandmother used to repeat came to mind. "You might get tossed in the pen with the pigs, but that don't mean you gotta roll in the mud with them."

Turning her back to him, she took in three long, calming breaths and strode toward the cafeteria line. *Lord, help me to be kind. Or at least to keep from doing and saying something I'll regret.*

Especially since she was hoping to land the next available teaching contract. Making enemies wasn't the best way to do that. She'd done way too much of that in her lifetime already. She was so ashamed of who she'd been—spending money on stupid things like clothes and bar hopping, racking up credit cards, jumping from one man to the next, one job to the next. Living off the men she dated for as long as they'd have her, believing they were the ones who would finally help her get a leg up in life. Then she'd met Stephen and had fallen hard for him—thought she was in love, though she knew now what they had wasn't anything like love was supposed to be. But at the time, she thought he was it, that he was going to marry her and she'd finally have that cute little house and happy life she'd always wanted.

Until he left her. And by then, she'd gotten so wrapped up in him, had quit her job to follow a stupid dream of opening a catering business, had broken her apartment lease and completely destroyed her credit. Leaving her homeless and out of options.

Almost. There'd been one option she hadn't expected, and that had been Ainsley. She and Chris took her in, helped her develop a relationship with Jesus, and encouraged her to go back to college to finish her degree. Then let her stay with them until she'd earned a bachelor's in education. At 48 years old. Ainsley would say better late than never. Angela hoped she was right.

The sound level rose as another classroom scurried in. Her heart skipped to see Sebastian among them. He looked her way and tilted his head, as if deep in thought. Or maybe sizing her up. She waved, and he flicked an almost indiscernible wave in return. As he continued forward, he cast frequent glances her way, and each time he did, she smiled.

"Ms. Meadows, hello!"

She turned to see Lynn, the receptionist,

approaching from the kitchen. She carried a tray piled high with fried chicken and mashed potatoes, two milk containers tucked under her arm.

"Please, call me Angela." Seemed she was telling her that whenever they met. But Lynn appeared to be old school. At least, in that regard. "How are you?"

"Hungry." She laughed and lifted her tray.

Angela's gaze drifted to the hall where Reuben now stood, talking with the fourth-grade science teacher. The two appeared pleasantly engaged. Come to think of it, though a bit stiff and snotty, Reuben seemed to get along with most everyone. Except her.

"Something wrong?"

Angela glanced over to find Lynn watching her with a quizzical expression. "It's nothing." She chewed on her bottom lip. "It's just . . ." This felt like high school. "Reuben hates me."

"Nah. Well, maybe."

What? She stared at Lynn. "What'd I do? Accidentally use his crossing vest? Stand on the wrong side of the asphalt during recess duty?"

Lynn laughed. "Funny, but no. His cousin applied to be a para this year. Word has it, she really needs the money. I guess she's been unemployed for a while." She gave a one-shoulder shrug. "But you've got a college degree. Who'd Reuben think the district would hire?"

Angela's eyebrows shot up, and she gave a slow nod.

"Listen, I've been meaning to tell you . . . I remember you saying you wanted to teach?"

"Yeah."

"You know Mrs. Carmichael, the third grade teacher, will be out for maternity leave soon."

"I wasn't aware."

"Well, by soon I mean two months. Or is it three?" She twisted her mouth to the side. "Anyway, I hear she'll be gone quite a while. I know you're looking for something more permanent, but it could be a foot in the door. Plus, I hear she might not return in the fall." She glanced at the clock on the wall. "Guess I better be getting back. Those phones won't answer themselves." She sauntered off, her silver curls bouncing.

Angela ran a hand along her collarbone. Could this be an opened door? Would the principal even let her do that—switch jobs midsemester? Or would that make her seem flighty? Maybe if she just hinted that she was available and looking to teach.

She scraped her teeth over her bottom lip, her stomach doing all sorts of acrobatics.

What if she couldn't cut it?

The memory of herself lying in a hospital bed, recovering from a botched suicide attempt, flashed through her mind. A hopeless, uneducated, unemployed, 40-plus woman who had run out of options.

She may have changed, but no one changed that much. Not in four short years.

Chapter 17

Mitch sat on his back porch, whittling a stick he'd found on his morning hike. Bones stood across from him, leaning against the railing and sipping a soda.

"Who's that lady I saw you talking with Sunday? The one in the getup?"

Mitch's cheeks heated. "Name's Angela. She's staying at the Martins' place."

"I heard about that." The note of caution in his voice made Mitch tense.

He kept his eyes trained on his stick. "Spill it, Bones." He sliced off a chunk of bark, the knife edging deeper than he'd intended.

"Guess she's had a rough go in the relationship department."

"What do you mean?"

"Not sure. I don't pay much mind to gossip, but old Netty was running her mouth again. Said something about the woman's daughter being all worried about her, that she'd fall into old habits and end up an emotional mess. Least, that's how Netty spun it."

Old habits? "She get that from the Martins?"

"'Spect so."

"When have you known Mr. and Mrs. Martin to gossip?"

"Imagine it wasn't gossip so much as wanting to look out for the lady. Encourage the church gals to reach out to her, keep an eye on her." He took another drink of his soda. Shifting, he hiked his pants up with one hand. "So, what happened with those renters?"

Mitch rubbed his forehead and relayed his encounter with Bianca. "I covered the difference myself. I don't know if I did the right thing. And I haven't told Dennis." The man wouldn't understand. Besides, it was Mitch's money. "I hate keeping things from him, but . . ." He inhaled, exhaled slowly. "Things are pretty on edge, know what I mean?"

"Seems to me it's been like that a lot lately. Think maybe it's time to walk away?"

"End the partnership, you mean?"

Bones gave a one-shoulder shrug.

Mitch shook his head. "We're incompatible for sure. But I can't walk out on the guy. Not after all he's done for me. I'd really like to see him come to Christ." He laid his knife-holding hand on his knee. "Everything would be so much easier." Not that coming to faith would turn Dennis philanthropic, but at least he and Mitch would have some sort of common ground.

Laughter sounded from the adjacent yard where his young neighbors had gathered. The dad, a tall guy with black hair and a bony frame, stood at the grill, smoke billowing up. His wife sat at their patio table, an infant balanced on her lap, while her toddler played peek-a-boo with the baby.

Just like Sheila used to with their boys, only she'd be the one holding them while he played peek-a-boo. Back when they made plans for family vacations and romantic getaways. And dreamed about who the boys would become someday.

He shook the memory aside and focused on his whittling stick.

"I'm going to have to figure out something in regard to the Douglases." He ran his fingers along the smooth inner wood. "I can't keep bailing Bianca out. It's not good for her, not good for the business. And it's not honest."

Bones nodded and then burped.

He stood. "Want another soda?"

Bones took a swig of his drink then crushed the can with his hand. "I got to get going. See you Sunday?"

After he left, Mitch returned to his porch. He spent the rest of his evening turning an old, knotted branch into a walking stick. Carving a face into the top, he left chunks of bark for a hat, hair, and beard. He'd just started on the old man's nose when his phone rang.

He set the wood and knife aside, grabbed his cell, and glanced at the screen. His oldest. "Nathan, how're you and Leza doing?" Mitch rarely heard from the kid. The last time he'd called, the conversation had ended in an argument over Eliot bailing on rehab. As if Mitch had any control over that.

"You got anything going on October 10th?"

"Not sure, why?" He put the call on speaker and pulled up his calendar.

"We're going to be out of town for Derk's birthday, so we thought we'd celebrate early." Mitch's grandson. "We figured we'd throw him a surprise party, considering this is the last year he'll be in the single digits."

"I'll be there." As would Sheila. "You invite Eliot?"

An extended pause, followed by a heavy exhale. "We haven't decided yet."

"I understand." And he did. There wasn't much he could say beyond that. How could he love somebody and be infuriated by him at the same time? How could he grieve someone who was still alive?

Bianca ran her fingers along the stitching in the hand towel Virginia had embroidered: "Come to me . . . I will give you rest. —Matthew 11:28."

Whatever that meant.

Math book opened in front of him, Robby sat with his arms planted on either side of his homework, leg jiggling so fast the entire table shook.

She approached and, placing her hand on his

shoulder, stood behind him. "Proud of you for doing your homework without me asking."

He grunted though a hint of smile emerged. It turned to a frown the moment he focused again on his paper. After making a few marks on the page, he erased them. He'd done this so many times, the sheet was a mess of smudges.

"Can I help?" Not that she understood this new math they were teaching him—something called a Common Core.

He shook his head and flipped a page in his textbook.

She glanced behind her to Sebastian who lay on the couch, hugging a pillow. An animal channel on TV.

C. J. had been in her room since she'd gotten home from school. Hopefully she was doing homework too. Bianca needed to check on her.

Turning back to Robby, she pulled out the chair beside him. "How about I just watch then. Maybe I'll learn something." She nudged him with her elbow.

His shoulders relaxed, and his smile emerged in full force. She ruffled his hair then pulled him into a sideways hug, kissing the top of his head. "Love you, big man. You know that, right?"

He nodded. "You too."

He wrote out another problem then drew a number line beneath it. He worked on this for a while, adding loops to his line, then set his pencil down. "Where's dad?"

Bianca's throat turned scratchy. "Don't know, baby."

"Is he in jail?"

She swallowed. "I don't think so." Reid had sent her a text a few days ago, and inmates didn't have access to cell phones. But the police probably had a warrant out on him. They might have found him. Locked him up. If they hadn't yet, they would soon. The man couldn't run forever.

Robby studied her for a moment longer, his eyes searching hers. "Why'd he leave us?"

"I don't know." She wrapped an arm around his shoulders. "But we're going to be all right. We've got each other. Always."

His bottom lip quivered, and his gaze dropped to his paper.

She cupped his chin with her hand and raised it. "I ain't going anywhere. You hear me? We're going to be OK."

She intended to follow through on that promise, even if it meant working herself ragged.

And leaving Reid? Her husband, the man she'd vowed to love until death?

Another question arrested her thoughts—one she couldn't answer. What if she had to choose between her husband and her kids?

Footsteps shuffled behind her, and she turned

to see Sebastian approaching. Face drawn, eyes hopeful, he looked from her to Robby then back to her again.

She smiled and opened one arm wide. "Come here, you. Give your momma some sugar." The dimples on his cheeks emerged, and he nestled close against her. They remained like that for some time, Bianca holding each son as close as she could without smothering them. Cherishing the moment.

The music drifting down the hall grew louder then muffled again. A moment later, C. J. appeared. Her gaze flicked over each one of them before landing on Bianca's. For a fleeting moment, Bianca caught a glimpse of the sweet little girl who used to ask to be held.

Resting her chin on Sebastian's head, she smiled. "You know what I'm thinking?" The sun would be setting soon, and with dusk came the fireflies and chirping crickets.

The boys squirmed to look at her, and C. J. raised an eyebrow.

"I bet it's cooled down a bit, and listen to how that wind's blowing, pushing the heat away." She grinned. "Ceej, grab your sketch book, and boys, get your bug nets. I need some fresh air. Come on."

That was all the encouragement her boys needed to send them bounding to their bedrooms. But C. J. remained where she was, her face void of expression. The girl needed some family time, some mom time. Whether she realized it or not.

Bianca drew near to her daughter. Tried to find the words to break through the wall between them, or at least say something that wouldn't thicken the barrier. "You finish that drawing you showed me a while ago? The one with the cherry blossoms?"

Her expression softened, and she picked at her thumbnail. "Not yet, but I need to. I want to give it to Grandma for her birthday."

"Why don't you bring it to the park with us?"

C. J. kept picking at her nail. Finally, she gave another shrug and plodded to her bedroom. She returned shortly after the boys, carrying her art bag.

Standing by the door, bug nets and mason jars in hand, the boys bounced with excitement. Sebastian swung his net around, bonking Robby in the head. A jousting match soon followed. Normally Bianca would've got on them for roughhousing indoors. Not tonight. Tonight they were all going to relax, have fun.

She chuckled and opened the front door. "All right, you little monsters, how about you take some of that energy outside?"

"Yeah!" Sebastian squirmed out from under Robby and bolted to his feet. "I'll race you to the playground."

The boys ran up ahead, waving their bug nets as they went, while Bianca and C. J. strolled behind. The sun was a fiery ball of light that reflected off the clouds in swirls of pink and purple.

They walked in silence for a few moments, C. J. kicking at stones along the way.

Bianca grabbed a twig off the ground and snapped it between her fingers. "You all right, Ceej? You seem quiet."

She shrugged.

"I know things have been . . . tough. Crazy. With the police and all."

"I'm getting used to it."

Bianca winced but kept her mouth shut. She'd rather C. J. lash out than not talk.

"I'm sorry." Bianca grabbed her daughter's hand and squeezed.

Something was going on—besides the Reid drama. If Bianca were to guess, she'd say it had to do with that low-life boyfriend of hers. Hopefully they'd broken up. C. J. didn't need to be throwing her life away chasing after some boy. Even so, she hated to see her daughter hurting.

They reached the park to find the boys climbing up a large, gnarly branched oak tree. Gripping a limb with both hands, Robby hung by his arms. He pumped his legs, swinging until he reached near horizontal. Then, with a high-pitched Tarzan call, he let go and soared through the air, landing on his feet. This of course stirred Sebastian's competitive side, and soon the boys were engaged in a long-jump competition.

Bianca plunked down on a park bench with her back resting against the table. She patted the wood beside her. C. J. sat and began pulling items from her bag—her sketchbook with the worn cover, her gummy eraser, a pencil, and sharpener.

For the next hour, her daughter drew, the boys played, and Bianca simply took it all in. Incredibly grateful for the moment of joy.

They were going to be just fine. She missed Reid something awful, but she'd get over him. Her heart had been broken before.

Stretching her legs in front of her, she watched a fat, furry caterpillar crawl over a large stone. Now this was rest.

Her phone chimed, and she pulled it out of her pocket. Her stomach twisted. Reid.

She stood and moved to the outer edge of the playground—out of C. J.'s earshot. "Hey."

"Hey, baby, I've missed you. How're you and the kids holding up?"

Her grip tightened around the phone. She cursed him. "How do you think we're doing?"

"I'm sorry. I know I really messed things up."

"You think?" She rolled her eyes. "You said no more. You promised." Her voice cracked. "I knew this would happen."

"I want to see you."

She closed her eyes to keep the tears from falling. "I don't understand, Reid. Why'd you do it? Why'd you throw everything away like that? They catch you, and you'll be facing some serious time."

"I know, but it wasn't my fault. We had it all planned out. It should've been an easy drop, but Maniac brought his cousin along."

Bianca swore again. "The drunk with the big mouth?" An extended pause followed. "What'd he do this time?"

"Dude got boozed up and started telling stories."

"Now what?"

"I want to see you. I need to see you." His voice went husky. "I need you with me."

"Where're you at?"

"The Saddle Inn. Caroll, Iowa."

"A hotel? How're you paying for that? Never mind. I don't want to know." She rubbed her face. "Aren't you tired of living like this? Of always having to watch your back?"

"What I'm tired of is seeing you and the kids struggle. Seeing you guys go without. Seeing you work yourself to the bone with little to show for it."

"So get a job!" She sucked in a breath of air, wishing she could take her words back. Knowing how deep they'd cut.

He didn't respond right away, and when he did,

his voice was soft. "I miss you. Please, baby, come see me."

His words, spoken with every ounce of love she knew he possessed, tugged at her heart. Broke it. Made it near impossible for her to say what she knew she had to.

"I can't do this, Reid. The police came to the house. Searched our stuff!" She slammed a fist against her thigh. "What if they think I'm caught up in the same garbage, huh? What then? What if they take the kids?"

"They won't do that. I wouldn't let them."

"Yeah? And how you gonna stop them?"

"I've got a plan. If you'd just give me—"

"I got to go." She ended the call and slipped the phone into her back pocket. Wiping the tears from her eyes, she straightened and faced her kids.

The next morning, Bianca paced her small kitchen, her pulse still spiked from her predawn dream. In it, Reid had been hiding out in an old, vacant hotel. Somehow he sensed she was there and began looking for her. Calling out as he walked down one dim corridor after another. The lights above him, faint and flickering, cast an eerie glow on the dingy wall.

Standing on the outside looking in, the sun behind her, darkness before her, she watched it all. Reid had looked so haggard, so . . . broken. Stubble covered his jaw, his hair long and unkempt. When he neared her, staring through the window, straight at her but not seeing, his eyes looked hollow. Desperate.

"Bianca, where are you?" His voice grew more urgent, and he began to run, throwing open doors and looking inside.

And still Bianca watched, only now from above, and the image morphed into a large maze covered in vines and grunge. A loud bang, followed by another, and another, shook the structure. Whirling around, his face pale, Reid stared as a side door burst open, cement chunks and debris flying.

"No!" He spun around as heavily armed men—hundreds of them—charged through the shattered opening, guns aimed. Faster and faster he ran, casting frequent glances behind him.

He turned a corner and stopped. Froze. A high, stone wall boxed him in on three sides. Behind him, the sound of pounding feet grew louder, causing the ground to tremble.

Bianca pressed her hands to the icy glass keeping her from her husband. "Surrender, Reid!"

He turned around, hands fisted, chin raised. His voice echoed, as if carried on the wind. "I won't go back to prison." He looked at Bianca, as if he could see her, and reached into his pocket.

Shots fired, shattering the glass in front of her. The air filled with the acrid scent of sulfur.

"Bianca!" Reid held her gaze as bullets shook his body. Falling to his knees, he extended his hands, as if reaching for her. "Bianca! I love you!"

When the final blow knocked him to the ground, her screams of "No!" had wakened her. Drenched in sweat and heart racing, she hadn't been able to shake the image from her mind or the thought that followed: *I never said good-bye.*

Chapter 18

Sketchbook and pencil in hand, Angela stood on her porch and inhaled the earthy, post-rain air. As September rolled in, the oppressive temperatures of summer gave way to cool breezes and late afternoon rains.

Across the street, young Robby and a kid she didn't recognize tossed a football between them. Every time Robby made a catch, he dashed to the other end of his yard, slammed the ball down, then did a knee-wiggling, elbow-flapping jig like an NFL player.

She giggled, and both boys turned. Offering a smile and a wave, she started to sit on her top step. Her lower back complained. She surveyed her porch and cocked her head. Surely the Martins had porch furniture somewhere—a folding lawn chair—anything would be better than the hard steps.

She set her art supplies down and headed into the very over-filled garage. Boxes were stacked four, sometimes five, tall. Behind them stood the top of an old yellow refrigerator, stacks of clay pots on top. In the far right corner, rakes, a ladder, random metal bars, and a rusted table stood, coated in a thick layer of grime and cobwebs.

She rummaged around a bit, releasing dust in

the air, then huffed. She'd never find anything in this mess. Someone could seriously get lost in here for days, devoured by the colony of spiders and rats that had no doubt taken up permanent residence.

A lovely thought.

As she moved away, a corner of teal, maroon, and navy fabric caught her eye. The long, rectangular edge protruded from behind a stack of rolled rugs. It was either a mattress or a seat cushion—a porch swing maybe? But getting to it would be horrendous.

Even so, she couldn't meet her neighbors, couldn't form a connection with the sweet children across the street, if she stayed inside. And her old bones were mighty tired of sitting on concrete steps. Besides, fall was coming. How lovely it would be to sit on her porch, leisurely swinging, iced tea beside her, sketchbook in hand.

Resuming her efforts, she began pulling various items from one side of the garage to the other. Thirty-five minutes in, sweat beading on her upper lip and forehead, she'd uncovered the coveted item. Wonderful! It was indeed a seat cushion. What appeared to be a swing awning was folded beside it.

Where was the frame? Then she remembered the random metal bars she'd seen earlier and trekked back to the front of the garage to unearth what she'd just barricaded. She lugged the entire contraption outside and up her porch steps, much to the amusement of more than a few neighborhood children. None of whom offered a hand.

Where were peoples' manners? Didn't matter. She wasn't looking for help anyway. She'd assemble this swing on her own, even if it took all night.

A laugh bubbled in her throat as the full reality of her thoughts hit. A wonderful, joyous, celebratory laugh. Three years ago, she would've been looking for some big, strong, handsome man to come help her. Would've fabricated a swing-assembling event just to get their attention. But now . . . now . . . she smiled. *Thank You, Lord.*

She grabbed the dusty seat cushion, lugged it up her steps, and rested it against the porch railing. She was heading back for the swing's awning when across the street Bianca pulled into her driveway. Her son clutched the football to his chest and bounded up to her. He met her at the car door as she stepped out. Pulling her son into a sideways hug, Bianca rubbed his head, casting a glance to Angela.

Angela smiled and waved. Bianca eyed her an extended moment, then, releasing her son, climbed the steps. She opened her front door and paused to glance back at Angela, her face hidden by the shadow of her house. Then she was gone, and Robby resumed playing.

Angela continued to watch the house, thinking back to when she first had Ainsley. Oh, how lonely she'd been. So frightened. So unsure. Wishing someone would see her. Really see her.

She smoothed her shirt, shook the dust from her hair. Made sure she didn't stink too terribly. And descended the steps.

Then stopped. That woman hated her. Besides, what was she going to say? *I have your sons in class? I pray for your family often?*

That'd get her thrown out for sure. Or laughed at. If Angela remembered anything from her non-Christian days it was the utter contempt and distrust she'd felt for anyone toting a Bible. Other than Ainsley. Sweet Ainsley, the daughter who'd loved her even when she was unlovable.

Like Angela needed to do with her neighbor.

Breathing deep to squelch her stomach jitters, she strolled down her walk. To her left, Mitch leaned against his parked pickup, talking with a man in a hard hat. He held what appeared to be blueprints. He glanced up as Angela passed and nodded a greeting, sending a nervous flutter through her midsection. He held her gaze for a moment, and her breath caught, not releasing until he resumed his conversation.

She stood there, stiff, watching him. The old Angela, the man-chasing Angela, rising up in full force. Fisting her hands, she turned back toward Bianca's and strode across the street.

Robby and his friend stopped playing and faced her.

"Hello, boys." She drew closer. "You fellas have great throwing arms."

Their faces lit up, and Robby began spinning his football between his hands. "What do you want?"

Taken aback, her mouth slackened. But his relaxed stance and features indicated he meant no disrespect. She looked at his house, catching a glimpse of his mother's face peeking out the window before the curtain fell back in place.

She faced Robby and donned her best teacherly posture. "I came to see if you'd finished your homework."

The boys looked at one another, their thin eyebrows shooting up, and she did her best to keep from laughing.

She failed. "I'm kidding." She stole a glance at Mitch to find him watching her once again. Cheeks hot, she turned back to the boys. "I'm just being neighborly."

"Oh!" Their shoulders visibly slackened and grins emerged.

Robby started tossing his ball in the air. "You an artist?"

"What?"

"An artist, like a painter and stuff."

"Um . . . no. What made you think that?"

"Cuz of how you're always sitting outside with that big ol' tablet. Like my sister has."

"Oh! My sketchbook." She smiled. "No, sweetie. I just doodle more than anything. For stress relief."

Forehead creased, he angled his head. "My sister must be lotta stressed, then."

Her heart ached at the truth in his words. No teenager—no human—could have police tear through their house without near losing it. Still, his comment seemed incredibly odd. "Why do you say that?"

"On account she's always drawing."

She raised an eyebrow, her heart skipping a beat. "Your sister likes to draw?"

"That's all she ever does, when she's not with her gross boyfriend." He scrunched his face as if he smelled something foul.

A smile tugged, and not just because the child looked absolutely adorable when he puckered his face like that. After all her prayers, she may have found a way to connect with Cassie Joe. If only she could figure out how to use this knowledge. Showing up at the Douglases' doorstep with a bag of art supplies didn't seem appropriate. Not unless she wanted them to think she was completely insane.

"Well, kiddos . . ." She faced her neighbor's house. Then, stomach doing 360s, she ascended

Bianca's steps and knocked. Inside, footsteps drew near then stopped.

Should she knock again or wait? She raised her hand, let it drop. Raised it again.

Robby clambered up the steps. "Need help?" He barged into his house before Angela could elicit a response.

"What the—" Bianca jerked backward, as did her son. "Boy, you better watch what you're doing." She looked from Angela to Robby with a deep frown.

"How was I supposed to know you were standing there?"

Eyes narrowed, the woman pulled him in then crossed her arms. "What can I do for you, Ms. Meadows?"

"I . . . uh . . ." She shifted. Swallowed. "I wondered if . . ." She cleared her throat. "You see, I was a single mom for years. And well, even when I wasn't—single, I mean—I still spent a lot of time by myself. Talking to kids. Wiping snotty noses." The more she talked, the faster her words flew, until she started repeating herself. This only made her more flustered, increasing her tempo.

Bianca shoved a hip out. "Uh-huh?" Behind her, Cassie Joe stepped forward, watched the conversation with something between a smirk and a laugh.

"Anyway, I figured, I mean, I wondered if you'd like a break once in awhile. The kids could come over to my house. We could do crafts, make cookies, or something."

At this, Cassie Joe laughed outright, and, shaking her head, traipsed out of sight.

"Oh, you want to *rescue* me." Bianca stretched the word out in mocked distress, clutching a hand to her neck. "Aren't you the kind one?"

Angela blinked. "I . . . uh . . ."

"What? You surprised I know such a big word?" She rolled her eyes. "Please. Save your charity work for someone else." And with that, she stepped back and slammed the door.

Angela flinched and stared at the peeling black paint in front of her. Then she scampered down the steps with the scant amount of dignity she retained.

"Angela?"

She startled and whirled around to find Mitch approaching. Heat climbed her neck. She stopped, willing her ricocheting heart to slow.

"You OK?"

"Yeah. Just . . . trying to be neighborly." She forced a nervous laugh. "It appears, however, that was a mistake."

"I doubt that." He offered a gentle smile. "Acts of kindness, regardless how small, or how they're perceived, are never a mistake." Her face reflected in his amber eyes.

She chewed her bottom lip, recognizing the truth in his words. Even if she cared not to.

"Some things just take time, is all."

She nodded. "Poor woman. That's got to be hard, raising those kids all by herself."

"I don't know. Might be good for her, having her husband out of the picture for a while."

"It's so sad." She wanted to ask more, to find out what had landed the woman in such a state, but that was none of her business. And she of all people had absolutely no right to judge. Who knew where Ainsley would be today if not for her third grade teacher, Mrs. Eldridge, who'd continually reached out to her. And what about Angela's first child?

She closed her eyes on the memory, one that still haunted her.

"I saw you fighting with the Martins' outdoor furniture. Need help?"

"I'm fine, but thank you."

"You sure? I don't mind. I used to help Mrs. Martin quite a bit, whenever her husband was deployed. Winterized her sprinklers, seeded and plugged her lawn. Do that for a few folks, actually."

"So you're the visiting Good Samaritan, huh?"

"More like the area handyman." He shoved his hands in his pockets, his biceps flexing. "For the widows and single moms."

"That's mighty nice of you."

"I fix their sprinklers, they bake me cookies."

He grinned. "I'm pretty sure I get the better part of the deal."

"Right." She smiled. "I did promise to bake you a treat, didn't I?"

He raised his hands, palms out. "I wasn't meaning to—"

"No, really, you should come over for coffee and dessert. We could—" She clamped her mouth shut. Less than ten minutes ago, she'd determined not to throw herself at every male she encountered, and here she was flirting.

She gave a nervous cough then shifted so her shoulder faced him. "Well, I should probably go. I've got . . . stuff to do." Like figuring out a way to untangle the porch swing's canopy from a long metal pipe that appeared to have no use.

"I'll come with you. Take a look at that swing."

"No." She blurted the word out then, softening her voice, "I'm fine, really. I enjoy challenges."

"If you're sure." He paused. "See you Sunday?"

"If not before then." She grinned, then her mouth flattened at his bewildered expression. "On account of your remodel, I mean."

"Oh, right."

Could their conversation have been any more awkward? Flirting she understood. Holding a normal conversation with a handsome, single man? Learning to be friends with said man? That she needed to learn.

Chapter 19

Phone pressed to his ear, Mitch waved to a few of his crewmen and stepped inside their 35th Street property. "Marble, you say? That's a bit upscale for this location." He paused on the stoop to glance Angela's way, hoping to catch her on her porch.

She wasn't there. The fact disappointed him more than it should have, especially after his conversation with Bones. What had he meant about old habits, anyway? Was he implying she wasn't good enough for Mitch? No, that wasn't like him. So what then? That Mitch would somehow trip her up?

Then again, maybe Bones was right. And if the woman was coming off a bad relationship . . .

He nodded a greeting to Jeremy and stopped in the entryway to survey the progress. "I'll talk to Dennis. Might stop by, give it a look over later."

Ending the call, he checked his watch. Once again, his son was a no-show. No surprise. Why'd Mitch even bother? All he got for his efforts was increased tension between him and Dennis and looks of pity from his crew. Pretty soon he'd lose their respect entirely.

He cracked his knuckles and surveyed the living room. The guys had ripped out the carpet and padding and were working to remove the tack strip, hopefully without destroying the hardwood flooring underneath.

Dennis strolled over, tapping his fist in his palm. "Not bad, huh? We really lucked out in this room. A bit of sanding and refinishing, a fresh coat of paint on the walls, maybe some crown molding . . . this space will pop."

"Good. Maybe that will make up for the tiny kitchen, bedrooms, and closets." The steady banging echoing through the house suddenly zeroed into focus. Mitch frowned. "What's the crew doing?"

He followed the sound of snapping wood and froze. Debris, splinters, and jagged shelf pieces covered the linoleum. One of their guys stood in front of a gaping hole where an overhang of cabinets used to be. To his right, another crewman was using a crowbar to tear off a piece of trim.

"What are you doing?" Mitch snapped.

Creases lining his forehead, the guy with the mallet looked from Dennis to Mitch. "Opening up the kitchen."

Mitch scowled at his partner. "I thought we decided to leave this space alone, other than upgrades."

"I talked to Chip last night."

Mitch groaned. That realtor was the biggest weasel around.

"He's got a client looking for a three bedroom with an open floor plan. Said the guy was in a hurry to buy and close."

"We've already got a realtor. One we can trust." So now Dennis was contacting people behind his back?

"This lead's legit, Mitch. Chip faxed me the preapproval letter last night."

"You couldn't call me?"

"I had to make a decision and go with it."

"Do you hear yourself? Some partnership, buddy." Words surged to his tongue, some he hadn't used in over a decade, but he bit them back. He refused to fight in front of his men. "We need to talk." He motioned toward the hallway then stomped off, halting when Dennis didn't follow. Turning around, he scowled, arms crossed.

Dennis glared at him. Mitch glared back. Then, cursing under his breath, Dennis marched out, pushing past Mitch and out the door. He didn't slow until he reached the end of their property.

Mitch followed, jaw clenched. He and Dennis needed to present a united front, even if they were on opposite ends of every spectrum. Bones's question, spoken only nights before, resurfaced, *"Think maybe it's time to walk away?"*

No. Not now. Not yet. Mitch could be Dennis's only exposure to Jesus.

Forcing his tight muscles to relax, he shoved his

hands in his pockets to keep them from fisting.

Dennis faced him, arms crossed, legs shoulder distance apart. "That kitchen was too small, and that wall only clunked up the space. Made everything feel smaller."

"It's still small, only now we've knocked out a chunk of storage."

"No one will notice."

Mitch huffed. "Right." As if their realtor, Kaden, hadn't told them the opposite a hundred times. "You know what? It's done. We'll move on. But from here on out, we make decisions together."

"So you want your hands in every detail, is that it?"

"The big ones, yes."

"And when we disagree?"

That was the big-money question. "I don't know, man."

"Heyya-heyya-ho!" Hollering drew their attention to the yard. "Where's the boss man?"

Eliot. Mitch's nerves ignited, his muscles snapping taut once again. He and his partner exchanged glances.

Dennis shook his head. "I'll let you deal with that."

Suppressing a sigh, Mitch crossed the yard to meet—or perhaps intercept—his son.

"Dude, this place is a mess." Eliot strolled toward the house, arms swinging—the exaggerated gait he always used when on something.

His loud voice gave further evidence to suggest the kid was drunk. Or stoned. Most likely both.

"Who's doing demo?" He grabbed one hand in the other and raised them above his head, as if holding a hammer.

"Why are you here?" Mitch asked.

"To get my work on, boss man." Eliot clamped his dad on the shoulder. "You been lighting up my cell phone like firecrackers. Pow-pow-pow!" He fisted then released his hands again and again then leaned his head back and laughed. "The bossss *man* been calling me! Ain't I the lucky one?" He cackled then, focusing on Mitch's boots, he straightened. "Dude. Those steel toed?"

"I was calling to see why you pulled a no-show the other day."

"No worries." He flicked his hair from his eyes. "I'm here and ready to go."

"Oh, you're going, all right." Mitch nudged Eliot's elbow. "Come on."

Eliot jerked back as if burned, rubbing his tricep. His eyes widened before crinkling with amusement. As if coming to a work site was the most hilarious encounter ever. Yeah, he was stoned all right, and he wasn't even trying to hide it this time. In fact, it was almost as if he was throwing it in Mitch's face.

"Dude. Am I in trouble?" He feigned sorrow, his bottom lip poking out. "Uh-oh. Boss man gonna beat my backside!" His high-pitched, exaggerated laugh grated on Mitch's ears, threatening to steal his last ounce of self-control.

"You're high."

"Dude! No way." The kid's goofy smile returned, his bloodshot eyes darting all over the place, his thin frame still twitching. "Where you want me? Need someone to knock out tile? Blast through a wall?"

"You need to leave. I can't have anyone working under the influence."

"Influence of what?"

"I'm not playing this game. I'm taking you home."

The tendons in Eliot's neck bulged as his crooked smile sank into a deep frown. "Right, Dad. Get rid of the problem kid." He backed up, hands raised. "Love you too, old man."

Mitch stepped forward. "Come on."

"Keep your hands off me. You want me to leave? No problem." He started to walk away.

Mitch ran up ahead of him, positioned himself in front of Eliot's car. "You're not driving like this. You don't want me to drive you, fine. I'll call you a cab."

Eliot's eyes hardened, sending a chill up the back of Mitch's neck. Then, turning, he stormed down the street, cursing. Mitch watched him go, tears burning his eyes, though whether from sorrow or anger, he didn't know.

Chapter 20

Sunday morning, Angela was up and dressed early, determined to reduce some of the clutter filling her home. Well, the Martins' home. Mrs. Martin had more knickknacks than an antique store, from clay figurines to strange metal pots. Not to mention a large assortment of furniture, much of it crammed into the basement. But Angela had yet to find a vacuum, or a mop and broom for that matter. Most likely all were buried somewhere in the garage, only she wasn't ready to reenter that chaos.

Besides, she really needed to mail that card to her aunt. She'd found a listing online, called the number, and left a message. But she wasn't expecting a call back. Not after all the cold shoulders she'd tossed her aunt's way. Maybe if Angela sent a note, explained herself and apologized . . .

Heart heavy, she pulled a card from a thin paper bag, grabbed a pen, and plunked down in front of the coffee table. How to start? Actually, the better question was how to fit it all in.

Dear Aunt Dorothy,

    I know I have no right contacting you after all these years. I've destroyed so many relationships and taken so many loving family members for granted, especially you. I never said so, but it really meant a lot that you tried to save my baby. I know you weren't focused just on my child but you truly loved and wanted to help me. I'm sorry I pushed you away.

I have so many regrets. I caused so many people pain, including my mother. I'd really like to reconnect with her, to apologize, and to pay back all the money I stole from her over the years, but I have no idea where she is or even if she's still alive. Do you? If so, could you please give me her phone number, or perhaps give my contact information to her?

With much love and deep regrets,

Your niece,

Angela.

She closed the card and slipped it into the envelope. She'd drop it in the mail on the way to work tomorrow.

In the living room, she knelt in front of one of her boxes. Across the front, Chris had written the word *mementos* in large, black letters.

She lifted the lid and began unloading the few belongings she'd kept over the years. A sealed, plastic bag containing the wristbands she and

Ainsley had worn when Angela had given birth. A photo album recording the first five years of Ainsley's life. A few pictures had been tucked within the plastic sleeves, the rest shoved in between the pages to be filed later.

Opening the page, she ran her hand along the smooth plastic. She smiled at the image of Ainsley, at three years old, dressed in a floppy hat and holding a paper fan. She wore a floral dress that fully engulfed her, the bottom trailing at least two feet behind. Beneath it poked a pair of gold shoes—women's. All from Angela's closet. That was the day she'd wanted to play rock star.

Angela flipped the page, soaking in every memory, nostalgia mixing with regret. But overriding it all swept a deep gratitude for all God had done. *I know I messed up something awful, wasted so many precious years. Thank You for Your grace and forgiveness. For Ainsley's forgiveness. And for restoring what I destroyed.*

She stood and glanced at the clock. Church wasn't for another hour, but she needed to get out. Take in some fresh air, shove down the painful memories with a brisk, mindless walk.

She grabbed her purse and slipped into a pair of dingy sneakers—pumps would never do—and headed out. The air was crisp, pleasant, and for once, the house next door was quiet, though two pickups and a four-door parked along the curb.

Mitch's vehicle wasn't among them—that didn't surprise her. Seemed he never worked Sundays.

The house across the street was equally quiet, curtains drawn, though Bianca's car occupied the drive. A few toys littered the dandelion-covered yard—Robby's bike and football. A red skateboard rested against the siding.

With plenty of time to spare, Angela headed toward the beautiful historic Field Club Neighborhood. It was her favorite neighborhood in Omaha, with its Victorian houses and their covered porches and wrought iron fences. If she had the money, this is where she'd live. But considering all her debt and the fact she had yet to land a permanent teaching position, that wasn't happening any time soon.

A handmade garage sale sign posted near the neighborhood entrance caught her attention. She could only imagine the treasures these residents could be selling.

Nearing the house, Angela slowed, taking everything in. The yard and garage were filled with sale items, everything from an old futon mattress, tables of books, to . . . a vacuum! A sign with red lettering was taped to it—$5. Perfect! Though she'd offer $2. She'd throw in another dollar for the beautiful, multicolored glass vase on the table next to it.

After some time browsing, and loaded down with numerous items, she dragged the vacuum behind her and approached a black haired woman sitting behind a metal box. "Will you take $20 for all this?"

The lady stood, pushed her lips first one way then the other. Planted her hands on her hips. "That vase is one of a kind."

"That's cuz our boy made it." A man wearing a straw hat called out from behind her. "In art class." He sauntered over, thumbs hooked through his belt loops. "Got an A." He winked.

Angela smiled, recognizing the parental pride in his voice. "I can give you $22.35 for all this." She pulled out her wallet and flipped it open. "That's all I got."

The woman studied her a moment longer then threw up her hands. "Fine." She plopped back on her chair and held out her hand.

Angela gave her the money then glanced at her watch. Where had the time gone? Church started in just over 15 minutes. That meant there was no time to drop her garage sale finds off at home beforehand.

"Mind if I pick this stuff up later? I'm out on a walk."

The woman crossed her arms. "Uh-uh. We're cleaning stuff out. Getting ready for the movers." She pointed at the sign in her yard that read Moving Sale.

Angela frowned. "Just for a short while? An hour and a half tops."

"Sorry. Can't do it. Imagine the mess I'd have on my hands if I started storing everyone's stuff. This ain't no layaway."

"Oh, come on, Patty." The woman's husband flicked her arm. "What harm will it do?"

"Uh-uh. We do it for her, we gotta do it for everybody." She glared at her husband, initiating an extended and awkward stare-off.

"That's OK." Angela stacked her things, nearly dropped them, then restacked them, differently. Any more bickering and she'd be late for church. Would miss the opening songs, and today she needed those more than ever. Balancing her purchased items between her arms and hips, she grabbed the vacuum handle and excused herself with a nod. "Maybe I'll see you around."

Heads turned her direction as she bumbled down the driveway to the sidewalk, dropping and retrieving items along the way. It didn't help matters that the early morning temperatures had started to climb.

She hobble-shuffled her way to church, evoking numerous stares. One woman in particular stopped watering her plants to stare. She watched Angela approach with wide eyes and mouth agape.

Angela flashed a grin. "Traveling housekeeper." She pressed her tongue to the roof of her mouth to suppress her giggles. "Would you like me to suck the dust from the carpets, ma'am?"

The woman stared a moment longer, deep creases forming above her raised eyebrows.

A horn behind Angela honked, and she spun around, hurling a lamp with a tasseled shade. She clutched the electric cord a moment before it crashed to the ground, knocking down her vacuum instead. Tripping over the handle, she landed, belly down onto the contraption, sending a plume of dust into the air.

Animal-hair scented grime coated her throat, nostrils, and eyes. Coughing, she swiped at her sweaty face with her hands.

"Oh, my!" The woman dashed toward her, and the engine behind her idled. A door opened then slammed shut. "Are you OK?"

Grit tickling her nose, eyes watering, she stared at the man and woman who now stood over her.

"I shouldn't have been so impatient." The man, a tall, muscular gentleman dressed in gym shorts and a Nebraska Cornhuskers jersey, extended his hand, which she accepted. "I was in a hurry and . . ." He frowned. "I was being a jerk, and I'm sorry."

Angela eyed her dirt-covered capris, the white now tinted a faint shade of brown. She forced a smile. "I'm fine, really." And to think, she'd chosen sneakers over heels to avoid situations such as this.

Bones and joints intact but pride bruised beyond recognition, she continued on.

When she neared the church, she considered heading home. She certainly had good reason to. Except she'd made a commitment to God and Ainsley to be serious about her church attendance, and she intended to honor it. Besides, it was only dust. That would brush off easily enough.

Plus she was starting to become incredibly lonely. She needed to find a women's group of some kind to join. Maybe an evening Bible study. Besides, if she felt too uncomfortable, she could slip in the back and slip out again as soon as service ended, before anyone noticed her.

The parking lot at Abiding Fellowship was full of cars but void of people. Not surprising, considering Angela was now ten minutes late. She glanced around for a place to store her garage sale finds. Not finding one, she continued down the sidewalk to the large glass entrance.

Inside the vestibule, chairs were stacked five tall. Beside this stood a metal umbrella rack. Surely no one would notice her belongings there. And if someone took them, well, then perhaps they needed the items more than she. She certainly couldn't bring her items into the sanctuary.

She had just tucked her armload behind the chairs when someone behind her cleared their throat. Startled, she spun around to find Mitch staring at her. He wore slacks and a mint green knit shirt. Faint stubble shadowed his jaw.

"Can I help you?" He watched her with an amused, and more than a little confused, expression.

"I . . . uh . . ." She swallowed, swiping at a brown splotch on her V-neck blouse. One would've thought maroon would hide dirt better. "I walked here, and," she shrugged, "did a little garage sale shopping."

He chuckled, his amber eyes dancing, the chocolate ring around his irises more pronounced. "Sounds fun."

Her tense shoulders relaxed at his genuine smile—not mocking, not condemning. Just . . . friendly. As if he were used to people lugging vacuums and random other items—like a wooden toilet paper holder—to church.

"How about I move this stuff behind the welcome counter?" He motioned toward the foyer.

"Are you sure that won't be a problem?" She reached for her lamp, the shade hanging lop-sided.

"Not at all." He grabbed the vacuum. "But you best go on in. Sermon's already started, and it's a good one today."

"Thank you." She bid him good-bye and, still wiping dirt from her clothes and out of the ends of her hair, strode toward the sanctuary.

Mitch beat her there, opening the door wide

with a finger pressed to his lips. He grabbed a bulletin from a basket on a nearby stand and handed it over.

She mouthed another thank you then slipped into the back row, where, hopefully, she'd go unnoticed.

She angled her head, remembering Mitch's crooked smile and golden, laughing eyes, as if he'd actually been happy to see her. And then she remembered her commitment to leave her man-chasing days behind. Far behind.

Chapter 21

Still chuckling, Mitch returned to the vestibule to gather the rest of Angela's things. Crazy woman. He'd think her completely insane if she wasn't so cute. Actually, it was her quirky behaviors he found the most endearing. He'd had enough of women putting on airs, guarding their words, and batting their eyes at everything he said.

Then again, Angela had done a fair amount of eye-batting herself, but that was probably due to the lint hanging from her left brow more than anything. He probably should've said something, but that would've only embarrassed her further. He'd never seen cheeks turn so red before. Poor girl. To think Mitch once thought he needed to protect the Martins from her. Seemed maybe Angela was the one who needed looking after.

Once again, his conversation with Bones came to mind. Whatever the reason, the people in Angela's life felt the need to protect her from men—if what Bones had said were true. For that reason alone, Mitch needed to proceed with caution. Act like a friend, not a suitor, regardless of how difficult that was proving to be.

Retrieving the vacuum last of all, he wheeled it to the welcome desk. He tucked it behind the counter next to her pile of junk. Which was what most of it looked like. Packing tape, a folded bath curtain decorated with paw prints, a box of pastels. Plastic food storage containers. A tiny book of cat slogans.

She exited the sanctuary less than 30 minutes later, just as the closing hymns began to play.

"Hi." He greeted her with a smile.

"Hi."

"Good message?"

She glanced at the bulletin in her hand. "I didn't see any women's Bible study listings. Except for this Mommy-and-Me program, and well . . ." She gave a nervous laugh.

"We've got a lot of options, some on Sunday morning, others on various weeknights." He motioned for her to follow him to the welcome desk and handed her a stapled stack of papers. "Some meet here at the church, others in folks' homes. Coeds, singles, ladies' groups, divorce recovery. You work days, right?"

She nodded.

"Let me know if you have any questions."

She remained where she was, looking from him to the double-glass doors leading to the parking lot. Was he supposed to say something? Ask her something? Did she want to ask him something? Did she want to ask him something?

"Er . . . did you need anything else?" He moaned inwardly. That sounded rude. "What I mean is . . ." How else could he say it? *"Why are you standing here staring at me?"* didn't seem appropriate.

"My vacuum?"

"Huh? Oh, right!" With a thumbs-up sign, he dashed around the counter, re-emerging with her belongings, the lopsided lamp barely hanging on. He frowned. "You said you walked here?"

"Uh-huh."

He surveyed the hodgepodge of items not so neatly packed within the sagging and misshapen cardboard, then to the vacuum. There was no way she'd be able to lug it all home. "How about I give you a ride?"

"Oh, no." She gave a dismissive wave. "I'd hate to put you out. Anyway, I could use the exercise. It'll give me an excuse to eat a chocolate bar later." Her smile lit her eyes.

"It's no problem. Besides, it's getting to be a hot one out there."

Angela chewed her bottom lip so fervently, he worried she'd bite clean through. Finally, she smiled and nodded. "If you're sure you don't mind . . ."

"Not at all." He started to gather her things, spilling plastic containers across the floor, then looked about for Bones.

The man wasn't around, but Phil, a guy from Mitch's Saturday morning Bible study was, and seeing Mitch fumble with his load, sauntered over.

"I'm so sorry." Angela dove for the spilled items and began shoving them into her box.

"Need some help?" Phil took a swig from the Styrofoam cup he was holding then set it on the counter.

Mitch grinned. "How about you grab the vacuum?" He reached for the box, now in Angela's hands. "You can catch the overflow."

"Absolutely." Taking the charcoal set and lamp, she walked with Mitch toward the entrance. Halfway there, Frances Archer and her gang of biddies stopped him.

"Are those for Takin' It To The Streets?" She peered through her glasses at the items. "I've got some coats I've been meaning to donate, but I just can't seem to make it down there. Do you think maybe you could stop by my place and pick them up?"

Mitch shifted his load. "Sorry, but this isn't a donation, and I won't be heading to the Streets anytime soon. But I bet Bones is."

Her lips puckered. "Oh. I see." She glanced from the box to Angela, eyebrow raised. "This is from the benevolence fund, then. How nice. I love how generous our church members are in caring for the less fortunate."

What was it about this woman that set Mitch's nerves on edge? Yes, she was nosy, but that was just because she wanted to feel included. In the loop. "I'd love to chat, but . . ." He smiled and raised his box then stepped forward.

"Before you rush off," Frances said, "a bunch of us are heading to Piggy's Corner for lunch. Would you like to join us?"

Lunch—with Angela—sounded great, although it'd also be venturing dangerously close to a date. He started to shake his head then caught a glimpse of Angela, looking so . . . hopeful? Definitely insecure, beside him.

"Um . . ." Couldn't be easy, being new. Every Sunday, she arrived just as the worship music was starting. Slipped into the back row, and hurried out as soon as the service was over. Someone really needed to help her get plugged in.

He caught her eye. "What do you say? You hungry?"

She examined each face in turn, her gaze lingering on Frances's before returning to him. "I . . ."

A frown deepened the wrinkles in Frances's forehead, and Mitch cast Phil an inquisitive glance.

The guy shrugged then turned to Angela with a grin. "We're not that bad. Just a bunch of kooky seniors who spend our time eating and flapping our gums." He laughed. "And reading the Word on occasion. Might as well join us now. Let us break you in easy." He winked at Mitch. "Imagine if this guy has any say in the matter, you'll be joining us soon enough."

Now it was Mitch's turn to blush. He shifted. The box wasn't heavy, but his fingers were starting to sweat. "What do you think, Angela?"

She breathed deep, releasing a smile on the exhale. "That'd be great."

Her response triggered a bigger grin than he'd anticipated. Fighting it, he cleared his throat, ignoring all the eyes staring at him. "All righty, then."

Chapter 22

Angela waited while Mitch deposited her things in the back of his truck then unlocked her door. Papers, a tape measure, and a pile of receipts cluttered the passenger seat. A pair of tan work boots and an empty, coffee-stained Styrofoam cup occupied the floor.

"Sorry." He reached past her, carrying with him the scent of musky sandalwood. He shoved the paper and tape measure in the glove box, tossed the remaining clutter in the back of the cab. Extending an arm, he motioned for her to get in.

As she did, she caught a glimpse of Frances standing outside a silver four-door. The woman's intense gaze made Angela squirm. Making eye contact, the woman's tight expression smoothed into a smile, and she wiggled her fingers. Angela returned the gesture.

Spine straight, she pressed her knees together and positioned her purse on the floor. The interior of the vehicle smelled like motor oil, old leather, and wood chips.

Mitch rounded the truck's cab then hopped in. "You been to Piggy's yet?"

"I can't say that I have." Eating out wasn't an option. Not if she hoped to pay off her debts within the next century. But today, she'd splurge, hopefully even make some friends.

"Then you're in for a treat." He cranked his engine, shifting into reverse. "It's a bit of a drive. Out near the cornfields, actually. But they've got the best bacon cheeseburgers in town. Best chili fries, pancakes, coffee, chocolate cake—"

Angela laughed. "You sound hungry."

He turned onto Hickory. "I am. Missed breakfast."

"Did you work this morning? I didn't see you at the remodel."

"Not on Sundays. Try to keep that day free for church stuff."

"You on staff?"

"Volunteer. Greet. Random stuff."

"I see." She'd met guys like him at her old church. Godly, responsible, respectable men. The kind that married Sunday School teachers and pastor's daughters. The kind who avoided women like her.

"You enjoying our church?" He turned onto a narrow, two-lane road. The truck hit a pothole, jolting the cab.

"I am." And she was, though it didn't feel like home yet. But that was probably because she didn't know anyone, well, other than Mitch. "So, you have kids?"

He frowned, studied her for a moment. "Three." He paused. "One with Jesus, two here in Omaha."

"I'm so sorry. I can't imagine."

A tendon in his jaw twitched. She wanted to ask him more but was afraid to push.

"How about you?" He tapped his brakes as a squirrel scampered across the road.

She smiled, thinking of sweet Ainsley and her growing belly. "My daughter lives in Kansas City with her husband." Her smile stretched her cheeks. "I'm going to be a grandma soon."

"Nice." They passed a Quick Stop with cars lined up behind every pump, a tattoo parlor, and a barbershop. "You just have the one, then?"

"Yes." *Alive.* A lump lodged in her throat as a shiver ran through her. What she'd done to her other child—one she'd never seen—still haunted her. Seemed maybe she and Mitch had something in common, except she doubted he'd caused the death of his child.

She hoped he wouldn't press her further yet felt a strange need to unload. She'd kept that secret for decades. Tried to drown the ache with shopping, liquor, men. Anything to avoid remembering that day. *Lord, Your Word says I'm a new creation. So why can't I forget?*

The rest of the drive they talked about random stuff, like typical Omaha summers, fall festivals coming up, and where to buy the best steak. By the time Mitch pulled into a small, gravel lot, Angela had begun to relax. Even enjoy herself. Perhaps a little too much.

"Here we are." The cab rocked as the truck's wheels sank into the uneven ground, pebbles pinging against its undercarriage.

In front of them stood Piggy's, a single story building with wood siding and a flat roof. The peeling paint, a faded peacock blue, left patches of blackened wood exposed. The trim was a pastel pink and a striped fabric awning stretched over the narrow wooden door. A neon "open" sign flashed in the grimy window. The upside? Lunch shouldn't take much from her pocketbook.

Mitch parked between Frances's vehicle and another Angela recognized from church.

"Looks like we're the last ones here." He fisted his keys, flashing that adorable, crooked grin she was coming to love. "You ready?"

Was she? Ready to eat lunch with near strangers, and godly ones at that? What if they hated her? Besides, what would she talk about? She knew few Bible verses. Had no nuggets of truth to share. Unless someone asked her how to restore the luster to rain-damaged suede shoes. But she was here. Too late to turn back now. Besides, these were fellow Christians. Her new church family. She needed to connect with them sometime.

She wiped sweaty hands on her capris. "Ready." She opened her door and slipped out.

Mitch rounded the truck. "Mmm. Smell that?"

She inhaled. "Nothing like the scent of fried food and bacon."

"Exactly." He winked, causing her heart to skip a beat.

After a momentary falter, Angela tried to match his long, confident stride as they approached the entrance.

Mitch held the door open. "After you."

His gaze captured hers and held it as she walked past him, so much so that she tripped over the rubber lining on the floor. He grabbed her elbow in his strong hand, steadying her and sending jolts of electricity shooting through her.

She was a mess. A mess headed straight for trouble, unless she figured out, quick, how to keep her emotions in check.

Chapter 23

Pulling away from Mitch's electric touch, Angela straightened and smoothed her blouse. The dim interior of Piggy's was as dingy and dated as its exterior. Black carpet with maroon swirls covered the floor. A potted plastic plant, covered in dust, stood near a metal podium, and on the wall of the lobby hung numerous framed posters.

"Mitch, good to see you." A short, bald man with tufts of hair around his ears greeted them.

"Hey, Cecil. How you been? How's your wife holding up?"

The man's smile faltered, and he gave a half-hearted shrug. "She'll make it." He grabbed menus from behind the hostess stand and raised them. "You need these?"

"Nah, but my friend here might. Cecil, this is Angela. She just moved here from Kansas City. Across from one of our rental properties, actually."

"Ah." The man gave a slow nod. "Brought her to the right place, then." His toothy grin returned. "I'm sure Mitch told you all about our buffalo burgers, made from the largest, grass-fed beasts around. So fresh you can hear 'em snarlin'."

Angela raised an eyebrow. "Um . . . not exactly."

Cecil laughed. "Don't worry. We've got regular beef too. And chicken. Better barbecue than Kansas City, hands down." He grinned, motioning them toward the dining room. The laughter and chatter echoing off the paneled walls and low-lying ceiling helped put Angela at ease.

Mitch trailed close behind. "Better be careful, Cecil," he grinned, "dissing the girl's hometown like that."

Cecil shot her a glance over his shoulder. "You a Chiefs fan, huh?"

"I . . . uh . . . not exactly." She'd watched plenty of football in her time but only because that allowed her to hang out with single men. The shameful memories made her blush.

Across the room, four circular tables, draped in red-checked vinyl, had been pulled together. The Abiding Fellowship crew was gathered around them. Only a handful of other patrons occupied the place. A few glanced up as Angela and the guys approached. Frances appeared to be watching her closely, her face tight.

"Smart girl you brought here, Mitch." Cecil's chubby cheeks bunched under his bright, blue eyes. "Now, if she says she's rooting for the Huskers, I just might bring her a nacho plate on the house." He sauntered off, a waitress carrying a tray of waters taking his place.

Mitch stood behind his chair, hands on the top of the seat back. "Everyone, this is Angela."

Hellos, smiles, and friendly nods followed. "She's been coming to Abiding Fellowship for, what?" He looked at her. "Three weeks now?"

She shrugged, taking her seat and pulling it close to the table. "Since August 14th, my first weekend here."

"Good for you." A woman with long, black hair and glass earrings smiled. "Where'd you move from?"

She told them, which initiated a string of stories, from cars overheating on the Paseo parkway to playing the banjo in one of Zona Rosa's outdoor concerts. This from the tall, lanky man named Marty.

Angela fought a full-fledged, proud-momma grin. "Are you a musician?"

"Just fiddle around some," the man said. "Had a buddy in the band. Started ribbing him about how I could play better than him. Just in fun, you know." He chuckled. "Long and short of it is, my friend challenged me to put my strumming fingers where my mouth was." He grabbed his water. "Most hilarious minute of my life."

"My daughter's a musician." She blurted the words before her brain caught up. If it had, it would've told the proud momma lurking within to keep her boasting mouth shut.

"Really?" Frances raised her water glass. "She does the nightclub circuit, then?"

All eyes on her, Angela shifted. "No. She

189

signed with a record company. Contemporary Christian."

Murmurs of admiration circled the table, more than a few offering approving smiles.

"That's lovely." The woman with the black hair, Joline they'd called her, glanced up as the waitress approached. "Perhaps she could play for one of our women's events." She sat an inch taller than most of the males and had a slender frame and angular face.

"We can talk about that at our next lifegroup meeting," Frances said.

"Great idea." Joline clapped her hands and turned to Angela. "Would you like to join us? We meet on Tuesday evenings at my house." Before Angela could answer, Joline grabbed her purse, plopped it onto her lap, and began rummaging through it.

"Lifegroup?" Angela glanced around, once again finding numerous eyes centered on her. The waitress had made it halfway through their group.

"Just a cozy word for Bible study." Joline ripped a deposit slip from her checkbook and wrote on the back. "And food. We always have chocolate, don't we ladies?"

Laughter ensued, although the taut skin around Frances's eyes told Angela she found this interchange less than comical. In fact, Angela was beginning to think the woman outright hated her, which was absurd, considering they hardly knew one another. Ainsley would say she was being paranoid, assuming the worst. That was probably true. And it was time Angela stopped.

She grinned at Joline, taking the slip of paper with her name, number, and address on it. "I'd love to come."

By then the waitress had made her way to Angela. Unfortunately, she hadn't given the menu more than a cursory glance. But she certainly wasn't about to hold everyone up further. Instead, she turned to Mitch, who was watching her with those deep, amber eyes of his. "I'll get what he's having."

The waitress nodded, jotted down her order, then dashed back toward the kitchen.

"Funny"—the corners of Mitch's mouth twitched upward—"I never would've pictured you as a blackened beef tongue fan."

She swallowed hard and nodded. Making small talk, but internally dreading the beef tongue sandwich. *Surely he was kidding. Right?* Relief overcame her like a wave moments later when the waitress brought her a cheeseburger. She exhaled and relaxed. The burger was good, and the conversation was nice. Quite pleasant, actually.

Her heart swelled at the smiling faces all around her. *Thank You, Lord. I needed this.*

She'd just taken her last swig of iced tea when

the waitress returned and began distributing checks. Chairs shifted as Angela's new friends rummaged in their wallets and purses. When the waitress got to her, she reached for the bill.

Mitch beat her to it. "I got this."

Heat flooded her face. She could feel everyone watching her. Did he think she couldn't afford it? "Don't be absurd." She tried to grab the check from him but he'd already returned it to the waitress with his credit card.

"Consider it our welcome."

She stared at her plate, the temperature in her cheeks increasing. How many of these folks knew she was staying at the Martins'? How many knew the story behind why she was staying there? That most of these people's grandchildren had been Christians longer than her?

Chapter 24

Angela's car puttered and trembled as she veered off the interstate in search of Helping Hands Thrift Store. The conversation she'd overheard at school replayed in her mind. She'd been headed to the office when voices drifting from the break room halted her.

"Someone really needs to talk to that woman." Angela had recognized Mrs. Wright's voice instantly. "Did you see how short her skirt was?"

"Completely inappropriate." Reuben. "She's an embarrassment to the school. And to think they hired her over my cousin. Unbelievable."

Angela hadn't heard the rest. She'd been too busy fanning her eyes while making a mad-dash for the ladies' room before tears ran down her face. Then she'd really look horrific.

Now where was that thrift store? She looked it up online before she left, and it was supposed to be at the intersection of 120th and Gardenia. But that's where she was, stopped at a red light, and she didn't see it. Had it gone out of business? That would be just her luck.

After looping around a few more times, she found the store tucked between an abandoned strip mall and a busy Laundromat. Nearby stood a massive, stone church with high, arching, stain glassed windows. Graffiti artists had destroyed the sign occupying the front grounds, and planks of wood covered what appeared to be a basement window.

Half a dozen cars dotted the Helping Hands's lot, some rusted and dented, a few new and shiny. Angela pulled next to a gray van and waited while a large family spilled from the vehicle. A short, broad-shouldered woman she presumed to be the mother grabbed a ginormous diaper bag and plopped a chubby baby on her hip. With a quick glance Angela's way, she shut her vehicle door, grabbed a feisty toddler by the wrist, and began making her way across the asphalt. Her children weren't cooperating.

Parenting truly did require village-sized help. Angela thought of Bianca and her sweet children. Oh, how she wished she could help them, but they refused her every effort. She was tempted to give up. If not for Sunday's sermon on long-suffering love, she might have. Even so, she was getting discouraged—about the Douglases, her job, the fact that she still hadn't made any real friends here in Omaha.

Well, except for Mitch. And Joline. Actually, all of the people she'd met from Abiding Fellowship had been great, everyone but Frances. Not that she bothered Angela much. Every church group had a sour crab. Sometimes once you got to know them, the people that frowned more than they smiled end up having the biggest hearts ever. Maybe Frances was like that. Angela chose to believe she was.

At least none of them, in their proper and respectable attire, had made mention of Angela's "embarrassing" clothes.

With a sigh, she glanced down at her silken blouse and suede skirt. Prior to today, this had been one of her favorite outfits. It made her feel young. Pretty. But now . . . why was her clothing such a big deal, anyway? God loved her just the way she was, short skirts and all . . . right?

She paused, tilted her head. Did God care what she wore? It wasn't like she was out in her undergarments. And she was showing much less skin than all the women she saw on television. Although she was older. Was that the issue? Were there some unspoken rules about how older women should dress? Joline's outfits were certainly much different, more . . . mature. Like what a librarian might wear.

She stepped out of her vehicle and gave the hem of her skirt a tug, causing the pull of her zipper to bite into her flesh. Unfortunately, the snug fabric wouldn't give, reminding her yet again of her recent weight gain.

Another reason she needed to go clothes shopping. Slinging her purse over her shoulder, she marched across the lot.

A high-pitched whistle stopped her as she reached the curb.

She whirled around to find an older gentleman dressed in a green-and-black T-shirt and faded jeans smiling at her.

"Hey, there, pretty momma. What's your hurry?" The man's gaze swept the length of her, making her skin crawl.

She straightened and pivoted on her heel, arms swaying staunchly at her sides.

The man's taunting voice followed her. "Ah, come on, now. Can't we be friends?"

She dashed inside, a gust of cold, musty air pouring over her from overhead vents.

To her left, a woman stood behind a long counter cluttered with stuffed garbage bags, piles of clothes, and plastic hangers. A line much longer than Angela had anticipated, especially considering the sparse cars in the lot, extended beyond this.

Signs denoting size protruded from the tops of clothing racks. Additional signs hung from the ceiling. Angela made a beeline for an area labeled Women's Dress Clothes, nearly tripping over a pile of fallen hats en route. She was halfway through a row of slacks when her phone rang.

Guessing correctly who it was, she practically jumped to answer it. "Ainsley! How are you?"

Her daughter laughed. "Wow, what an enthusiastic greeting. Way to make a girl feel special." She paused. "You OK?"

Angela didn't want to launch their conversation with her poor-me's. "How are you feeling?"

"Ready. And it appears, so is little Joey. The Braxton-Hicks are starting."

Angela's heart skipped a beat, a large grin forming. "That's so exciting! What's your doctor saying? Any chance the baby will come early?"

"I suppose there's always a chance, but the doctor's still saying sometime around the 29th. Do you think you'll be able to come? I mean, I understand if you can't, with your new job and all."

"Oh, I'll be there." She'd make it happen somehow because she couldn't—wouldn't—miss the birth of her first grandchild.

They talked for a while longer, Ainsley sharing silly stories from her and Chris's recent shopping trips. Apparently Angela's son-in-law managed to turn every conversation with every random stranger into one about his first ever child. It was absolutely endearing.

"He's going to make such a great father." The love radiating from Ainsley's voice warmed Angela.

Thank You, Lord, for grabbing hold of my little girl and giving her the life I never could.

"But enough about me. How are you? How's

your job? How're Robby and Sebastian? Making any progress?"

"Not really. Robby still seems to hate school, though he appears to be trying. Except he tries to hide it. I guess maybe it's uncool to study."

Ainsley laughed. "Boy, am I glad to be in the adult world. Whew! How's work going? You making any friends?"

Angela bit her bottom lip as a wave of sadness washed over her. She moved toward a far wall, away from eavesdropping ears. "Do you . . . ? Is there something wrong with me?"

"What are you talking about? Of course not! You're letting negative thoughts get the best of you again, aren't you?"

"I guess." She watched a toddler climb into a box of stuffed animals. "I just . . . what about how I dress?"

An extended pause followed, causing her gut to knot.

"What happened?" Ainsley's voice was soft, almost maternal.

Pressing her back against the cold, concrete wall, Angela told her all about the overheard conversation. "I've always known I didn't fit in with church people. Now I know why."

"Oh, Mom. I'm so sorry. People can be so unkind. But as to whether or not you fit in—the Cross says you do. Remember that verse I sent you?"

"Yeah." She had it taped to her mirror, read it every morning.

"Therefore, if anyone is in Christ—"

"He is a new creation. I know." She fingered a string of beads hanging from a nearby stand. "You never answered my question. Is there something wrong with the way I dress? Am I too stylish for the Midwest?"

Another pause.

Angela huffed. "Your silence answers that. So what should I do? Start shopping in the old ladies' section? Stick with neutrals? Go plaid? Help me out here."

"It's not the style as much as . . . well, I suppose you could tone things down a bit. Maybe less bling and geometric shapes?"

"OK. Fine." So drab it was, apparently. "I can do that." She migrated back toward the women's dress clothes and pulled out a pair of charcoal slacks. "Earth tones, then?"

Another pause.

"What? That's not enough?"

Ainsley sighed, and Angela could envision her sinking deeper into the couch cushions. "If I were to guess, though I've never liked making assumptions regarding other people's behavior . . ."

"Just tell me already."

"It's . . . well . . . you show a little more skin than . . . is, perhaps, best."

Angela moved sideways and gazed at her

image in a standing mirror. Her cleavage did show. Not a lot, but more than the other ladies at church, perhaps? She tried to remember what Frances and her clan wore. Straight-necked collars. Sometimes button-ups. V-necks, though she couldn't recall how low.

"How much skin is appropriate?"

"Well . . . I suppose everyone has a different idea on what constitutes as modest, but I usually try to choose shorts that reach the end of my fingertips or longer. And I don't show any cleavage. Ever."

"I see." Still facing the mirror, she extended one hand, the hem of her skirt hitting mid-palm. "Who makes up these rules, anyway?"

"Private schools and moms of teenagers?" Ainsley laughed. "There aren't any specific rules, per say. It's really more of a heart issue. Choosing to be modest."

"Modest. Right."

"I can send you verses, if you'd like."

"So basically Mrs. Wright thinks I look like a tramp."

"I wouldn't go that far. But you might get a better response if you dressed more conservatively. Looser clothing. Not so low-cut."

She thought of Mitch and how nice he was being, and her face heated. Surely he didn't think she was . . . surely he wasn't trying to . . . ? No. Of course not. He was a good, godly man.

Who steered clear of immoral women, the type, apparently, she'd been dressing like. Her stomach sank as shame overtook her.

She closed her eyes and pinched the bridge of her nose. "Why didn't you tell me this before?" If only someone had given her a list of do's and don'ts when she became a Christian, everything would be so much easier. Less confusing.

"Mom, life change takes time. Sanctif— growing more Christ-like is a process. For all of us. Besides, it's not my job to change you. That's up to the Holy Spirit."

"Yeah, well, you could've at least given me a hint. Maybe helped me chisel away at the biggies."

"Yeah, that would've been fun. And productive. Overwhelm you with a long list of faults and expectations."

"So there's more then?"

"What?"

"You said it was a long list. What else am I doing wrong?"

"Mom, stop. You've come a long way. I'm proud of you, and I know Jesus is too."

"Yeah, well, apparently I've still got a long way to go."

"Don't we all? Just keep stepping, Mom. Keep drawing near to Christ, reading His Word, going to church, and trust Him to do the rest."

"You make it sound so easy."

Chapter 25

At the end of her shift, Bianca stopped into Virginia's room before leaving. The woman sat in her wheelchair, crocheting what looked to be miniature flowers. A lawn care infomercial played on her television screen, indicating Virginia's lack of attentiveness.

"Hey." Bianca rapped on the doorframe.

Virginia dropped her needlework in her lap and smiled. "Well, hello. I thought you were off today."

"No. Just covered a different section, is all."

"The Alzheimer's unit?"

She nodded.

"I heard Christine quit. Sue, from occupational therapy, said it was because she didn't like the new director."

No one did, but talking about that with the residents wouldn't help matters any. "So she said."

"I know she was close with Marissa." Virginia adjusted the blanket on her shoulders. "Is it true what they say, that she and Summer were fired for fraudulent billing practices?"

"No one knows the real story, and I doubt we'll find out." That wasn't a can of worms she wanted to open. All she cared about was the fact she still had a job.

"Well, I'm sure it will hit the papers soon enough."

"I hope not." The last thing Hillcrest Manor needed was more folks pointing fingers their way, getting headquarters all worked up again. She looked at her watch. "I was about to head home but wanted to stop in first." She remained a moment longer, her gaze falling on a pink journal sitting in the windowsill. According to Dawn, the nosiest nurse's assistant on staff, that book recorded Virginia's prayers. Was Bianca's name in there? Would it matter if it were?

Obviously not, considering what a mess her life was.

"See you tomorrow." Forcing a smile, she hugged the woman, then left.

She arrived home just as the sun started to dip below the horizon, filling the Omaha sky with vibrant shades of orange and pink. It made Bianca want to pour herself a glass of sweet tea, pull out a lawn chair, and spend the evening outside. But she couldn't. She needed to make dinner, gather the laundry to take to the Laundromat, make sure Robby studied for his math quiz, and finally get all the munchkins tucked in bed. Hopefully during all that, she and C. J. could have a bonding moment.

As she stepped inside, the smell of cooked hamburger swept over her, and she smiled. C. J.

had made dinner, and, it seemed, cleaned up after. Raising an eyebrow, Bianca stepped into the kitchen. The counters were spotless, not a dish in sight. Even the living room had been tidied.

What was that girl up to?

Bianca deposited her purse on the counter and headed down the hall. She froze midstep at the familiar, male voice emanating from her youngest's bedroom. Nerves fired with a strong mixture of hope and dread, she poked her head inside. It was all she could do to keep her knees from buckling.

Reid lay on Sebastian's bed, reading. Robby laid in his bed across the room, on his side, pillow tugged to his chest. She glanced at the book cover—*Green Eggs and Ham.* Sebastian's favorite. One he could recite by memory. The boy's head nestled between Reid's arm and chest, reminding her of the many winter nights when the three of them had curled up in her and Reid's bed, Sebastian squished beneath them. Most times Robby would join. C. J. never, though every once in a while she'd hover in their bedroom doorway, as if considering it.

"Hey." Her voice came out froggy.

"Hey." Reid held her gaze, as if pleading with her.

"Hi, Mommy." Sebastian grinned and snuggled in closer to his father. The vice around Bianca's heart tightened.

Such a good father. But he was still a criminal, running from the law. No amount of love for her or the kids would change that.

Blinking back tears, she straightened, still gripping the doorframe for support. "We need to talk."

Reid's face fell. He stared at her for a long moment then kissed his son's forehead. "You sleep good, bud." He slid out from under him then lingered in the center of the room, as if reluctant to go.

Bianca didn't want him to leave either. But he had to. For the kids' sakes, he had to. She wouldn't lose her children. Wouldn't raise them in a life of crime.

She waited in the kitchen, her back to the hallway, every muscle in her body so tense, she quivered. Reid's slow, shuffling footsteps drew near, then stopped.

"Baby." His strong hands gripped her shoulders, his breath warm on her ear. "I've missed you."

She stepped away, shrugged loose of his embrace, and turned to face him. Her heart squeezed at the pain etched on his face. *Oh, Reid!* "Where's C. J.?"

"In her room. Moping. She's not too thrilled that I came back."

Bianca nodded, craning her ears. Odd she didn't hear music coming from her daughter's room. Maybe she should check on her. "You have to leave. Now."

He winced, his eyes searching hers. "I love you, B. Please. Don't do this."

She swore. "You really messed up this time, Reid."

His gaze fell, his shoulders dropping. "I know." His voice, hoarse, was barely above a whisper. "I'm sorry. It wasn't supposed to go down like this."

"It wasn't supposed to go down at all. You promised. Said you were done. Seriously, how many times are we going to have this conversation?"

"Baby, I—"

She raised a hand, palm out. "Don't. Just don't." She sighed. "I need to check on C. J."

Rubbing her forehead, she approached her daughter's room. The door was locked, the other side oddly quiet. Bianca's stomach plummeted. Surely the girl hadn't done anything stupid.

Holding her breath, she knocked, "Ceej?" She waited. Nothing. She knocked again, harder this time. "Ceej, you OK?" Still no response.

She used a bobby pin from her hair to disengage the lock, eased the door open, and poked her head inside. Her heart ached at the image before her. C. J. lay on her bed, legs pulled to her chest, head buried in her pillow, back to Bianca. Her thin frame shook, as if sobbing, but no noise came out.

Bianca plodded to her daughter's bed and sat

on the edge. "Ceej?" She nudged her shoulder. The girl startled, looked at her with red, puffy eyes, the wire of her ear buds crossed beneath her nose. "Sweetie, can we talk?"

C. J. glanced at her again, eyes narrowed. "Leave me alone." She pushed Bianca away then grabbed a pillow and pulled it over her head.

"Sweetie, please." Bianca rubbed her daughter's back in slow, wide circles, just like she used to do when C. J. would wake up with nightmares. "Let's talk about this."

C. J. bolted to a sitting position, her face hard. She yanked the ear buds from her ears. "Why can't you just leave me alone? I'm tired of you pretending like you care."

"I love you. You know that."

"Really? Because it sure seems like you love that loser husband of yours more."

Bianca stared at her, mouth dry. She'd do anything for her kids. Would die for them, if she had to.

And yet, there was Reid, the man who'd caused her children such incredible pain, the man whose actions could get her children taken from her, sitting in her living room.

Leaning close enough to smell C. J.'s honeysuckle lotion, Bianca smoothed the hair from her sweet daughter's face. "I'll take care of this. I promise."

C. J. continued to hold her pillow around her

ears, gripping the fabric so tight her fingertips blanched.

"Can you hear me?" Bianca tugged on the pillow. "I'll take care of this. I'll take care of you."

The color returned to C. J.'s fingertips as her grip loosened on her pillow.

"I'm so sorry for everything that's happened." She placed her hand on her daughter's shoulder. "For what you've had to go through. It's not right. Not fair." She swallowed, her throat scratchy. "I won't let him stay."

Though C. J.'s pillow remained, the rhythmic movement of her back slowed, her breaths steadying. Wrapping her arms around the child, Bianca held her, C. J.'s torso trembling beneath her. When C. J. looked up, tears streamed down her face.

Bianca wiped them away. "I'm so sorry, baby. I'm gonna take care of this. Everything's going to be OK."

C. J. took in a shuddered breath. They sat like that for a moment longer then Bianca inhaled and stood. "I'll see you in the morning?"

Eyes red, C. J. nodded, rolling onto her back.

Bianca smoothed the child's hair away from her face then pulled the covers up, tucking them around her. "Sleep good, sweet girl."

She trudged out, easing the door closed behind her.

When she arrived in the living room, she found Reid sitting on the edge of the couch cushion, hands folded tightly in his lap, eyes trained on her. Stomach knotted, she sat beside him and looked into his sapphire eyes. "You can't stay here. Not anymore. You gotta turn yourself in."

"I can't. I won't go back to prison, B."

"You have to. For us. For the kids." A tear slid down her cheek, causing tears to form in Reid's eyes as well. "Otherwise we're done."

"Don't say that." He reached for her but she jerked away.

"Do the right thing, Reid. Be the type of father your kids can be proud of."

He hunched forward, elbows propped on his knees, his face in his hands. He sat like that for a long time. Long enough Bianca worried her resolve would crumble. She hated to see him in such pain. Hated to think of him in prison.

Why does it have to be so hard?

If God heard her, He didn't answer. Not that she expected Him to.

Reid sat up, rubbed his fisted hand, studied her. "I could face serious time."

She swallowed, nodded. A felony drug charge was a big deal, especially since this wasn't his first offense.

"Will you wait for me?"

A sob wrenched from her throat. She took his hands in hers. "I will. You know I will."

"And you'll come with me to the police station?"

"Of course." She was supposed to work tomorrow. She'd just have to call in.

He breathed deep, blew it out through tight lips. "All right."

"Oh, baby." She grabbed hold of him, burying her face in his chest, her heart feeling as if it'd been wrenched in two. "I'll be here."

"I want to say good-bye to the kids." His voice wavered. "Walk them to school in the morning, then we can go."

"I think that'd be good." She leaned her head against his shoulder and closed her eyes. Wishing this would all go away, that they could go back in time. Wishing he'd never lost his job, that she earned more at hers. That she didn't have to choose between her kids and keeping her husband home.

"Come on." He stood and pulled her to her feet. "Let me hold you for one last night." Twining his fingers through hers, he led her to the bedroom.

He pulled her toward the bed but she resisted. "I gotta call in."

Releasing her hand, he nodded, sitting on the edge of the mattress.

She grabbed her phone. Each ring caused her stomach to knot tighter. Things at work were tense enough. Three salaried staffers had been let go, headquarters had sent in a new director.

Others had quit. Besides that, Bianca needed her hours. But this was her husband. She had to stand beside him. Especially now.

"Hillcrest Manor. May I help you?"

Bianca wiped a clammy hand on her pant leg. "Hi, Jean. It's Bianca. Is Mr. Homer in?"

"Nope. What do you need?"

Mr. Homer was their new director. Corporate brought him in. He was a hoverer, scrutinizing everyone with a heavy-browed frown. Like he was waiting to catch them messing up. So far, Bianca had largely stayed off his radar. But after today . . . ?

"My kid's sick. Puking all over the place. I'm going to have to keep him out of school tomorrow, so I won't be able to make my shift."

"Oh." Jean's voice sounded flat. "I'll tell Diana you called."

"Thanks. I owe you."

"Whatever."

She ended the call, and Bianca dropped her phone on the dresser and massaged her forehead.

"Everything all right?"

She looked up to find Reid studying her, tender love radiating from his deep blue eyes. "Yeah." She closed the distance between them and sat on his leg, hers between his. Holding tight to him, she pressed her cheek against his chest, breathing deep of his earthy scent. Oh, how she'd miss him.

They'd lock him up for good this time. By the time he got out, the kids would be grown. Maybe even married with families of their own.

"Love you, babe." His breath tickled her hair, his hand rubbing her back. "We'll get through this."

"I know."

Her night was restless and filled with horrendous dreams of Reid dragged away in shackles, crying out to her, begging her to help him. Of him in prison, getting beaten down by large, hairy men covered in tattoos. Of Reid walking out the door while Sebastian clung to his leg. That image haunted her the most.

Am I doing the right thing? Reid would never turn her in. She knew that much. He'd do anything to protect her. He'd give her the world if he could. It was his love for her that got him in this mess in the first place.

"You all right?"

Rolling over, she found Reid sitting up in bed, watching her. She pulled herself up and inched backward until her spine rested against the back wall. "Did you get any sleep?"

He shrugged, his bloodshot eyes answering for him. He glanced at the clock on the bedside table. "Guess we better wake the kids, huh?"

She nodded, slipped out from under the covers. The sun pressed through the blinds, striping the carpet. A neighbor's dog barked, a low, gravelly sound, followed by a series of yips.

She followed Reid into their youngest's room, hanging back while her husband nudged the child awake.

"Hey, bud." Reid smoothed the hair from Sebastian's forehead.

The child's eyelids fluttered. Then a huge smile emerged. "Daddy."

Tears stung Bianca's eyes. Moving to Sebastian's bedside, she gave her husband's arm a squeeze then leaned over to kiss her son. "Time to get moving, little man."

Reid stood there for some time, stroking his son's head, his brow pinched. She knew that look. Had never seen the man cry, though he came close the night before.

Bianca gave his hand a gentle squeeze. "I'll start breakfast."

Everything was falling apart.

You still praying for me, Virginia? For us?

Giggles cascaded down the hall, her boys following shortly after.

"After school can you throw me batting practice?" Robby pulled out the kitchen chair and plopped into it, his eyes bright.

Sebastian scurried behind him, taking the adjacent seat. "Me too! Can I come?"

Reid and Bianca exchanged glances, then she turned back to the stove, swiping at a stray tear.

Wood scraped against linoleum, and Reid cleared his throat. "I wish we could. I've got to take care of some stuff, bud."

"After that, then?"

The hope in Sebastian's voice tore at Bianca's heart. Drying her cheeks, she took in a deep breath and scooped fried eggs onto a plate. She brought it to the table, hovering behind Reid, her hands on his shoulders. "We've got some things to talk about." But first, they would eat. This would be her boys' last meal with their father for some time, maybe decades. She refused to take that from them.

Chapter 26

Standing in the center of the kitchen of their remodel, Mitch surveyed the progress. "We might be ready to schedule our open house soon."

Dennis nodded. "Think we should call the stager?"

"Will do. I'll get Kaden to send his photographer out too. Let him know we'll be ready to list . . . what? By a week from Wednesday?"

"Sounds about right." Dennis hadn't mentioned in some time the snake realtor he'd been talking to. Mitch assumed that meant the guy had flaked out, as he expected. But Mitch wasn't going to say anything. That would only put his partner on edge.

"You're picking up the sink for the master bath, right?" The old one was cracked. Unsalvageable.

"Yeah. I'm heading to pick it up now. Going to hit the coffee shop on the way back. Want me to grab you something?"

Dennis grinned. "A cappuccino shake would be awesome."

"I'm on it." He pivoted toward the arched entryway. "Should I get some for the guys?" They'd been working hard. More than expected and they'd made up a chunk of the time they'd lost dealing with the mold issue. Truth was, they deserved extra pay, but Mitch and Dennis didn't have that to give.

"Bet they'd appreciate that." He studied Mitch, his eyes softening. "How's your boy?"

"Haven't heard from him." He pulled out his phone and checked his text messages for the fifth time in half as many days. He'd sent ten, asking Eliot where he was, telling him to call him. No response.

"Sorry."

So was he. It killed him to see his son continue to self-destruct but he had no idea how to help. "He'll show up eventually." When he ran out of drug money. Then Mitch would be forced, yet again, to make the most painful choice any father could face—help his son out, hoping the next time would be different, or show tough love in the hopes of saving his life.

The decision was crippling, he wanted to avoid it altogether. In truth, that was how he usually dealt with Eliot. He should do better. But a guy could only hit his head against the same brick wall so many times.

"Oh, man." Ted's voice arrested his thoughts. The electrician's heavy boots clomped down the stairs. "Mitch, Dennis, you better come see this. Yo, Jeremy!" He raised his voice. "Check this out, man."

Mitch gave an inward groan.

"What now?" Dennis spun around and stomped out of the kitchen.

Mitch followed to find Jeremy, Big-man Alfie, and Ted gathered at the foot of the stairs.

"The wiring's all messed up." Ted shook his head. "It's old school. Probably have to be redone."

"What're you talking about?" Mitch asked.

Ted fidgeted, clicking the metal tab on his measuring tape. "I was up in the attic to wire that new ceiling fan you ordered." His gaze shifted to Dennis then flicked away. "It's a mess up there. They've got knob-and-tube wiring, and it's breaking down. We're gonna have to rewire all of it."

Dennis cursed again and blew out a gust of air. "How much?"

Ted shrugged. "Can't tell, but I wouldn't be surprised if the mess ran through the whole house."

Mitch turned to Dennis. "What about the kitchen? Did you notice anything when you knocked out the hanging cabinets?

Dennis shook his head. "Didn't open the walls."

Jeremy cracked his knuckles one finger at a time. "The bathroom electrical seemed fine."

Mitch nodded. "Hopefully this is an isolated problem and the rest of the house was updated."

"Won't know unless we open things up." Ted said. "So what're we gonna do?"

Mitch rubbed the back of his neck. "Can you handle this, Jeremy? Figure out what needs fixing?"

"No problem."

He checked his watch. "I've got to get going. The guys are holding a sink for me." He eyed Dennis who stood with his shoulders hunched, rubbing his face so hard the skin turned a deep red. He looked ready to blow.

Mitch clamped a hand on his shoulder. "We'll get through this."

Dennis's eyes narrowed. He stared at Mitch, his mouth flattened, lines fanning from his lips. Then, shaking his head, he turned around and left, slamming the door behind him.

Mitch followed him out and released a slow breath. *Lord, help us out here. Show me what to do, what to say.*

He stopped on the porch and watched his partner stalk to his vehicle, gun the engine, and peel away, a trail of exhaust following him. That man was an explosion waiting to happen. He'd already lost his cool in front of the guys way more times than Mitch liked. It was bad for morale. Stressed everyone out.

The door behind him creaked open. Jeremy. "Hey, can I talk to you for a minute?"

"Sure." Mitch leaned with his back to the porch railing.

Jeremy scratched at the back of his neck. He

looked toward the street then back at Mitch. Whatever he wanted to say, he sure wasn't in a hurry.

"Everything all right?"

"It's probably nothing . . ."

"What is it?" A thousand possible catastrophes flooded Mitch's brain, each one high dollar.

"It's . . . Dennis." Jeremy shifted.

Mitch waited.

"I heard him talking on the phone the other day. About legal stuff like . . . what his options were, what'd it take to buy you out . . . without losing the crew." His fingers kneaded his forearm. "Wanted to know about the legal options, should you fight him."

Mitch felt like he'd been punched in the gut. Dennis was turning on him? Talking to lawyers, even?

He took in a deep breath. "Thanks, Jeremy."

The kid nodded then started to leave.

"And Jeremy?"

He turned back around.

"Let's keep this between us, OK? No sense getting the guys all worked up over something that's bound to blow over by the time we list."

With another nod, he slipped back inside.

Mitch had felt torn over this business for some time, having to fight Dennis over every little thing, always pulled between the bottom dollar and doing what was right. He'd been praying about the situation for over a year now. Maybe this was God's answer? But if it were, it'd cost him a friend.

He gazed toward Angela's house, where she sat, swaying gently, on her newly erected porch swing. The image of her was like a ray of sunshine on an otherwise gloomy day. It bothered him like crazy that she had this kind of effect on him. Probably meant he should steer as clear of her as possible. Except today, he really needed a dose of sunshine.

He decided the sink could wait and ambled over.

"Mitch. Hi." She set a sketchbook and colored pencil down. On the page, she'd drawn the beginning of what looked to be a child standing on an old, wooden porch.

"Nice. You're very gifted."

"Thanks." She blushed. She wore her silver hair pulled up in a clip, loose tendrils framing her delicate face. Her baby-blue T-shirt brought out the gray flecks in her blue eyes. "It helps me relax. Think."

"The church could really use someone like you in our kids' department."

Her eyes lit up, but then her gaze dropped, and she gave a halfhearted shrug.

Didn't like children? No. That didn't make sense. Her career choice was all about kids. "You go to Joline's?"

"What?"

"Her Bible study. I heard her invite you."

"Oh." She paused. "Not yet."

Had something happened? She'd seemed so excited when Joline had invited her. Had been all smiles and chatter during lunch. Had really hit it off with the other ladies, as far as he could tell. Maybe he should talk to Joline about it later, encourage her to invite Angela again. Being the newbie had to be hard.

"How're things at work?" he asked.

"Good. Most days." She gave a fleeting smile. Tilting her head, she chewed on her bottom lip. "Reid's back, huh?"

"You saw him?"

She nodded. "Yesterday, walking the kids to school."

His muscles tightened, and he gazed toward Bianca's. The boys were in the yard, but her car was gone. Her curtains were drawn. She never did give him the remainder of the rent money. Never mentioned it again. If anything, she avoided him. Not that he could blame her, nor did he care about the cash. Least, not when he thought she was in a place to finally get her feet under her. But with Reid back . . .

The words of his son's first rehab counselor flashed through his brain. *Can't help someone who won't help himself. Sometimes the best thing you can do is let them feel the stink of life's consequences.*

That idea didn't sit with him any better now than it did when they were talking about Eliot.

"I really worry about Robby and Sebastian." Angela broke through his thoughts.

"Yeah." He tried to shake off the ever-present cloak of regret. "They're in a rough spot for sure. You make any progress? At school, I mean?"

"Some. They're pretty reserved. Quiet. A lot of the teachers have labeled Robby as a lazy troublemaker, but that's not it."

"Kid's just hurting. They all are."

She nodded. "Wish I knew how to help. I've tried reaching out to their mom." She shook her head. "For whatever reason, that woman hates me."

"She just doesn't trust you. Doesn't trust anyone."

"I can understand that." She cupped her knee with her hands. "How long have you known them?"

"Seven years. No, eight. I had just remodeled her place and was about to put it on the market when I got a call from one of our church members. Bianca had hit a rough patch and was about to be homeless. She comes from a pretty rough family—had no one who could really help her. I don't know a lot about her mom. I'm pretty sure her dad's not in the picture, and her brother's been in and out of jail. Juvie before that."

"Wow. I guess they call it generational poverty for a reason, huh?"

He nodded. "It's hard to do better if no one's taught you how and you and everyone you know are always living in crisis. When I met her, she just had Cassie Joe and Robby, her husband wasn't in the picture." He'd thought he was doing something significant, helping her start over, but she kept slipping the other way, heading right back to where she started. "I never did hear the whole story, figured I didn't need to. I let her move in that afternoon, much to my partner's dismay."

"Why?"

He chuckled. "Seemed he liked the idea of making money."

"Do you support her, then?"

Mitch shook his head. "She had a job, just not the money for first and last. She wasn't earning much more than minimum wage. But that's not what my partner was upset about. He was concerned about her poor credit. Said she'd drain us. I couldn't imagine a mom and her kids living on the streets. Found out later,that happens all the time."

"That's so sad."

An extended silence followed as both of them gazed toward Bianca's. Robby had gone in but

Sebastian remained outside, tossing and catching a football. A guy on a motorcycle rode by, going at least 40 miles an hour. Totally oblivious to the Kids at Play sign.

"Would you like something to drink?" Angela's sweet voice recaptured his attention. "Lemonade? Iced tea?" Her smile, a light, glimmering pink, drew his attention to her full lips.

She seemed to grow more beautiful every time he saw her. If he weren't careful, he'd fall for this woman. And that would be a mess waiting to happen, once they broke up. Which they would. He stunk at relationships. His failed marriage was proof enough of that. Besides, from what Bones said, this woman was probably still on the mend. Mitch didn't want to be a rebound or responsible for hurting her further.

But it was just lemonade. "Sure. That sounds great."

Her smile grew, and, gathering her things, she sprang to her feet. She wore white capris and a blue, crewneck T-shirt. The outfit hugged her curves without strangling them, and the colors were nice. Soft. Accentuated her femininity.

He followed her into the house then stood in the center of the living room, the scent of vanilla wafting from a candle on a nearby end table. Portions of drywall were exposed, the yellow and green striped wallpaper torn from it in jagged strips. The removed wallpaper lay scattered about the floor and still more filled a bulging plastic bag.

"Sorry about the mess. I'm doing some remodeling. Well, trying to."

"I'm impressed." From the looks of it, she still had a long way to go, and at the rate she was going, she might not have any wall left by the time she was done. "Would you like help?"

"Oh, no." She spoke quickly, flicking a hand. "I'm fine, but thank you."

Stubborn little thing. Mrs. Martin never had a problem letting him help out. But maybe Angela was one of those independent types.

"The Martins said this was OK. Thought it was a great idea, actually. They have been so kind to let me stay here, the least I could do is freshen the house up a bit"

Renovating. Brilliant! Funny he'd never thought of it before. He peered through her opened doorway to Bianca's. It'd be a great way to pour into those boys too. Give them something productive to do, something they could be proud of.

He turned back to Angela. "If you run into a snag or simply get tired," he grinned, "you know where to find me."

"Speaking of . . ." She headed toward the kitchen, Mitch following. "How are things going? Everything looks great from the outside. I love the color you chose for the trim."

"Thanks. My partner picked it. Isn't it crazy what a fresh coat of paint can do?"

Pulling two glasses from her cupboard, she studied him, head cocked.

He fought a chuckle. Was the pretty lady thinking of painting her house? Now that was a project she'd definitely need help on because he couldn't see that woman up on a ladder. Least she'd stopped wearing those heels, though. Those things were an accident waiting to happen.

When his gaze met hers, the questions in her eyes caused heat to crawl up his neck. She'd caught him staring.

He gave a nervous cough and leaned against the counter. "Sure is getting nice out there. Supposed to be in the midseventies all week."

"I love autumn." She opened the fridge, revealing near empty shelves. "It's my favorite season."

Rubbing his knuckles under his whiskered chin, Mitch watched her pour the lemonade. Housesitting for the Martins, sparse in the food department . . . was she low on cash? How much did a para make, anyway? Not that it was any of his business, though he should keep his eye out, just in case. Without acting like a creep.

"Here you go." Angela handed Mitch a glass of lemonade.

"Thanks."

She brought her drink to her lips then lowered it, glancing around. Should she ask him to sit? Would that be appropriate? Should he even be in her house? She thought back to her conversation with Ainsley. So many unspoken rules she didn't understand. Her daughter had sent Angela verses—something about women focusing on their inward beauty, not their outward. Another about being humble, and yet another about not doing anything to cause another Christian to stumble. She had read them all, really read them. But she still didn't understand where the line between appropriate and inappropriate behavior lay.

"Would you like to . . . ?" She swept her hand toward the kitchen chair but then noticed the clutter piled on the table. Lying on top—her debt repayment schedule.

She faced Mitch, finding him also noticing her mess. Based on his tight expression, he'd seen more than she'd wanted.

"Um . . . how about we go to the living room. It's more comfortable." She groaned inwardly, the heat in her face accelerating to near combustion. Comfortable? Had she really said that? How many men had used that line on her? "Actually, why don't we sit outside? The porch swing is so love—" That sounded like a pickup line too. She stunk at this friendship thing. Of course, it didn't help that the man was so incredibly attractive.

And honorable. It was the latter that grabbed her most. What would it be like to date a man with integrity? Who cared about others, even those like Bianca?

Except she was done with men. She'd promised herself that three years ago when Ainsley and Chris first took her in. For good reason. She had absolutely no business dating. None.

"So . . . outside then?"

Jolted from her inner discourse, she found Mitch watching her, with a hint of an amused, or perhaps confused, grin. "I . . . er . . . yes. Wherever."

She resisted the urge to fan her fiery face or climb under the nearest rock and followed him onto the porch. A cool breeze swept over them, carrying with it the scent of fresh cut grass. A baby rabbit scurried across her yard, darting beneath a nearby bush.

Angela lingered on the stoop. She glanced first at her porch swing then her steps. Mitch's work boots clomped behind her, then the swing's hinges creaked.

Not wanting to appear forward, she meandered over, leaning against the side railing.

"What do you do, anyway? At church, I mean?"

"Go to a lot of meetings, pray for folks, and eat lots of pound cake."

"Sounds fattening."

"Oh, I don't know. I'm pretty sure there's a

'thou-shalt-not-gain-weight-while-volunteering' clause."

She laughed, then, sobering, studied him. Funny he wasn't married. Which meant he was divorced, right? Either that or he had kids out of wedlock.

"What?" He took a swig of his drink then, still holding it, rested it on his thigh.

She startled. "Huh?"

"You look like your mind's churning."

She followed a drop of condensation on her glass with her finger. "I just . . ." She studied him, his gentle eyes, his accepting smile. "I just . . . I mean, I hope this doesn't sound rude, but are you divorced?"

An eyebrow shot up, his mouth opening before curling into a grin. "Yep. Not proud of it. Hate the fact, actually, but yeah." He studied his hands, rubbing his index finger with his thumb. "If I had it to do over . . ." He released a huff of air. "It was a tough time for our whole family." He looked past her, his forehead wrinkling, as if lost in a memory.

She didn't push him, but rather, lowered to the porch's floorboards, back pressed against the railing, legs extended. He remained silent for a long time, long enough that she thought their conversation was over. Which was fine. Almost nice, actually, that they could simply sit.

But then his expression changed, as if things

inside him had shifted. "My son died. He got killed in a car accident. His twin brother was driving. Ran a red light, straight in the path of another vehicle."

He stared into his glass, swirled the ice cubes. "Eliot made it out untouched, other than some bruising." A tendon in his jaw twitched. "Ray and the driver of the other vehicle died. Her name was Phyllis Hough, a single mother of three grown children. According to the article, she'd been driving home from watching her grandson's basketball game. The medics air-rushed her and Ray to the hospital. They lost my boy in transit, Phyllis the day after. And Eliot . . . he's been slowly killing himself ever since."

"I'm so sorry." She suddenly wished she'd sat beside him, so she could reach out to him. Comfort him somehow, not that anything she could do or say would ease the pain of losing a child.

"We all fell apart after that, my marriage included." He took in a deep breath. "If only we'd turned to Christ instead of running from Him, everything would've been different." He leaned back, the swing hinges creaking. "Least I've got Him now, right?" He gave a slow, sad smile. "I turned my life over to Him a few years later."

"So you're a late bloomer too, huh?"

Forehead wrinkled, he scratched his cheek. "What's that?"

"A late bloomer—someone who wasn't born in the church."

"Oh!" He grinned. "I guess you could call it that, though bull-headed would probably be more accurate."

"The church doesn't care that you've been divorced?"

"They don't love it, but they understand grace. They see me like Christ does—forgiven."

How many times had Ainsley said the same thing of Angela? She knew it was true. Her Bible said it was.

So what kept that truth from settling deep into her heart?

Chapter 27

Sitting in the hard plastic chair meant for a child half her size, Angela suppressed a sigh. She checked the clock above Mrs. Wright's desk. Only five more minutes. If these kids could handle it, so could she.

This was her least favorite class of the day, and not because of the subject matter. Not because of the kids, either, though the group she'd been assigned to could do a better job of paying attention. And trying. Even so, they were like saltwater taffy compared to the scowling Mrs. Wright.

She popped her knuckles one finger at a time.

Ayden laughed. "You sound just like my grandpa."

Angela gave the boy a weary smile. If he gave his grandpa this much trouble, she could understand why. How come the child refused to do his homework, and what could she do to change that?

Straightening, she clapped her hands on her thighs, looking from one young face to the next. "I've got an idea."

Eyes shifted her direction, even Robby's, though he watched her with a sideways, guarded look.

"I'm going to bet you all like chocolate."

"Not me." Barry scrunched his nose.

"You do so." Ayden elbowed him in the arm. "You stole my brownie yesterday. Shoved it all in your big, fat face."

"Shut up!" Barry shoved Ayden back, which initiated a pushing war, creating all sorts of racket as metal chair legs scraped against the linoleum.

"Boys." Angela raised her voice a notch—not yelling, but firm. "Enough."

They glowered. Barry crossed his arms while Ayden jammed his elbows on his desk, dropping his chin onto fisted hands. His chubby cheeks bunched beneath his hazel eyes, nearly swallowing them.

Angela pressed her tongue to the roof of her mouth to keep from laughing. Difficult or not, these children were absolutely adorable. "Here's what I'm thinking." She pulled her chair closer. "But let me start by saying, I know you all are much smarter than you think."

She made eye contact with each child, holding Robby's gaze the longest. But then he looked away and began tearing at the edge of his paper.

"I know you all can pass the test tomorrow, if you study. I think you just need a little incentive." More accurately, evidence that someone actually cared. "So, here's the deal. If you do one grade better on tomorrow's test than you did on your last, I'll bring you a candy bar of your choice. What do you think?"

"Yay!" Violet grinned, and for once, she didn't fall into her normal habit of talking with herself.

But Barry's frown only deepened. Why? Did he believe he couldn't do it? If only she could catch a glimpse into his mind, hear his thoughts. Leaning forward, she placed a hand on his back.

She lowered her voice. "I know you can do this. If not this time, then next for sure. What's your favorite candy?"

He shrugged.

"Sweet-and-sour balls?"

He shook his head.

"Carmel Zotz?"

Another head shake.

"Chocolate covered pickles dipped in Tabasco sauce?"

This triggered "ews" and giggles all around, and a raised eyebrow from Robby who watched her with brightening eyes. Even his mouth was beginning to lift slightly.

She dusted her hands off and said, "Chocolate covered pickles it is," then smiled at Robby.

The bell rang, followed by the sound of metal scraping against the floor, zippers opening and closing, books and papers rustling.

"Hold on!" Mrs. Wright clapped her hands, her narrowed eyes making a hard sweep of the classroom. "Don't forget to do your chapter review tonight." She peered over her glasses at a thin kid with near white hair. "Tomorrow's test will account for 10 percent of your grade. I expect you all to do well. You're dismissed."

Angela grabbed a crumpled piece of paper from the floor and strolled to the trashcan.

"Ms. Meadows?"

She stopped, turned.

"I would like to speak with you, please."

Mrs. Wright's icy tone caused Angela's stomach to tighten. "Yes, ma'am. Of course." Squaring her shoulders, she walked, stiff-legged, to the front of the room. She fought to keep her smile in place. "How can I help you?"

The teacher perched on the corner of her desk, arms crossed. She studied Angela for some time, long enough to cause her mouth to grow dry. Something told her, if this woman had the power to do so, she'd fire Angela on the spot.

"Did I hear you bribe the children, Ms. Meadows?"

"I . . . uh . . . *bribe* might be a strong word. I was simply—"

"Offering to pay your small group of students, who have notoriously shirked their duties, to do that which everyone else, including themselves, is routinely expected to do. Now tell me, is that fair?"

Angela searched for the best words. "I didn't mean to cause problems or to slight any of the other children in any way. If you'd like, I could offer them—"

Mrs. Wright raised a hand. "I'm sure you meant well, but bribery is not the answer. Especially for those children. They've been coddled enough. That, Ms. Meadows, is why they consistently perform so poorly. They expect everyone to cater to them, to excuse their behavior." She stood and rounded her desk, grabbing her purse from the back of her chair. "What they need is accountability. Perhaps flunking a test or two, should it come to that, will provide the consequences they need to do better."

Surely that wasn't the answer. "But they're just kids. Isn't it our job to help them succeed in any way we can?"

"Which is precisely why you are here. To help them better grasp the concepts I teach. Not to reward them for poor behavior."

"I'm not—"

"I don't have time to argue with you." She slung her purse over her shoulder. "You're an idealist. I get that. I was once as well. You'll learn and adapt in time." She started to walk away then stopped, rotated. "Have a good day."

Angela stared after her, mind spinning. Was she right? Were the children's poor study habits due to lack of accountability and pampering? There was no way to know, except for with Robby. She knew better with him. He was hurting, so much

236

so, he'd almost given up entirely. She just wanted to give him hope, somehow.

With the laughter of newly recessed children drifting through the glass window beside her, she crossed the room into the hall. Kids thronged the narrowed walkway, their high-pitched voices piercing Angela's ears. Following close behind, teachers boomed the familiar "walk, don't run" mantra.

With each command, chubby legs would slow to a jerky walk-jog-walk stride, arms waving staunchly at their sides. But in a few steps, the admonition would be forgotten, and the pattering of running feet would resume. And each time, Angela's heart would swell with laughter.

She slowed as she neared the office. The principal's strong voice quickened Angela's pulse, reminding her of the decision she'd made during her morning devotions. The Bible said God hadn't given her a spirit of fear. And this morning her study guide had encouraged her to approach new opportunities with confidence. Walking in the knowledge that one was deeply loved and that God had a glorious plan for her life.

Of course, that didn't mean God's plan and hers would align. So what happened if God didn't want her to obtain a full-time teaching position?

She massaged her temples, forcing her raging

thoughts to slow. *Lord, help me trust You. Help me surrender to whatever Your will is.*

Even if I make a complete fool of myself.

On second thought, maybe she should pray about this more. She'd only been on the job for a month. That was hardly enough time to demonstrate her competency. And yet, if she waited any longer, someone else could snatch the position. Probably already had.

Ugh! She fisted her hands and stormed around the corner.

And barged straight into her boss, sending the papers she was holding spewing across the floor. Snickers erupted behind them, and a handful of teachers stopped to stare.

"Oh, my! I'm so sorry." Angela clutched a hand to her mouth before darting for the dropped documents. She quickly gathered them into a pile, inadvertently bending the corners of some.

"Please, Ms. Meadows. Allow me." The principal knelt beside her.

Angela's nail snagged the woman's skin when they reached for the same paper.

"Oh!" Angela shrank back, clutching the papers she'd retrieved, two of which were high-resolution, glossy, full-colored graphs with bold lettering typed across the top. The bottom right corner had bent backward, forming a long crease along the cover.

Her stomach plummeted as she read the

brochure more closely. It appeared to be a proposal of some sort. One that was supposed to look nice.

Angela stood and did her best to smooth the shiny page flat, rubbing her finger along the crease, leaving a very noticeable smudge. "I'm . . . uh . . . here." She shoved them at her boss then wrung her hands.

Frowning, Mrs. Allen grabbed the items and began straightening them into a neat stack.

Angela swallowed, the verse she'd read that morning tangling with her thoughts, most of which urged her to turn around and walk in the opposite direction as quickly as possible.

God hasn't given me a spirit of fear. I have nothing to fear. God has a wonderful plan for me.

"Did you need something, Ms. Meadows?"

"I . . . uh . . . no. I mean, yes." She gave the bottom hem of her blouse a tug. The hallway was now near empty. Even so, this was not the place to discuss career matters. "Do you have a moment? I'd love to talk with you about a position I heard will be opening up soon."

Mrs. Allen checked her watch. "Actually, I'm heading to a meeting at the district office." But then her expression softened. "You can walk me to my car, if you'd like."

"Great." Angela quickened her step to match the principal's, a woman who appeared to know two speeds—fast and faster. "As you probably remember from our interview this summer, I have a teaching degree from UMKC."

Mrs. Allen nodded, pausing outside a classroom door to peer through the window of one of the special needs classrooms. She watched for a moment, then turned back toward the hallway exit. Resuming her hurried pace and unwinded, she was completely oblivious to Angela's deep breathing beside her. Thank goodness she'd traded her cute pumps for flats.

"I heard Marlene Carmichael will be taking maternity leave soon, and . . ." Perhaps restating rumors wasn't the best course of action. "And . . . well, I wasn't sure what she planned to do after that."

Mrs. Allen slowed. "Yes?"

Having reached the side doors, their long, frantic strides stopped. "Well, I . . ." Angela forced what she hoped to be a confident smile. "I'd love to be considered for that position, ma'am."

"And who, pray tell, would take your position?"

The woman's intense gaze silenced her for a moment but she recovered quickly. Did she forget that Angela's job as a para was only temporary? "I was thinking in terms of next year, ma'am."

Mrs. Allen gave one quick nod. "I see." She paused. "As I'm sure you're aware, we receive a great number of applicants each school year."

Angela bobbed her head.

"Many with years of teaching experiencing."

More head bobbing, enough to make Angela dizzy.

"However . . ." Clutching her papers between her chest and forearm, she tapped her chin with her index finger. "I believe Hartman Elementary has a few openings next fall. Check their website."

Angela's heart sank. "I'll do that, thank you." This was a brush off if she'd ever heard one, and a familiar one at that. Why should anyone hire her when they had so many other, more experienced candidates? But how could she ever gain experience if no one hired her?

"I'd be more than happy to write you a letter of recommendation."

"That'd be wonderful, thank you." Surely that would mean something. Enough to get her hired?

Except . . . switching schools would mean she'd limit the time she had to influence Robby and Sebastian. And based on the way he was hanging out with the sixth grade troublemakers, it wouldn't be long before Robby began to follow in the footsteps of his father.

Chapter 28

Bianca checked the time on the microwave. She was late for work. Where was C. J.? She should've been home 20 minutes ago.

"I can't do this." Sitting at the kitchen table, Robby dropped his pencil and fisted his hands on either side of the paper. "Who cares how many zebras were left over?"

Bianca rubbed his back in circular motions. "You can do this." If only she had time to help him. If only Reid were here . . . She swallowed, her eyes stinging as an image of her husband locked up in a cold prison cell came to mind. "When C. J. gets home, she can help you."

"Uh-uh. She'll be hanging all over her boy-friend." He accentuated the last word in a mocking, winey voice.

"No she won't. She knows good and well he's not allowed in the house while I'm gone." He never came around when she was here, which said a lot about the kid's character. Or lack thereof.

"Then she'll be on the phone with him."

"I'll make sure she helps you."

"That'll make her mad."

Which meant she'd take her frustration out on the boys. "I know. How about you and I work on it together in the morning?"

Robby's fisted hands uncoiled, his posture straightening a bit. Looking at her with his big, brown eyes, he gave a slight nod.

She ruffled his hair, glancing toward Sebastian sitting in the living room. "What about you, little man? You gonna study your spelling words?"

Sebastian looked up, frowned.

"Remember, I don't want to see nothin' lower than a C."

Car tires crunched on the gravel driveway. She recognized the shrieking music that blared then muted when a door slammed shut. A moment later, footsteps sounded on the rickety porch steps and the door screeched open.

Bianca's jaw tensed when her daughter entered wearing a skirt so short, a slight bend would reveal all. Thick, black eyeliner gave her a bold look, and her bright-red lipstick was smudged. It didn't take much imagination to guess why.

Bianca crossed her arms. "Where you been?"

She dropped her backpack to the ground. "Studying."

"Uh-huh." Bianca held her daughter's gaze. "You're late."

"Sorry."

"I bet you are." Now wasn't the time to fight with the girl. That'd only set her off, leaving the boys to pay. Or else she'd storm out, and Bianca would be without a sitter. Still, Cassie Joe was throwing her life away. How could Bianca help her see that?

She grabbed her purse and water bottle. "Ground beef's thawed in the fridge. Rest of what you need is on the counter. Please clean up when you're done."

"I've got plans." C. J. pulled a piece of gum from her pocket and popped it in her mouth.

"So change them because I need you here."

"I can't. Alexis and I are going dress shopping for homecoming. J. C. Penney is having a huge sale."

"You don't have money for that. And you better not plan on hot-fingering nothing."

"Alexis gets an allowance. Gets paid for babysitting too."

Bianca sighed. "I'm sorry. I know it's tough. I really wish I could give you some spending money, but . . ." Bianca shook her head. "I'm broke."

"Story of our life. I'm sick and tired of it. Of working for nothing, never getting anything. Always being broke. Why do I have to suffer from your stupid choices?"

Bianca tensed as a jolt of electricity shot through her. Fighting to maintain self-control, she spoke slowly. "Like I said, I'm sorry. I know it's tough." She glanced from Robby to Sebastian then back to her daughter. "But we've got to pull together."

"What if I don't want to? You ever thought of that?" She started to walk away.

Bianca grabbed her hand. "Don't you get it? I'm trying to get you out of this mess. All of you. I want so much better for you, Ceej. I don't want to see you end up pregnant, throwing your life away to raise a kid."

"Like you did with me?" Her eyes narrowed.

"That's not what I meant."

"Whatever." She walked to the kitchen and grabbed a glass. "I'm playing Mom already."

Bianca held her gaze, wishing she could say something to cut through her daughter's anger. To restore the sweet relationship they once shared. How could a person miss someone so much when they were standing right in front of them?

"You know I love you, right?"

C. J.'s face softened, and her eyes misted. Then, with a visible breath, she turned back to the sink and filled her glass.

They'd get through this. Somehow.

Chapter 29

"Stager's here now." Phone pressed between his ear and shoulder, Mitch grabbed his things from the passenger seat. "I'll call you when she's done."

"OK." Dennis coughed. Evidently the cold he'd picked up on Monday still lingered. "Just make sure she knows we're on a tight budget. No leather furniture or the latest TVs."

"I hear you." But if the stager said high quality, they'd be best to follow her advice. She had helped sell more houses than Mitch could remember. Many that had been stagnant, eating up their margins with utility fees and taxes.

Mitch tucked his phone in his back pocket and stepped out of his vehicle. The air carried the scent of fried onions and something else. Garlic? His stomach rumbled. He glanced toward Angela's place, disappointed she wasn't in her usual spot on the porch. Maybe he should stop by in a few, see how she was doing.

And ask her out for coffee? Had they progressed to that point? Did he want to? Did she? Had she even entertained the notion? Not likely, considering how far she'd sat from him, the day she offered him lemonade. You would've thought he carried a virus or something.

"Mitch, how you been?" Rebecca, the stager, a

short, boxy woman with black hair streaked with blond highlights approached, free hand extended, clipboard in her other. Her thick ring, a gold band with an oval ruby center, glimmered in the sun.

"Ready to get this property listed and off our hands." Grinning, he accepted the handshake. "Thanks for coming."

She nodded and faced the house, tapping a painted nail against her lip. "The place has great curb appeal. How many square feet?"

"Just over 1,700. Two stories, two and a half baths." He led her across the yard and toward the remodel. "Wood floors in the living room, dining room, and kitchen."

"Nice." She waited on the stoop while he opened the door.

He motioned for her to enter. He glanced back at his vehicle to lock it, then paused. On the street corner, young Robby stood talking to Pockets, a neighborhood thug known for hawking drugs. Which meant, based on the way those two were acting all buddy-buddy, he was hoping Robby would do some running for him. Those thugs always picked out the struggling kids. Sweet-talked them with the promise of money, girls, and a bunch of other garbage.

Still holding the door ajar, he turned back to Rebecca. "Think you can handle this for a minute? I got something I need to do."

"Sure." Clipboard in hand, she glanced around. "I'll check out the place, take notes. Should be able to send you an estimate by this evening. You want me to get my cleaning lady out here too?"

"Wouldn't hurt. Thanks." Mitch left with a parting nod, letting the door close behind him. He crossed the street, watching Pockets, grabbed his gaze and held it. The snake backed up, mouth still flapping.

As Mitch drew closer, the guy tried to ditch. Probably to find another kid to reel in. Like they'd done with Mitch's son. An image of the first time he caught Eliot high filled his mind, igniting his pulse. After that, the boy had made a rapid decline, and no amount of love, tough or otherwise, had been able to keep him from self-destruction.

"Hey." Mitch called out to Pockets and hustled to catch up with him. "Don't make me chase you."

Pockets turned around and glared. "What's your beef, old man?"

"Stay clear of the Douglas boys."

"Or what?"

"You want to push me on this?" He had an inkling that he should be nervous, getting in the guy's face, but he didn't care. Bianca's kids needed someone to look out for them, to stand up for them. "You really want me up in your business? Watching your every move, letting the police know where you go when?"

"Never took you for a stupid man."

The threat was clear, but Mitch refused to back down. Besides, Pockets talked a tough game, but that's all he was—talk. "Stupid and stubborn, and prepared to be your biggest headache." Though the kid was no pansy, Mitch was banking on his laziness in this instance. Hoping if he got in his face often enough, the jerk would back off. And if that didn't work, he'd call the police, encourage them to up their patrols in the area. Matter of fact, he should've done that long ago. He'd take care of that this afternoon.

With a sneer and a string of curse words, Pockets sauntered off, talking about how Mitch was a waste of his time.

Just keep walking, buddy.

Satisfied Pockets wouldn't be coming back around anytime soon, and determined to keep an eye out for when he did, Mitch approached Robby. Stopped at the edge of the driveway. "What're you up to?"

He shrugged, sauntered over. "Just hanging out."

"You have school today?"

"Yeah."

"How'd it go?"

"Boring."

Mitch chuckled. "I hear ya. But it's good

learning, right? You never know when you'll need to multiply the width of a two-by-four or calculate the square root of a wood floor." He winked. "Your mom home?"

The kid visibly tensed. "Uh . . . not sure."

Either he forgot Bianca's car was in the drive, or he hoped Mitch wouldn't notice.

"Guess I'll go see, then."

His heavy work boots clomped as he made his way up the stairs and onto a faded welcome mat. Inside, a television blared from one end of the house while a shrieking guitar sound emanated from the other.

He knocked, waited. Knocked again. Nothing. He knocked again, louder, his free hand reaching for his phone. With all that racket, might be best to call the woman. Let her know a fella was standing on her front porch, banging on her door.

Bianca answered the door before he had a chance, her face pale. "I'm sorry. I've been meaning to call you." She spoke fast. "About my rent, I know I owe this month and the rest of last's, and I'm going to pay you. I'll give you what I've got now and the rest . . . soon as I can."

"Actually, I think I've got a solution that'll work for both of us."

She studied him, clearly wary. "Yeah? What's that?"

"Seems this place could use a few repairs." He glanced back toward her yard to find Robby watching him. The boy had inched closer and stood near the bottom step. "Fence could use fixing, a fresh coat of paint. This porch too." He tapped his foot on a loose board beneath him. "Looks like the trim around your front windows might have dry rot."

"OK?" She leaned against the doorframe.

"So, I was thinking . . . would your boys be willing to help me out with the repairs? I'd knock it off your rent." He'd pay the difference himself, to get her caught up. He had some funds to spare. Not a lot, but enough. For now. He'd cover whatever she couldn't until she got her feet under her. And if she never did? He'd deal with that later. But for now, he had to give her every chance, for the sake of her kids.

"I don't know." She chewed her bottom lip. "They've never done nothing like that before. What if they mess it up?"

He smiled. "Then I'll show them how to fix it. Truth is, it won't be that complicated. They'll pound some nails, slap on some paint. Figure their time's cheaper than if I had to send a crew over here." So maybe that wasn't entirely true, but the words were out. Too late to take them back now.

She stared at him for a long moment, looked at her son, then back at him. "Seeing how you're my landlord, I guess I can't really say no, huh?"

He shrugged. He wasn't going to force these

projects on anyone, but he was sure hoping she'd agree to it. If only for her boys' sakes. They needed a positive male influence in their lives. And the place was a mess. Really, he should've fixed it up long ago, but Dennis had never been too keen on the idea. Plus, Mitch had always had enough to manage dealing with house-flips and keeping his more demanding renters happy. Not to use that as an excuse. Come to think of it, his lack of attention to this place was downright shameful.

He pulled up his calendar on his phone. "This weekend, then?"

"Yeah, sure. Whatever you want."

He grimaced as recollection surfaced. That was the day of his grandson's birthday party. "Actually, make that Wednesday." Most likely Sheila and Eliot would both be at the birthday party. Working off each other and getting everyone else stirred up. Mitch's stomach flopped just thinking about it.

Bianca stood with her hand on the knob, staring at the closed door in front of her. What kind of mess had she walked into now? Not that she'd had a choice in the matter, considering how much money she owed that man. Course, the bigger question was, what was he up to?

What if he truly wanted to help?

She squelched the thought as soon as it came.

People weren't like that except on TV. Well, maybe Virginia was, but that was only because she didn't have nothing to lose. And she was old. Folks got sentimental when their time drew near. She shuddered, wrapping her arms around herself. The realization that she could very soon lose the woman she'd grown to love so dearly left her hollow. But no sense dwelling on what-ifs. For all she knew, Ms. V still had years ahead of her.

Soft footsteps approached her door, and Robby entered. His sweet little face was all crinkled, making her want to pull him close. Which would only make him fuss.

"Mr. Kenney says he's hiring me?" Though the boy frowned, his eyes lit up like they used to when Reid handed him a wrench and called him outside.

Robby needed a man in his life, and now he had one. Maybe God had heard Virginia's prayers after all. Fighting a smile, she planted a hand on her hip and angled her head. "He'd like to, but he's worried about your grades and what they say about your work ethic."

Robby's shoulders slumped, and his gaze fell.

Truth or not, she needed to work this. Might be the best opportunity she had to get her son to pull his grades out of the gutter. "I told him you'd do better." She lifted his chin and looked him in the eye. "Cuz I know you will. You're smart." She tapped her finger against his sweaty temple. "I keep telling you that. Just got to work a little harder than some, is all. But you can do it. You hear me?"

He shrugged and started to slump again but she lifted his chin a notch higher.

"I asked, do you hear me?"

He took in a deep breath, his thin frame straightening, and nodded.

"Good. And don't let anyone tell you otherwise." She glanced around for her purse. It lay on the counter next to Sebastian's leftover breakfast plate. Her stomach growled as she eyed the half-eaten peanut butter sandwich, growing stale. Grabbing it with one hand and her handbag with the other, she shoved the dry bread in her mouth. It clung to the back of her throat.

"C. J.?" She raised her voice above the nerve-grating music pouring from her daughter's room.

No answer.

"Ceej, I gotta go." She dashed down the hall and knocked on her daughter's door. "Cassie Joe?" Bianca poked her head inside. "I'm heading out."

C. J. looked up, her expression smooth. She nodded. "Can you pick me up some women's stuff on your way home?"

"Sure." She forced a smile, inwardly calculating the cost. Why they got to make feminine hygiene products so expensive?

"Thanks."

Bianca lingered, wanting to soak in this peaceful moment. "I'm off this Sunday. Maybe we could go for a walk or something?"

C. J. studied her, as if engaged in an intense mental debate. "Maybe."

It wasn't the resounding yes Bianca had hoped for, but it left her with hope. That hope kept her spirits high as she drove to work, adding energy to her fatigued muscles. Walking toward Hillcrest's front entrance, she almost had a bounce to her step. Maybe things were looking up. It'd been tough, sure, and her heart still ached something fierce whenever she thought of Reid—he'd taken a plea, had received ten years. The boys would be grown before he got out. Maybe that was a good thing.

At least now she felt like she and the kids would make it.

Standing in front of the time clock, she glanced through the small, square window toward the cloudy sky. *You watching me, God? This You, turning things around?*

As usual, there was no answer. She huffed. If He did have anything to do with the recent turn of events, it was only because of Virginia.

Speaking of, today was Ms. V's salon day. Bianca smiled as she traipsed out of the room and down the hall. Oh, Virginia would be excited about that one. Her daughter would probably come a little after to take her momma to dinner. Those two were like a bright ol' rainbow in the middle of a hailstorm. They always made Bianca want to try harder with her own kids.

"Where've you been?"

Bianca whirled around at the sound of Mr. Homer's stern voice. She blinked. "Excuse me?"

The tall man, shoulders so broad he blocked out the light streaming from his office, frowned, arms crossed. "You were supposed to be here an hour ago."

Her stomach twisted. "No, sir. My shift starts at four." She glanced at the clock on the far wall. She was two minutes late, which was normally not a big deal. But with Mr. Homer towering over her, she felt every second of those two minutes.

"Wrong." He pulled a folded sheet of paper from his front pocket and handed it over.

She opened the page and studied the dates and times on it. No. It couldn't be. She swallowed past a dry mouth. "I'm so sorry. I must've gotten my days mixed up."

His expression hardened.

Voices drifted behind her then stilled as the footsteps neared then receded. The dry, stale sandwich she'd forced down weighed heavy on her queasy stomach. Everyone said not to get on Mr. Homer's bad side, that he was looking to clean house, for folks to make an example of.

She'd have to be extra careful now. Step it up.

Her eyes stung as she continued to hold his gaze. Should she look away? Apologize again? Why didn't he say something?

She cleared her throat, took half a step backward. "I'll get right to work, sir."

He continued to watch her as she took two more backward steps before turning on her heels and marching, arms stiff, toward her assigned hallway. Turning the corner, she barreled into Dawn, knocking a Styrofoam cup from her hand. Ice chips spilled across the linoleum.

"Whoa, girl, watch where you're going! What's with you?"

Bianca knelt and scooped the ice into a pile. "I just got my first Homer talking-to."

"Man." She shook her head. "You better hustle, then. Ms. V's been asking for you. That gal's all worked up about something."

Bianca nodded and hurried down the hall and into Virginia's room. She found her friend sitting in her recliner reading her marked-up old Bible. Her journal lay open on her bedside table, and she held a pink highlighter in her hand.

"Bianca, dear." She closed her Bible and pushed the table aside. "I've been so worried about you."

"I'm sorry. I got my schedule flipped." She angled her head. But . . . why would that worry Virginia? Bianca had been late before. Unless she'd overheard something. The way the other nursing assistants ran their mouths, Bianca wouldn't be surprised. Even so, Ms. V was never the type to listen to rumors.

She crossed the room and moved Virginia's wheelchair into place next to the recliner. "We best get you down to the salon." Spreading her feet shoulder distance apart for stability, she grabbed Virginia by the arm. "You ready for your makeover?"

"I'm in no hurry." She glanced at her clock. "They swapped my appointment with Dottie. Seems her son decided to pick her up early today." She grinned. "You have a second?"

Time was the last thing Bianca had. If she didn't hustle, she'd have more than Mr. Homer breathing down her neck. Nothing got her co-workers riled up like when one of them didn't pull their own slack. Even so, she did need to change Ms. V's sheets. That'd give her a minute.

"Sure. I got a few." Bianca started to move toward Virginia's bed but the woman grabbed her hand.

"I've been praying for you." Her fingers, soft and cold, squeezed Bianca's. "God woke me up in the middle of the night."

"For what?" Her voice came out croaky.

Virginia motioned toward her empty wheelchair, and Bianca sat.

"He loves you so much, dear. Can't you see that?"

Tears stung Bianca's eyes. No. What she saw was everything around her falling apart. Sure, there'd been a glimmer of hope—Mitch asking to spend time with her boys, C. J. acting pleasant. But then, just when she started to reach for that sliver of joy, *bam!* She ran into Mr. Homer. Next time he could send her packing, then what would she do?

Not to mention Reid was still in prison. No amount of prayers would change that.

And it was her fault. She'd urged him to turn himself in, knowing he could be locked up for the duration. Knowing her boys would lose their father. Had she done the right thing?

"Oh, sweetie." Virginia reached up and thumbed away a tear Bianca didn't realize had fallen. "I've asked God to show you just how much He loves you."

Oh, how she wished that were true.

Chapter 30

A shrill ring jolted Angela awake. It took her a moment to orient herself. Her room was dark, her bedside clock flashing. 3:45 a.m. Who would be calling at this hour?

Adrenaline shot through her. *Ainsley!*

She lurched for her phone, sending something crashing against the wall as cold liquid sprayed her arm. Her water glass. Wonderful.

Her cell trilled a third time.

She grabbed it, answered. "What's wrong?" Her chest felt heavy.

"It's time. Will you pray for me?"

"You serious?" Angela jumped out of bed, her sheet entangled around her feet, narrowly missing a face-plant into the carpet. She grabbed the closet door, nearly yanking it from its hinges."What? Now? But he's not supposed to come until—Where's Chris?" She kicked free of her bedding and hobbled to her dresser. "I'm on my way."

"What about work?"

"I'll call in sick."

"That's lying."

"This is my first grandchild. My baby's first baby."

"Oh, Mom." Warmth radiated from her voice.

"How about I have Chris video chat you? Then it'll be like you're right there."

"Uh-uh." Phone between her shoulder and ear, Angela wiggled into a pair of jeans, catching the end of her nightgown in the zipper. "Oh, drat. Stupid thing."

"Mom?"

She tugged the fabric free with a grunt. "Sorry. I'm, uh . . . hold on." She dropped the phone on the dresser and exchanged her nightclothes for a T-shirt, and grabbed her cell again. "I was just—never mind. What hospital are you going to?"

"Mom, listen." Ainsley sucked in a breath and moaned softly. "Come first thing Saturday. Please. I really don't want you to lose your job over this."

"I'll take a sick day. I'll call in once I get to Kansas City." Combing her hair with her fingers, she dashed into the living room to search for a duffel bag. She found one—filled with art supplies, of course. She dumped the contents on the floor and hurried back to her bedroom.

"Fine." Ainsley's breathing deepened. "We're going to—" She made another soft, moaning sound. Chris's voice could be heard in the background. Poor kid was probably terrified. Both of them. "Northland Mercy."

"I'm on my way."

She arrived at the hospital two hours and 43

minutes later. Luckily Ainsley told the hospital staff Angela would be coming.

"She's in room 348." The lady behind the desk smiled. "Down the hall on the left."

"Thank you so much!" Angela flicked a wave then walk-ran down the hall, her arms swinging staunchly at her sides. Her breathing came out in quick bursts.

From outside Ainsley's door, she watched the organized chaos playing out before her. What she could see anyway. A curtain had been drawn around her daughter's bed, keeping her and the doctor from view. A nurse emerged, glanced at Angela, then continued on.

"Hello? It's me. Mom."

Ainsley let out a loud moan, followed by panting breaths.

"Come in, Mom." Chris poked his head out from the curtain. His face was pale, his eyes bloodshot.

Angela swallowed and crossed the room, coming to her daughter's side.

"Mom, I'm so glad. You're here." Grimacing, she spoke between pants.

Oh, Ainsley. My sweet Ainsley. Angela took her daughter's hand, wincing when Ainsley squeezed all circulation from it. "Breathe, baby girl." She leaned close and brushed her daughter's hair from her face. "You got this." She looked around. "Where's your father?"

Ainsley gave a part-smile, part-grimace. "He'll come later." She spoke between pants. "Wanted you here with me."

Tears stung Angela's eyes. Such a sweet man. After all she'd done to him, he still showed incredible grace and compassion. Pulling her lips in over her teeth, she nodded. "Tell him how much I appreciate that."

How surreal. Less than five years ago, Ainsley had wanted little to do with her, and now . . . tears Angela had been fighting spilling over her cheeks.

"Hey!" One of the nurses laughed. "No tears, Grandma. This is a happy day."

"Absolutely." She blinked. *I don't deserve to be here, Lord. Thank You for allowing me to be a part of this.*

She'd barely finished her prayer when Angela's precious grandchild began to wail. It was the most beautiful, robust sound, one that nearly brought Angela to her knees. But what did her in completely was when the doctor placed the wailing baby boy in Ainsley's arms.

Thank You, Lord, for the gift of life and . . . for offering me a second chance. Please don't let me blow it.

Saturday morning before the birthday party, Mitch paced his small kitchen, making frequent glances at the clock. He'd gotten maybe four hours of sleep. Even that was fitful and filled with the strangest dreams, all of them revolving around Ray and Eliot. Sitting at the dinner table, everyone laughing, the entire family together. Throwing a ball around in the yard. Getting into the car on that haunting night, grins wide on both their faces, Sheila waving them off. While Mitch sat, oblivious, in his recliner.

Had he even told Ray good-bye? He couldn't remember. Couldn't remember the last time he'd told the boy he loved him.

He rubbed his face and grabbed a mug of coffee. Today would be a doozy. If history held true, something would happen—Eliot would show up drunk, make a fool of himself, and Mitch would be forced to ask him to leave.

Either that or Eliot wouldn't show, and Sheila would spend the afternoon in hysterics over every worst-case scenario, most of which ended with their son being dead on the side of the road somewhere. Great lunch conversation.

His phone chimed, and he startled, nearly spilling his coffee. He checked the number on his screen. Dennis. "What's up?"

"My granddaughter's in the hospital, on IVs."

"Oh, man. What happened?"

"Not sure." Dennis's tone sounded tight. "They think maybe some sort of bacterial infection, food poisoning, maybe. She's pretty dehydrated. They're running tests now."

"Man, I'm so sorry."

"I'm heading that way now. Doubt I'll be answering my phone much."

"No problem. I'll take care of things on this end." Their property had listed that morning. The open house was scheduled from one to three, with another one scheduled for the same time on Sunday. Though their realtor would be handling all the details, Mitch would need to be near the phone in case offers came in or folks had questions. "Want me to stop by the hospital? Bring you a sandwich or something?"

"No." His tone was clipped.

An extended silence followed. "I'll pray for you."

Dennis scoffed. "Yeah, whatever. Listen, I gotta go."

The line went dead. Whatever headway Mitch had made spiritually with Dennis appeared to have vanished.

Chapter 31

Mitch slipped his phone into his pocket and grabbed his grandson's present—a gift card to Derk's favorite gaming store. As he opened the garage, a cool, moist breeze swept over him. Cleansed after a midmorning rain, the air carried the scent of damp earth and a hint of fermenting silage. The sun poked through clouds hovering in the pale blue sky.

At least the weather would be nice for Derk's party.

Would Eliot show?

By the time he reached Nathan's, vehicles already clogged the drive and lined the curb on either side. Mitch parked behind a maroon van. A woman with poofed haired ushered a half dozen kids out. The children, ranging from chubby-faced toddlers to late-elementary age, darted across the street. Wrist gripped in his momma's hand, the youngest tugged forward, his face squished between a smile and a grimace.

Mitch chuckled, remembering Ray at that age, always in a hurry to keep up with the big kids. He followed the energetic family up the walk, waiting on the stoop while a boy with spiked black hair and neon green sneakers rang the bell again and again. And again.

"Cooper, stop." The woman pulled the kid back and offered Mitch a sheepish grin. "Kids. So impatient."

Laughter, chatter, and upbeat music drifted over the wooden fence.

"Don't blame him," Mitch said. "From what I hear, this party is going to be epic." He winked, stretching the last word out in his best teenage-voice.

The mom laughed. The boy rolled his eyes then focused back on the door. "No one's coming."

Mitch peered through the living room window. Streamers and balloons hung from the ceiling, and presents were piled on the coffee table. Other than that, the room was empty.

"Everyone must be around back." He jerked his head toward the side fence. "I know the secret entrance." He led the way toward the sound of laughter and throbbing bass.

The side gate hung open, the iron railings adorned with decorations. A giant bounce house centered the yard, children spilling in and out of it. Adults sat in folding chairs, others stood in circular packs of four and five. A group of ladies occupied a blanket spread in the far corner of the lawn. Two of them held babies; a third infant lay on her back between them.

Mitch searched the crowd for Sheila. He located her sitting at the patio table, her back to him. Her blond, permed hair flowed from beneath a yellow and blue party hat. Leza, his daughter-in-law, stood a few feet away, pouring lemonade into paper cups while Nathan manned a nearby grill. Eliot wasn't among them, a fact that brought Mitch great relief and sorrow.

It's party time, and, Lord, please help it stay that way, if only for little Derk's sake. Especially considering he'd practically had to talk his son and daughter-in-law into inviting Eliot. Mitch squared his shoulders and approached his family.

Leza saw him coming, and a frown shadowed her face as her gaze flicked from him to Sheila. But then she donned a wide smile and greeted him with outstretched arms. "So glad you could make it."

He hugged her, feeling his ex-wife's eyes boring into him. Pulling away, he glanced around. "Quite a setup you've got here."

"You know." Nathan deposited his grill tongs on a platter of steaming hot dogs and sauntered over. "It's one of those unbreakable rules of suburban parenting—moms gotta throw their children the biggest party on the block, even if it kills them." Skin around his eyes crinkling, he nudged Leza's shoulder.

She swatted his hand. "As if you weren't the one demanding the largest available bounce house. And the multilayered pirate cake."

Nathan laughed. "Can't a man live vicariously through his kids?" He and Mitch embraced. "Can

I get you something to drink?" He motioned toward a cooler near Leza's feet.

"Water's fine, thanks." Accepting a chilled bottle with melted ice dripping from it, he deposited his gift bag on the table. "Where's the little man?"

Nathan tipped his head toward a pack of kids spread out on the grass.

"I'll be back." Mitch excused himself to say hi to his grandson.

Mitch ribbed Derk about the amount of potato chips piled on his plate. He asked him all the routine, grandfatherly questions—how's school? How's baseball? Your team heading to the play-offs? The conversation had just ventured into the discussion of moray eels when Derk caught sight of a lizard and jumped up.

"Help me catch that thing!" The kid and several of his friends darted after the reptile.

Feeling like a rusted nail poking from new wood, he returned to the patio. Though he would've preferred to avoid his ex altogether, he wanted to spend time with Nathan and Leza. That and he didn't know anyone else, except for his daughter-in-law's parents. But they didn't seem to like Mitch much, and he'd never been good at talking with acquaintances. Especially those who knew, from past parties, about their family history. They eyed him like he was the model of ineffective parenting.

Probably was.

He grabbed a paper plate from the rolling tray beside the grill and loaded it with hot dogs, potato chips, and coleslaw—Leza's specialty, the kind with purple cabbage, carrots, raisins, and apple chunks.

Sheila looked up as he sat across from her. She'd lost weight. The sharp angles of her face made her look ten years older. But her eyes pained him most. Once bright and full of laughter, they were now dull and bloodshot, shadowed by dark purple bags. He'd loved her once, deeply. Still cared for her now.

"How you been?" The wrinkle between her brows deepened.

"Good. You?"

"Same ol'."

"You still working at the dentist's office?"

She nodded, her gaze falling to her plate. She'd been answering their phones for going on 15 years now, working toward a retirement she'd never see, thanks to Eliot. As far as Mitch could tell, that's where most of her money went. According to Nate, that's where most of her savings went too. Always bailing their youngest out, never making headway.

"Mitch Kenney." Metal scraped against concrete as Charles Palmer, Leza's father, pulled up a chair. He dragged a second one for his wife Darlene who followed close behind. "Sheila." He shook hands with each greeting, his wife echoing her husband's sentiments.

Settling back in his seat, Charles popped his soda can. He eyed Mitch for a moment, scraping his teeth over his bottom lip. Most likely, Leza had given him a talking to, telling him not to stir things up. Based on his narrowed gaze, her preemptive efforts were about to fail.

"Glad you chose to come." Charles dusted imaginary crumbs off his designer sport coat, a thick class ring flashing in the sunlight. "It means a lot to Derk, I'm sure."

As if Mitch had considered not coming?

"Then again, family gatherings can be . . . complicated. Am I right?"

His wife gave a nervous chuckle.

"Dad." Leza frowned.

He raised his hands, palms out. "Just stating a common fact of life, sweetie."

His wife shifted, looked from her husband to Leza then back to her husband again. An awkward silence followed, the unspoken elephant crushing them all. A loud wail from across the yard broke the tension and catapulted Leza to her feet. Boyish snickers followed.

"No! Derk Kenney, you turn that water off now." She dashed across the lawn toward her son, who stood mud splattered to mid-calf, hose in hand aimed at one of his friends.

"Boys." Mitch laughed. "Leave it to them to

make a mess of things, huh? Literally speaking."

"I can only imagine." Charles cleared his throat. "This has to be tough. For all of you, Leza and Nathan included." He took a swig of his soda. "I must admit, I've enjoyed this peaceful gathering. And my daughter . . ." he glanced across the lawn to where Leza was hosing down a dozen muddy feet, "is more relaxed than I've seen her in some time."

A tendon in Mitch's jaw twitched as he clenched his teeth. He watched Sheila, who visibly stiffened, from the corner of his eye. *Don't take the bait. Just shake it off.*

She breathed deep and dipped a carrot in ranch dressing, her expression smooth though her eyes sparked. Mitch watched her a moment longer, holding his breath, exhaling when her gaze shifted to a group of toddlers picking flowers from a bordering bush. He leaned back in his chair and picked up his hot dog, searching his brain for a more pleasant topic.

"How's your court case going?" Keeping his expression smooth, he folded his hands in his lap. "The one with the lady with the broken leg?"

Charles reached for a tortilla chip. "It's dragging on. The defense keeps filing bogus motions in the hopes of wearing down my client. Which means they're worried."

Mitch nodded.

"What about you?" The man's wife joined the

conversation. "How're things going with your house-flipping business? Leza says you listed another one?"

"Went live today."

"Speaking of . . ." Charles ran his finger along the top rim of his soda can . . . "I heard you hired your youngest on?"

Mitch stared at the guy. He just couldn't let it drop, could he? "We discussed the possibility." Which was true enough.

Charles shook his head. "Like I said, tough situation." He paused. "Course, some would advocate using tough love. Letting the kid suffer the consequences for his decisions."

"If we did that, he'd be dead." Acid laced Sheila's voice. "We've already buried one son. I have no intention of burying another. Now, if you'll excuse me." She stood and started to leave.

"I'm sorry," Charles said. "I shouldn't have said anything. It's really none of my business."

She turned back around. "No, it's not."

"Except that it affects my daughter. And grandson."

Sheila's lips pressed into a firm line. While Mitch worked his jaw until the muscles cramped, unlike his ex-wife, he refused to let this guy chase him off. That'd only add fuel to his insults.

Charles raised his hands. "Stay. I'm leaving." He turned to his wife. "James and Rita are here with their new baby. Let's go say hi."

Darlene nodded and rose, offering everyone a parting, albeit tentative, smile. Poor woman, it was clear her husband embarrassed her. Probably embarrassed Leza too, a lot more than Mitch's son did. OK, that might be stretching it, but the guy wasn't exactly the draw of the party.

Sheila rubbed at the back of her hand, glancing about, her face flushed. Mitch did the same, relieved to see everyone else engaged in conversation. Finally, she sat, one arm hugged around her torso, her other kneading her tricep.

Mitch picked at his half-eaten lunch while she traced the condensation sliding down her glass with her finger.

She pushed her drink away. "Have you heard from him?"

"Who?" As if he didn't know, but a man could hope. Right now he hoped the conversation had shifted to something more pleasant, like mud-splattered children and deep-fried potatoes.

"Eliot. I told him to call you."

"About what?"

"Getting his job back."

Mitch exhaled. "It's not gonna happen, Sheila. That kid burned his bridges so bad, there's nothing but a pile of ashes left."

"But he's your son."

"And I've got a business to run. I don't call all the shots, anyway. You know that."

"Does that matter? We both know you wouldn't hire him."

Mitch leaned forward. "You're right on that. I've hired the boy three, no, four times now, and regretted every one. Why would next time be any different?"

Looking down, she blinked numerous times, the telltale sign she was on the verge of tears.

"This isn't working, Sheila." He softened his voice, hating to see her in such emotional pain. But her refusal to face reality wasn't helping anyone, Eliot least of all. "He'll never change if you keep rescuing him. Remember what the drug counselor said?"

"What did he know? Eliot was nothing but a case number to him."

"I'd say 20 years working with addicts and drunks count for something."

"Drunks?" Her tone rose, wobbling. "Is that how you see him?"

"Passes out in his own vomit. Can't go a day without a drink. Can't make it to work sober. Sounds like a drunk to me."

"So much for that unconditional love your church preaches." She shoved to her feet, her chair scraping against the concrete.

"Hey, hey, hey!"

Mitch's stomach roiled at the sound of Eliot's overly loud voice. He turned, wincing when his son stepped through the sliding glass door and onto the patio. At least three days' worth of stubble covered his chin, and his dingy hair stuck out in all directions.

He stopped, looked around, then approached Mitch. The kid's eyes were bloodshot, his cheeks sunken in. And he wore that stooped, crooked half smile, walked with the exaggerated swagger, like he always did when drunk or stoned.

"Where's the boy of honor?" He held a plastic shopping bag in his hand. His gift for Derk? Where'd he get the money for that? Bigger question—what was inside?

Mitch stood, lunging toward his son. "Let me see what you've got there."

Eliot jerked his hand away with a sour-breathed laugh. "Dude, don't be greedy. You've done had your birthday already. A boatload of them."

"What're you doing, son?" He formed a barricade between Eliot and the rest of the partygoers.

"Bringing the birthday boy a present." He lifted his sack and rolled his eyes. "Duh." He stepped aside and looked about. "Where's the little man, anyway?" He turned toward his sister-in-law who stood, staring, at the other end of the yard, and cupped his hands around his mouth. "Yo, Leza? Nate, man, where's the little stud?" Squinting, he shielded his eyes. "There he is, chillin' with the ladies like a boss! Right on."

"Eliot, sit." Sheila rushed to him, grabbing him by the elbow. "Want some coffee?"

"Nah. That battery acid makes dudes hairy, 'member, ma?" He laughed and slapped his chest. "But I am starved." He eyed the platter of hot dogs. "Can I get me some of that?"

"Sure. You wait here. I'll bring it." She started to guide Eliot toward the table.

Mitch intervened. "I thought Nathan said you could only come here if you were sober."

"Dude. What's with Mr. Party Police here?" He swore and grabbed a chip off a vacated plate, tossed it in his mouth. "Don't get your hackles up. Everything's fine." He smirked. "I'll be a good boy."

"No. Everything's not fine. You're drunk, and you're disrespecting your brother and sister-in-law."

"Disrespecting?" He raised an eyebrow, his face hardening before the lopsided grin reappeared. "Oops. I must've forgotten my manners." Straightening, he twined his hands, his expression pinched. "Excuse me, sir." He donned a British accent. "May I please have a sizable amount of nourishing deli-dela—food?" He ended his sentence with a cackle, spittle flying, then wiped his mouth with the back of his hand. "For real, though, my stomach's about to eat itself." He looked at Sheila. "Think I can get a couple hot dogs?"

Mitch shook his head, curse words he hadn't spoken in years swelling to the tip of his tongue.

Sheila raised her hand. "Leave him be. Don't make a scene."

"Right." Mitch scoffed. "Let's pretend like this is all normal. Clean up after him, and give him a wad of cash for his troubles. Because that's working out great, isn't Sheila?" The peripheral noise stopped, and he looked around to find everyone staring at him.

Frowning, Charles stalked toward them, heading straight for Eliot.

"Dad, please!" Leza hurried after her father and reached for his arm.

He stopped, patted her hand, then plucked it off. "Let me handle this, princess." He stood less than two feet from Eliot, his chest puffed. "Son, you'd best leave now."

"Or what, big fella?"

Leza brought a fisted hand to her mouth.

A vein in Charles's temple pulsated. "Or I'll have to make you leave."

"You think?" Eliot scoffed. "Well, Mr. Stiff Neck, it just so happens this ain't your house. And you ain't my daddy. You know what that means, right, big guy? You don't get to tell me nothing." He grabbed a partially filled glass of Coke, sniffed it, then set it down.

Charles stared at him, red climbing up his neck and into his face.

"Dad." Leza hurried to him and rested her hand on his shoulder. "Please, just let him be. He'll settle down once his mom gets him something to eat, isn't that right, Eliot?"

"Girl, you're on my wavelength." He tapped his heart, pointed to her, then tapped his heart again.

Sheila set a full plate and opened soda can in front of him, her gaze darting from one face to the next. Mitch would almost feel sorry for the woman, if he wasn't so mad. It was behavior like this that kept their son strung out.

Eliot flopped back into his chair, grabbed a hot dog, and shoved half of it in his mouth. Watching him eat, it was as if everyone gave a collective sigh, thankful to have avoided a blowup.

"Some things never change." Mitch glared at Sheila. "You're killing him. Can't you see that?"

Leza stepped closer, eyes moist. Nathan came beside her and wrapped an arm around her shoulder.

She pulled away. "I'm tired of this. And at your son's birthday party?"

"Leza's right." Nathan looked from his mom to Mitch. "We've gotta do something. Can't we call that drug counselor? Do an intervention or something?"

"What's the point?" Mitch faced his ex. "It doesn't do any good to throw a bunch of empty threats at the boy. He's on to you, Sheila. Knows all he's got to do is come crying to mommy. She'll fix everything. Fix him right into the grave."

Tears spilled over her lashes. With a shuddered breath, she nodded. "OK. You're right. I'll stop."

Mitch released the air he was holding, his tense muscles relaxing. "Really?"

She nodded.

"You've got to stick with it, you know. Even if it gets tough. Even if . . ." Mitch swallowed. "Even if he gets bad. Desperate. Or angry." That would be the hardest, when, jonesing for his next hit, Eliot started hurling hate speech at the both of them.

"I know. I can do it." She pressed the back of her hand beneath her nose. "I want our son back."

"Oh, Mom." Leza practically lurched on Sheila, enveloping her in a hug, while Nathan drew near, one hand on his mother's shoulder, the other on his wife's.

"I do too." Mitch whispered. And now that he and Sheila were in this together, maybe they actually had a shot of making that happen.

Chapter 32

"You kids ready?" Bianca stuffed a jug of water and package of crackers in a backpack. "And bring your soccer ball, boys."

"Yay!" Sebastian ran to his room, returning with a ball tucked under one arm, his bat and baseball shoved under the other. All gifts from Reid.

That man was the most generous person she'd ever met. It was that generosity that sent him to jail—his desire to take care of her and the kids. If only he'd waited. Filled out a few more applications. Someone would've hired him eventually. They would've been OK, and he'd still be here.

C. J. walked down the hall wearing a short pencil skirt, dark lipstick, and a snug, pink T-shirt. "We're leaving?"

Snug enough to rile Bianca's momma bear, but she kept her opinions to herself. "Yep." She had the day off, had all her kids together, and it was a beautiful, Sunday evening. She intended to enjoy every minute of it. "Soon as Robby gets off the toilet." She wrinkled her nose and pointed to the bathroom.

"Oh, no!" C. J.'s eyes widened, and she burst out laughing, waving her hand in front of her face. "I'm out of here!"

This led to a great deal of teasing once Robby finally emerged, releasing a mighty stench when he opened the bathroom door. This of course only fueled the child who, claiming every stink, grinned and puffed out his chest.

Bianca shook her head. Boys. She opened the front door, casting a backward glance to her oldest son. "Get your smelly self out here already." She and C. J. shared a wonderful, conspiratorial smile. Bianca's heart felt ready to burst.

She paused on the porch to fill her lungs with the autumn air, looked at the sky. Beams of sunlight streaked through diffused clouds. It almost looked like God Himself was reaching down. And for a moment, watching her boys dart ahead while her daughter fell into step beside her, Bianca almost believed He was.

You still praying, Virginia?

She glanced toward the property Mr. Kenney and Mr. Gibbs were remodeling, and a wave of guilt rushed over her. She still hadn't paid Mr. Kenney the rest of the money due him. She owed just under $400, not counting what he'll cut off from the odds and ends her boys did for him. He'd come looking to collect soon enough. She'd best start saving her pennies.

They continued through their neighborhood then rounded the corner at a crumbling, old, two-story apartment complex. Out front, a little girl with wild, curly hair squatted on top of a mound of dirt while a boy, maybe a year older, scurried about, dragging a stick in the dirt behind him. Across the street, two men leaned against the cab of a dented pickup, beer cans in hand.

At the park, the boys sprinted toward the jungle gym while Bianca and Cassie Joe settled onto a nearby bench. The play equipment, painted blue with patches of rusted metal showing through, stood in the center of a patch of wood chips. A steep, grassy hill bordered the park to their left, a wooden staircase dissecting it, tall trees flanking the top. A quiet, one-lane road stretched from their right, and behind them stood single-story, mid-eighteenth century houses.

Hands tucked under her thighs, C. J. swung her feet, watching her brothers. No cell phone? No texting?

Bianca smiled, feeling as if every weight she'd been carrying all week had lifted from her. "So, how's McKenzie?"

C. J. shrugged. "She doesn't talk to me anymore."

McKenzie had been C. J.'s best friend for years, almost a decade. Then something happened, something to do with a boy. That was all Bianca knew.

C. J.'s legs kept swinging as they watched the boys monkey up a plastic rock wall. Looked like they were racing. Bianca cast a sideways glance at her daughter, searching for something to say. Something that wouldn't lead to a fight. Something to initiate conversation before the teen pulled out her phone, got bored, and left.

Bianca picked up a golden leaf that had fallen near her feet and tore it vein by vein. "You like your classes so far?"

"They're OK, I guess."

"What about your art teacher? He as strict as everyone said?"

She shook her head and ran her finger along a gouge in the park bench. "He's kinda regal, know what I mean? But he's nice. Treats everyone the same. Doesn't have favorites."

"I really like the oil painting you're working on. The one with the part rock, part peacock."

"I turned it in Friday. Want to see it?" Her blue eyes sparkled, and Bianca's heart swelled.

"I would."

The teen's excitement to make Bianca proud reminded her of the sweet little preschooler she once was. The one who made Bianca pictures of stick people and scrawled, "I love you," across the top in bright crayon.

C. J. got her phone out, swiped the screen a few times, then angled it so Bianca could see the image she'd pulled up. Painted in varying shades of gray to show depth, bulges, and crevices, she'd painted a rock with vibrant blue, violet, and teal feathers cascading from it. Beyond this stood a thicket of trees, a setting sun dipping behind them.

"That's beautiful." Bianca gave her daughter a sideways hug. "You're crazy-talented."

"Thanks." Still encased in Bianca's arms, C. J. leaned her head against Bianca's shoulder.

She closed her eyes, breathing in her daughter's coconut shampoo. How she loved this girl!

They sat like that for a while, the sun warming Bianca's back as a cool, autumn breeze swept over her, and the boys' giggling voices drifted toward her. If only they could stay here forever, but tomorrow she was scheduled for a double shift. Then the stress of life would start, her needing C. J. to act like an adult, all three of them basically fending for themselves.

"Angela draws," C. J. said.

"Who's Angela?"

"Our new neighbor."

She snorted. "That crazy old woman with the nasty spaghetti and teenage wardrobe?"

C. J. laughed then sat up, ending their hug. She tucked her hands under her legs once again and resumed her leg swinging. But then she stopped, head angled downward.

She cast Bianca a sideways glance. "What's going on with Reid?"

Reid, not Dad. Ever since the raid. It was as if C. J. had closed her heart to the man. Maybe that was a good thing—what they all needed to do, so they could move on. Heal. Start over.

Bianca breathed in, let it out slowly. "He did a good thing. A brave thing."

"Brave?" C. J. scoffed. "Drug dealers are heroes now?"

She studied her daughter. An icy glare had replaced the sparkle that once lit her eyes. "No. What your father—"

"He's not my dad."

Bianca spread her hands flat on her thighs. "What Reid did was wrong. Stupid. And he'll be paying for that for a long time. Probably ten years, maybe more."

C. J.'s shoulders dropped, her expression softening.

"But taking responsibility for what he did, even though he knew it'd mean serious jail time . . ." Bianca held C. J.'s gaze. "That's brave. Something to be proud of." Words toppled from her brain in a fierce desire to defend her husband. To tell C. J. why he'd fallen back into crime, that he only wanted to provide for them, help pay the bills. But that'd only hurt her more, make her feel like Bianca didn't understand—or didn't care—about her pain.

Like she didn't have a right to be angry.

"I'm sorry, baby." Throat tight and scratchy, she reached her arm around C. J.'s shoulder and gave her a gentle squeeze. "I know it's been tough. Scary. You deserve better." She lifted

C. J.'s chin so the girl's eyes met hers. "I'm going to see that you and the boys get that."

"Are you getting a divorce?"

Bianca sucked in a breath of air, feeling as if someone had squeezed her lungs. "I don't know, baby."

Sunday evening, Angela held baby Joey close to her chest and pressed her lips against his peach-fuzzed head. Her heart swelled as she inhaled his milky-sweet baby scent. He was so precious, so tiny. So absolutely perfect. She looked up to find Ainsley and Chris watching her with soft smiles.

"I wish I could stay here, holding him forever." She touched his tiny, curled hand and slid her finger beneath his. She glanced about the living room, decorated with suede furniture, ocean paintings, and lacy curtains. "I've missed this place. Missed you guys." If only Angela's mom could be here to share this moment, to see all God had done, and to be the final piece in His restoring work. But she still had zero information as to her whereabouts. Did that mean she didn't want Angela to find her?

Shaking off the thought, Angela gazed down at her sweet grandbaby. So much had happened in the span of a few years. So much healing, rebuilding. Lazy, Sunday afternoon walks with just her and Ainsley, and their late night mother-daughter chats. Her old church and all the friends she'd made there. Friends who loved her even though she flubbed it half the time, misquoted Scripture, and usually left her Bible at home. It'd been nice seeing those ladies this morning. Talking with them again, as if she'd never left. Those were the kinds of friends Angela needed, the kind, hopefully, she'd soon make in Omaha. If she could muster up the courage to go to one of those Bible study groups listed on the sheet Mitch gave her.

"Hey there," Ainsley recaptured her attention. "What's with the long face?"

"Just thinking."

"About?"

"How much I enjoyed living here, with the both of you. How special that time was to me."

"I thought you liked Omaha and your new church," Ainsley said.

"I do. But I still miss you." She raised Joey to her face and kissed his cheek.

"Well," Chris leaned forward, elbows planted on his knees. "I'm glad you're close." He grinned. "Because we'll need you once we start touring again."

"Absolutely." Ainsley yawned and leaned her head on Chris's shoulder. "Though I might be calling for your help sooner, so I can actually get a night's sleep once in a while."

"Definitely." Watching her grandson, thinking of her long drive home, she almost wished she'd stayed in Kansas City. That was absurd, of course. She was a grown, educated woman and needed to behave like one.

Besides, she'd prayed long and hard about her move—about every step of it. She'd felt certain she was following God's will.

And Mitch? Her mind shot to him unbidden, initiating a smile.

"What's so funny?" Ainsley watched her with a raised brow.

Angela blushed. "Nothing." Her daughter would be less than thrilled to learn Angela was developing feelings for her handsome new friend. Although . . . would her opinion change if she knew Mitch was a Christian?

Angela checked the clock. Almost eight, with a three-hour drive ahead of her, and she had to work tomorrow. She stood. "Unfortunately I have to go." She kissed the baby a few more times, nuzzling her nose into the folds of his neck.

You're too good to me, Father. I don't deserve any of this.

She could almost hear Kathleen, her old Sunday School teacher responding, "That's why it's called grace, sugar."

Indeed.

Chapter 33

Wednesday afternoon, Mitch and Dennis spoke with their realtor, a meeting that left Mitch more than a little discouraged. According to Kaden, the market itself appeared to be doing well. He'd sold three houses that week alone. The neighborhood their remodel was in, however, had remained stagnant. No, not stagnant. Home values were declining.

"Maybe we should lower the price." Mitch ran some numbers in his head.

Dennis sighed, face drawn, everything about his body language screaming defeat and exhaustion. "And what? Throw away almost two months' worth of work and any chance at turning a buck?"

Kaden stood a few feet away, hands in his slacks pockets.

Mitch grabbed a stack of flyers off the shiny, new granite counter and studied the photos, read the blurb. Hoping he could discover the problem in Kaden's marketing efforts but knowing he wouldn't. If Kaden couldn't sell this place, no one could. The truth was, they were asking too much. Because they'd spent too much on repairs.

He dropped the paper. "If we hold on to this place much longer, we're going to end up in the red." He turned to Kaden. "What would we need to list this at in order to sell?"

Pulling on his chin, Kaden gazed past him. "Like I told you when you bought, this is a transitional neighborhood, which means it could go both ways. Y'all could be the first step in turning it around, or the crime could take hold. And with . . ." He shook his head, not needing to voice his concerns for Mitch to know what he was thinking. The police raid that had taken place at the Douglases' hadn't done them any favors. "Another property was just foreclosed half a block down."

That made three in a half-mile radius.

Kaden shrugged. "You could always rent the place for a year, till things settle down and more investors move in."

"No way." Dennis's frown deepened. "That's part of why we're in this mess." He glared at Mitch. "I'm finished with freeloaders, and Mr. Do-Gooder over here," he hooked a thumb in Mitch's direction, "keeps turning every rental into a charity project. I'm done."

A heavy silence fell between them, an equally pressing weight descending on Mitch's shoulders. Especially considering his plans for the afternoon.

Kaden looked from Dennis to Mitch then back to Dennis. "What if I lined up a rental management company? So that neither of you had to deal with collecting rent, making repairs, whatever."

Dennis shook his head. "Too expensive."

"Actually, those folks are cheaper than you might think." Kaden pulled his phone from his shirt pocket and tapped the screen a few times. "$900 listing fee then $90 a month. I know someone. Might even be able to talk them down a bit, considering how the rental market's slowing."

Dennis studied Kaden. "What's your cut?"

"I get a referral commission, paid out by the rental company."

Dennis gave a jerk of a nod. "See if the guy has wiggle room then get back to us with the numbers."

"Will do." Kaden grabbed his briefcase from the floor and shook both men's hands in turn. "I'll be in touch."

Dennis nodded as his phone rang. He answered and shook Kaden's hand at the same time. "Thanks for coming."

"I'll walk you out." Mitch wasn't thrilled with this recent option, but there was no sense raising a stink until it happened. For all they knew, this house could sell tomorrow.

Although considering less than half a dozen potential buyers had come to look at the place, that wasn't likely.

Following Kaden outside, he closed the door behind him.

Across the street, Bianca's car was parked in the drive, but her boys wouldn't be home for a few hours yet.

That'd give him time to hit the office, go over their company's financials, leave yet another message on Eliot's voice mail. If his phone hadn't been shut off by now.

Except he doubted Sheila would let that happen. She might have promised to stop funneling money the boy's way—Mitch could only hope she'd follow through—but his cell service was attached to hers. And Mitch and Sheila both needed a way to stay in touch with Eliot.

Mitch climbed into his truck and cranked the engine. He flipped to the sports radio channel, letting the broadcasters' arguments drown out his thoughts. He returned exactly three hours later and parked along the curb, waiting for Robby and Sebastian to appear.

Bianca shot frequent glances out her window, peeking through parted blinds before they snapped shut. Each time, Mitch tried not to chuckle.

He turned toward the street in time to see Angela's rusted car round the corner. She slowed then pulled to a stop beside him, engine idling.

She rolled down her window. "Everything OK?" She glanced at Bianca's then back to him.

The alarm in her face, evidence of her tender heart, warmed Mitch. Made him want to reach out and trace a knuckle along the smooth curve of her cheek.

"Yeah." His gaze dropped to her soft, pink lips. "Just waiting for the boys. I've got a project for them." A grin broke loose, big enough to make him feel goofy, but he couldn't help it. He had a great plan, one that could even turn those boys' lives around.

Angela laughed. "Sounds conspiratorial."

"Something like that." Man, was she beautiful when amused. He needed to distance himself soon, before all hope was lost. Who was he kidding? He'd reached that point a while ago, and with every encounter, his feelings for this woman only grew.

"Anything I can do to help?"

He considered this. Made sense, allowing her to join hisefforts, and it sure would be nice to have her around. Although she didn't strike him as the handy type.

"What?"

"I guess you could . . . uh . . ." Angela could reach out to C. J. in a way he never could, but how? "You can stop by if you want, maybe . . . bring some lemonade?" He told her of his plan, her eyes growing all the brighter.

She clapped her hands. "What a splendid idea. And a batch of those cookies I promised." But then she sobered. "You're such a kindhearted man, Mitch Kenney."

Heat climbed up his neck, and he averted his gaze. "Here come the boys now."

"Oh." Angela glanced in her rearview mirror. "I better go, then. I'd hate to blow your cover." She shot him a wink, and a jolt of electricity ran the length of him.

She rolled up her window with a wave then pulled into her driveway. Mitch watched her leave, shaking his head. That woman was something else, and that something else was gonna land him in a heap of trouble. Between Dennis, their rentals, Eliot, and the never-ending Sheila drama, he had enough to deal with. And that was way more drama than Angela needed.

But when had he last met a woman so compassionate, so . . . real, silly behaviors and all? A woman who not only understood his need to help kids like Robby and Sebastian out but who seemed to want to do the same?

Chapter 34

Casting a glance over her shoulder, Angela suppressed a giggle and scurried into her house. That Mitch Kenney—all gruff and whiskers on the outside but softer than melted butter beneath. If only she'd met him earlier, before . . . who was she kidding? She'd thrown her life away long ago, back before she'd even learned to drive.

And though Mitch seemed interested now—made her stomach all jittery—the minute he knew about her past, he'd be disgusted. But maybe she didn't have to tell him. She was a new creation, after all, and everyone had a history. Some were just more sordid than others.

Regardless, right now she had a job to do, and she wouldn't let shame keep her from it.

She dropped her purse onto the counter and dashed into the kitchen to make lemonade and cookies. Opening cupboard doors, she searched for baking ingredients, none of which she had, of course, other than a bit of brown sugar purchased to go with her oatmeal. She rummaged through her handbag, ignoring the debt repayment schedule lying on her table.

What was a few dollars? Not enough to make much of a dent on her debts. But a little spent on groceries could do a lot of good, as far as those sweet boys were concerned.

And Mitch. Her pulse quickened at the thought. They said the way to a man's heart was through his stomach. Angela had plenty of anecdotal evidence to back that up.

Was she being manipulative? Ugh! Why did relationships have to be so complicated? Fine. No cookies. Just lemonade.

Except she was out of mix, which meant she'd have go to the store anyway. Besides, she'd said she'd bake cookies. So long as she made them for the boys, not Mitch, she'd be fine. If he happened to eat one and enjoy it, so be it. She moaned again, sensing her thoughts about to venture down the same manipulative rabbit trail she'd just torn herself from.

She glanced at the clock. If she didn't hurry, those boys would be finished with whatever project Mitch had planned, and she'd still be standing around in her kitchen arguing with herself.

Grabbing her purse, she preheated her stove and dashed out of the house, returning exactly 14 minutes later with two expensive tubes of premade cookie dough. She plopped dough onto a cookie sheet, pacing her kitchen while she waited for them to bake.

Ten minutes after that, she headed across the street carrying a jug of lemonade in one hand

and a package of plastic cups in the other.

All eyes turned to her as she approached.

"Wow, does that look good." Grinning, Mitch wiped sweat from his forehead onto his sleeve. A pile of unpainted 2-by-4s lay on the ground by the partially dismantled fence. Another stack, broken and with peeling paint, had been tossed aside.

"Hi." She smiled, first at him then the boys. "Sebastian, think you could pour everyone a glass?" She raised the cups before setting them on the ground.

His face lit up as a grin bunched his sweet little cheeks before he fought it back into a save-face frown. He gave a quick nod, his thin brow furrowed, as he did his best to pour. A fraction of the liquid made it into the cups. Good thing Angela bought the large tub of mix because at this rate, they would go through it all.

After distributing drinks to his brother and Mitch, Sebastian handed a cup to Angela.

"Thanks." She took a drink then set it on a porch step, planted her hands on her hips. "Y'all wouldn't be hungry, would you?"

Sebastian and Robby exchanged glances, looking like she'd asked them to try raw octopus.

"Uh . . . no, thanks." Robby chewed on his pinky nail.

Strange. Angela had never known boys to turn down food before. Unless . . . her eyes widened, her mouth forming an O. The spaghetti! That mess had tasted something awful—she'd tried it herself once she got back home. Greasy, bitter, not enough salt but entirely too much pepper and garlic. Not to mention the bit of lemon juice she threw in hoping to spice it up a little.

She'd spiced it up, all right, enough to pucker her lips. Why did she always feel the need to experiment when cooking for others?

"Actually, I . . ." Her cheeks flushed. "I was going to bring over some cookies."

"That sounds awesome." Mitch took a gulp of lemonade.

Once again, the boys exchanged glances.

"From the store. I mean, I baked them and all, but I bought the premixed dough."

The boy's suddenly hopeful expressions did little to ease Angela's embarrassment. She glanced at Mitch. If there was any truth to that old cliché of a man's stomach being the way to his heart, she had a lot to learn. Not that she hadn't fed men before, but usually she opted for take-out or meal-kits. Charged to one of her many credit cards.

"All righty then." She reached to ruffle Robby's hair then stopped herself. She didn't want to scare the boy any more than she already had. "I'll be right back." She darted across the street, returning with a plate piled high with still warm, chewy, chocolate chip cookies.

Sebastian grabbed three, and Robby started to do the same, cast Angela a sideways glance, then let two of his cookies drop. The boys plopped onto the grass and focused intently on their treat. Mitch did the same, making Angela laugh.

"What?" Robby looked up, crumbs falling from his bottom lip.

"Oh, nothing." She grabbed a cookie and sat between Mitch and Sebastian, the four of them forming a circle of sorts. "So, you ready for your math test, Robby?"

He frowned. Shrugged.

Time to change the subject. "I hear you boys have a pretty cool field trip coming up. Some pumpkin patch not far from here with a giant corn maze, peddle carts, and such."

Sebastian's head shot up, bobbing. "Yeah!" This loosened his jaw, and before long, he and his brother were sharing stories of past trips from the biggest pumpkin found ever to zooming past their classmates in their go-carts.

All the while, Mitch and Angela exchanged amused, knowing glances, as if they shared a wonderful secret. And they did, for they'd finally managed to break through the boys' defenses.

Robby reached for another cookie. "I saw you doing your art stuff yesterday. What were you making?"

"I . . . uh . . . I was sketching the sunset." Angela grabbed her drink. "Trying to, at least."

"You ever sell your stuff, like in that art place downtown?"

She laughed. "Hardly. I'm nowhere near that talented."

"I disagree." Mitch drained his lemonade then crushed his cup with his strong grip. "From what I saw, you've got talent."

Angela's gaze faltered, her face heating. Did she detect admiration in his tone? How often did a man regard her with true admiration, not lust? For something she did and not how she looked, or what she might or might not do on the first date?

Standing, Sebastian picked up his hammer, ran his hand along the smooth metal bell. "I want to be a . . ." He scrunched his little face and turned to Mitch. ". . . what you do, when I grow up."

"Do you, now? Well, you're well on your way." He winked at Angela.

The butterflies in her gut swarmed once again. What was it with this man? The more she was around him, the more she wanted to be around him.

"Really?" And clearly, these boys felt the same because the hope shining in Sebastian's eyes was so tangible, it brought tears to Angela's.

Those precious children, so desperate for a positive male role model. Thankfully God provided them with Mitch because their father was anything but. Where was their dad, anyway?

She'd thought the cops had carted him away, until she saw him that one morning, walking his boys to school. The two boys had looked so happy, bouncing, grinning. They'd practically glowed at school all day. But she hadn't seen the man since, and a day later, Robby and Sebastian were back to their sullen selves.

Something had happened. Most likely their dad had ditched. She watched Mitch as he shared a demolition story with the boys. Men like him were rare.

And much too good for women like her.

"Really?" Robby's eyes went wide. "A dead cat, stuck between the walls?"

Mitch nodded. "Nothin' but bones and fur by the time we found it."

Sebastian grimaced. "Must've stunk. I found a dead chipmunk behind our house this summer, and it smelled nasty!" He shook his head. "My dad wrapped it in a bunch of plastic bags and tossed it in the trash. Said the garbage men were in for quite a surprise."

Mitch chuckled. "I bet they were." He sobered, studied Robby who sat, hunched, tugging grass from the lawn. "Haven't seen him around lately."

Sebastian shrugged. "He's in jail."

"Shut up, you idiot!" Robby shoved his brother with enough force the kid toppled on his side, knocking over his glass of lemonade.

"What? Mom never said—"

"Just close your stupid mouth, OK?" Robby glared at him.

Sebastian teared up, his chin dimpling.

Angela suppressed a sigh, wishing she could scoop the child up and hold him close, wishing she could hug them both. Wishing she could help their poor mother. It stunk being a single mom, knowing everything—everything—fell on you. And with her husband in prison . . . Angela couldn't imagine.

Robby jumped to his feet. "So, we gonna finish this thing or what?"

Mitch looked at Angela. He nodded. "Sure. Might as well knock out what we can."

Conversation squelched, Angela moved to the porch stairs to watch them work, hammering new boards in place where old ones had been torn down. Mitch alternated between the boys, always patient, always gentle and encouraging. Every once in a while he'd shoot a grin Angela's way, causing her face to flush.

What would it be like to be married to a man like that? Would he stay kind and patient, or would his charm wear off once their vows were spoken?

As if that was where their relationship was heading. Was he even interested in her? She thought for sure she could see an attraction in his eyes whenever he looked at her. No, more than an attraction . . . he was caring. Almost protective.

Shrieking music jolted her from her thoughts as a vehicle Angela recognized drew near, stopping along the curb.

The driver, whom she'd come to assume was Cassie Joe's boyfriend, swept a biting glare from Mitch to Angela. Sitting beside Cassie Joe, his face, framed by long, jagged, black-and-blue hair, he looked ghostly pale.

After glaring at Angela a moment longer in what appeared to be a challenge, he yanked Cassie Joe to him. Angela turned away as the two engaged in an extended kiss. Then a door slammed, the engine revved, and the annoying music faded.

Cassie Joe stood at the edge of the sidewalk, backpack draped over her shoulder.

Sebastian ran to her, as if seeking a hug, but stopped a few feet away, hands limp at his sides. "Hey."

She looked from Angela to Mitch then to Robby. "What's going on?"

Still holding the hammer, Robby crossed his arms. "We're working. To help with the rent."

"Does Mom know that?" She glanced toward her front door. "She inside?"

Robby nodded. "She told us to do it. Said she was tired of us sitting around watching TV all the time."

Cassie Joe continued to study Robby, revealing the same distrust Angela often saw displayed by

Bianca. Displayed by all of them, actually. "For how . . . what are you doing, anyway?"

Mitch sauntered over with his usual lazy, nonthreatening grin. "They're helping me repair this fence so we can paint it." He ruffled Sebastian's hair. "Figure your mom is doing me a favor, considering how I should've taken care of this a long time ago."

Cassie Joe squinted at him, as if deciding whether or not to believe him. Then her gaze shifted to the plate of cookies. There were five left.

Angela picked up the plate. "Want one?"

The teen watched her for a long moment. Finally, she shrugged and grabbed a cookie. "Thanks."

Angela poured her a cup of lemonade. "Thirsty?" She handed it over.

The girl took this with less reluctance, and stood, hip cocked, nibbling on the edge of her cookie. She looked at her youngest brother. "You doing what you're told?"

Sebastian nodded, his grin reemerging. "Mr. Mitch says I'm doing real good. Worth my weight in chocolate."

Cassie Joe snorted. "Yeah, well, chocolate's cheap." Her lips curled up, her face softening.

"I hear you're quite the artist," Angela said.

Cassie Joe shrugged. "I like to paint. Helps me relax."

"Me too."

Cassie Joe hesitated, gave a brief nod.

"I'd love to see your work sometime."

Cassie Joe brought her cup to her mouth, observing Angela over the rim. "It's nothing special."

"No. It's awesome." Sebastian spoke with such energy, he practically bounced. "Mom says she'll be a regular Picante someday."

Cassie Joe rolled her eyes. "Picasso."

"Whatever. All's I know is she's real good. Hold on, I'll show you." He spun around and bounded up the porch, grabbing the door handle.

"Sebastian, she's not in—"

The door slammed shut, cutting Cassie Joe short. Before the teen had time to react, her brother returned, clutching a spiral sketchpad. Cassie Joe reached for it, but her brother ducked and spun, holding the page in front of Angela.

"Wow, this is amazing." She surveyed the image—a night scene with a vibrant, shaded moon framed by clouds, its silver light spilling onto a tree-encased lake. "The depth . . ." She shook her head, staring at the picture. "This is phenomenal." And it truly was, like nothing she'd ever seen.

Cassie Joe blushed and looked at the ground. "Thanks."

Angela handed it to her. "Think you could teach me how to do that sometime?"

"Maybe."

"You know . . ." She rubbed her forearm. "I've been wanting to go to Fontenelle Forest, bring my travel easel, try out my new charcoals. Maybe we could go together?"

"I want to go!" Sebastian lunged forward, eyes bright.

Angela laughed, as did Cassie Joe, although hers came with an eye roll. "Do you even know what that is?"

Sebastian frowned. "A forest. Duh."

"Whatever." She faced Angela—"thanks for the cookies"—and ascended the steps.

Angela caught a glimpse of Bianca watching them through the window above the porch. Meeting Angela's gaze, the woman's eyes widened, then she darted away, the blinds falling closed. Cassie Joe disappeared inside the house, the door slamming behind her.

Angela sighed. She'd been so close. Had her invite pushed the girl too far?

Mitch strolled over, nudged her shoulder. "It was a start, right?" He smelled like sandalwood and cedar chips. He turned to the boys. "So, you really want to go to Fontenelle, huh?"

"Yeah!" Sebastian bounced on the balls of his feet.

Robby laughed.

Mitch looked at him. "What do you say? Wanna join us?"

He swiped his bangs from his face. "Sure. Whatever."

Mitch grinned. "I'll shoot your mom a text, and if she's OK with it, next Saturday, I'll pick y'all up."

His gaze hovered on Angela, his warm amber eyes drawing her in, stealing her breath. She was falling hard. The smartest thing would be to walk away, establish an impenetrable "friend zone." Instead, she found herself agreeing to a midmorning hike. One of the most romantic endeavors she could think of.

Oh, Lord, what am I doing?

Ainsley would kill her.

Chapter 35

Early Saturday afternoon, Mitch pulled into the Midtown Children's Hospital parking lot and called Dennis.

His partner answered on the first ring. "Any news?"

"No." A couple had toured their remodel on 35th Street three times now. They said they had their short list narrowed down to two properties, but Kaden hadn't heard from them or their realtor. "Kaden thinks they're trying to sweat us out. Says they might low-ball us."

Dennis cursed, and Mitch waited.

"That's not why I'm calling." A siren blared in the distance, growing steadily louder. "I'm at the hospital. Wondered if you'd like to join me for lunch."

"Not really, no." His voice came out flat.

"How about I come to you?"

A tense silence followed, causing Mitch's jaw to clench. Why was he trying so hard? The guy was mad, irritated, whatever. He and Dennis were as compatible as plastic and wood glue.

He thought back to his morning devotion—it'd been on long-suffering—and the inner fire he'd felt upon reading it. The committed prayer he'd made after. Fine. He'd reach out yet again.

Doubted it'd do much good, but for obedience's sake, he'd do it.

"I've got burgers. Maybe I could drop them off?"

No response.

"Where you at?"

After a short pause, Dennis's breath reverberated across the line. "West tower, ninth floor."

"On my way." He grabbed the two fast food bags with one hand, a drink tray with the other, and stepped out. A warm, late-autumn breeze swept over him, carrying the aroma of burgers mixed with diesel fuel.

Inside, recessed, fluorescent lighting reflected off polished linoleum floors, the distinct scent of disinfectant filling the air. Bypassing the guest services desk, Mitch turned left, heading straight for the elevator.

On the ninth floor, Mitch stepped into an area decorated with colorful murals set between orange, red, and yellow walls.

Across from him sat a cozy waiting room filled with over-stuffed armchairs, a few recliners, and two suede loveseats. Puzzles and board games were spread on end tables, and a rack of books lined the far wall. On the right, two women, one older with silver hair, the other maybe 30 years younger, sat in side-by-side chairs.

Mitch placed his and Dennis's lunch items on top of a circular table near the juice and coffee counter. He called his partner. "I'm in the waiting room across from the elevator."

Machines beeped on the other end. "I'll be there in a minute."

Dennis appeared a moment later, expressionless.

Mitch shoved one of the fast food bags his way as his partner sat across from him. "Half-pounder, extra cheese, no mayo. Large waffle fries." He slid Dennis's drink across the table. "Chocolate cookie-chunk milk shake, no whip."

Dennis grabbed his drink but made no move to bring it to his mouth. "Thanks."

They sat silent for some time, Mitch sipping his soda, Dennis staring at his shake. Footsteps echoed in the hall behind them, voices approaching then receding.

Dennis broke the silence first. "She's doing better. They ruled out kidney failure and cancer— the doc thinks she has a bad case of adenovirus. They're pumping her with fluids, still need to run more tests." He swiped a hand over his face. "She's still pretty weak, but the doctor said he anticipates a full recovery."

"That's good. That's real good." He paused. "Can I pray for you and your granddaughter?"

Dennis narrowed steely eyes. "You can do what you want."

Mitch swallowed.

Dennis cleared his throat. "My daughter's got a

high deductible. Emma's hospital stay's going to eat her alive."

"How about we do a fund-raiser?"

He snorted. "Right. A spaghetti dinner's really going to help." The crevice between his brows deepened. "I've got a better solution. How about we unload the freeloaders and start turning some properties? Start acting like a business instead of a—" he cursed "—charity."

He didn't have to ask who Dennis was referring to: Bianca and her boys, although Mitch had been covering for them with his own funds. But Dennis still wanted the family out, had been dead set on finding a reason to evict them since Bianca's husband gave him mouth over late rent about six months back. Then there was the elderly lady on West Hemlock who lived on disability and had been grandfathered in on a crazy-low rate. Same with Old Man Howard, who stayed holed up in his house with no cable ever since his wife died. People who would never find a place on their incomes.

"I worried she was on her death bed, Mitch. They were talking kidney failure."

"I'm sorry. I didn't know she was that sick."

"Yeah, well."

He caught the meaning laced in Dennis's unspoken words. The two of them hadn't been close in some time. Did Dennis blame him for that? "I'm here now."

"How considerate of you." He pushed back in his chair and stood. "You care more about a bunch of leeching strangers than the success of our business."

"That's not true. You can't believe that."

"Know what? I don't even care anymore." He scowled. "All I know is you've got 60 days to clean out two properties and get them on the market. You can do what you want with the rest."

"What are you talking about?"

"I'm done, Mitch. It's been a great run, but it's over."

He stared at him, mouth ajar. "You can't be serious. I know we haven't seen eye-to-eye lately, but break our partnership? Really?"

"I've got a lawyer. Don't fight me on this. It'll only get messy and expensive."

So that's what their partnership meant to him? Their friendship? Fine. If this was how Dennis wanted to play things, so be it. Clearly they weren't as tight as Mitch thought.

He started to say as much when a snippet from his morning devotion came to mind, defusing him: *If we want to reach the world for Christ, we need to show radical, unexpected love, especially to those we feel deserve it least. Isn't that what Jesus did for us?"*

He breathed deep and unfisted his hands. "I'm sorry it's come to this, but I understand."

He paused. "You've been a great friend." He extended his hand, holding it out as Dennis stared at it, unmoving. "If you ever need anything, anything at all, I hope you'll ask."

Chapter 36

"I'm so glad you slept well." Phone pressed to her ear, Angela added a swipe of blush to her cheeks then studied her reflection. Did she always have such puffy bags under her eyes? And when had the lines on her forehead grown so deep? It gave her a perpetual scowl. If not for her subterranean crow's feet giving evidence to an occasional smile, she'd appear the epitome of an aging grouch.

"So, what about you?" Lullaby music played in the background. "Do you have any plans for the day?"

A quiver swept through Angela's midsection, her gaze shooting to her alarm clock. "Um . . . actually, I do." Mitch would be by within the hour to pick her and the Douglas children up, which was why she'd tried on three pairs of shorts, capris, and enough T-shirts to bury her bed. It wasn't that she worried they'd be inappropriate. She'd given her entire wardrobe a modesty makeover. The challenge was finding a cute outfit—hiking attire—without looking like she was trying to look cute. "I may have found an in with the Douglas children."

"Oh, Mom! That's so wonderful. Tell me all about it."

Angela did, trying to downplay Mitch's involvement, or, at the very least, to hide her enthusiasm regarding it.

"Is this the 'handsome' remodeler you told me about when you first moved in?" Ainsley's voice was tight.

"I . . ." Angela gave a nervous laugh. "Maybe. But don't worry, sweetie. He's a wonderful man. Very godly. He goes to my church. He's quite involved, actually." She winced and chewed on her bottom lip, smudging raspberry lipstick into the fine lines fanning her mouth. Beautiful.

Her daughter sighed, the long, drawn-out breath Angela had become quite accustomed to over the years, the one that warned of a coming lecture. The irony of which—daughter scolding mother—didn't escape her.

"I thought you'd decided to avoid the dating scene. So you could focus on launching your career and . . . you know, making progress."

Getting my life back together, you mean. "So I should remain lonely and single forever?"

"Of course not. But you've only been in Omaha a few months. And I don't meant to sound condescending, but—"

"Then don't." Her words came out more clipped than she'd intended, and Ainsley gave a sharp inhale. A tense silence followed.

Angela closed her eyes and pinched the bridge of her nose. This wasn't how she wanted their conversation to go, but she was growing tired of hearing her daughter play parent. True, Angela had given her reason to do so in the past, but at some point Ainsley needed to give her the opportunity to change. And, should she make a mistake, to deal with it on her own.

"Listen, sweetie." She grabbed a tissue and began de-smudging her lip wrinkles, "I know you're worried. I appreciate your concern, truly." Well, partially. "I really am trying to live how God wants."

"That's my point. You've come a long way, and I'm so proud of you, but you haven't been a Christian very long. I think you should focus on that right now—on spending time with Christ, reading His word, getting to know other believers."

Angela suppressed a laugh. "Mitch is a—"

"I mean *women* believers, Mom. Are you serious about this guy?"

That was the jackpot question. "Honey, you worry too much. We're friends who feel called to help the same family." She glanced again at her reflection and frowned. Her attempts to remove her lipstick from her mouth wrinkles only served to spread the gunk around, resulting in a ring of pink-stained skin. "Listen, sweetie, I'd love to chat more, but I really need to go. Can I call you later?"

"Fine. But Mom?"

"Yeah?"

"Please be careful. There are a lot of users out there."

"I know, dear." *I used to be one of them.* "Give that sweet baby a hug and sloppy-old-grandma kiss for me. And tell Chris I said hi."

She set her phone on her dresser and dashed into her bathroom for a rushed face-scrub. Ten minutes later, she returned to her vanity mirror with dry, reddened skin and raccoon eyes. Moaning, she grabbed her under-eye cream and began to massage it into her skin while simultaneously removing traces of mascara. And she hadn't even started on her hair yet!

By the time Mitch arrived 30 minutes later, she'd given up on her beautification efforts and opted for a hair-hiding visor, a thin layer of foundation, and a hint of blush. Which was probably for the best, considering she was bound to do a fair amount of unfeminine sweating.

After dabbing on an extra layer of deodorant, she dashed for the door. Mitch stood on the stoop wearing a snug, gray T-shirt, Husker's ball cap, and faded jeans. A hint of stubble shaded his jaw, and a gentle breeze swept the scent of his familiar sandalwood aftershave toward her.

"Hey." Hands in his pockets, he gave a boyish grin. "You look . . ." He coughed. "I mean, you ready?"

"I am. Oh, wait . . ." She frowned. "I probably

318

should've packed drinks and snacks. Hold on."
She raised a finger then ran to her kitchen where
she rummaged through her fridge and cupboards.
When was the last time she'd gone shopping?

After five minutes of searching, she came up
with little more than half a box of crackers, half
a tub of peanut butter, and two overripe bananas.
She didn't even have refillable water bottles,
and she certainly couldn't take a pitcher and
mismatched coffee mugs.

"We can pick something up on the way, if you'd
like," Mitch called out.

Reminding her that she'd rudely left him
standing on her stoop. "Oh!" Carrying her dented
box of crackers, she hurried back to the entryway.
"Sorry, I . . ." She glanced at the package in her
hand, filled largely with crumbs.

"Do you think the kids will be hungry?" Of
course they would be. They were on the free
meal system at school, after all. How could she
not have thought of that? "Buying something on
the way sounds perfect. Let me grab my purse."

She started to dash off again, but he snagged
her by the arm, sending a jolt of electricity
through her.

His smile crinkled the skin around his eyes.
"I've got it."

Fifteen minutes later, Angela, Mitch, and
the Douglas boys were crammed into Mitch's
semiclean truck, milkshakes in hand, heading

south on I-75. Sebastian chattered in the back, barely pausing to take a breath while Robby stared through the side window. Angela was somewhat surprised Bianca had allowed the boys to come. Maybe she needed childcare or, hopefully, was beginning to believe that she and Mitch truly did care about them.

Angela glanced back, caught Robby's eye. "It's too bad your sister couldn't come." She hated to think of the teen holed up in her house all day while her mother worked. "But I'll take a few pictures for her. That way she can sketch things out when she has time."

"When she's not getting all smooch-face with her boyfriend, you mean." Sebastian scrunched his nose, causing Angela and Mitch to laugh.

"Right." Mitch looked at the rearview mirror, laughter dancing in his eyes. "When she's not doing that." Merging off the highway, he cast her a lingering glance.

Face hot enough to melt her rouge, she cleared her throat and looked away.

When they reached Fontenelle's parking lot, Mitch parked, and the boys spilled from the truck. They'd made it to the visitor's center before he and Angela had a chance to close their doors.

Mitch cupped his hands around his mouth. "Hey, boys. Wait for us, will ya?" He turned to Angela. "You bringing your easel?"

She shook her head. "Maybe next time."

"I've got a digital camera in the dash. Use it for work. Before and after shots, stuff like that." He moved past her, his hiking boots crunching the gravel, and opened the passenger door. Once retrieved, along with a plastic bag of water bottles, he handed the camera over.

"Thanks." She looped the strap around her neck and fell into step beside him.

Mitch showed his park pass to the clerk manning the desk. Then she followed him outside and onto a long, wooden bridge that cut through the trees. Holding maps, the boys darted ahead, then hurried back, pointing to various things they saw on the way.

A gust of cool, dry air swept over them as they entered. The boys bounced from one indoor exhibit to the next.

Mitch laughed. "You'd think we brought them on some mysterious adventure, the way they're acting."

"Boys turn everything into an adventure."

"True."

"This was a great idea. I just wish I could figure out a way to draw Cassie Joe in. I'd hoped my pastels would entice her."

"It's always harder when they get older. They've got more layers you gotta break through." He grabbed a water bottle, offered it to Angela.

"No thanks."

"Don't give up. It'll get easier."

"You sure?"

He studied her for a long moment, a hint of sadness shadowing his expression. Then, with a shrug, he looked away. "That's what hope says, right?"

"Yeah, I guess."

The rest of the morning, their conversation was frequently interrupted by Sebastian's enthusiastic discoveries. The boy found everything from snails and fat earthworms to flowerlike fungus.

"Oh, Sebastian!" Her eyes widened, and she grabbed his wrist a moment before his handful of treasures dropped into his pockets, soon to be squished. "I'm not sure your mom would appreciate that, sweetie." She and Mitch exchanged glances, laughter lighting his eyes. "Besides, don't you think your snail—?"

"Hermie."

She pulled her lips in over her teeth to keep from laughing. "Don't you think Hermie would like to go home to his family?"

Sebastian opened his hand, palm up, treasures balanced in the center, dirt clumped between his fingers. He observed his newfound friends for some time before slumping his shoulders with a gusty exhale. "I guess. But can I at least make him a fort?"

Angela rustled his hair. "That sounds very considerate."

Sebastian beamed and plopped onto a moss-covered log. He deposited his finds gently onto a pile of fallen leaves then set about his task, building a barrier of twigs, stones, and pine needles.

Angela smiled. "He has such a tender heart."

"That he does." Mitch shielded his eyes from the sun, gazing up the path to where Robby stood, hacking at a tree branch with a twig. "I just hope he stays that way—the both of them." He shook his head. "Saw Robby talking to the neighborhood gang-bangers the other day. Kids like him are the perfect targets, and with their dad's history, even more so."

"What do you mean?"

"Dealers love making friends with kids, enticing them with the lure of instant cash, getting them to run drugs for them."

"Why?"

"Couple reasons, I imagine. Kids won't face the same jail time as the dealers. Plus, I suspect starting young leads to stronger loyalty."

"That's terrible."

He nodded, his eyes hardening, as if lost in unpleasant thoughts. "Not much anyone can do about it, though, except maybe catch the big dogs. But even then, another dealer pops up, ready to take his place."

"But if we could reach the kids before then, give them something else to strive for, convince them that they could actually make something of themselves . . ."

His expression smoothed back into his adorable smile. "I like how you think." His eyes searched hers with an intensity that stole her breath. "You got plans tonight?"

"Other than knocking down cobwebs and matching washed socks, nope." Her heart hammered against her rib cage, the stomach flutters that had caused her to forgo breakfast returning with a vengeance. Was he asking her out? Like on a real date? Hadn't Ainsley just warned her against this very thing?

She'd just told her daughter she was trying to listen to God more, to follow His will, but in truth, she hadn't even prayed about Mitch. Except to ask God to guard her heart against him. So if He hadn't, did that mean He was giving her a green light?

Or that she was completely inept at discerning His will?

Chapter 37

Bianca's youngest bombarded her the moment she stepped from the car.

"Look what I found!" He raised a plastic bag full of dirt. "I'm going to plant it in the backyard, and it'll grow into a giant tree."

"You don't know that." Robby sauntered over with an I'm-much-older-and-wiser frown. "For all you know, that seed could be from some kind of stinging nettle plant."

Bianca deposited her phone, with its two missed collect calls from Reid, into her back pocket and raised an eyebrow. "What you got in here, little man?" She pulled her youngest to her, kissing the top of his sweaty head. "Besides a bunch of dirt."

"A seed, from Fontenelle." He told her about all the plants, birds, and bugs—lots of bugs—he'd seen on his hike with Mr. Kenney and their crazy neighbor lady. Listening to him ramble on, adding in occasional stories or tidbits Ms. Angela told him, Bianca couldn't help but smile.

The boy's eyes radiated joy, and that always lifted her heart. Almost enough to make her forget the stabbing pain shooting through her tired feet.

"Tell you what." She moved to Robby, giving him a squeeze. "How 'bout you two unload my groceries." Her grin widened as she envisioned the looks on their faces when they saw what she'd bought, thanks to the clearance bin. Along with ten dented cans of vegetables and three pounds of day-old hamburger.

"Fine." Robby slumped but obeyed, and Sebastian followed. Soon, they were both loaded down with bags, trying to grab them all in one go. For once, she had too many. Mm-hm, they'd eat good tonight, and the next night too.

Padding ahead of them, Bianca shoved open her front door and heaved a sigh. Today had been insane, with trainees running around and Mr. Homer breathing down her neck. Like he was waiting for her to mess up, so he could send her packing.

Music emanated from her daughter's room, though softer than usual. Maybe C. J. had one of her headaches.

"C. J.?" Depositing her purchases on the counter, she continued down the hall and rapped on her daughter's door.

As expected, no answer. C. J. probably had her earbuds in. Bianca eased the door open and poked her head in. C. J. sat on her bed, back to the headboard, her sketchbook on her lap.

Bianca watched her for a moment then ambled over. "Hey." She gave her a sideways hug, waiting until her daughter removed her earplugs. "Want to help me bake a cake?"

She offered a hint of a smile. "For real?"

Bianca nodded. "Got stuff for meatloaf too." C. J.'s favorite, smothered in sugary ketchup. "Come on." She led the way to the kitchen. Sebastian sat hunched over the dirt-speckled table, his hiking finds, a glass of water, and an empty soup can in front of him.

C. J. raised an eyebrow. "What are you doing?"

"He's trying to plant himself a forest." Bianca laughed, moving to the counter to unload groceries. She set the cake mix, eggs, and cooking oil beside the stove. She turned the oven on and glanced at her daughter over her shoulder. "How 'bout you get this started while I mix up the meatloaf?"

C. J. gave a genuine smile and moved to the counter. "I got my language arts paper back. The one on *Frankenstein*."

"Oh?" She plopped two pounds of ground beef into a bowl. "How'd you do?" She added oatmeal, eggs, and her favorite spices while her daughter told her all the nice things her teacher had to say about her project.

Elbow deep in goo, she nudged C. J. with her hip. "Proud of you."

She glanced at the clock on the stove. Visiting hours were tonight. Reid would be upset if she didn't come. She hadn't even filled out all the necessary paperwork. Because she didn't know yet what she was going to do. He'd never change. Didn't this incarceration prove that?

So why should she wait for him? So she could live with a career criminal? Raise her kids in a life of crime? Robby was already starting to lean that way. She saw the way he watched Pockets and his gang, like they were the coolest thing since iPads. And the way Pockets weaseled up to Robby, it was only a matter of time before they got their hooks in the kid. If Reid were here . . .

She snorted. If Reid were here, he'd be bringing his own hoodlums around.

Still, she loved him. And he'd been there for her when she needed him most, had accepted all the kids as his own. She sighed and rubbed her temples.

"Mom, you OK?"

She looked up to find C. J. watching her with a furrowed brow. "Yeah, baby." She forced a smile. "Just a little tired."

"Want me to take care of this?" Still stirring the cake mix, she pointed her elbow toward Bianca's meatloaf mixture.

"I'm good." She leaned toward her daughter and kissed her cheek. "Wouldn't trade this moment for nothing."

The day had started out rough, but it was ending better than she could have hoped. Huge sales at the grocery, a fight-free evening with her daughter, and . . . she glanced over her shoulder at her boys, still sitting at the table.

One of them had brought in a bunch of fallen

leaves and twigs, and the two were piling everything into an old soup can. Like they were trying to build a terrarium or something. She chuckled to herself. Boys and their love for dirt. Sure'd been nice of Mr. Kenney and Ms. Angela to take them out.

Virginia always said God was trying to love Bianca through others. Tonight, Bianca almost believed her.

Angela stared at her phone on the dresser. Why did she feel like she was being deceptive? She was a grown woman, for pity's sake, one that did not need her daughter's permission to spend time with a man. Besides, this was one date, and for all she knew, their last. There was no sense getting Ainsley all worried over nothing.

With a huff, she paced back to her closet to try, yet again, to select an outfit for tonight's dinner. She really should've asked Mitch what type of restaurant, or even where they were going. With her luck, she'd choose a dress and heels, and he'd take her to fast food. Then she'd know for sure this wasn't a date. Nothing but a couple of church friends getting together.

Her heart sank at the thought, indicating something she already knew but was trying to ignore. She was falling for this man, and fast. The last time she'd fallen for a guy, she'd landed in the hospital on IVs. But she was much better now, stronger. Had purpose and a life goal. She didn't need a man to make her happy.

So why was she trying on every piece of clothing she owned? With a groan, she grabbed a pair of jeans and a blouse purchased from the thrift store and put them on. She'd barely donned clean socks when her doorbell rang. So much for fixing her windblown hair.

After powdering her face and glossing her lips, she dashed out and down the hall. She fluffed her limp locks in route. Grabbing her purse from a nearby end table, she opened the door.

Mitch stood on her stoop, hair damp, dressed in jeans and a teal knit shirt that deepened his tan. "You ready?" His lazy smile accelerated her pulse.

"Ready."

He moved aside, and she stepped out into the crisp autumn air. A crescent moon peeked out from behind the adjacent houses,and a handful of twinkling stars dotted the evening sky. Crickets chirped over the hum of distant cars.

He fell into step beside her. "Beautiful evening, huh?"

"It is." She paused outside his car and glanced toward an especially bright star. God had given her so much. A college degree, a restored relationship with her daughter, a grandchild. Could He give her a godly husband as well?

Listen to me, on my first real date with the man

and already jumping to the altar. She suppressed an eye roll and waited for Mitch to open her door. Rather than dreaming of the rest of her life with him, she should focus on making it through dessert without sending him running.

He rounded the truck and hopped in, his familiar yet subtle cologne filling the cab. "You been to the Old Market yet?"

She fastened her seatbelt and settled in. "No, but I've heard a lot about that area."

He grinned. "Plank it is, then." He eased into the street and headed downtown. "Those kids sure were something else today, huh? Man, can that Sebastian talk."

"And tells quite the story."

He nodded. "Always thought girls were the chatty ones, but after today, I'm not sure."

"That was true of my Ainsley-Bear. Oh, the tales she could spin, most of them involving herself in heels and a flowing gown. And a tiara."

"Girls got to have their bling." He winked, causing her cheeks to warm. "How's she doing, anyway?"

"Great." Angela grinned, reliving the memory of her baby holding a baby of her own. "She's a wonderful mother. So attentive, perhaps too much so, but you know how it is with first-time parents."

"Oh, do I ever." He went on to tell of times his ex would call him at the job site, frantic, convinced their twins were having seizures. He'd rush home every time to find an apologetic wife and two content baby boys. "Figured it'd get easier when they grew up a bit." He gave a low whistle. "Boy, was I wrong."

She laughed, then sobered. "Tell me about him, the son you lost."

He stopped at a red light, staring straight ahead. A tendon worked in his jaw, and she regretted asking the question.

"I'm sorry for prying." What would she do if he asked about her history, her past? If he found out what she'd done? Not just to her sweet, innocent, aborted baby, but in all her pre-Jesus years?

She'd rather not find out.

"He was a good kid. Focused. Responsible." He swallowed and cleared his throat. The truck rocked and bounced as he turned onto a cobblestone street. Pedestrians swarmed the sidewalks. "Always said he'd be a Husker someday. Man, could that boy play! Made the varsity football team a week before his death." His voice turned raspy.

"I'm sorry."

"It's OK. I like to talk about him. To remember the good times."

"That must have been hard for your other boys."

He studied her for a long moment, as if deciding on what to say, or maybe on whether or not to share. The skin around his eyes grew taut, then, with a loud exhale, he gave another shrug. "Death isn't easy for anyone to deal with, but yeah, it was hard. Destroyed our family. And Eliot." He pulled between a motorcycle and two-door and cut the engine.

Her heart squeezed as she thought about what Mitch had said about his son slowly killing himself ever since the accident. Shame and guilt could destroy a person. She shivered and hugged her torso as memories of herself in the hospital bed, IV drips in, came crashing back. Any other questions she might have had were squashed by an overwhelming sense of shame.

"Hope you don't mind walking," he said. "Because this is as close as we're going to get."

Good thing she'd opted for flats tonight. "An evening stroll sounds lovely."

She stepped out, breathing deep the scent of fried fish and roasting garlic. Music and laughter drifted from every direction—jazz from a nearby store, country from the street corner. A group of men, clearly drunk and loud enough to gain more than a few gawkers, gathered on the sidewalk maybe ten paces down.

"We're this way." He took her by the arm.

His warm, strong hand sent goose bumps up her skin as he guided her past a coffee shop to a chic restaurant bustling with people. Holding the door for her, he flashed a smile that melted her heart and almost made her believe the man was falling as hard for her as she was for him.

But that wasn't true. Mitch was falling for the woman he thought she was. If he knew who she really was, what she'd really done, he'd want nothing to do with her.

Chapter 38

"How many?" A brunette woman with a ruby studded nose ring greeted Mitch and Angela with a smile.

"Two, please." He stepped forward and placed his hand on the small of Angela's back, breathing in the soft strawberry scent of her hair. Catching her eye, he smiled. "What do you think?"

She surveyed the area, her gaze lingering on the granite counter in front of the oyster bar. "It's lovely."

The waitress brought them to a red booth beneath the long boat frame hanging from the ceiling.

Angela glanced about, her expression tight, dropped her purse on the seat beside her, and slid in. "So, what do you recommend?"

He sat across from her. "They make a mean blackened catfish."

"Sounds perfect."

"My kind of gal." That statement was proving truer with every encounter. He could tell she liked him, but what did she want out of this?

They weren't young anymore, after all. Lots of folks their age were through with romance, and if she'd recently come out of a bad relationship . . . maybe he should ask her. So he would know what he was up against. So he didn't push her the wrong way, unintentionally hurt her. Or ruin his chances with her.

Although . . . finding out about the drama with his son would take care of that all by itself.

"You OK?" Water glass raised to her mouth, she peered at him over the rim.

"Huh?" He straightened, stretched his back a little. "I'm good. Just thinking."

"Work been tough? I noticed your remodel is still for sale."

"The market's slowed down some."

"That must be stressful."

How much should he tell her? Maybe it was too soon to unload all his issues on her. She'd probably think him a terrible father, might even blame him for his son's addictions. Except he'd never been one for secrets. That'd been Sheila's thing, and look where that got them.

No. If he and Angela were going do this thing, he wanted to do it right. No lies, half-truths, secrets, or deceptions. She'd either fall in love with him for who he was, or they'd end it right now.

He shifted. "I wasn't thinking about work."

"Oh?"

"I was thinking about my son—my youngest."

"The one who died?"

"No. The one who lived through the crash—his twin."

She folded her hands on the tabletop, eyes compassionate.

He pushed his knife forward a notch until the end matched the bottom edge of his napkin. Then, beginning with the accident, he told her everything, ending with finding his son passed out in his own vomit.

"I'm so sorry." She reached across the table and placed her hand over his. "That must be so painful."

He nodded. "Worst thing is, there's nothing I can do about it."

She opened her mouth like she wanted to say something but the waitress arrived.

"Sorry to keep you waiting." The girl glanced over her shoulder toward a long table of very loud customers, at least 14 strong. "I've got—" She flicked a hand. "Never mind." An orange curl plopped into the center of her forehead and just sort of dangled there, bouncing as she spoke. "What can I get you?"

Mitch ordered lobster rolls to start them off, and then the waitress left, allowing them to resume their conversation. "So, anyway, that's where I'm at." He took a long swig of his Arnold Palmer. "What about you? You always been a teacher?"

She halted mid-drink, her gaze faltering briefly, then deposited her glass. "Actually, I'm an assistant, though I have my teaching license."

"Right. But you used to teach, right? I figured maybe you decided to slow things down a bit, sort of ease into retirement."

"No. I . . ." Her gaze faltered. "I recently got my degree. This is my first . . ." She glanced up, her eyes searching his, then looked down again. "This is my first experience working in education."

"Ah. A career change. That must have taken some courage." He pushed his lemon into his glass. "Good for you." His cell vibrated in his pocket. He pulled it out and checked the number. Sheila. Stifling an eye roll, he hit ignore and put the phone away.

"I suppose you could say that." She picked at a cuticle, her expression tightening. "I'm just waiting for a full-time position to open."

Before he could ask her anything else, the waitress arrived with their appetizer. After this, their conversation turned to when Omaha first became known for their steaks and who had better barbecue. By the time they finished their desserts, Angela seemed to be thoroughly enjoying herself.

First date—a success. Hopefully one of many to come.

As they were leaving, his phone vibrated again. Sheila. *For the love of—*

"Excuse me." Leaving Angela outside a storefront window, he stepped away to answer.

"What? Eliot's out of money and can't upsize his French fries?"

"Must you always be such a smart aleck?"

He inhaled, exhaled slowly. "Sorry." He let his voice soften, his gaze shooting to Angela who stood a few feet away, watching a horse-drawn carriage roll by. "What do you need?"

"Eliot called. I'm really worried. He didn't sound good."

"He's an addict, Sheila. He never sounds good."

"No, I mean, he sounded so sad. Depressed. He can't get a job—"

"Because he never shows up for work."

"And even if he did, he doesn't have a car—"

"Let me guess, got it impounded. Again."

"This is serious, Mitch. I'm afraid he'll—I'm afraid he'll . . ." She began to cry, and he'd never been good at resisting a crying lady.

"Fine. I'll check on him."

"Thank you."

He closed his eyes and rubbed a hand over his face. Here we go again. "Yeah." He hung up and returned to Angela.

"Is everything all right?"

"Just my ex-wife. Having a panic attack about our son."

"You need to leave?"

"No. We're good." Better than good. Angela was one special lady. He was glad he'd opened up to her. No secrets, no half-truths, no lies or omissions. For once, it seemed, he was actually going to enjoy a healthy relationship with a woman.

Chapter 39

4:35. Bianca had 25 minutes to shove some food down and get to work. She almost regretted picking up the extra shift, except she needed the money.

Opening the oven, she glanced over her shoulder at C. J. "This chicken should be ready in about 45 minutes." For once, her daughter wasn't holed up in her room. Actually, she'd hardly done that at all lately. Had even initiated conversation a couple times.

Roasting pan sitting on the bottom rack, Bianca closed the oven and faced her daughter. "Got rice cooking with it. Tell the boys no milk. What's left is for breakfast tomorrow." She started to wipe her hands on the dishtowel Virginia gave her, then stopped.

Rest in Me . . . What did that mean? "Lean on me" she could understand but *rest?* In? Maybe she'd ask Virginia tonight.

She moved to the fridge, grabbed a chunk of cheese, and tossed it into her mouth. Then, she stepped closer to her daughter.

"I appreciate you watching your brothers for me." She wrapped an arm around the teen's waist.

C. J. rolled her eyes but the corners of her mouth turned up. "Did I have a choice?"

Bianca laughed and playfully punched her shoulder. "Boys, you be good for your sister, you hear me?" She walked into the living room to embrace each of her sons in turn. "Do your homework, and—" She cupped Robby's chin and lifted his face until his eyes met hers. "—study for your spelling test. I expect a C or better."

He moaned and gave a half-hearted shrug.

"Good enough." She stepped back and draped her purse over her shoulder. The doorbell rang as she reached the door. Eyebrows raised, she moved aside to peer through the side window, then shook her head. "Angela Meadows. What's that crazy woman up to now?"

She opened the door. "Hello?"

Angela stood before her looking like a timid preschooler thrown into a class of kindergarteners. "Hi . . . I . . . uh . . ." She glanced past Bianca. "Is Cassie Joe here?"

Bianca frowned and crossed her arms. "Can I ask what for?" Just because this woman and Mr. Kenney took her boys on a hike didn't give her the right to poke her nose into Bianca's business. Why was she so interested in her kids anyway? If Bianca didn't know better, she'd say this woman was doing someone else's bidding, getting ready to rat her out for poor parenting or something.

Angela handed over one of those photograph envelopes, the kind you get at a photo center at the grocery store. "I know she likes to draw and

I, well . . ." She scratched the side of her neck. "I do too, and I find nature so inspiring." Her words tumbled out so fast Bianca struggled to keep up. "I thought maybe she'd, I mean . . ." She took in a deep breath. "I took some pictures during our hike with your boys. I thought maybe she'd like to . . ."

Her gaze lifted as footsteps approached behind Bianca, then she smiled. "Hi."

"Hi."

Bianca glanced back at her daughter who now stood beside her, studying Angela.

Angela repeated her spiel about the hike, pictures, and art. "Maybe you can come over some time, help me with my shading, depth."

C. J. shrugged. "Yeah, maybe."

"Anyway . . ." Angela looked from the teen to Bianca then back to the teen. "I won't keep you." With that, she left.

Bianca stared after her, wondering again why that woman was so interested in her kids.

"Here." She handed the photographs to C. J. "Have fun. And lock up after I leave."

"Right. Because the boogeyman's waiting to get us." The teen rolled her eyes, a hint of a smile emerging.

Considering Reid's friends and the fact he'd turned himself in, there could be more truth to that statement than either of them wanted to admit.

In her car, Bianca cranked the engine then eyed the time on the dash. Visiting hours started at 5:30. Should she have gone to see Reid instead of picking up this extra shift? Should she go see him at all? Or was now the time to let their relationship end quietly?

He needed her. She knew enough about prison life to know that. But so did her kids.

She slammed a fist on her steering wheel. "Reid Douglas, I hate you for forcing me to make this choice!" A sob hiccupped in her throat as tears pressed to her eyes. Sitting with her engine idling, she let them fall. For just a minute, then, with a long, deep breath, she palmed her face dry and put her car in reverse.

She arrived at work 15 minutes later, clocked in, and headed straight to the east dining room to help with feeding.

Dawn was in her usual dinnertime spot, spoon in hand, positioned between Cranky Clyde and Goofy Gus, two men affectionately nicknamed by the staff long before Bianca hired on.

"Hey." Bianca hovered near the end of the table, glancing about to see who she should take to their room first.

"Hey yourself." Dawn scooped up a blob of applesauce and moved it toward Clyde's mouth. "What're you doing here? Thought you finished your shift and went home already."

"I did. Covering for Mandy now."

Dawn gave a slow nod, glancing conspiratorially over her shoulder. "Well, be careful. Matthews came on at four and is fit to be tied. Done set on making everybody miserable."

"Great." There was little worse than working with an angry charge nurse. "What's his problem now?"

Dawn glanced about then leaned toward Bianca. "Don't know. But from what I hear, Mr. Homer pulled him into his office. Gave him a talking to."

Her eyebrows shot up. "For real?"

Dawn nodded.

She rubbed her temples. "Guess I better get hustling then, huh?"

Dawn laughed. "You know that's right. Unless you want the jerk to write you up. For something stupid."

Bianca wouldn't put it past him. The guy'd been wound tighter than a corroded yo-yo ever since headquarters started nosing about. Hopefully that meant he was on his way out, but knowing him, he'd take a bunch of folks with him.

She moved to the center of the dining room and scanned the area. Sweet Betty sat at an empty table, leftover food caked on her face, blowing raspberries. Walking toward her, Bianca chuckled. That woman was one of the few bright spots in this place. Her and Virginia.

After cleaning Betty's face, Bianca rounded

the wheelchair and took the handles. She leaned close to the woman's ear. "Hey there, Ms. Betty. You ready for some TV time? I hear there's a *Name That Phrase* marathon going on tonight."

This perked Betty up. Didn't take much to make these folks happy. Just a kind word and speaking to them like an adult, treating them with dignity. Like everyone needed.

"What phrases you think they'll pick this time? Unexpected ways to say good-bye? Maybe how many ways you can invite someone to dinner. Grub. Supper. Sup. Stuff your face." She turned the corner and headed down the hall, acknowledging other residents as she passed. Chatting all the way to Betty's room, Bianca didn't stop, or slow even, until she'd lifted the frail woman into bed.

She raised the bed rail, propped some pillows behind her, then positioned her tray in front of her. "Glad I got to be the one to tend to you, Ms. Betty. Been wanting someone to share my wordsmith ideas with." She tucked the covers under her chin then gently patted the woman's cheeks. "I'll be back to check on you in a bit. And to see who's winning that game show of yours."

She darted back into the hall, returning to the dining room again and again until almost all of her patients had been cleaned up and put to bed. On her last trip down, she paused outside Virginia's room and checked her watch. She was running late—by this time in her shift she had usually moved on to the next task, but she wouldn't be here long. She really needed advice, and Virginia was about the only person she knew who actually had a lick of sense about her.

Bianca poked her head in the doorway. "Hi."

Sitting in her overstuffed recliner, Virginia looked up and laid the book she'd been reading on her lap. "Bianca, come in, dear. I saw you earlier, but you were so busy scurrying all over the place, I never had a chance to say hi."

Bianca entered and sat on the edge of the bed, her hands folded tightly in her lap. "Sorry about that."

"Pshaw." Virginia waved a hand. "You work much too hard." Her smile fell. "You OK, dear? Looks like something's eating at you."

Bianca cast a glance toward the hallway before looking back at Virginia. "I've . . . you know I'm married, right?"

She nodded. "And that you have three wonderful children. I pray for your entire family daily."

"Thanks, I . . . thanks." Bianca chewed on her bottom lip. She hated to say something that would make Virginia think badly of her, but she really needed help. Someone who wasn't always caught up in drama. "Well, things are sort of . . . he's . . ." Dragging this out only made it harder. *Just blurt it, girl.* "He's in jail."

Virginia flinched, resuming her smile so quickly, Bianca almost wondered if she'd seen the woman react at all. "I see."

"And I'm . . ." She breathed deep. "I love him, you know? I told him I'd wait for him, but I worry about the kids."

"I see."

Bianca frowned. Was that all Virginia was going to say? "I haven't been to see him since he turned himself in. I can't." She paused to keep her emotions in check. "Plus we're married. And divorce is bad, right?" Not that she believed in all that stuff self-righteous Christians spewed all the time, but religion or not, she'd made a promise. Vows were vows, right?

Virginia watched her for a long moment, her expression unreadable, her eyes soft.

Bianca resisted the urge to groan. *Say something!* "What do you think I should do?"

"Can I give you something?"

Bianca blinked. "Huh?"

"Can I give you something?"

"Sure. Yeah, I guess."

She reached for the books on the shelf behind her, shuffling about until she'd wrested a thin pink one from within the pile. She held it to her chest and closed her eyes. Then, looking at Bianca once again, she handed the book over. "I bought this for you. Actually, my grand-daughter purchased it on my request. I've been waiting for the right time to give it to you."

Bianca read the cover. *Cherished, Loved, Set Free.* Was that some kind of hidden message or something? One of those God-speaks things? And if so, what did it mean? Were the authorities gonna set Reid free, or was God saying she and her family would be set free from Reid?

She suppressed a snort. Since when did she believe God spoke to people? Except maybe Virginia? Still, this was a kind gift, offered from a woman that meant a great deal to her.

"Bianca." Ellis, one of the older nurses assistants, poked her head into the room, startling her. "Jordan's running his mouth, talking about you leaving Mr. Boggs sitting at the table. I'd hurry and get him, if I were you."

Bianca sprang to her feet. "I better go." She hugged her friend. The woman smelled like roses and arthritis cream. "Thanks for the book."

"Of course." Virginia patted Bianca's back. When Bianca pulled away, Virginia grabbed her hand. "I love you, dear. So does God." Her eyes grew moist. "I wish you could see that."

Chapter 40

The scent of cinnamon cider filled Angela's nostrils as she passed the craft store's candle display. Where was the painting section? She scanned the signs hanging from the ceiling. Ah! There it was, in the back right corner.

Rubber soles squeaking on the linoleum, she dashed across the store, weaving around dawdling customers. Reaching the aisle, she stopped in front of an acrylic starter set. How much painting had Cassie Joe done? The sets were costly, but they included all the necessary tools along with some basic colors. They'd make a nice gift.

Except . . . what about the boys? If she purchased something for their sister, would she need to buy them something as well? Although she had supplied the both of them with plenty of candy—on the sly, so as not to irritate Mrs. Wright.

Was that being deceptive? She sighed. So many confusing gray areas.

"Angela, hello."

She turned at the sound of a familiar voice.

Joline stood behind her. "Fancy seeing you here." She grinned. "You paint?"

"I dabble."

"Well," Joline leaned closer, covering her mouth as if about to share a juicy secret. "I've got an extra coupon, if you'd like it. I won't use it." Her expression sobered into all seriousness as she began to sift through her purse. She produced a wad of advertisement clippings and began flipping through them one by one. "Here it is." Smile returning, wider, she handed over a torn slip of newspaper offering 40 percent off total purchase.

"Thank you so much!" With such a discount, Angela could probably buy the starter set, though she'd be wiser to purchase supplies for herself. That way Cassie Joe would have to come over to use them. Then Angela wouldn't have to worry about slighting the boys.

"My pleasure." Joline patted her shoulder. "We missed you last night."

"I'm sorry. I . . ." Joline had been inviting her to Bible study for weeks now, extending the invitation whenever they met. One of these times Angela needed to take her up on the offer, if only to be polite. Besides, she really did need to make friends with people from church. As much as the thought terrified her. "I'm sorry. What time do you all get together again?"

"6:30." She plunged her arm back into her mammoth purse, embarking on another extended fishing expedition. Finally, she pulled out a pink slip of paper decorated with an image of a steaming teacup, gingerly writing her address, telephone number, and meeting time and then handing the slip of paper to Angela with a smile. "We'd love to have you. And we'll have chocolate."

She turned to leave then stopped, facing Angela once again. "You know . . ." She angled her head. "Our women's ministry has a service project coming up. I know it's not as fun as crafting, but it'd be a good way to meet other ladies. If you're interested."

Having something to do would certainly make things less awkward. "What would I be doing, exactly?"

"Oh, this and that. Sorting donated diapers and clothing, making gift packages for new moms."

"Where is this at?"

"My house, but we're doing the project for the local pregnancy center. They serve single moms in our area and women in crisis, showing them they have options, that they don't have to abort their children."

Angela's chest tightened, and her hand flew to her queasy midsection.

Joline's forehead creased. "Is everything all right?"

Her, serving at a crisis pregnancy center? Surely she was the least qualified to do such a thing, and yet . . . the idea drew her. "Yes, of course. Just . . ." She shifted her basket from one arm to the next and forced a smile. "I'd love to come."

"Wonderful!" After reaching into her handbag a third time, Joline pulled out a spiral bound, pocket notebook, and pen. "What's your number?"

She raised an eyebrow. The woman was playing hardball now, getting Angela's contact information so she couldn't back out. Maybe that was what Angela needed.

Phone to his ear, Mitch made a right turn. "I'm heading to my son's now." It was past time he checked on Eliot, though he dreaded the encounter. Or more accurately, the fight that was certain to follow. "Not sure how long I'll be . . ."

This could be the time he followed through on his threats, grabbed Eliot by the scruff of his neck, and carted him off to rehab. Except he wouldn't stay, and Mitch couldn't make him. Any efforts to do so would result in nothing but hefty bills. A person couldn't even think of stepping into one of those facilities without racking up charges.

"I know this is hard, will be hard," Angela said. "I'll be praying for you. For both of you."

"I appreciate that." He hit "call end," then dropped his cell onto the passenger seat. On second thought, he'd best keep his phone handy, in case Eliot had overdosed. Wouldn't be the first time. Bones once joked that Mitch's son had more lives than a stray cat.

Apparently, Eliot had concluded the same thing. Either that, or he had a death wish. Everything the kid did and said indicated the latter. He was given the gift of life—a gift his brother never got the chance to experience—and he was treating it like trash.

As he neared his son's apartment complex, if you could call the crumbling brick structure that, the homes became more dilapidated. Many had been abandoned, though they were probably filled with squatters and their refuse.

He parked and surveyed the bed of his pickup with a frown. Why hadn't he unloaded his supplies before coming? Oh, well. He was here now. If someone had the nerve to snag a bunch of bricks and 2-by-4s, let them.

He stepped out of his vehicle. The stench of rotting garbage merging with a hint of marijuana swept over him. Oil and trash clogged the gutter and littered the crumbling concrete.

Inside the complex, a dim hallway stretched to his left and right, fluorescent light flickering above. The others had burned out. The stench of vomit, urine, and—gasoline?—stung his nose. Shouts emanated from one of the closed doorways, and sweat beaded on his upper lip. He wasn't a pansy, knew how to swing a hammer and haul dry wall, but no strength could stand against a drug-crazed meth addict.

He clomped up the steps two at a time. His heavy footfalls echoed against the dingy concrete walls. His son's apartment, if he hadn't been kicked out yet, stood midway down the hall. Mitch reached it to find the door ajar, the inside dark and silent.

"Eliot?" His heart hammered against his rib cage as he nudged the door open wider with the toe of his boot. The acrid scent of mildew and rotting meat made him gag. Dripping water pinged on metal. Muted voices seeped through the wall.

He turned on a switch. Nothing. The lights were out or his son hadn't paid his electric bill. Maybe he'd bolted. Owed money to his dealer and ran. Or worse.

Mitch tapped the flashlight app on his phone, taken aback by the filth that surrounded him. Though he shouldn't have been. Eliot had been living like a sewer rat for years, but it never made the reality of seeing it any easier.

Two paper grocery bags, one lying on its side, the other upright, sat on the counter. He bit back a curse. As if the fact that his son never purchased actual food wasn't proof enough, the label of his ex-wife's favorite grocery was.

"Sheila, what are you doing?" A slip of paper, no, an envelope, lay beside the sacks. He moved closer, flipped it over and read the bank logo printed on the back. How'd she expect their son to turn his life around if she kept bailing him out? He should've known she'd cave. Truth was, he had known, but he'd desperately hoped this time would be different. That Sheila would actually do what was best for Eliot.

Why was Mitch wasting his time? His son wasn't here, and even if he were, nothing Mitch could say would make any difference.

Whirling around, he stormed out, slamming the door behind him. It bounced back against the wall. Someone had broken the latch. Probably kicked it in. *Great place you got here, son.*

He'd hardly stepped outside when loud music pulsated to his left, followed by the screech of brakes gone bad and the scent of burning rubber. He turned just as his son was stepping out of a low-riding, rusted two door. A blond with frizzy hair and black roots got out on the other side. Whose car had Eliot finagled this time? Or had he stolen it?

"Yo, Daddy-O." Eliot grinned, showing blackening teeth. A stiff breeze carried the stench of alcohol and marijuana.

Mitch's hands clenched into fists. "Drinking and driving. Smart." Blood pulsated in his ears. "Who'd you kill this time?" He blinked, swallowed, and took half a step backward. Had he really just said that?

Eliot froze, his lazy grin morphing into a fiery-eyed scowl. He swore. "So that's how you feel, huh? Your loser son killed your precious boy." He let out another sling of curse words, then, grabbing his girlfriend around the waist, he jerked her forward. "Forget this jerk."

Mitch watched him leave, the words he'd just spoken to Eliot replaying in his mind.

Chapter 41

Angela peered at Bianca's house through her own living room window. As usual, the blinds were drawn and her car wasn't in the driveway. Were the kids home? Robby and Sebastian, most likely. She'd seen them during crosswalk duty, but what about Cassie Joe? Should she stop by, invite the teen over? Thanksgiving was only a week away. What if she invited the entire family over? Or would that be too weird?

Probably. Besides, they undoubtedly had plans. If she could just figure out a way to connect with Cassie Joe . . .

The teenager reminded her so much of herself when she was that age, and Angela feared, if no one intervened, she'd end up exactly how Angela did—with a lifetime of regrets.

She sighed and turned back around. One couldn't force these things. Doing so would only push the teen further away. But then how was she supposed to form a connection? That girl hardly stepped out of her house, and when she did, she usually jumped straight into her boyfriend's car. Maybe now that Mitch and the boys were repairing the fence, and if Angela kept baking cookies . . .

Am I doing this right, Lord? Why am I not

making any headway? These sorts of things were so easy for Chris and Ainsley. All they had to do was walk up to someone and start sharing the gospel. Something Angela had never done. Matter of fact, she didn't even know how to go about it. How did one learn to do such a thing, anyway?

She plopped onto her couch and grabbed the painting magazine she'd purchased. *How to Draw Horses Using Charcoal.* Not the easiest subject, perhaps, but one more teen-friendly than the others she'd seen.

Who was she kidding? Cassie Joe wasn't going to come over to paint, bake, or do anything else. Like the kid wanted to hang out with some old lady she barely knew.

But as long as she'd purchased the material . . .

Sinking deeper into the seat cushions, Angela flipped through pages until she settled on a picture of a mare with her foal. The mother's muzzle was pressed affectionately against her offspring's neck. The foal leaned toward the mare, his eyes lidded, lashes thick and dark. Such a beautiful picture of parental love. How could she capture that emotion in art?

She grabbed her sketchbook in one hand and picked up a piece of charcoal in the other. She'd just started to form the mare's head when her doorbell rang. Setting her things aside, she answered.

Mitch greeted her holding a gallon of paint in each hand. Based on the splatter dried on the outside of the containers, one was cream, the other periwinkle blue.

"Hi." His crooked smile weakened her knees. His hair was mussed, and sawdust clung to his clothes. Speckles of paint decorated his hands and forearms, and a large smear of pale blue colored his temple.

"Hi." A mischievous giggle rose to the surface. "So, you came to borrow my hose?"

"Huh?"

Her laughter bubbled out. "Seems you've been busy."

He wrinkled his brow, studied her for a moment, then glanced down, probably catching a view of his disheveled attire. "Sorry." His lopsided grin returned, and he deposited his load and began untying his work boots, which, considering all the twine and loops, would take him a while.

"Oh, don't worry about that." She touched his shoulder, and his head jerked up, his face dangerously close to hers. She took a quick step back. "How about you . . . ?" She still didn't feel right about inviting him in, despite the fact they'd been on numerous dates, and she was growing quite comfortable with the man. Actually, that was all the more reason not to. As Ainsley said, you can't get burned if you don't dance near the fire pit.

"Have a seat." She motioned toward the porch swing. "I'll get you some lemonade." She started to dash back inside then turned around. "Um . . . what's the paint for?"

"Your bathroom." He glanced past her. "You still planning on changing it up? Tearing out the wallpaper?" He indicated his paint cans. "I know these colors might not be your first pick, but we're not going to use them. Figured no sense throwing them away."

"Thanks." Warmth spread from her toes to her cheeks. He'd been thinking of her at work? Did that mean he thought of her often? As often as she thought of him? Silence followed, until she realized she'd quite rudely left him standing on her porch.

"Sit. I'll be back in a moment." She darted inside, leaving her front door ajar. When she returned, he was relaxing in her porch swing, hands twined behind his head.

"Here." She handed him an iced drink then settled in beside him—but not too close. "How was your day?"

Taking the glass, he looked at her for a long moment than shrugged. "Tense. My partner's throwing a fit."

"I'm sorry."

"I knew this was coming. He's making a break, and will probably take most of our crew with him."

"Oh, wow. What happened?"

Mitch kneaded his shoulder. "Nothing really. We were just on opposite pages. On everything." He went on to tell her about their rentals, the money they brought in, and the tenants who were behind. "I've got less than 60 days—less than 50, actually—to clear out and sell half our properties or face a lawsuit."

"That doesn't seem right."

"Oh, he's bluffing. No judge would enforce terms like that. I could be made to sell, sure, maybe even put properties up on auction . . ." He sighed and rubbed a hand over his face. "And I could be forced to evict."

"I see." Glass sweating in her hand, she gazed across the street. "The Douglases?"

"Might have to."

Her heart ached for Mitch and the poor family she'd prayed for so many times. God had formed a deep love in her for each of them. If only there were some way she could help, but on her salary? Besides, she had a mountain of debt to pay herself.

The swing creaked beneath them. An old, sputtering car drove by, a swirl of blackened exhaust following.

"Wanna . . . pray?" she asked.

His features relaxed as his gaze landed on hers, his eyes soft. "I'd like that." He took her hand in his, sending a surge of heat up her arm. "Father, show me what to do. Give me a way to help Bianca and her kids. And be with them, Lord. Whatever happens, may it draw them closer to You." When he finished, he kept Angela's hand in his. "Sometimes it takes losing everything to find the only thing that truly matters."

"I know what you mean." She closed her eyes as the memory resurfaced of the day she woke in a hospital bed after having tried to take her life. Though that had been an incredibly painful time, it also brought her to Christ. Opened her eyes to grace.

He pushed his foot against the porch railing, causing the swing to sway. "So, how's that little grandbaby of yours?"

She grinned. "Growing like a weed. I'd show you pictures, but . . ." She pulled out her prepaid flip phone. "This contraption isn't so smart."

He gave a throaty laugh, but then, looking into her eyes, his gaze intensified. "Maybe I can meet him sometime. And the rest of your family."

Her breath caught. That was serious, right? Him wanting to meet her family? What did that mean? Forcing her smile steady despite the butterflies doing cannonballs in her stomach, she nodded. "You should." How would Ainsley react to her mother dating? "Does that mean I get to meet yours as well?"

His smile faltered, and his hand stiffened in hers. But then, with a deep breath, he nodded.

"Sure. At least my oldest. My other son . . ." He shook his head. "He's pretty messed up. Whenever I go to see him, I wonder if it'll be the last time."

"I'm so sorry. I can't imagine what that must feel like."

"I went to check on him the other day. Didn't want to. I hate seeing him like that, you know? Seeing how he lives?" He leaned back, gazing into the distance, then went on to tell about his son getting out of a car, obviously under the influence. "So I lost it. Got in his face." He gave an audible exhale. "He thinks I blame him for his brother's death."

"Do you?" She clamped her mouth shut. She had no business asking questions like that. None.

He searched her eyes for a long moment then gave a slight, almost indiscernible shrug. "I don't know . . . I don't know."

Bianca entered Fred's room with a heavy heart. Though he wasn't part of her rounds, a deep compassion had drawn her to his bedside. She'd caught a glimpse into his room on her way to the kitchen, and she knew the man was dying. She needed to alert the nurse. Fred's breathing was raspy, shallow. Would his family come?

Probably not. In all her years at Hillcrest, he'd only had one visitor that she knew of, a nephew or something. The kid had hardly stayed through lunch, and even then, he'd been distracted. Checking his phone, looking about. Why he came at all was beyond her.

In the hallway, Mr. Davis's voice, loud and sharp, approached, his rubber soles squeaking on the linoleum. "Where is that woman?" The squeaking stopped not far from Fred's opened doorway.

"Last I saw her, she was laying Marlene down, but that was like 20 minutes ago." That sounded like Wendy, one of the new hires.

Mr. Davis cursed and muttered something under his breath. "Bianca Douglas!"

She startled, but Fred clutched her hand all the tighter. "Don't leave me." Though his voice was weak, his eyes beseeched her.

"I'm not going anywhere." She rotated slowly.

The charge nurse stood in Fred's doorway with a scowl. "Eugene's been laying on his call button looking for someone to help him to the john. Hurry up."

She blinked, looked from Davis to Fred then back to Davis. Could he not see what was going on here? "I'm sorry sir, but I . . ." How could she say this without coming right out and saying it, for Fred's sake? "It's time." As acting charge nurse, she needed to alert Davis anyway. The fact that he was here now only made things easier.

"I'll take care of this."

"I'm sorry, sir, but I really feel like I need to

stay. Can you ask Dawn to check on Eugene for me?"

The man's eyes about bugged out of his head. "No. I'm telling *you* to do it."

She swallowed hard, a rush of anger spiking her temperature. Holding Fred's gaze, she talked slowly to keep her voice steady. "I can't leave just yet. I'm sorry."

Mr. Davis's breathing grew louder behind her, and she envisioned veins bulging in his neck.

Such heartlessness. Fred was dying! True, this was expected—the man was on hospice, but still. Couldn't Davis see that or did he just not care? She continued to look into Fred's eyes, which soon gazed past her, as if seeing something. He muttered, words that made no sense, and then, with a final raspy breath, his features relaxed.

He was gone.

She wiped her eyes then tugged his blanket tighter around him. "Bye, Fred. May you rest in peace."

Then she left and headed straight toward Eugene's room. Turned out, he'd spilled his nutritional shake and needed someone to help clean it up—before he or someone else slipped and fell. Mess cleaned and Eugene happily sitting in his recliner with a new drink and his remote, Bianca hurried out to finish her rounds. She nearly collided with Mr. Davis en route. Mr. Homer was with him.

"Excuse me." Her gaze shot from the fuming charge nurse to Mr. Homer, the equally scowling director.

"Bianca, would you come with me, please?" Mr. Homer turned on his heel and walked swiftly toward his office.

Ignoring Mr. Davis's smirk, she marched after her boss. His arms swayed stiffly at his sides, his crisp slacks swooshing, his heavy footsteps echoing in the hall. Reaching his office, he opened the door and advanced toward his desk. He pulled his chair out and sat, features hard.

Bianca crossed the room on wobbly legs, forcing herself to look the man in the eye. "Sir, I'm sorry if I—"

"Sit." He motioned toward the chair across from him.

She complied and folded clammy hands in her lap.

"I understand you defied instructions from your charge nurse. Is this correct?"

"Yes, sir, but Fred was—"

He raised a hand. "I will not tolerate insubordination."

"I'm sorry, sir. I meant no disrespect."

He swiveled his chair, pulled a manila folder from a nearby filing cabinet, and laid it on his desk. He flipped it open and began reading. "You've been late four times this quarter, including missing almost half of your shift.

You've called in . . . three times, not to mention the fact that you've been written up on more than one occasion for failing to care for your patients in a timely manner."

"I got a little behind, is all." If not for Mr. Davis hating her like he did, those instances wouldn't even be on her record. Besides, they were given way too many people to look after. There was hardly time to get them cleaned and changed, let alone really care for them.

"I'm sorry to inform you, but we're going to have to let you go." He rose. "Gather your things. We'll send your final check by mail." He moved toward the door then stood with his hand on the knob.

Her mouth went dry. This couldn't be happening. She still owed Mr. Kenney money— her landlords would evict her for sure this time. What was she supposed to do? Especially with it being so close to Thanksgiving. To Christmas. What would she tell her kids? That Santa got busy? Couldn't find their house?

She sprang to her feet, feeling sick to her stomach. "Give me another chance, sir. I can work faster. Harder. I'll be more punctual."

"Good day, Mrs. Douglas."

Bianca stared at him, her hands trembling, then, lifting her chin, she walked out.

Dawn grabbed her arm as she neared the break room. "Where you going?"

Mouth flattened, Bianca shook her head. She continued to her locker, gathered her things, and left. What was she going to do? If she didn't find work soon, she and the kids would land on the street.

How dare Mr. Davis chastise her for staying with a dying man! She'd done the right thing. She'd do it again, if given the chance.

Even if it meant losing her job?

She stomped to her car, swearing, threw the door open and got in. Why did she always have to choose? Huh? Why? Glaring at the sky, she slammed a fist on the steering wheel. If God loved her so much, why hadn't He protected her?

Rest. Right. Like You care. I'm done chasing fairy tales.

Chapter 42

Angela hummed as she arranged pinecones on her kitchen table, decorated with colorful, artificial foliage found on clearance at the local craft store. Turkey roasted in the oven, and two pies—one pumpkin, the other pecan, just like her mother used to make—cooled on the counter. The rich aroma of sage and buttery crust filled her nose, making her stomach growl.

Her heart swelled as she imagined Ainsley and her sweet family, and any of Angela's old church friends who chose to make the drive, gathered around the table, giggles and coos filling her home. How long had it been since she'd hosted Thanksgiving dinner? Decades.

If only her mother were coming, but as of yet, Aunt Dorothy still hadn't responded to Angela's letter, and she didn't know who else to contact. But at least she'd tried, and she refused to allow regrets from her past to dampen her Thanksgiving celebration. She had way too many things to be thankful for.

Her phone chimed. She glanced at the number and smiled. "Mitch, good morning. I was going to call you later." Her stomach dropped as she thought about the imminent disclosure she'd be making to Ainsley. But she couldn't keep Mitch from her daughter forever, nor should she.

"Hi." His voice sounded strained. "Listen, about this evening, I'm not sure if I'll be able to make it."

"Oh." She frowned.

"Family stuff is always tense on my end, and I feel like I really need to stick around, to support my son and daughter-in-law."

"I understand." So maybe she could delay her revelation a little longer. "I'll be praying for you."

"Thanks."

"You talk to Eliot?"

Silence, followed by a loud exhale. "Not yet. I'm praying on that."

"What's there to pray on? As Christians we're supposed to resolve things, right?" She shut her mouth and squeezed her eyes shut. *Way to go, Angela, putting your nose where it doesn't belong.* "I'm sorry. That was uncalled for."

"It's fine." His voice sounded flat. "Listen, I got to go."

"Call me later?"

"Sure."

She dropped her phone onto the couch cushions and paced her living room. Why had she said that? She was the last one to speak on reconciliation! Besides, Mitch's issues with his son were none of her business. Except she understood the deep regret of letting things go until you'd lost contact altogether. She didn't want him to experience that same pain, but still, that was God's arena, not hers. Right now, she had plenty of other things to worry about, like making this the best Thanksgiving celebration ever.

She couldn't wait to scoop her sweet grandbaby in her arms and kiss his pudgy little cheeks. Giggling, she flitted about the house, dusting, vacuuming, rearranging miniature pumpkins and other decorations. By the time Ainsley and Chris showed up two hours later, she'd worked herself into quite an unattractive sweat.

"Come in!" She threw open her door and ushered her family inside, hugging first Ainsley then Chris. "Oh, look how big he's grown!" She took Joey in her arms and breathed in the sweet scent of baby powder. "How's my favorite grandson?" She kissed each of the infant's cheeks.

Chris set a polka-dotted diaper bag near the door. "He's healthy as an ox. Off the charts for growth and height."

"But of course. The Meadows women know how to make babies." She hip-bumped her daughter then led the way into the kitchen. "You thirsty? I have sodas and iced tea in the fridge. Sweetened with peach syrup."

"My favorite," Ainsley said.

"I know." Angela handed Joey over to check

the turkey. "There will be a lot of your favorites today, my dear." Maybe she was trying to make up for Thanksgivings past, or maybe she was just milking this one for every memory it was worth. Either way, it was going to be special.

Grabbing a dishtowel, she turned around and leaned against the stove. "Any of our old Bible study gals coming?"

Ainsley shook her head. "Sorry, Mom. They're all either out of town or have family coming in. But Mrs. Loomis sent a card." She pulled an orange-and-tan envelope from her purse and handed it over.

"That's nice." Angela set the card on the counter to read and cherish later. "Now, I bet you're hungry. Chris, would you mind grabbing the crackers from the pantry? I'll get the cheese and hummus."

They spent the rest of the evening chatting about Angela's new job, the Douglases— Mitch never came up, though she considered mentioning him a few times.

"I made a lot of food." Angela smoothed a lock of hair off her forehead. "Figured I could take the leftovers across the street."

"That's kind." Ainsley smiled. "You have such a tender heart, Mom."

"Well, no more than you two. Speaking of, how's the café?"

"It's going well." Chris popped a loaded

cracker into his mouth. "Still holding to my original vision."

"Which means he has a lot of turnover." Pride radiated from Ainsley's eyes. And rightly so, with all the battered and homeless women Chris employed over the years. Once they got back on their feet, many went back to school or found other jobs, leaving openings for the next woman.

Angela lifted her tea. "How many mothers have you helped, do you think?"

"All total?" A blush crept into his cheeks. "Maybe 15? Twenty?"

That was a lot, considering he'd only bought the place five or so years ago. She couldn't remember exactly. She started to ask him when her phone chimed, and she glanced at the returned number. Not one she recognized.

"Excuse me a moment." She answered. "This is Angela Meadows. How may I help you?"

"Hello, I'm Shirley Russel. I'm Dorothy Ludwig's stepdaughter."

"Yes?" Her grip tightened on the phone.

"I found a card you sent my mother. She's in an assisted living facility, and I don't get back to her old house much. We need to sell it but can't settle on a price. Anyway, I just found your letter."

And? She fought to keep her impatience at bay.

"I thought you should know . . . your mother

374

passed away last year. Congestive heart failure."

Angela's knees felt like they'd give way. Grabbing the back of a chair for support, she lowered into it. "Last year?" Meaning, if she'd tried to contact her mother sooner, she could've said good-bye. Could've apologized for all the pain she'd caused her, told her how much she loved her.

"I'm sorry," Shirley said.

Angela laid the phone gingerly on the table.

"Mom?" Ainsley touched her shoulder, and Chris moved to her other side. "What's wrong?"

"Your grandmother's dead." Her voice trembled.

"Oh, Mom, I'm so sorry." Ainsley wrapped her in a tight hug.

"I never had the chance to pay her back. To make up for all the pain I caused her."

Ainsley took Angela's hands in her own. "You can't always make up for the past. But that's what grace is about. I know it's hard, but you've got to let all that go. Your past is gone. You've been forgiven and redeemed. You need to walk in grace. Know what I mean?"

She nodded and wiped her tears away. "I just wish I knew how."

"God will show you," Chris said. "Let's pray."

They all bowed their heads as Chris prayed for healing, emotional freedom, and an ever-deepening understanding of grace for each of them. The oven timer chimed at the same moment he said amen.

Angela gave an awkward laugh. "Well, if that isn't a sign to move forward, I don't know what is."

Chapter 43

Bianca's steps echoed through the 12-by-100-foot concrete tunnel, her chest tight. Though she'd arrived almost two hours before scheduled visitation, grim-faced people already sat in the chairs lining the walls. An old woman with scraggly hair and a sunken mouth glanced up as Bianca passed, her eyes hard. Angry.

Beside her sat a pregnant woman dressed in a flannel shirt and exercise pants. Sitting cross-legged, she bounced her foot so fast it looked ready to take flight.

Clutching her pass in sweaty hands, Bianca found a vacant chair. This was a first come, first served deal. Did that mean she might not get to see Reid? It didn't help that this was Thanksgiving. She thought of Virginia's prayer, of God. If she didn't get in to see Reid, did that mean God was telling her to walk away from Reid for good?

She closed her eyes and rubbed her temples. While she waited, she planned what she might say to her husband, anticipating what he might say to her.

An hour ticked by, then another. She shifted, her back sore. Glanced about once again. Wished she'd brought a book. Wished she hadn't come at all, that she was at her mom's eating ham and mashed potatoes with her kids. But no; once again she'd put Reid first. And because of that, she was on her own. None of her family would help—they'd never liked Reid. Not that they'd be much help, regardless. All her siblings were either in jail or fighting their own battles, and her mom could barely make ends meet. Didn't help she had a fierce attachment to alcohol.

"Bianca Douglas?"

She startled and rose on shaky legs, walked to the long metal desk.

"Remove your shoes and belt."

She complied, proceeded through the metal detector, then waited in a small room while a female officer patted her down. What was she doing? She didn't belong here. She wasn't the type to throw her life away for a felon, waiting for him to get out for a month or two before falling back into old habits and getting thrown back into prison.

And yet, here she was, and on Thanksgiving, no less.

Once cleared, she continued, stiff, through a lobby area and into a concrete room with rectangular tables. Her lungs tightened, making it hard to breathe. Reid sat in the center of the room.

His eyes lit up when he saw her. "Baby."

Four officers were positioned throughout the room, faces stoic. Security cameras filled the corners, and cheap beige carpet covered the floor. A glass window stretched across one entire wall.

She looked at a blond officer to her right. The man nodded, and Bianca continued forward and pulled out the chair across from her husband.

"Hi." She studied his face, searched his eyes. Though he'd lost weight, he looked good, healthy. "They treating you all right?"

He gave a lopsided smile and one shoulder shrug. "It's not a party, but I'm doing all right." His face sobered. "Where're the kids?"

She glanced at her hands but then lifted her gaze, forcing herself to maintain eye contact. "My mom's."

He nodded. "Tell them I said hi." His voice went husky, and he cleared his throat. "That I love them, and I'm thinking of them."

"I will." Should she have brought them? He was their dad, after all. But just once, she wanted them to enjoy a drama-free holiday.

Who was she kidding? There'd be plenty of drama at her mom's house, especially if Bianca's brothers showed up. Even so, it was better than spending the day at the state penitentiary.

She pulled a picture Sebastian drew from her pocket and handed it over. "Little man made this for you." Two stick figures stood in a grassy field, one of them holding a football.

Reid took the page, his Adam's apple bobbing.

He stared it for a long time before looking at Bianca with red-rimmed eyes. "How're you holding up?"

She frowned, holding back an angry retort. Breathed deep, emptied her lungs slowly. "It's been tough. Real tough." *Didn't I tell you selling drugs wasn't the answer? That it'd only make things worse?* "I got fired."

Hands flattened on the table, his eyes widened. "For what?"

"Bunch of garbage." She relayed all that had happened at Hillcrest Manor since he'd been locked up. "I don't know what to do."

"Can you apply to another nursing home?"

"Maybe. But what if they call my references? Find out I was terminated for insubordination and 'continual patient neglect'?"

"Is that what your boss is saying?"

"Who knows? I wouldn't put it past him."

"What're you gonna do?"

She stared at him then her tightly twined hands. Neither spoke for some time. The conversations around them rumbled a steady buzz. A man to her right let out a loud, long cackle that caused her teeth to grate. As if this was the place for a party. Then again, folks did what they had to in order to survive, and if humor helped the guy out, more power to him.

"I know someone who might be able to help you."

"Uh-uh." She raised a hand. "No more games, Reid. One felon's all our kids need."

He jerked back as if slapped. Paused long enough Bianca thought about leaving.

When he finally spoke, his voice was soft, defeated. "Remember Shawn, the scrawny guy with the sleeve tattoos?"

She shook her head.

"He owns a gas station a few miles from the house. Go see him. Tell him I sent you, that you're my girl. Probably won't pay much, but he'd hire you on. He owes me a favor."

"Right. Because a part-time, minimum wage job's going to help me feed our kids and keep a roof over their heads."

Mitch waited until nearly eight o'clock, watching the door, hoping Eliot would stop by. Family members gathered in packs of fours and fives, everyone from his son and daughter-in-law to great aunts and distant cousins. For the most part, everyone behaved, and only a few mentioned Eliot. Which was a welcomed change.

So often these get-togethers turned into brainstorming sessions. Everyone thought they had the best solution. Problem was, Mitch and Sheila had already tried them all—interventions, counseling, forced rehab.

But there was one thing Mitch hadn't tried, and it was time he did. Fisting his hands on the table as a wave of emotion he couldn't name swept over him, he stood.

He glanced about, smiled at his aunt, his oldest son Nathan, and his third cousin twice removed. "It's been great, but I better go." He'd planned to gather up some leftovers to take to the Douglases, but considering some folks were still eating, thought better of it. He could pick up something on the way home, if only to make Bianca's night a little brighter.

Nathan rose to meet him, gave him a handshake that turned into a hug. "Thanks for coming, Dad."

He nodded and said good-bye to the others on his way to the door. Outside the air was cold, the night sky an inky black. A thick blanket of clouds hid the moon except for a faint glow. Only a handful of stars poked through. Cars lined the street on either side, his five houses down. But he welcomed the walk. Maybe it'd help him clear his head, figure out what to say to his son.

He'd never been good at that—voicing his emotions. He didn't even know what he was feeling half the time, except he couldn't use that excuse now. God made this one as clear as a bowed plank in a wooden floor. Eliot was his son, and he refused to walk away, not without letting the boy know just how much he loved him. And that he didn't blame him for his brother's death.

An image of Eliot lying in some ditch inside a totaled vehicle flashed through his mind, spiking his pulse and increasing his nausea. Tossing the visual aside, Mitch climbed into his vehicle and cranked the engine.

As he drove through the near-empty streets toward his son's apartment complex, the silence ate at him. He flicked on the radio, tuned to sports talk, and let arguing commentators dominate his thoughts. Didn't help much, and by the time he arrived at his son's, every muscle felt ready to snap.

He waited outside, prayed for peace, for courage and strength. Clenching and unclenching his hands, he stepped into the dark hallway and continued to his son's unit. Loud music vibrated the floor beneath him. He listened for the sound of voices, hoping he wasn't walking in to one of his son's drug-fests.

He raised a fist and knocked. The door inched open. "Eliot?" He nudged it open further, waited, then stepped inside. As usual the place was dark and putrid.

His son sat on the sunken couch, staring at the flickering television. Empty liquor bottles were scattered across the floor and covered the lopsided table in front of him. Mounds of cigarette butts and ashes spilled from Styrofoam cups.

"Eliot?" Adrenaline pricked his veins as he stepped forward.

His son glanced his way then stared straight

ahead, lifting a vodka bottle to his mouth. He took a long swig then rested it in his lap.

Mitch moved in front of him. "Hey."

Eliot raised cold eyes and took another drink.

"Listen, I . . ." Mitch made a visual sweep of the area, shoved his hands in his pockets. Looked at his son again. "I've got something I've . . ." He raked a hand through his hair and released a puff of air. "I forgive you."

Eliot flinched, and when he raised the bottle again, his hand trembled.

"I know it probably felt like I blamed you for your brother's death, and I'm sorry. That must've been hard. You must have felt so alone. Can you forgive me?"

Eliot's shoulder's caved forward and began to quake. The bottle slipped from his hand onto the floor.

Mitch drew closer, cleared the garbage off the cushions beside Eliot. "I'm so sorry, bud. I messed up big time. I should've been there for you." He drew his son's shaking body to him, held his head in the crook of his arm. After a few moments, he pulled away and lifted his son's chin until their eyes met. "Whatever you need, I'm here, you got that?"

Eliot sniffed. Wiped his nose on the back of his arm. After what felt like five minutes but was probably only two, Mitch stood. What else could he do? What else could he say? What he should've said long ago. "I love you. Always have. Always will."

Eliot stared at him. Mitch turned toward the door, a deep ache filling his chest. He wasn't sure what he'd been expecting, but this was a start, right? Least now his son knew how much he loved him. Shoulders slumped, he reached for the doorknob.

"Dad?"

He turned around to find Eliot standing.

"I need help."

Mitch's heart leapt, painful memories fighting against rising hope. "Really?"

Eliot nodded. "I can't do this anymore. Can't live like this."

"Son!" Tears sprang to Mitch's eyes, and he dashed across the living room, grabbing his boy in a tight embrace. "I'm with you every step, bud. We'll do this together."

"I told you, I don't want to hear it." Bianca pulled a sharp right, sharper and faster than she'd intended. Her headlights reflected off the dark, rain-slicked road. Exhaling, she relaxed her grip on the steering wheel and cast her fuming daughter a sideways glance. "It's Thanksgiving. I wasn't going to let him spend it alone."

"Yeah, well, he did it to himself." C. J. slouched further into her seat and leaned against her window.

Bianca sighed and watched her sleeping boys through the rearview mirror. At least they'd seemed to have a decent night at Grandma's, despite the fact that over half the family ended up drunk.

She pulled into her driveway, grinding her molars together to keep from crying. Staying angry was easier. Before she'd put her car in park, C. J. jumped out and dashed up the stairs. Bianca let the engine idle, closed her eyes, and leaned back against the headrest.

She thought of the devotional Virginia had given her, with the sweet note written on the cover page: *God has a plan for you, and even now, He's working out that plan.*

Some plan this was. Jobless, husband in jail, daughter who hates her. Too broke to pay next month's rent.

You still praying, Virginia? Because if you are, you best stop. I don't need these kinds of blessings.

She'd do better to stay off God's radar completely.

Car parked, she swiveled toward her boys, tapped her youngest's knee. "Hey. We're home."

Sebastian's head drooped forward at an awkward angle, his mouth open. Robby leaned against the window, snoring. Looking so peaceful, so innocent, reminding her of everything that was good in the world. As long as she had them, held tight to them, provided for them, everything would be fine. And first thing tomorrow, she'd head down to the GasMart to see about getting a job.

She opened the door and started to step out when C. J.'s voice stopped her. "You going to answer me?"

Bianca huffed. "What're you griping about now?" Snapping at the teen wouldn't help, but exhaustion had seeped the patience straight from her.

"What's all this?"

"What're you talking about?"

"All this junk." Beneath the porch light, C. J. rummaged through one of three bags. "Dude! Smoked salmon and fancy cheese, with crackers! And some of that fancy chocolate, like the kind in those TV commercials."

Bianca stared from her daughter to the bag with a wrinkled brow. "I have no idea." She rounded to the back seat, jostled Robby awake, and scooped Sebastian into her arms. Fighting to keep her grip, she lumbered up the steps, Robby's footsteps crunching behind her.

"Let me get your brother to bed." She passed C. J. "I'll be back."

"Looks like a turkey too, in this roasting pan." Tinfoil rustled as C. J. continued to go through the mysterious deposit.

"Turkey? From who?" Supporting her son with

a bent knee, she unlocked the door and huffed inside. From that crazy Meadows lady most likely.

That was kind of nice. Real nice, actually. Especially now, with her being as broke as she was.

"Can I have some of the chocolate?" C. J. called after her, not letting up until Bianca had laid Sebastian in bed and shuffled back outside.

She stood, staring at it all—three packages worth along with a pie dish and two roasting pans, both covered in foil. "You can have whatever you want." A smile tugged. When had she ever said that in regard to food? It felt good. "After you help me bring all this in."

Without hesitating, C. J. grabbed two bags, deposited them, then returned for more. Bianca reached for one of the pans, stopping when an envelope caught her eye. She picked it up. Her name was written in cursive across the front. Sliding a finger under the flap, she opened it.

I hope you all had a great Thanksgiving. I've been thinking about you a lot. I pray for you daily. I know how hard it can be as a single mom. I was one myself, for a long, long time, and it was tough. I felt so lonely. What I longed for most was to have an adult to talk with.

Anyway, just wanted to extend another

coffee invitation. And thanks for letting me borrow your kids for a hike the other day. I can use more childish laughter! Love your neighbor and hopefully, friend, Angela.

Bianca gazed across the street at the lit house. An extra car sat in the driveway, and the faint flicker of a television set glowed from the living room window. Reid always said Christians had an agenda, that they acted all nice to get you to come to their church then dropped you the moment you got dunked. If not sooner. But that didn't seem true with Angela. Not Mitch, either. Matter of fact, they asked nothing from her. Seemed to expect nothing, either.

Now two women were praying for her.

She leaned against the porch railing and stared at the starry sky. What if she prayed? Would God listen?

Chapter 44

Angela sat on Joline's floor, empty bottles, reels of ribbon, pacifiers, and bibs to her right, scissors and gift tags to her left.

"This is such a wonderful idea." She smiled, first at Joline then at Ginger, the director of Midwest Crisis Pregnancy Center. "How many women do you help in a given month?"

Ginger sat back on her feet. "On average, anywhere between 30 and 40. Most of those receive walk-in care. Pregnancy tests, formula. Some take parenting classes. We also help women study for their GED, learn life skills, that sort of thing." She grabbed a pamphlet from her purse and handed it to Angela.

Angela thought about her own crisis pregnancy, so many years ago. Would she have made the same choice, had she known of a place like that?

Joline touched her shoulder. "You OK?"

Angela nodded. "I'm just . . ." She watched Ginger, so patient, so gentle, so . . . accepting. Then she looked at the gift packages she'd made—five so far, each for a woman in crisis. And each made with a joy she couldn't quite express. A joy that felt so . . . purposeful. So very important. "I'm just really glad to be here."

Ginger smiled and patted her hand. "I understand completely."

"I'm really glad you're here as well." Joline pulled Angela into a sideways hug.

"I've been meaning to come before." She glanced from face to face, faltered for a minute when her gaze landed on Frances sitting in a corner recliner. The woman almost appeared to be glaring at her, but then again, Angela had a tendency to think everyone hated her. Frances was probably just a sour apple.

Forcing a smile, she shifted in Joline's direction. "What I mean is, I've been wanting to join your Bible study for a while now. I've just been so . . ." Lying didn't become her, and admitting she'd allowed her fear of rejection to paralyze her seemed childish. So instead, she flicked her hand. "I hope to start coming more often. Not just for the service projects."

The rest of the night, Angela listened to the stories Ginger shared—of a young woman who changed her mind about having an abortion on the procedure table. Of a young man who had prayed fervently for his unborn child, feeling powerless against the mother's choice only to find himself holding a healthy, plump baby boy seven months later. Of another woman, a child, really, who felt she had no choice but to get an abortion but who had chosen life instead and went on to not only have the child but also finish high school and college.

But there were sad stories too. Of women who had not chosen life and had been plagued by regret and shame for the rest of their lives.

Like her.

Why did You bring me here, Lord?

She thought back to the first day she saw Cassie Joe, climbing out of her boyfriend's car, and the deep, haunting pain that had filled her heart. How she'd seen herself in the teen, and how that had triggered an incredible longing to help. Before the teen threw her life away, like Angela had done.

And now she was here. Could it be that God had brought her here, not just to Omaha, but to this living room with these ladies, filling gift packages for unwed pregnant moms? Pregnant teens?

Teens she could help, because she'd been there. She'd never be able to undo what she'd done, but she could help keep other pregnant teens from making the same mistake. *I'm going to make things right, Momma. I will.* If only her mother were still around to see how much Angela had changed. How much she would still change. *Oh, Momma, I miss you.* She'd wasted so much time, time she could've spent repairing their relationship. But now it was too late. She blinked back tears and busied herself filling a basket with baby items, casting frequent glances Ginger's way.

She waited until Ginger migrated to the kitchen alone to approach her.

"Hi." Her stomach knotted. "Can I . . . ?" She smoothed her hair behind her ears, clutched her hands in front of her. "I was really touched by the stories you shared."

Ginger smiled. "Thanks. God is good."

"He is." She tugged on her necklace. "I . . . I understand what those women feel. What it's like to carry a child when you're still a child yourself." Her words came out slow at first, halting, but soon picked up speed. "I never thought about getting pregnant. I know I should've, but I was too young. Too stupid. Too in love to care about anything other than making my boyfriend happy."

Ginger's eyes softened, and she gave an encouraging nod.

"But then, well, it happened." Her voice hitched. "I wish I would've kept the baby, but I was so scared. I was sure, if I did, my boyfriend would leave me. He paid for the abortion, set me up with a sleazy doctor in the back of a rank warehouse." A tear slid down her cheek, and she wiped it away. "It was a different time, you know?"

"I'm so sorry."

"Anyway, I guess what I was wanting to say

393

is, I'd really like to serve. If you could use me."

"Absolutely. Actually, I was planning on starting an abortion recovery support group. It would be great to have someone who's been there, who's had an abortion herself, to help these women heal." She reached into her back pocket and handed Angela a business card. "Call me Monday?"

"I will." Heart lighter, she grabbed a cookie and turned around, startled to find Frances watching her.

The woman raised her eyebrows. Then, with a curt nod to Ginger, she entered the kitchen and reached for the teapot. "That was a touching story." Her flat tone contradicted her words.

Angela released the air she'd been holding. "Thanks." Her cheeks flamed, and yet, embarrassed or not, there was no sense hiding her past. Especially not if God wanted to use it to help someone else. "God's grace still amazes me."

"Indeed." Frances poured steaming water into her mug. "Is that how you and Mitch came to know one another then? Because of your past?"

"Um . . . I don't understand."

She shrugged. "The church pairs him up with folks needing his help all the time. He's quite giving in that way, always ready to reach out to the broken. I'm sure you agree."

"I—" Was that why Mitch had been so nice to

394

her? If Ainsley had told the Martins of her past, and considering the family went to his church . . . surely she hadn't . . .

But of course she had. It made perfect sense. Why else would a man like Mitch Kenney be interested in a woman like her? And if he didn't know about Angela's past, he would find out soon enough and leave her anyway. All men did eventually. Either way, their relationship was over. If not because of her past, then something else. There was always something else. She'd never been able to hold on to a relationship for long. Nor had any of her past relationships ended well.

Ainsley had been right. Angela had no business meddling with romance.

Chapter 45

Wednesday morning, Mitch rapped on Pastor Kaplan's opened office door.

"My man, come in." The pastor smiled, meeting Mitch halfway. Tall, muscular, and often dressed in faded jeans and trendy T-shirts, the man looked more like a college student than someone nearing 40.

"Thanks for seeing me." He extended a hand and the two shook before sitting, Pastor Kaplan behind his desk, Mitch across from him.

"My pleasure." The pastor settled back in his seat. "How've things been?"

"Good. Well, mainly." Not counting the increasing drama between him and Dennis.

"You ever sell your remodel, the one on 35th Street?"

Mitch shook his head. "There's a greater demand for rentals right now. Got a military family moving in next month—they signed a one year lease with the option to buy later."

"Nice. How's Eliot?"

A grin stretched Mitch's cheeks, the tension seeping from his shoulders. "Awesome." He relayed his recent encounter with his son. "I know what you're thinking. Sheila and I have been down this road before. But I think this is the real deal this time. Eliot wants to go. Asked for help."

The pastor's eyebrows shot up. Then he chuckled. "Now that is an answer to prayer."

"It is. Nothing short of a miracle."

"What do you need from me?"

"Besides a boatload of prayer?" Though he passed it off as a joke, the truth of his words laid heavy. Fighting addiction wouldn't be easy or quick. More likely, it'd be a lifelong battle for Eliot, one ready to rear its head at the first hint of weakness. Which was why Mitch felt certain they'd need support from his church family. But he'd find that with his Bible study group. "Although that's not why I'm here."

"Oh? Is everything all right?"

"Sort of. I'm trying to help a single mom I know." He explained Bianca's situation, including her impending eviction.

"So your partner's pretty set in his decision, then?"

"I'm afraid so." Mitch sighed. "To be honest, I know this is for the best. The Bible tells us not to be unequally yoked with nonbelievers." Of course, Mitch and Dennis had gone into business together well before Mitch came to Christ, complicating things once he had. "I'd really like to be as amicable as possible, to salvage what I can of our friendship. With minimal collateral damage."

"I see. And you wanted to know more about our benevolent fund?"

"Correct."

"Unfortunately, that money is typically ear-marked for members, and with Christmas coming up, those donations are pretty tapped dry." He rubbed the back of his hand under his chin. "I'm not sure there's a whole lot we can do, except maybe offer the young woman some gift cards."

"I see." Mitch stared at the small plastic container of paperclips on the pastor's desk, thinking. "Are there any ministries who could maybe help her out?" Except he'd already called everyone he knew of. They were all low on funds and high on needs. Which is why he kept coming back to the church. With over 800 congregants, many of whom worked white-collar jobs, surely they could come up with something. If they knew of the need.

"You could try Midland Family Restoration. Maybe New Beginnings." The pastor rolled in his chair to a low-lying shelf behind him, returning to his desk with a binder. He opened it and pulled out a few information sheets, which he handed over, none of the contacts new to Mitch.

"Thanks. I've tried all those." He paused, an idea forming. "Have you seen those gift-giving trees set up in the malls? The ones with ornaments on them listing kids' names and needs."

"Yeah. Hannah's Heart organizes that, I believe. Want me to find their number?"

"No. I mean, you could, but . . . what if we did something like that? Started an adopt-a-family program? We've got some crazy-generous people at our church. I'm certain they'd help, if they knew how."

"You might be right." The pastor pulled a pen from his holder and jotted something onto a sticky-note. "I'm meeting with the elder board later this week. I'll mention the idea. Tell them you'd be willing to head it up?"

Oh. Mitch hadn't considered that, and yet, he knew better than to suggest a new ministry unless he was willing to help with the heavy lifting. "Sure. I can do that."

He stood, and the pastor walked him out, sending him off with a friendly clamp on his shoulder. "I really appreciate all you do for Abiding Fellowship, Mitch. Keep up the great work. And I'm thrilled to hear about your son."

"Thanks." With a parting nod, Mitch rounded the corner and headed down the empty hall toward the main sanctuary.

When he reached the welcome desk, the front door swooshed open, ushering in a gust of cold air. Frances approached, pulling a rolling cart packed full of partially filled plastic tubs. They seemed to contain various craft supplies.

"Mitch, what a pleasant surprise." She stopped

a few feet away, carrying with her the scent of pine and . . . some sort of flower. "What're you doing here?"

"Had a meeting with the pastor." He'd never been one to brag about his ministry efforts. Besides, there was no sense talking about something that might not happen.

"Your lady friend came to our Bible study last night."

"Oh?" The word popped out with more enthusiasm than he'd intended. But then again, he was falling hard for that woman. Why hide it? This wasn't junior high. "I'm glad. I was hoping she'd get plugged in."

"Well, you certainly did all you could to help in that regard." She propped her forearm on the counter. "I really admire your tender heart and how you always try to help women like her out."

Women like her? "Newcomers, you mean?"

"That and . . . the downtrodden and shame-filled." She shook her head. "Poor thing. She's been through a lot, through her own poor choices, of course. But even so, there's always grace."

Mitch frowned, thinking back to a previous conversation he'd had with Bones. What had happened in Angela's past to worry her daughter so? Come to think of it . . . she never invited him into her house, was always quick to suggest they sit on the porch. Had she been violated? His temperature soared. No wonder Angela's daughter wanted her to stay away from men. She was probably terrified, having her mom live alone like she was. Angela as well. All the more reason for him to tread gently, show her he could be trusted.

Frances started to walk away then turned back around. "I do suggest you remain cautious. Considering her past and all. We both know women like her can grow accustomed to using manipulation to get what they want. Not on purpose, mind you. It's simply all they know. Which is why we, the spiritually healthy, must make sure we're not reinforcing those negative behaviors, don't you agree?"

"What are you talking about?"

She angled her head. "You mean you don't know?"

A tendon in his jaw twitched. He was not a fan of playing games. "Know what?"

"About her . . . promiscuous lifestyle."

Mitch's teeth ground together as Frances went on to tell how Angela had experienced numerous sexual encounters, beginning when she was but a teen, one of which resulted in an abortion.

"She admitted to the one, but I suspect she's had more, as is often the case with . . . well, you know." Frances shrugged. "Of course, I'm glad she came to our study. And that she felt comfortable sharing so much of her past. Yet, with such a history . . ."

"I have no interest in the woman's past, nor is it appropriate for you to be sharing it, with me or anyone else."

"Oh, I'm not trying to gossip."

Yeah, right. He started to walk away.

The rhythmic click of her footsteps followed. "I just . . ." She sighed and shook her head. "I'm worried about her."

Mitch stopped in midstep and faced Frances. "About what?"

"Are you two dating?"

"What's this about, Frances?" This conversation was beginning to remind him of middle school, and he had no intention of regressing.

"I just think she needs some space. Did you know she's serving at the pregnancy center?"

He nodded.

"Being around those women, counseling them against abortion and hearing about their . . . relational choices . . . I think it's just too much for her, you know? I think maybe she needs some time, to sort everything out."

"Is that what she said?"

"Not in so many words, but . . ." She paused. "From what I hear, she's never had much luck with men, and I think . . ." She flicked a hand. "I'm sure you'll do what you feel is best."

Mitch watched her leave, questions swirling through his mind. What had happened to leave Angela so wounded? Domestic abuse

402

wasn't uncommon, especially when unwanted pregnancies were involved. Should he ask her about it? Except if what Frances said were true, now wasn't the best time. No. It sounded like maybe Angela needed to process some old hurts. Hopefully that processing wouldn't cause her to end things between them. Until then, there wasn't anything Mitch could do but wait. And pray.

Chapter 46

Humming to herself, Bianca pulled open the blinds, allowing the midmorning sun to flood her living room. Ice crystals glistened on her front lawn beneath a deceptively blue sky. According to rumors, they were in for an early and heavy snow.

She laughed, remembering her kids' conversation over breakfast, the three of them already hoping school would be canceled tomorrow. At least they'd agreed on something! A morning without a fight had done Bianca a mess of good. Didn't hurt that she actually had plenty to feed them. Over a week since Thanksgiving, and they were still enjoying all the food Angela dropped on their doorstep.

She glanced at the clock. Already 10:45. No sense wasting any more of her day. Starting tomorrow, she'd be working splits all week at the GasMart. Nothing like losing an entire day to pick up a handful of hours, but at least she had a job. Until she found something better or got promoted. She could be a store manager, right? There had to be more money in that. Benefits too.

Musing over what life would look like should she ever get a career—she liked the sound of that, *career*—she strolled into the kitchen. Her place was a disaster, and something in the kitchen smelled foul. She wrinkled her nose and pulled the garbage out from under the sink. The stench of soured milk rolled her stomach.

Turning her face away, she dragged the container from room to room, tossing in junk and emptying other cans. She spent a full ten minutes in Robby's room, digging garbage out from under his bed, from the corners of his closet, his sock drawer even.

By the time she'd reached the bathroom, she'd worked up a sweat.

"Children, can you make it inside the trash for once?" She tossed a wadded tissue into the garbage. Then, grabbing the bathroom container, she poured it into the kitchen can.

Spilling a chunk of it onto the floor.

She fell to her knees with a groan. Nastiness. And now she'd have to vacuum too. She lifted a wad of paper towels and froze.

Surely that wasn't . . . a white plastic stick lay on the floor. "Oh, Cassie Joe, what've you gone and done now?" She picked up the wand with a shaky hand and stared at the plus sign in the window.

Her daughter was pregnant. "Not my baby. Please, no." She was throwing her life away, just like Bianca had done. "What are we going to do now?"

The question swirled again and again through

her brain as memories of when Bianca had been C. J.'s age flashed through her mind. Of her telling her boyfriend, certain he'd stand by her.

He'd only sneered at her. "This ain't my kid."

His words had stunned her. "What are you talking about?" She'd reached for him, but he jerked her hand away.

"Girl, you've been giving it up since I met you. Best get rid of that thing, before you balloon into a whale."

Her mom had said the same thing—told her to "take care of it" before she threw her life away. Bianca hadn't listened, and she'd been paying the price ever since.

But not C. J.

She sat at the kitchen table, staring at the front door, while the clock ticked above her.

Robby and Sebastian came home first, barging in. Robby tossed his backpack on the floor. "Hey." He angled his head. "You off tonight?"

"Something like that."

He studied her a moment longer then moved out of her peripheral vision and into the living room. The television clicked on. "Can I have a hot dog?"

"Yeah, me too?" Sebastian asked.

"Whatever."

She could feel them watching her. But their steps entered the kitchen. The fridge opened, shut. Footsteps shuffled past, back into the living room.

And still Bianca sat.

She was still at the table, hands folded in front of her, when C. J. arrived an hour later.

"Hey." She smiled and dropped her backpack by the door, her smile soon fading. "What's up?"

Bianca's lips pressed together so firmly, they began to tingle. "Sit."

She did, the chair legs squeaking beneath her.

"Found something in the garbage today." Bianca pulled the pregnancy test, wrapped in a paper towel, from her pocket, and set it in front of her daughter.

C. J. just stared at it, her bottom lip quivering.

"Go ahead." Bianca flung a hand her direction. "Open the paper towel. Let's see what kind of surprise you got waiting for us." C. J. remained stock-still, so Bianca did it for her. "Why? Why you got to throw your life away like this?" Her voice trembled.

"I didn't mean to." C. J. spoke so softly, Bianca could barely hear her. Tears flooded her face. "I'm sorry. I'm so sorry."

"Lot of good sorry will do you." She closed her eyes and rubbed her face with both hands. "What now, huh? Tell me that. Because I for sure know you've got no business raising a child."

Nor could Bianca raise the baby for her. She had trouble enough keeping her own kids fed. Besides, with her crazy hours and C. J. in school, there'd be no one to watch the child. And no way could she afford day care.

"I'm going to tell Gabe, and he'll—"

Bianca cursed. "You think that loser's going to stand beside you? Play the daddy role?" She shook her head. "You're not keeping it, I can tell you that much." She straightened, breathed deep. "I'll make you an appointment at the clinic tomorrow."

"I don't want an abortion." C. J.'s hands flew to her stomach.

"Yeah, well you don't have a choice. You gave that up the minute you got knocked up." She stood. "This conversation is over."

In Ginger's office at Midwest Crisis Pregnancy Center, Angela perched at the edge of her seat. A heavy binder filled with training manuals and procedures rested on her lap. On top of this lay *Rescued From Darkness: One Woman's Post-Abortion Story*.

"I'm so excited to begin serving here." A lump filled her throat. "This is such a good fit for me. Such a very good fit." Lyrics from a song Ainsley wrote, one she often sang as she flitted about the house on Sunday afternoons, came to mind. "Restoring Love."

Forget what has gone before
The past need not haunt you anymore
God's grace is pouring from above
Rest in His restoring love.

Ginger smiled. "I agree. Having experienced the psychological effects of abortion yourself, you'll connect with these women like many of my other volunteers can't. Simply because they haven't been there."

She nodded, thinking back to that eerily dark day when she lay on a cold table, staring at the stark white ceiling. As the sedatives began to take control, her heart had thrashed against her rib cage. A scream welled up within as a desire to run overcame her. And yet, she'd pushed those thoughts aside, told herself again and again she was making the right choice. That it would soon be over. She'd had no idea how false those words would be.

"I'll see you Tuesday afternoon, then?" Ginger stood.

Angela grabbed her purse and jacket from the back of her chair. "Four o'clock." As a full-fledged, fully trained volunteer. Her smile grew as she exited the office. She couldn't wait to call Ainsley.

Except Ainsley didn't know about the abortion.

She frowned, her step slowing. She'd have to tell her eventually, of course. It was only a matter of time before word got out, and she didn't want Ainsley to hear it from someone else.

What about Mitch? He'd find out too. Things like this traveled fast in church circles. He'd be disgusted. Maybe even hate her. If she knew anything about Christians, it was how much they hated abortion and everything to do with it.

Hadn't she known better than to get involved romantically with a man? It never worked out, not for her. She was damaged goods. Shameful. Mitch deserved someone better. He'd realize that soon enough, and then where would she be? Heartbroken, like always. All her life, men had easily discarded her. How many men told her they loved her only to leave once they really got to know her? Mitch would do the same, especially when he learned of her abortion. Matter of fact, she hadn't heard from him or seen him in a while. Not since . . . the Bible study? Could be he was busy, or that he found out and decided he was done with her. Experience told her it was most likely the latter.

But he could only hurt her if she let him. She needed to add distance between her and Mitch. She couldn't handle yet another rejection.

Ignoring the ache within, she slipped on her coat and stepped out into the cold. It'd begun to rain, and was quickly turning to sleet. Her feet sloshed in the parking lot, moisture creeping into the canvas of her shoes. Thick, dark clouds advanced across the gray sky, a dull glow giving a hint of where the sun stood.

She reached her car, shivering, and pulled her coat collar tighter around her neck. The temperature must have dropped ten degrees since she'd first arrived. Sliding behind the steering wheel, she started the engine and cranked the heat, cringing when a blast of cold air flooded her face. Her car didn't warm up until she was a block from home.

As she neared her house, a huddled form to her right caught her peripheral vision. She pulled to the curb and idled. What in the—? Cassie Joe sat on the bottom of the Douglases' porch, sopping wet, face buried in her knees.

Had something happened? Another raid? Worse? Bianca's car wasn't in the drive, and the house shades were drawn. Where were the other children?

Angela lowered her window, a gust of icy rain spraying her in the face. "Cassie Joe?"

No response. Probably couldn't hear her over the wind.

"Cassie Joe?" She called out a few more times with no response then pulled into her driveway. Throwing the car in park, she jumped out. Rain pelted her face and back and caused goose pimples to erupt on her arm. By the time she reached Cassie Joe, she was soaked through, as was the teen.

"Sweetie, what are you doing out here?" She placed her hands on the girl's shoulders and squatted in front of her. Cassie Joe's eyes were bloodshot, red-rimmed, and swollen, her lips tainted blue. Mascara streaked her face. "Honey, you're freezing."

She slipped off her jacket and wrapped it around the girl. Then, gently urging Cassie Joe to her feet, she placed a protective arm around her shoulder. "Come on. Let's get you warm." *Oh, Father, help me. Help her. Give me the words to say.*

Casting a glance at the dim house behind her, she guided the whimpering teen across the street and inside. "You wanna take a shower?"

Cassie Joe didn't respond so Angela led her into the bathroom and pulled a stack of towels—three, all that she owned—from the cupboard.

"I'll be back with some dry clothes." Angela left her standing in the center of the bathroom, water dripping from her and pooling at her feet, and dashed to her bedroom. She returned with exercise pants, a T-shirt, and her bathrobe. Then, she turned the water on and let it run until it reached a comfortable temperature.

She rested a hand on the doorknob. "I'll have some hot tea and toast waiting for you."

Cassie Joe lifted teary eyes and gave a slight nod. "Thanks."

Closing the door behind her, Angela hurried

to her room to change clothes. Then, grabbing a T-shirt to dry her hair, she went to the living room to wait. Cassie Joe didn't emerge for 45 minutes, long after the tea Angela made went cold. But the color had returned to the teen's lips and cheeks, and though her face was still drawn, she was no longer crying.

"You hungry?" Angela guided Cassie Joe to the couch. A plate of cinnamon toast waited on the coffee table in front of her.

She shrugged and began to tear off chunks of crust, lining the pieces along the edge of her plate.

"I'll reheat your tea." Angela took her mug and hurried to the kitchen. By the time she returned, Cassie Joe had eaten half of her toast. Good. Hopefully that meant she was beginning to relax.

Angela waited until she'd finished it all before initiating conversation. "What happened, sweetie?"

Cassie Joe gave another shrug, and her eyes teared up once again. "My mom hates me."

"Oh, honey." Her heart squeezed. She placed an arm around Cassie Joe's shoulder. "That can't be true. She's your mother. She loves you, and she always will."

Yet, Angela didn't know Bianca. Some women did indeed behave as if they hated their children, especially if drugs or alcohol were involved.

She peered through the living room window

413

and thought again of all the police cars that had been lined outside Bianca's house not long ago. What was life like over in that house? To hear Mitch talk, all the criminal activity was the husband's fault, but what if he was wrong? Oh, those poor children.

She turned back to Cassie Joe and handed her some folded paper towels left over from painting. She didn't have tissue. "What makes you think she hates you?"

Cassie Joe swiped at her tears then her nose. "I really blew it this time. I thought he loved me. But the minute he found out I was pregnant, he ditched."

"Oh, sweetie." Nausea bubbled as Angela remembered the day when she sat in Cassie Joe's place—the overwhelming fear and shame.

"My mom wants me to have an abortion, 'cept she says we can't afford it. Said she hopes the women's clinic will do it for free or I'm in real trouble." Her voice trembled. "But I . . . But I . . . what about those people who say abortion is murder?"

Oh, Lord, give me the words. "How long has it been since your last period?"

Cassie Joe tugged on a strand of hair. "I don't know. Four weeks. Maybe six."

She nodded, so grateful she'd just completed her four-day training session at Midwest Crisis. "At 28 days your baby is the size of a poppy seed, and all of his or her organs are beginning to develop. By the sixth week, his or her little nose, eyes, and mouth are beginning to form."

Cassie Joe lifted her head.

"And you . . ." Angela playfully poked Cassie Joe in the side, "are going through major hormone changes. Let me guess—you're beginning to wonder if you have split personalities, feeling goofy happy one minute and utterly heartbroken the next?"

Cassie Joe smiled. "Something like that. Doesn't help my mom won't hardly speak to me. Like I did this on purpose or something."

"She's just scared. Us moms act crazy when we get scared. Because we love our kids so much and want the absolute best for them."

"So getting an abortion's for the best?"

"Honestly?" She paused. "Many people think getting an abortion will fix everything, but they're wrong. It only makes things worse. The sorrow and guilt—" She swallowed and shook her head. "It's relentless. The pain never goes away." She enveloped Cassie Joe's hands in her own. "I know, because I'm one of them. Having an abortion is the biggest mistake I ever made."

Cassie Joe was quiet for a long moment. She took a shuddered breath. "So what do I do about my mom? If I choose to keep my baby, how do I tell her?"

"Want me to go with you?"

"I'd like that."

But first, Angela needed to pray because this was going to be one of the most difficult, and urgent, conversations she'd had in some time. *Lord give me the words, and show me the proper time. More than that, give me courage.* This would be a tough conversation, and the stakes couldn't be higher. Angela couldn't mess this one up.

Chapter 47

Mitch dropped the letter he'd received from Dennis's lawyer onto the coffee table and paced the living room. He couldn't believe it'd come to this. After all he and Dennis had been through. To think his longtime friend would even consider suing him. And for mismanagement? As if Dennis hadn't been an equal partner this whole time. True, he'd fought Mitch on numerous decisions, but no judge would rule in his favor.

Right?

Most likely Dennis and his lawyer were bluffing. Even so, the longer Mitch let this garbage drag on, the greater the barrier between him and Dennis would grow.

He sighed and flopped onto the couch. What now?

Seemed he was boxed in. Only way out was to liquidate, which meant evicting the Douglases. The other tenants were safe, until their leases ran out. And maybe even after that, if Mitch could get the judge to award him those properties, giving the other listings to Dennis. Wouldn't he prefer that? Their flips would provide much higher payouts.

No sense getting all worked up over a bunch of what-ifs, however imminent. Mitch needed to check on their 35th Street property. Make sure the recent snowfall hadn't frozen their pipes. And check on the Douglases one last time to see if, by some miracle, Bianca had managed to scrape up rent money. And if not . . .

It was out of his hands.

He pulled on his jacket and headed out the door. A thin layer of powdery snow covered the ground and his truck's windshield, enough to require a bit of scraping. He'd hoped the activity would use his pent up energy, but in reality, it only gave his thoughts more time to spin. By the time he arrived at the property 15 minutes later, the muscles in his jaw ached from all his teeth grinding.

Pulling into the driveway, he paused to watch Angela's house. How was she holding up? He thought back to what Frances had said about her abortion and needing space. Was Frances telling the truth? Why would she lie about something like that? Angela was in her Bible study. Maybe she'd said something. Maybe she'd even said something about Mitch. Part of him wanted to march on over to her house and ask her, but that was selfish. Right?

Lord, show me what to do.

He'd never been good at initiating tough conversations. Most of the time, his attempts only made things worse. And this wasn't a relationship he was willing to blow.

Zipping up his jacket, he turned off his truck and got out, stalking straight for his remodel. A car engine hummed to his right. He paused with a foot on the bottom porch step and watched Angela pull into her drive. She looked at him, her face stoic. Then, she looked away.

What if she was done with him? Decided she needed space permanently?

Shoulders slumping, he turned back toward his property, stomped the snow from his boots, and opened the door. His skin tingled when warm, centrally circulated air swept over him.

He made a visual sweep of the decorated living room. Leather couch, matching love seat and recliner. Forty-inch flat-screen television. Coffee table and one end table with a silver vase on top. All rented. Time to return everything to the rental company. Make sure his new tenants got the utilities switched over into their name.

He moved into the kitchen to check the faucet and under the sink. Then he continued from room to room, giving everything a once-over. The place was beginning to smell a bit musty, but other than that, everything looked good.

Locking up, he stopped on the porch to study Bianca's property. Her car sat parked in the driveway, free of snow, indicating she hadn't been home long.

Too bad he hadn't made more progress on the adopt-a-family ministry, but those things took time. Time Bianca didn't have. If not for his son's rehab expenses, he might've paid more of her rent himself, though he'd already helped her out quite a bit. But, looking at a $20,000-plus bill coming his way, he didn't have that luxury anymore. And that's where his priorities needed to stay right now—with his son. Hopefully sobriety would stick this time.

He crossed through the yard and street, continuing to Bianca's stoop. He rang her doorbell then waited as footsteps approached.

A gust of wind swept over him, sending a chill up his exposed neck. He tugged his jacket collar tighter and rang again.

After an extended moment, Bianca answered, her body slumped. "Hi." She wore jeans and a red T-shirt, the name of a nearby gas station written on the right.

She'd changed jobs? Why? She couldn't be making more than minimum wage. A woman could hardly provide for herself on that kind of income, let alone feed three kids. No wonder she hadn't paid her rent. And here he was about to take money from her. The fact that she owed him didn't make him feel any better.

Fighting to hold her gaze, he shoved his hands in his pockets. "Listen, I know things are tight, but I—"

"I know why you're here, Mr. Kenney, and I wish I had my rent money for you. But all's I got is a couple hundred." She raised a hand to her neck, her eyes sad. Defeated. "Hold on. I'll get you what I got." She eased the door closed so only a sliver remained open.

He took in a long, slow breath. It felt as if a heavy stone had settled in the pit of his stomach. He'd had to evict people before. It came with being a landlord, but never a woman with kids. And especially not one he'd tried so hard to help.

Bianca returned with a bank envelope. "Here's $235. All I got." Her voice trembled.

He swallowed hard and opened the envelope. He pulled the two Benjamins and handed the rest over. "Here. I don't want to take your last dollar."

"What's a little cash gonna do for us when we're out on the streets?" Her voice held a bite, though she took the money. "Dennis called. Said y'all were gonna start the eviction process. That true?"

Unless God intervened. "Might have to."

She nodded, stared at him a moment longer, then stepped back. "You do what you gotta do." She closed the door.

Chapter 48

Angela stared out her living room window, her heart aching. She couldn't get Mitch's dull expression out of her mind. His face used to light up when he saw her, as if that were the best part of his day. Clearly something had changed. And Sunday at church, he'd barely said two words to her. Even then he'd acted strange. Guarded.

He must've found out about her past—stuff like that traveled fast in church prayer chains. Obviously, her abortion had disgusted him. Did she blame him? She was disgusted herself. To think she once used men—and her daughter—for money. Now she was paying the consequences. But at least Christ had restored her and Ainsley's relationship, helped Angela get a degree, a job. Even if it was a temporary position. She'd find another soon enough.

But right now, she had other things to worry about. She grabbed her phone to once again read the text message Cassie Joe had sent her: *When R U gonna talk 2 my mom? My abortion's Saturday.*

Those people at the women's clinic moved fast. Angela had hoped to talk to Bianca earlier but kept missing her. Her neighbor's schedule, it seemed, had become more unpredictable than ever. But after watching, through the front window, the interchange between Mitch and Bianca, Angela felt certain now wasn't a good time to initiate such an intense conversation. Though she couldn't see their faces, Mitch's body language as he walked away said it all. Something wasn't right. If she had to guess, she'd say Bianca had come up short on her rent, if she'd paid at all.

Another text chimed, making her jump: *I'm scared.*

So was Angela—for Cassie Joe and the potential conflict she was about to insert herself into. She wasn't any good at these types of things. But she had to do something, to say something. She'd promised Cassie Joe. Besides, it was the right thing to do. Regardless of how Bianca responded.

Angela closed her eyes. *Lord, help me.*

She didn't have time to wait for His answer. Angela texted Cassie Joe back. *I'm on my way now.*

She slipped on her coat and stepped outside. The wind picked up, whipping her hair about her face and making her eyes water. Her legs felt shaky, and her heart pounded so hard and fast, her chest hurt.

What am I doing? That woman hates me. I'll only make things worse.

Except a precious life was at stake, two actually.

Reaching Bianca's porch, she paused to breathe warmth over her chilled hands, then tapped the heel of her palm against the door.

It opened a moment later. Bianca stood on the other side, face drawn, eyes bloodshot. "Yeah?"

"Hi. Uh . . . can I come in?"

Bianca studied Angela. A car engine neared and passed behind them. A horn honked in the distance.

Angela shivered, icy wind biting at her cheeks.

Bianca sighed. "Come on." She stepped aside.

The aroma of roasting beans swept over Angela as she entered, warmth seeping into her wind-chaffed cheeks. Robby and Sebastian sat on the couch, completely engrossed in television.

Bianca walked into the kitchen and grabbed a wooden spoon. "I appreciate all the food you brought me on Thanksgiving. I've been meaning to thank you."

"My pleasure." She combed her fingers through her tangled hair then dabbed at the moisture, streaked with mascara, no doubt, below her eyes. "There's something I'd like—"

Cassie Joe approached from the hall. "Hi." She looked from Angela to her mom then back to Angela again.

Angela smiled. "Hi."

Bianca dropped her spoon and crossed her

arms, resting her rear against the counter. "What's this about?" She glared at her daughter. "You got something else you need to tell me?"

Cassie Joe's bottom lip quivered, her gaze shooting between the two ladies.

"Can we talk?" Angela motioned toward the kitchen table. "Please?"

Bianca glared at her daughter a moment longer then threw her hands up with a huff. "Sure. May as well throw another one at me." She yanked a chair back, and sat. Her daughter occupied the seat to her right.

Angela sat across from mother and daughter and rested tightly folded, clammy hands in her lap. It felt like stampeding caterpillars had taken up residence in her stomach. She lifted a leveled gaze. "Are you familiar with Midwest Crisis Pregnancy Center?"

Bianca swore. "You came to my house to get all religious on me. Is that it?"

Angela blinked. "Not at all. Your daughter came to me upset." She wiped sweaty hands on her thighs. "She thinks you hate her."

Tears shone in Bianca's eyes, and she turned to her daughter. "I don't hate you, Cassie Joe. I love you. You know that." Facing Angela again, she stood. "I appreciate you letting me know."

Angela remained seated. "Actually, there's more I'd like to talk to you about, if you don't mind."

Bianca remained standing, eyes wary, then slowly lowered to her seat. She waved a hand, as if motioning Angela on.

"I got pregnant when I was 16. My boyfriend was older. I was convinced he loved me, and I felt if I didn't do certain things, he'd leave me for an older, prettier girl. Then I got pregnant. I was terrified. I didn't know what to do." She swallowed. "My boyfriend said he knew of a place I could 'take care of it' downtown, so I went." She rubbed her arm to ward off a sudden chill.

"I see." Bianca's eyebrows pinched into a deep scowl.

"My aunt tried to stop me. Told me I'd regret it, but I didn't listen." She paused. "She was right. I've regretted that decision the rest of my life."

"Yeah, well. That was you." Bianca stood once again, her chair scooting behind her.

"But Mom, I don't want an abortion."

Bianca whirled to face her. "Girl, how you know what you want? You're just a kid. A kid who's got no business raising a child. And don't you think for a minute I'll raise it for you. How'm I gonna do that, being at work all the time?"

"I can handle it. I'll be responsible, I promise."

Bianca snorted. "Uh-huh. And who's going to pay for all the formula and diapers? You thought of that?"

"There's help," Angela said.

Bianca slammed both fists on the table, resting her weight on them. "How's any of this your business? That's what I want to know."

"I care for your daughter. And I want to help her. All of you."

"How you gonna do that? You going to pay my rent? Watch my kids and grandkids? Help C. J. here finish school so she can make something of herself?"

"I, ha—you could stay with me." The words flew out before she had time to process them. But her heart told her this was the right thing to do. "Until you get your feet back under you."

Bianca blinked, mouth agape. She stared at her for a moment longer, then slid back into her seat.

"I could help with the baby, and Cassie Joe could finish her schooling at home. I've got a teaching degree, so I could help."

"You'd do that? Take us in?"

Angela nodded.

"Why?"

"Because I wouldn't be sitting here today if someone hadn't offered me grace."

Bianca studied her hands, then pushed up from the table. Cassie Joe and Angela exchanged glances as Bianca walked to the counter, leaning her backside against it once again. She stood like that for some time, staring straight ahead.

Lord, soften her heart. Give her courage.

Angela resisted the urge to bite a fingernail.

427

Cassie Joe shifted, and Angela shot her a nervous glance, hoping the teen wouldn't say anything to startle her mother into a rash decision.

After what felt like an eternity but was probably only a few minutes, Bianca sighed. "Tell me about this pregnancy place."

Angela nodded, and released the breath she'd been holding. "They'll meet with Cassie Joe, present all her options."

"Like abortion?" Cassie Joe's eyes were wide.

Angela placed a hand over hers. "That is one of your options, yes, but not the only one. You can choose adoption, or raise the baby yourself, with help."

Bianca crossed her arms. "What kind of help?"

Afraid to misspeak, Angela tried to remember her training. "They've got nurses on staff who can take care of Cassie Joe's prenatal care, whether she chooses to raise the baby or allow another loving family to do so. Volunteer teachers can help her with her classes. Or, if she wants to get her GED, they can help her study for that as well."

Bianca returned to the table and sat. Cassie Joe visibly relaxed, offering Angela a hint of a smile.

"Plus, if Cassie Joe takes classes—they've got a bunch," Angela said, "parenting, financial management, life skills—she can earn shopping dollars to buy things she needs." Her stomach began to settle as she shared all the information she'd learned in the short time she'd been serving at the center, which was a lot. "I can take you there, if you'd like. So you can talk with the nurses directly. Discuss your options."

Bianca looked at Cassie Joe, her eyes soft and shiny. "That what you want to do?"

Angela held her breath.

Cassie Joe nodded. "I think so. To find out my options, like Ms. Meadows said."

It wasn't a resounding yes, but it was a first step. And if Angela had learned anything over the years, it was that God could do a lot with those tentative first steps.

Later that night, after the kids were in bed, Bianca grabbed a hot mug of tea and the devotional Virginia had given her and ambled into the living room. She curled into the corner of the couch and opened to the first page.

> If you have children, you understand the depth of a mother's love. The indescribable joy that fills your heart at the sound of their laughter. There's nothing you wouldn't do to keep them safe. If only you could walk beside them every day of their lives, guiding them away from danger and toward the very best. And as they grow and become more and more independent, to hold them close one last time.

Sweet Sister, God loves you with that same fierce, protective love. He longs more than anything to gather you close in His arms and lead you toward His very best—which is Himself. He alone will bring you rest.

She closed the book and held it to her chest. *I want that, God. Show me how to get that. Show me what to do.*

Chapter 49

Mitch stood in the hallway of Second Chance Recovery Center, blinking back tears. Eliot's admittance counselor, Mr. Vernet, waited a few feet away while Mitch and Sheila said their good-byes. Mitch's Bible study group had wanted to come, to support him more than anything else. And he'd wanted Nathan and his family to be here, but Eliot wanted to keep this simple. As unemotional as possible, as if walking your son into a treatment center that could quite literally save his life wasn't emotional.

Eliot stood across from him, a duffel bag in one hand, and in the other, an old, raggedy, flannel-cased pillow, one he'd kept since he was young, back when he and his brother shared a bedroom. "Guess this is it, huh?"

Mitch thought Eliot had tossed that thing, or forgotten it, long ago. Him clutching it now reminded him of the boy he once was, the boy he still was, vulnerable, scared. But incredibly courageous to take this step.

"Guess so." His voice turned husky. "Proud of you." He tousled his son's hair then pulled him in a headlock hug, casting Sheila a sideways glance.

She stood to his right, dabbing her nose with

wadded tissue. "Me too, son." She stepped forward, arms outstretched.

Mitch moved aside so the two could embrace. Sheila held Eliot for a long time, her shoulders quivering.

Pulling away, she took his hands in hers. "You can do this. It'll be hard, but you gotta push through."

Eliot nodded. "About time I manned up, huh?"

Mitch's phone chimed a text, the tenth one this morning. He glanced at it. The pastor had mentioned the adopt-a-family program in the church's e-blast. Only a week in, and he'd already paired three single moms with Bible study groups. Only two more to go, and everyone on his list would have a very merry Christmas.

Turning his phone off, he tucked it in his back pocket. "You got this." They fist bumped. "I'll be praying every day. Call as soon as you can."

Eliot wouldn't be allowed outside contact for the first ten days. According to the counselor, that was the most intense time of the treatment plan, a time when many patients wanted to give up. They didn't need any outside drama to tip the already weakened scales.

Sheila gave their son another hug and they said their last good-byes. Then Eliot disappeared behind the big, double doors separating the lobby from the treatment center. Exiting the building,

Mitch's steps felt lighter than they had in years. Since Ray's death, actually.

He looked at the clear blue sky. *Thank You, Lord.* After all these years, after countless sleepless nights, God had finally answered his prayers. *Please give Eliot the strength to see this thing through to the end.* Though it'd never really be the end. He understood enough about addiction to know that much, but God had brought Eliot this far. He wouldn't abandon him now.

Crossing the street, Mitch caught a glimpse of Dennis sitting in his car, and the tears he'd fought against all day almost spilled out.

Inhaling, he approached his former business partner, old college roommate, and longtime best friend. "How'd you know?"

Arm resting on the opened car window, Dennis gave a one-shoulder shrug. "Ran into Sheila at the grocery. Asked her how she was holding up, she got to talking."

Mitch nodded. Sheila had always processed verbally, with anyone who would listen, and though she and Dennis weren't on "friends" terms, he'd been around enough when Mitch and Sheila were married to form a friendly acquaintance. "I'm glad you're here."

"I care about the kid too. Glad to see he made this choice."

A thick silence stretched between them. There

were so many things Mitch wanted to say, he just didn't know how. But he couldn't leave things the way they were. They'd been friends for far too long.

"Listen, I'm really sorry about how things turned out. I never meant to hurt you."

Dennis's features hardened and his gaze intensified. But then his face softened. "I know. It's that stupid heart of yours; always gotta rescue the stray. I just wish . . ." He shook his head. "Doesn't matter. It's better this way, you know."

"You're probably right. And I'm willing to work with you on this. However you want to divide things. But if you ever need anything, you know I'm here. Always."

Dennis nodded. "Guess I better go. I wish you and Eliot the best." He looked at the rehab center. "I hope this works out for him."

"Thanks." Mitch stepped back. *I'm praying for you.* Saying it aloud would only irritate his former partner, for now. But there'd come a day when Dennis would welcome those prayers, Mitch was certain of that. Maybe even when the two could pray together. Until then, he would continue to beseech God on his friend's behalf.

Arm linked with C. J.'s, Bianca paused to read a verse painted in black calligraphy on the pregnancy center's wall. " 'For I know the plans I have for you,' declares the LORD, 'plans to prosper you and not to harm you, plans to give you a hope and a future.' —Jeremiah 29:11"

Across from this stretched a mural of Jesus lifting a bulging bag off the bent shoulders of a tired-looking woman. Bianca read the words written below it, also in beautiful calligraphy. "Come to me, all who are weary and burdened, and I will give you rest. —Matthew 11:28" An image of Virginia handing her the hand-stitched dishtowel with the same verse on it came to mind.

"I'm praying for you. . . . That you would know how much God loves you."

Tears stung her eyes as she looked at Angela, walking a few paces ahead. That she'd open her house like she had, bring Bianca and C. J. here, come with them . . .

Angela glanced back. "Everything all right?"

"Yeah. I'm good." She sniffed and, with a smile, gave her daughter's hand a squeeze. Maybe God didn't hate her after all. Maybe He even loved her.

Bianca stopped in the middle of the hallway, a deep longing pulling on her heart. "But I think I could be better."

Angela and Ginger exchanged glances and stepped closer.

"How is that?" Angela's brow furrowed. "Do you need something?"

"I do." She couldn't keep her smile in check

any longer. "I think I need to make friends with Jesus."

"What?" Angela gave a laugh-gasp, and for a moment, Bianca feared the woman was about to fall over. Or to launch into a hallelujah dance, if there were such a thing. "You mean . . . like . . ." She looked from Bianca to C. J. then back to Bianca, her grin stretching so wide her cheeks had to hurt. "You want to get saved, right here, right now?"

Bianca frowned. "I'm not sure about all that." Christian jargon gave her a headache. "But I'd like to get to know Jesus. Learn how to get right with Him. If He'll have me."

"Of course He'll have you." Angela's eyes danced. "Like my old pastor used to say, 'Forgiveness is only a prayer away.' "

Ginger nodded, taking Bianca's hand. "That's right. The Bible says, 'If you declare with your mouth, "Jesus is Lord," and believe in your heart that God raised him from the dead, you will be saved.' That means your sins will be forgiven and you will be given new life, for now and eternity."

Warmth spread the length of Bianca, and tears—happy tears—surfaced.

Angela grabbed her free hand. "Want to pray?"

She nodded. "I'd like that."

After the tour of the pregnancy center concluded, Angela led the way to the front doors, pausing to give Ginger a hug. "Thanks so much for all you do. This was such an answer to prayer. In so many ways."

"My pleasure."

Angela couldn't wait to call Mitch and tell him all that had happened.

She frowned, and a dull ache settled in her midsection. She and Mitch were over. She needed to quit thinking of him. It'd only make it harder to move on. Besides, he obviously had never really cared about her. If he had, he wouldn't be acting so distant. It was like he'd pulled away completely—and not long after she'd shared the truth of her past with the Bible study ladies. Clearly he'd found out about her abortion, her past promiscuity—the type of woman she really was—and wanted nothing to do with her. But had she really expected any different?

"Do you have a minute?" Ginger asked.

Angela glanced at Bianca who waved her on. "Don't worry about us. We're in no hurry. With your friends watching my boys, I'm in no hurry at all." She laughed, as did everyone else.

Angela turned back to Ginger. "Well, then." She followed her into her office.

Three of the walls were painted a powdery blue with one gray accent wall. Her desk sat in front of mahogany shelving loaded with Bibles, study material, and various curriculums, most written by her or her staff. A slender floor lamp stretched over her computer and a decorative vase sat in the corner. Apparently, a local church passionate about the choice for life had donated all the furnishings.

"Have a seat." Ginger motioned toward the armchair in front of her desk then took hers.

Angela complied, her stomach doing an unsettling flop. Would Ginger turn Cassie Joe away? Considering she was talking about keeping the baby rather than pursuing adoption? If she did, she'd need support, a lot of it. Maybe the center was low on resources or had all the clients her center could handle. Then what would Angela tell Cassie Joe? Would Bianca still let her keep the baby? Would Cassie Joe still want to?

Straightening, she pressed her knees together and cupped her hands around them. "Is something wrong?"

"Not at all. My educational director has been offered a position with another company."

"Oh, no. I'm so sorry."

"We are too, and yet, we believe God may have provided someone to fill that role. Someone passionate about helping women in crisis, someone with the perfect combination of grace, truth, and heart-felt compassion."

Angela exhaled. "I'm so glad! You had me worried there for a moment, wondering what these poor, sweet women were going to without someone to teach and mentor them."

"Of course, she hasn't agreed to take the position yet. In fact, I haven't even asked her." She paused, grinned. "Angela, I showed the board of directors your volunteer résumé, and with your education degree, experiences, love for others, and unique giftedness, you'd be perfect for this position. I've seen how you interact with our clients—how they interact with you. They truly love you."

Angela clasped a hand to her chest. "And I love them."

"I know you do." Ginger's smile grew. "So, when does your position at Rockhurst end?"

"After the new year."

"Perfect." Ginger stood and started to round her desk then stopped. "I suppose I should ask, are you interested?"

"Yes!" Angela clapped her hands together. "Absolutely. Nothing would make me happier."

Chapter 50

Flitting about her kitchen, Angela hummed with the Christmas carols playing from Ainsley's smartphone. She and the boys—Robby and Sebastian—gathered around the table, rolling dough out in preparation for cinnamon rolls. Her son-in-law Chris sat on the floor, playing with his chubby-faced angel while, last Angela had checked, Cassie Joe was helping her mom get all dolled up for church.

A memory surfaced of a Christmas some 40-plus years ago. Her mom had been baking all morning—pies for dinner, cookies for munching on beforehand. Angela had pranced in singing "Jingle Bells." Seeing her mom baking made her think of braided bread she'd seen at one of her friends' houses, and she'd asked her mother if they could make it. Without so much of a pause, her mom had turned to her with a wide grin and said, "Absolutely." They'd spent the rest of the afternoon elbow deep in bread dough, covered in flour, and chatting about everything from why Rudolph was the only reindeer with a red nose to why people decorated their trees with lights.

Mom would've made a lovely grandmother, great-grandmother.

I miss you, Mom.

Shaking the thought aside before the tears building in her eyes threatened to run her mascara, she checked the time on the microwave.

She turned to Ainsley. "Y'all better hurry. We need to leave in 15 minutes." Otherwise they'd never get a seat. She bit her lip, wiping her hands on a towel. Would the large number of people crammed in the sanctuary intimidate Bianca?

Would Mitch be there? Of course he would be, and probably serving as a greeter. She'd spoken to him half a dozen times in the past month, always hoping he'd initiate deeper conversation. Something to convince her maybe they could in fact have a relationship. Prove to her he cared—enough to overlook her past. But he never did. Oh, he'd called twice, sent her a card. All surface conversation. *"I hope you're doing OK. Let me know if you need anything."*

Clearly, Frances had been right. Angela had been nothing more than a project to him, and apparently he'd moved on. Not that she was surprised. She'd been rescued by her share of do-gooders enough to know where that road led. If only she'd seen this coming, then maybe she could've kept her heart from being shattered.

"You all right?"

She turned to find her daughter watching her with a concerned expression.

"Of course." She forced a smile. "I best go check on the ladies." She dropped her rag on the counter, hurried to Bianca's bedroom at the end of the hall, and rapped on the opened door.

Standing beside her daughter, Bianca was on the phone, and based on her tone, the conversation was unpleasant. Was she talking to Reid?

"I'll do that. Love you, Ms. Virginia." Bianca set her phone on the dresser and grabbed a brush.

Angela stepped into the room. "Everything all right?"

Bianca cast a glance Cassie Joe's direction before returning Angela's gaze. "That was Ms. V."

She nodded.

"She's pretty excited about me going to church this morning. Said she's been praying about this, praying for me, ever since she met me. Said God's got His hand on me and won't let go." Her voice turned husky.

"I'd agree with that." Bianca had told Virginia about her decision to follow Christ shortly after she'd made it, and her sweet friend had sent the most touching card. Said she wanted to be there when Bianca got baptized. Angela planned to make sure that happened.

Bianca watched her daughter a moment longer, then said. "Hey, girl, can you check and see how your brothers are getting along?"

Cassie Joe sighed and trudged off, hollering their names en route.

Bianca faced Angela with sorrowful eyes. "We

talked about Reid. He wants me to come see him."

"I thought he might." Angela sat on the edge of Bianca's bed and patted the mattress. "What're you going to do?"

Bianca sat beside her, shrugged. "Don't seem right to leave him. I mean, we're married. Divorce is a sin, right?"

Angela frowned. "I'm the last person to ask for spiritual advice. I'm still learning how to dress right." She forced a tight laugh.

Picking at a cuticle, Bianca was silent for a long moment. "Don't know I'm ready to leave him. And I for sure don't know what the right thing to do is, Jesus-speaking and all. But I need space."

"Like a separation?"

Bianca swiped her fingertips under her teary eyes and nodded. Gave a shuddered breath. "This is so hard."

Angela pulled her into a sideways hug. "I know. And I'm sorry."

They sat like that for a while, neither saying anything. Angela praying—for Bianca's heart, for her family, for Reid—that somehow God would get a hold of him while he was in prison.

Bianca pulled away, dried her eyes. "Guess I better redo my makeup, huh?"

She stood and faced the mirror, forehead

creased, short hair shiny and spiked on top. She tugged at the bottom hem of her sweater on top of her faded jeans. "Are you sure this is appropriate? Shouldn't I be wearing a dress or something?"

Angela glanced at her own attire, suddenly wishing she'd chosen something more casual. Was it too late to change? She offered Bianca her best smile. "Nope. You look beautiful. Matter of fact, this fabric is making me itch something awful." Which was true enough. "Give me a minute." She turned toward the door then glanced back over her shoulder. "Be ready to leave in ten?"

Her eyes widened, and the poor thing looked like she'd swallowed a marble.

Angela laughed. "Relax. It's church. Not kickboxing."

Bianca's eyes danced with mirth. "True that."

Still chuckling and praising God for the miracle of His grace, Angela dashed to her room to exchange her favorite new dress for jeans and a sweater. She returned to the living room to find the others gathered at the door. The boys spilled out first, pausing to hurl snowballs on the way. Then, divided into two cars, they caravanned to church, Angela with Bianca and her boys, Cassie Joe with Ainsley, Chris, and Joey.

Pulling into the lot, Angela slowed to search the massive number of parked cars. Mitch's vehicle was parked in its usual spot in the far northeast. Which meant there'd be a good chance she'd run in to him. She still didn't know how to act when that happened. Which was why, most of the time, she chose to do whatever she could to avoid him. With her large crew, that should be easy.

She stepped out of her car and faced the boys with a forced smile. "You ready to get your fa-la-la-la-las on?"

Sebastian grinned and Robby rolled his eyes, though laughter danced within them. Silly kid, always thinking he had to play the tough guy, but he was getting better.

Once inside, she scanned the foyer for signs of her new Bible study friends, but it was too crowded with strangers. Looping an arm through Bianca's, she waited for Cassie Joe, Ainsley, Chris, and Joey to catch up, then slipped into the sanctuary.

The lights dimmed until everything went black, then a soulful violin played. Above the stage, a spotlight flicked on, showing a woman dressed in black, two others, dressed the same, standing beside her. A melody followed, one that seemed to tell a story of beauty and longing.

"Imagine." A deep voice sounded above the quartet. "Sending your son, your beloved, to a place ravished with anger, hatred, sorrow. Pain. Knowing the moment you did, the clock toward his death would begin to tick. Knowing the very people you sent your son to save would, one day, pound nails into his hands and feet."

The music continued, and the spotlight shifted, illuminating a wooden feeding trough filled with hay.

"Imagine the Son, the Prince of Heaven, stripping Himself, willingly, of all His heavenly glory to come to earth as a tender, vulnerable babe. To be despised by the people He created. To be born not in a palace with attending servants, but instead, in a stable to a couple of peasants. To a mother some rumored to be a harlot, to a father others considered foolish. All for the sake of the lost. For this sin-ravished world that God so loved."

Angela pressed a hand to her mouth, her chin quivering. Mary, Jesus' mother, had endured rumors. Though the Bible didn't say so, it had to be true. People could count the days, figure out when she'd first conceived, and later, when she and her husband had wed. Assuming the worst rather than choosing to believe the truth. Like many were probably doing with Angela.

You understand, Lord.

And He loved her. Deeply. He'd loved her when she'd been living a life of sin, and He loved her now, when she'd turned from her old ways to live in a way He desired. Through it all, He'd been faithful.

She glanced down the pew at Chris, Ainsley,

and their precious little one, then to Bianca and her kiddos on the other side of her. Amazed at all God had done through His restoring love.

The deep voice continued. "Imagine a group of rough shepherds, society's refuse. The kind you crossed the street to avoid. Then one night, as they lay on the hard ground, smelly, surrounded by bleating animals, the sky lit up, and angels filled the horizon, singing, announcing the birth of the Savior of all mankind. And when they heard, they were so overjoyed, they told everyone. Because that's how grace works. It overflows until it saturates everyone around us."

The spotlight shifted again, back to the trough, and the music turned gentle, soothing, as the pastor walked onto the stage. "And now, friends, we must ask, why did God choose to come to earth as a helpless baby? Why would He choose to come to such lowly, impoverished parents? And why would God choose to use a group of dirty and scorned shepherds to proclaim such glorious, miraculous news?"

The music stopped, and a hush fell over the crowd.

"Because He wanted us to know without a doubt that no one, no matter what you've done or where you've been, is beyond God's transforming grace."

Angela's heart stilled as realization swept

through her, bringing a deep peace. That was the very reason God wanted to use her down at the center, and wherever else He might choose. To show those poor broken women like Bianca and Cassie Joe that grace was meant for them too. In light of God's grace, there was absolutely nothing for Angela to be ashamed of. Not anymore.

It felt so good to be forgiven, to rest in Christ's forgiveness, a gift she'd received the moment she trusted in Jesus Christ as her Lord and Savior. It was time she offered herself that same grace.

Mitch hurried toward the foyer, trying to keep an eye on Angela as she and her family made their way out of the sanctuary. He couldn't shake the stiff, almost distant expression she'd given him when she'd come in. If her tight frown wasn't a brush off, he didn't know what was.

No more waiting. No more guessing. He needed to find out, once and for all, where he stood with her.

Frances caught him as he passed the information desk. "Mitch, Merry Christmas. Do you have plans this evening?"

He glanced her way then back at the door as Angela slipped out, soon hidden by a throng of people. "I . . . yes, you too. Excuse me."

Maneuvering through the idle crowd, he dashed outside into the cold night air. Conversations drifted from every direction as families crossed the parking lot, got into their vehicles, and drove away.

Too late. Most likely she'd left. He should probably wait till after the holidays to talk to her. He turned and started to walk back inside when he heard a familiar laugh. Robby.

He and his brother were climbing up the hill leading from the lot to the side of the church, hurling fistfuls of snow at one another while a group of adults gathered a few feet away. Mitch squinted, trying to make out forms and faces in the dim streetlight. Hope blossomed. There was Angela. And Joline, and Joline's husband.

Swallowing hard, Mitch strolled over. "Hey."

Angela spun around, her eyes wide, her expression unreadable. "Hello."

"Good evening, Mitch." Joline smiled and extended her hand, giving his a squeeze.

He nodded and gave everyone the obligatory greeting, made small talk for a moment, then faced Angela. "Can we talk?"

Angela exchanged glances with her daughter, whose eyebrows rose. She didn't appear pleased. Was that why Angela had suddenly pulled away?

Angela clutched the collar of her jacket and nodded. "Sure. I've got a minute."

They moved a few feet away, their breath fogging in front of their faces. He searched her eyes, hoping to see a hint of tenderness. "Are you mad at me?"

"What?" She blinked. "No, of course not."

He frowned. Shifted. "Then what is it? Why the cold shoulder all the sudden? I thought we were friends."

Her eyes softened. "Oh, Mitch, we are. You've been a great friend, a true Christian. But everything's good now. You don't have to . . . you can . . . I appreciate all you've done."

This didn't make any sense.

"I'll see you later?" She started to walk away.

"Why are you so afraid of men?"

She turned around, visibly stiff. "I'm not." Her voice trembled.

He'd hit on something, but what? Why couldn't she just tell him? "Listen, I know you've had some bad relationships in the past, but I'm not like that. After all this time, can't you see that?"

"Sweet man, it's not about you." Tears filled her eyes. "At least, not in the way you think."

"Then what's it about? Tell me."

"My momma done told me, I'm not the marrying kind." She sang the words to an old country music song, one he vaguely remembered, then turned to leave. Then recognition hit. The lyrics were about a tainted woman who'd fallen in love with the preacher's son. She wasn't afraid of men, she was afraid he'd be the one scared off.

• • •

Angela felt as if her heart was literally being sliced in two. If she didn't leave now, she'd be reduced to a sobbing, snotty-nosed mess.

"Wait!" Mitch called out to her, and she turned back around. He stepped closer. "I know about the—" *abortion*. He closed his mouth abruptly, and his eyes softened, compassion radiating from them. "I know . . . about everything."

The air squeezed from her, and she froze. What was he saying?

"I don't care. I know you've had some bad relationships—"

"A lot of relationships." He only knew a fraction. "Way too many."

"But that was before Christ, right?"

A tear slid down her cheek, and she nodded. Was it possible he would offer her the same grace Jesus had? That maybe he could love her, truly love her, despite all she'd done? Who she'd been?

Stepping closer, he thumbed her tear away then dropped his hand until it cupped her chin. "Then it doesn't matter. None of that does. Jesus paid for it all when He died on the Cross, so who am I to hold it against you?"

"Oh, Mitch." Her tears fell unhindered now, and she clumsily swiped them away.

He smoothed back her hair then held her face in his hands. "When did I fall in love with you,

Angela Meadows? And whatever can I do about it?"

She let out a half laugh, half sob. "Just hold me tight?"

He pulled her close and buried his face in her hair. "That's what I plan to do."

A cough sounded behind them, and she turned to see her daughter watching them with a tense expression. "Mother?"

What would Ainsley say? Angela wasn't sure she cared. Yes, she wanted her daughter's approval but this—she glanced back to Mitch, and her heart leapt—oh, how she loved that man. And he loved her. She almost laughed aloud at the thought. Mitch Kenney loved her, deeply. He knew all about her—everything!—and loved her anyway.

To be known, fully known, and loved—the sense of freedom was so overwhelming, it stole her breath.

She smiled, twined her fingers with Mitch, and faced Ainsley. "You remember me mentioning Mitch."

She nodded. "Hello."

An awkward silence followed.

"What are your intentions with my mother?" Ainsley asked.

Mitch blinked. "Uh . . . my intentions?" He glanced at Angela, who, hand covering her mouth, was doing all she could to keep from giggling, then back to Ainsley. Facing Angela, he grabbed both of her hands in his. And in that moment, she knew, she could not live without this amazing man God had brought in to her life. And the love radiating from his eyes said he felt the same. "I intend to marry this woman, if she'll have me."

Ainsley and Angela gave a collective gasp, followed by laughter. Then there was so much hugging—by the entire Bible study, it seemed, who, at some point had joined the huddle—Angela thought for sure they'd be plowed over. Once all the talking, laughing, and whooping and hollering, the latter largely by Bones, concluded, Angela twined her fingers through Mitch's and tugged him away from the crowd. "Can we talk?"

He nodded. "I'd like that." He turned to the group. "Y'all, we'll catch up with you later. This beautiful lady and I need a minute."

Bones gave a whistle. "I'll bet. Don't do anything Pastor wouldn't do." He winked, then he and everyone else, still chattering, migrated to their respective cars.

"Want to go for a drive?" Mitch asked.

She nodded then followed him, still holding his hand, to his truck.

They drove in silence for a while, thoughts and questions raging through her mind. She wanted to believe what she and Mitch had was real, that he'd truly stick around when things got hard or she didn't act like the good Christian wife she should.

Because no matter how hard she tried not to, she knew she'd mess up. She still had so very much to learn, and honestly, a lot of healing yet to do.

As they drove out into the country, his profile lit then shadowed in between the streetlights they passed, she studied him. Watched his expression, his body language, waiting for the best time to broach the subject. Hesitant to break the magic she'd felt when he'd declared his love but needing to know where she stood. Needing to know if she could truly trust him with her heart.

She took in a deep breath and released it slowly. "What happened?"

One hand on the steering wheel, he cast her a sideways glance. "What do you mean?"

"You were so . . . distant. You just sort of quit coming around."

"I knew you needed your space."

"What do you mean? Space from what?"

He hesitated. "Me, I guess. I knew you had a lot going on, a lot of emotions getting kicked up with your work at the pregnancy center. I didn't want to push you."

"What if I needed you to be there for me?"

"Frances said—"

"Frances?" It was starting to make sense now. Obviously that woman had planted doubts in both their minds, fueling Angela's insecurities. Hoping . . . what? That Mitch would quit paying attention to Angela and start looking her way? "She loves you."

Mitch snorted. "Who, Frances?" He shook his head. "She's just a Nosy Nettie, is all."

"A Nosy Nettie with her sights on a handsome house-flipping contractor."

He turned right onto a dirt road and put the truck in park. Facing her, he took both of her hands in his. "Well, someone ought to tell her, this house-flipping contractor's got his eyes set on someone else, and he ain't letting go. Ever."

Tears blurred her vision, and she gave a hiccupped sob. "You have no idea what you're getting into."

"So you think." He tilted her chin up, and his gaze intensified. "Woman, you done stole my heart, and there's no tossing it back now." He grazed her cheek with the back of his hand then traced her lip with his thumb. "I'm yours, now till I'm old, decrepit, and gray. If you'll have me."

So this was what love felt like. It was better, sweeter, and purer than anything she could ever imagine. She opened her mouth to respond, but as he leaned closer, his breath warm on her face, the words escaped her. Closing her eyes, she gave in to his kiss, warm and gentle at first, then deepening as she melted into his embrace. One she felt clear to her toes.

And to think, he'd be holding her close for the rest of his life.

Books are produced in the United States using U.S.-based materials

Books are printed using a revolutionary new process called THINKtech™ that lowers energy usage by 70% and increases overall quality

Books are durable and flexible because of smythe-sewing

Paper is sourced using environmentally responsible foresting methods and the paper is acid-free

Center Point Large Print
600 Brooks Road / PO Box 1
Thorndike, ME 04986-0001 USA

(207) 568-3717

US & Canada:
1 800 929-9108
www.centerpointlargeprint.com